THE LANDLORD

~

KEN MERRELL

KAY DEE BOOKS™

Published by
Kay Dee Books TM
P.O. Box 970608
Orem, Utah 84097-0608
USA
e-mail sales@kaydeebooks.com
www.kaydeebooks.com

ISBN: 0-9678510-1-7

Printed in the United States of America

April 2001

THE
LANDLORD

PROLOGUE

CENTRAL DISPATCH: "All units! Missing child in the area of Sixth and Fir. All units respond!

The scream of sirens pierced the frigid night air of the small Utah town. Of the seven police officers on the force, five were on duty. The second missing child in town, fifth in the county this year. Last time, Lieutenant Barker had vowed to be prepared when it happened again.

Officer Rick Stacey wheeled his patrol car around. Sig, his three-year-old German shepherd, lurched to attention and began to bark as the tires spun on the gravel at the side of the road. "Are you ready?" he yelled to Sig as he keyed up the mike. "One-thirty-nine responding."

"You got Sig?" The dog's ears snapped to attention, as he released a deep, throaty growl.

"Ten-four."

"She's been missing only ten minutes," crackled the voice on the other end.

"We're three minutes away." Stacey, dark brow drawn down around black eyes squinting to penetrate the moist night air beyond the glow of headlights, maneuvered down the center line.

Sig was one of just two K-9s in the county. The rookie team of man and dog was as ready as could be expected. Together they'd trained hundreds of hours just for this kind of crisis.

Eleven-year-old Ashley Gardner swung her arms and legs frantically, hopelessly trying to fight off the masked attacker who had pulled her from her bicycle only minutes earlier. He had dragged her into the thick undergrowth, taped her mouth shut, and now struggled to secure her arms.

She struggled for breath, precious air becoming harder to draw in. She knew of the other attacks. Who didn't? That's why her mother had been on her way to meet her. The entire town lived in fear— and now she was experiencing it. Fight! she thought. Mama said to fight.

Ashley could hear sirens above the pounding of her heart throbbing in her ears. Her lungs burned, starved for air. She reached to her face to tear away the tape, but her attacker caught her arm in a powerful grip, practically pulling it from its socket. The pain instinctively sent the girl's other hand on a desperate mission to pry open her attacker's fingers. With both arms now in reach, the child-killer acted quickly, taping her wrists together, leaving only her flailing feet as defense.

Stacey jammed the gas pedal; his right leg started to shake like half-chilled gelatin. Thick, meaty hands, white at the knuckles, gripped the wheel as if in a stranglehold on the elusive perpetrator. Sig stalked anxiously, pivoting side to side across the tattered rear seat, sensing the buried fear, smelling it, registering his owner's change in demeanor.

Stacey's squad car skidded to a stop on Fir's dead-end gravel road. His headlights, in concert with those of the three other patrol cars, shone on a bicycle laying on its side in the gravel. He scrambled from the car and opened the door for Sig.

"Stacey, this is the girl's jacket, and the mother, Mrs. Gardner." Lieutenant Barker, keeping control of his voice, stood near the woman, dust billowing around them. A single thin vein jutted from his forehead like a faintly smeared tattoo. "She was walking to meet her daughter, on her way home from a friend's house. This is where she found the bike and coat."

The woman was dressed in a three-piece suit that bulged at the buttons. Sag-chested, wide-hipped, her knees protruded recklessly from a high-cut skirt. Her dark curly hair was wrapped around her painted face, mos-cara smeared by tears.

Several neighbors milled about nearby, talking with the gathered policemen. Stacey reached down and picked up the coat. He dropped to one knee in front of Sig, shoved the jacket under the dog's muzzle, and held him by the ears. "This is important, Sig. We have to find her."

Determined to live, Ashley continued to kick violently at her attacker. A contemptuous grunt came from behind the mask as two strong hands slapped her legs to the side. Within seconds, her shoes were flung from her feet and her pants yanked from her slender legs as she continued to kick in her own defense. The distant sound of voices could be heard over the rush of the swollen river nearby. Grabbing Ashley's bound arms, the perpetrator hauled her to her feet and pressed his covered face close to hers.

The girl stared into eyes as black and hollow as the senseless acts they had witnessed over the past year. His breath billowed from his lips, rotten, suffocating. Ashley ceased her struggle as powerful hands encircled her youthful neck.

Sig struggled to break free from his master, then raised up to lick Stacey on the mouth with his rough tongue. "Seek!" Stacey commanded. The dog leapt forward and began to sniff the ground. Suddenly he bolted sideways, scattering bits of dirt and rock behind him.

"He's onto her!" Stacey sprinted to keep up with the dog, heading directly north.

"Mitch, you go northeast," Barker shouted, pointing to the right. "When you get to the river, turn toward the old Bunnell farm. Deek, you head east. Keep in touch on channel one." The second man jogged off, following the beam of his flashlight.

Barker unfolded a map on the hood of the car and addressed the small crowd. "If you men want to help, form a line 20 feet apart and head through the trees toward the Bunnell farm." He motioned toward the trees. "I don't want anyone hurt. Don't do anything stupid; just try to find the girl."

"Sig's movin' real fast. I think we're getting close," the radio reported. Stacey had been moving at full speed; their quarry couldn't be far off. "We're now headed east," he added, "almost straight for the river."

Lieutenant Barker gently took the arm of the mother. "Come on, Mrs. Gardner, let's find your daughter. Officer Stacey's on his trail. Been less than half an hour. I think he'll drop her and run."

Again the radio, it was Mitch. "I see him on the other side of the river!" he yelled between ragged breaths. "Don't know how, but he got across."

Captain Bingham snatched the device, his voice booming. "Has he got the girl?"

"It's dark...can't be sure. He's movin' real fast. Don't think so."

"Take him out if you can," the captain roared. "Just take him out."

A shot rang out—then a second.

"Don't shoot! I repeat, don't shoot." The radios fell silent. Everyone knew Chief Anderson's voice.

Stacey stopped to listen through the trees. The shots were close; he heard them clearly over the rush of the river. Sig began to bark. "He found her—I can tell by his bark."

"Is she alive?" sobbed the mother.

Barker patted her arm. "He'll let us know as soon as he gets to her."

Judging by the sound of his barks, Stacey figured he'd meet up with Sig just around the bend. He'd never seen a homicide up close—and didn't want to see one now, especially a girl the same age as his sister.

Officer Stacey's flashlight beam swung up from the ground. There was Sig, pacing wildly back and forth in front of the girl. "Off Sig!" Stacey commanded, wading through the thick brush toward the girl. Sig, obeying his master, backed up and crouched down. Stacey's beam shone on the girl's face. "She's alive!" he called over the radio.

The distressed mother collapsed to the ground. Deep sobs of relief shook her body. Lieutenant Barker stooped to comfort her. "Come on, Mrs. Gardner. She needs you now." He helped her to her feet and led her toward the river.

Officer Stacey knelt by the frightened girl and pulled her close. Tears coursed down her cheeks, broken only where tape covered her face. Her hands were also taped. "Don't be afraid. I'm Rick and this is Sig. That's short for Siegfried. Do you like dogs?" The girl nodded warily. "This is going to hurt a bit," he warned, gently peeling the tape off her mouth. "What's your name?"

"Ash—Ashley," the girl stuttered between whimpers.

"Ashley, you hurt?"

"I don't know."

"Let's undo your hands." Ashley bravely stretched her arms in front of her to allow the officer to remove the tape.

Just then she gazed upward. "The moon's out," she said. "I knew it would come from behind the clouds."

Stacey realized the girl was in shock. "Do you want to meet my dog?" She nodded. "Sig, come." The dog trotted over and began to lick the tear-stained face. Hands now free, Ashley hugged its neck. The clouds once more slid like a curtain over the moon. Officer Stacey lifted the girl and strode toward the vehicles, Ashley holding tightly to his neck.

About halfway through the undergrowth to the road, the bushes rustled and out stepped Mrs. Gardner and Lieutenant Barker. The woman flinched slightly as the lieutenant's light beam fell on the young girl wrapped in the arms of the approaching officer. She rushed to take the girl in her embrace. "Oh, Ashley," she cried, "thank goodness you're alive."

The girl, with long, dark hair cascading across a face streaked from dirt, burst into tears at the sight of her mother. Her pants were gone, but she still wore her shirt and underwear.

Sig, clearly proud of himself, pranced about nearby. Bathed in the light reflected from his owner, his ashen coat gave him a ghost-like glow.

Barker slapped Stacey on the back. "Good job, Stace.

Good job."

Stacey, in turn, knelt to pat the head of the "real hero." "We did it, Sig. This time we did it!" Emotionally spent, he settled himself on the ground. He blinked in a vain attempt to hold back tears. Sig stepped up to lick the droplets away.

ONE

NIGERIA 1945

YOUNG KIN RO SAWA and his father Gi Ra Sawa hunkered on a hillside overlooking the green fields of farms and grazing land. Huge slopes rose behind them. Scattered iroko trees, their upraised limbs angling into the sky were silhouetted against the horizon, reluctantly giving way to the lazy lowland rivers. Further to the west, fading light struggled from a sun slowly being swallowed by the ocean beyond.

"My son," the old man spoke in his native tongue of Khana, his black skin calloused and creased from a lifetime of exposure to the harsh African sun. "We have lived on this land ten generations. My father, a great chieftain, served before me. I now serve in his stead, old and weary from the loss of those I love. We must find a better way or perish."

The small boy of eight gazed lovingly into the old man's face, wishing he could read the stories that lay hidden deep beneath the lined wrinkles of his aged father. The 90-year-old had outlived all other men in the tribe. Kin Ro Sawa was his prized possession, his only living son. The stoop-shouldered Gi Ra gazed out over the land, his arm resting motionless across the boy's shoulders. "I have seen many wars and much bloodshed," he sighed. "The time is at hand for us to make peace with our neighbors and unite to defend our homes and land."

Kin Ro had witnessed how the recent war between his tribe and the neighboring Tie had taken many lives on both sides. His two older brothers, each born of a different mother, had been lost in the series of scattered border skirmishes. Though Gi Ra had sired many sons, only a few had died of natural causes: all the rest had succumbed to war. Of his seven wives, two yet lived. The youngest of them was Kin Ro's mother. Still, the old man's posterity was vast, many sons and daughters having lived full lives, given him grandchildren, and passed to the beyond.

"There are those who oppose my feelings of unity with our enemies," he continued. "But if we remain divided, again we will be conquered. I must teach you all that you can understand. I have seen the Europeans take claim to our land. It was many, many years ago. They brought their guns and cannons."

Gi Ra ceased speaking as he reflected on the conflict that took the lives of not a few of his friends, brothers and eldest sons nearly seven decades earlier. "The Europeans love money and power more than happiness. They will destroy us if we allow them to take that which does not belong to them. They fight between themselves. They oppress us in our desire to be heard. We must rise up and unite our people in peace for a better land. The Holy Quran says, 'All those who fight when oppressed incur no guilt, but Allah shall punish the oppressor.'"

ELEVEN MONTHS LATER

KIN RO crouched outside the elders' counsel chamber, his only covering a loosely-wrapped loincloth draped about his waist. He peered through a narrow opening in the bamboo walls, straining to hear the heated voices of the men who ruled their tribe. Kin Ro could tell by the expression on his father's face that he felt that he was not being well-represented. The meeting went long into the night. Each day his father grew more feeble. The journey home would not be easy.

Finally the head elder intoned, "The counsel has heard all voices. We must now vote...All who wish to adopt the peace treaty, show." All were counted. "All against, show." Again, all were counted. "The treaty will stand."

Kin Ro studiously watched his father's reaction. It seemed as if a lifelong battle was drawing to a close; his face slackened and his body slumped in the shadows cast by the dim torch light. The young boy waited for the men to disperse. A mixture of anger and excitement filled the air. Some cursed as they emptied into the darkness of the night.

"Father, come, I have your mount," Kin Ro urged, as the old man shuffled outside. "I have set up camp. We will spend the night before our long journey home."

Gi Ra was escorted to a mule tied at a nearby tree. As the two of them trudged down the dusty path leading from the village, the father made his request: "You must press forward in my quest for peace and unity. When you reach age, you must return to take my seat in the counsel and win freedom for our people."

Then his countenance abruptly changed. "How was your first day in the British school?"

"I would rather be at your side, learning the way of our people."

"Times have changed. You now must learn all you can to become a great leader and deliver our people from their captivity."

Kin Ro helped the frail old man to the makeshift bed, and carefully drew the linen over his shoulders. "I will learn," he whispered.

NIGERIA 1964

The local Bori government, consisting of Khana, Tai, Eleme, and Gokna, met in the Otegal council chambers. "We wish to recognize our newest representative. Some of you will remember his father, Gi Ra Sawa. Let me present the youngest delegate, Kin Ro Sawa." The 110-member counsel stood and offered their applause as Kin Ro waited to speak.

"My fellow elders, it is because of a promise I made to my father many years ago that I stand before you this day. It was the same night you voted to unite in peace to create this governing body that I, just a boy, looked on in amazement through the slats of the hut. It was the last night my father spoke to me before he was murdered as we slept."

Kin Ro's eyes softened and his head bent to the earth. Then he straightened to resume his address. "I have sounded my voice in strong accord for this great cause. Our country has won independence from the British. We must continue to educate our children in schools and colleges. We must insist they leave the farms to learn. Only by learning can we become free. We still have much to do. We are a small minority in this country, but our voice must be heard."

The crowd broke into wild clapping.

When the noise had died down, Kin Ro, his face drawn and earnest, went on. "Now we have another monster in our midst. Our land is being sucked dry by those who wish to take its rich black blood from the earth. Our brothers are being trampled by the machinery that mows across our land in search of oil. Our forests are being savaged and the wildlife disappears. We must stand together to deliver ourselves from this tyranny. The Ogani people must fight against those that take the oil; they become rich while we live in poverty. And we are ever-burdened by our leaders' fight for power. They fight among themselves to see who would rule over us. Instead we must take a first step along the road of democracy. We must create a new society, one governed by the people. For at present we stand at the edge of disaster."

Several miles to the west, a caravan of machinery, escorted by a small patrol of government soldiers, plowed across a field of yams. A bent old farmer scurried from his shack, waving his arms in protest. "No, no it is not ready to harvest! You said you would wait until we gathered the crop. I will not have enough food for my family."

The column of machines rolled on; almost no one gave any notice to the distraught old man.

Finally a soldier stepped forward. "Move aside, old

man. Here are the papers and your fee."

The old man stared down at the paper he was handed. "This is nothing. It is not the value of my crop. Please, please you must wait." He hobbled to the front of the foremost bulldozer and stood with his hands in the air. "Please, two more weeks. I will harvest early." The huge machine groaned to a stop as the operator looked to the soldier for instructions.

Again, "Step aside, old man," came the stern warning, "or we'll bury you where you stand."

"It will be better than to starve!"

The soldier's hand shot into the air, his voice rang out, a puff of smoke rose up, and the bullet found its mark. "Have it your way, then!" Seemingly in a slow motion, the farmer's body crumpled to the ground.

The operator dropped his blade and rumbled forward, a smear of soil and yams in its wake. Within seconds the machine had rolled up and over the old man's body, burying it beneath the dark, rich earth he had so carefully tended.

"Push him far to the side," ordered the soldier. "Make sure it's buried so we won't smell it while we work."

TWO

NIGERIA 1994

I HUNCH BEHIND THE BARS of my cell as I speak to the American sitting across from me. He's slight of build, middle-aged, and is lacking hair. He leans to one side as he adjusts himself to get comfortable. I am weary from the many years of struggle and disappointment. And now I await my execution, two short hours away. I don't know how this man gained access to interview me. I've not had but one visitor in my brutal two-month-long incarceration—except for the government-paid lawyer who has pretended to defend me through the entire abomination.

I shift nervously in my seat. The prison hall is empty, except for an inmate who is mopping the concrete floor at the opposite end. I answer the man's question, briefly recounting a little about my life, starting with my father, who was murdered in his sleep almost 50 years before, the same night he cast his vote for peace and unity with our neighboring tribes. The American thrusts the microphone further under my chin as I begin to relate my appointment to the tribal counsel some 13 years afterward.

I tell him how our land once appeared when, as a young boy, I sat on the hillside with my father. The rivers were full of life, so pure that we drank from the water used to irrigate the fields. I hunted plentiful game in the surrounding foothills. The land was green and lush, stretching to the ocean. I had never seen an oil rig or a bulldozer. I wore nothing on my feet but callouses. We had no schools in those days. I was raised to speak only the native tongue of my people.

I tell him that we once stood a chance of overcoming the powers of a greedy government, reclaiming our children who were being taught how to read and think. But alas, my people of less than five hundred thousand were now a lost nation, drowning in a sea of one hundred million Nigerians. A scattered minority race, we live between the Yoruba to the south and the Bura to the north. We are neither northerners nor southerners, trampled under foot for over a hundred years.

I explain how we fought for independence with others of our country, driving the British from our borders, yet we are still invisible to our government. Now they own the rights to our land, a land blessed—or cursed—with more than two hundred billion gallons of oil, much of which has since been bled from the ground. More than 90 percent of our foreign revenue comes from oil dollars. Our government boasts that the richest and purest oil in the world is contained beneath our once-fertile fields, soil now polluted by puddles of mud and slurry. Our rivers are empty of life; a film of deadly oil, which has killed fowl, mammals and fish alike, floats like a shroud.

My people are the poorest in our country. I tell him of the hundreds of villages I have seen burned to the ground. The thousands that have been killed as they stood up for their human rights. Yet our rights continue to be trampled under foot by the military rule, funded by the very revenues taken from the Ogani people.

I don't know why the guards do not come and send this brazen American reporter packing. Why don't they come and destroy his tapes on which I describe my people who are dying from a sickness no one can cure? Their bodies weep and stiffen from open sores, until they are drained of life. From the smallest child to the most ancient elder, all are affected. I sigh as I explain: We have been told by those in authority that it is a genetic sickness, one not caused by the oil that pollutes our wells. How odd it is that this malady seems only to affect those who openly oppose the continued rape of our land.

The American pauses to change the tape. He is a pleasant man—appears to be sympathetic to our plight—but displays an insolence in his manner that I do not like. I proceed to tell him I have stood before His Excellency, the Military Governor, to plead our cause, but to no avail. I now stand accused of murders, crimes of which I am innocent. Five of my fellow countrymen and I will be hanged this day for the death of our leaders, assassinated during the recent riot at Sogho. I tell him I am a man of peace and ideals, that I am appalled by the effects of poverty and oppression heaped upon my fellow citizens. Three of those who will be executed were not even present when the riot took place. I am one of those innocents. There was ample evidence that the two chiefs who died in the uprising were fired upon from a distant rooftop. The assassinations were not at our hands.

The American quietly asks who, then, would have done such a thing. I suggest to him that more than likely the assassins were recruited by owners of the oil companies. Surely their wish is to squash our uprising of freedom.

He asks me what evidence I have of such a theory. I explain that information has been smuggled into me through the prison walls and the evidence agrees with my theory. He asks several more questions regarding the matter—and I give him as many answers as I can—before we move on.

In answer to his original question, I say, "What do *I* want? I want a place where our ministers cannot be jailed and detained for weeks on end without reason; a place where the Ogani people are consulted about the laws, and where the powerful oil companies that rule our lands and steal our livelihood are not the first and last word. The constitution should protect minority rights. I want free choice! I'm not merely begging for it; I demand it! I quote the Holy Quran like my father before me: "*All those who fight when oppressed, incur no guilt, but Allah shall punish the oppressor.* Come that day!"

Somehow the American has petitioned to allow me a few brief moments with my family. Then two guards enter the room and wait as my loved ones bid their final good-byes. Tears are shed as I am chained hand and foot. Then I am led from the barred room, escorted to a barbed wire compound, and marched up the steps to the waiting gallows.

I stand with the five others, their heads bowed and already covered. My head also is bowed, my eyes fixed on the metal trap door below me, staring at the crack of light that flashes around its edge. I think back to the time I looked through the slim opening in the hut, and, in my mind, can still see the faces of the counsel members seated alongside my father.

A black hood is drawn down over my head, then tied loosely around my neck. It is suffocating. I struggle to take a breath, my heart pounding so loudly that I no longer can hear the cries of the protesters outside the prison gates. The sun beats upon the hood as a heavy noose is pulled down and tightened at my neck. My chest rises and I mumble my final words: "May Allah take my soul unto him. My fight is over; the struggle continues."

I feel the heavy door collapse beneath me, and hear the thunder of metal striking metal. I am falling....

"It's not fair," murmurs the American as he watches the bodies twitch under the gallows floor. He struggles to his feet and hobbles from the compound, whispering to himself, "Something must be done to end this crime."

THREE

THE HORIZONTAL RAYS from the morning sun played against the far wall of the hallway as Kate and Christina approached the guard station. Either because they didn't care or they were too preoccupied, the security guards never broke from their conversations, never even looked their way as the young woman and girl stepped through the metal detector.

"Do you want to stop at the restroom before we go up?" Kate asked.

Christina nodded, flipped her hair to the side like a drill team cadet, and scanned the ornate walls and ceiling of the old building. In her 12 years she'd never been in such a place. After sidestepping the "Wet Floor" sign in the hall, Kate pushed open the door and they both entered.

Outside, the sheriff's deputy helped his prisoner step from of the rear seat of the squad car. Manacled at the wrists, Don Rodriguez, a 29-year-old Hispanic man, towered above the guard. Six-foot-two, an athletic body built from hard work Rodriguez looked the part of a movie star, though his once black hair already had gray streaks running through it. His broad smile stretched across a black goatee belied the fact that he was a convict on his way to plead for leniency.

"Gonna' smart-mouth the judge today?" asked the smirking deputy.

Don grinned. "I think I'll keep my mouth shut this time."

"I hardly recognize you in the suit. Maybe the judge

will have forgotten." The deputy rinsed his mouth in a brown ooze of chew before spitting it on the newly planted flowers that ran next to the walk. Then he reached up and wiped his chin with his sleeve. "Hear about the excitement last night?"

"No."

"He got another kid. We know it ain't you. You been in the county resort the last few weeks." The deputy laughed at his own joke.

"Kill her?" Don asked.

"Nah. That K-9 unit got to her in time. Cap'n Bingham said he'd stop 'em if he could. Done some shootin', though. Someone's butt's in a noose this mornin.'"

The deputy stepped in front of his prisoner. "Lemme take off them bracelets. They don't match your suit." Don rubbed his sore wrists as the handcuffs fell away. "Sorry ya' had to wear em, Don. Regulations, ya' know."

"No problem." Don's calloused hands, badly scarred at the knuckles, fiddled with the tie that hung awkwardly from the collar of his crisp, new shirt. The wool suit, charcoal-colored with pinstripes, chafed at his knees.

The deputy swung wide the door to the courthouse. One of the two security guards standing close by spoke quietly as they neared the metal detector. "Hey, Tony, what you think of the shooting last night? Did you hear? They found blood this morning."

"They got him?"

"Just a few drops," the guard answered. "Never found the guy."

Don passed through the metal detector without a beep. The deputy followed, loaded down with gear. The machine went crazy. "Must be the new hip," he chuckled.

The building was old but still grand. Its marble floors were well worn, ground by the wheels of justice that had rolled thanklessly along for almost a century. Don Rodriguez had been there many times before. He turned left as they passed a yellow "Wet Floor, Caution" triangle near the restrooms. Strange that the floors weren't the least bit wet, he noted as he started up the stairs.

"Room 210," the deputy said.

"I know—Judge Demick," replied Rodriguez.

The old staircase, its polished handrails of brass, twisted around a towering marble column. When they reached the landing at the main level, both men paused to take in the view. The grand rotunda stretched upward another 50 feet. Built just after the turn of the century, the building took its design from ancient Greece. Six massive pillars held up the ceiling; the main floor opened up to the mezzanine above, its ornate entrances guarded by marble balustrades. The edifice was a magnificent work, pride of the county.

"My attorney is supposed to meet me here," Don said. "He's probably on the next floor." He and the deputy turned up the stairs.

"Don...I'm up here." They both pivoted and craned their necks to see who was calling. Dee Brady, Rodriguez's attorney, clad in his customary western-cut suit, stood on the second floor, talking to the prosecuting attorney. He motioned toward his client, smiling, waving his arm.

Don smiled back. "We'll be right up."

"Ready to go?" asked Kate as she dried her hands. Glancing in the mirror, she straightened her dress and tussled at her short blonde hair.

"Yes," Christina nodded.

A bosomy woman in her late twenties, reeking of cigarettes and perfume, and wearing a short, tight skirt meant to complement her shapely figure, stepped from an adjoining stall, tucked an application for marriage in her purse, and approached the sink to wash her hands. Christina sneaked a longing glance as they exited the room toward the stairs.

"Do you think she was born with that beautiful hair?" Christina asked when they were out of hearing.

"I don't think so, dear."

"I wish I had blonde hair like you and mom."

"You have the most beautiful hair of anyone I know."

The girl's mouth puckered and drew to the side. "But it's almost black," she sighed.

Kate smiled. "That's part of what makes it so pretty." They continued up the stairs. "Your dad doesn't know you're coming. Don't be surprised if he's a little angry. His attorney thinks it's best if you're here."

"Will he be in jail clothes?"

"No, I gave his attorney the new suit we bought."

Christina was small for her age, mature, emotionally stable, full of life. Her tenacious personality had carried her through the ugly divorce that seemed to have broken her father's heart. Their close relationship stemmed from the countless hours he had spent with her, in the years when her mother started roaming. After the divorce Aunt Kate stepped in to pick up the pieces of a family broken by her sister's reckless lifestyle. To Kate, her niece wasn't at all one of those fractured pieces; she was more like her own daughter.

Christina caught sight of her father, standing on the floor above them amid the filtered light, shining like an angel. "Daddy! Daddy!" her voice ricocheted from the marble structure.

Don turned an angry eye at Dee. "What's she doing here?"

"Relax, Don. She's been living with your sister-in-law the last three weeks."

"Three weeks? Where's Monica?"

"We're not sure. Kate thinks she's in Europe with...a new boyfriend."

"Figures." Don shook his head in disapproval. "Probably has lots of money. Won't last long. He'll get tired of her shoving it up her nose."

He and Monica had been married ten long years, years laden with infidelity, mistrust, vicious arguments, hollow promises. She was the one who finally filed the divorce papers, launching a tug-of-war which had raged for the past two years, costing both of them their savings, their home, and every last shred of friendship.

"If you get your act together, maybe you can gain permanent custody," Dee suggested.

Don shot his attorney an angry glance, clearly embarrassed to have his daughter see him like this. "I don't want her here!" he growled.

"It's up to you, Don. I think it's in your best interest to let the judge know you have responsibilities to see to." Dee was serious. Rodriguez could tell by the way he spoke that the outcome would rest solely on his own shoulders. "Now put on a smile and let her know you love her."

Christina rounded the corner of the stairs and dashed into her father's embrace. He knelt to greet her. Then he stood to cradle her in his arms, lifting her feet well off the ground.

"Daddy! I missed you!"

"I missed you, too."

"I don't want you to go away again. I need you," she whispered in his ear.

He swallowed hard, "*I need you.*" The phrase echoed in his mind. She did need him—and he needed her.

The courtroom was situated at the south end of the building. Huge sliding windows stood watch over the street below. The high ceilings, towering wood work and massive bench where the judge sat made Christina feel small. A clerk was seated at a desk off to the side, solemn-faced, tapping on her computer keyboard, glancing up occasionally to see who was present. Her father and his attorney took their places at a well-worn hardwood table to the right of the room. The sheriff's deputy stood behind the railing to the side. She'd seen enough television to know the man at the other table must be the prosecutor, the enemy. She and her Aunt Kate were the only other people in the vast room. Christina glanced up at the clock: 9:05. "What time does it start?" she whispered.

Kate leaned over. "Nine o'clock, but they're never on time."

"Why is that sheriff here?"

"He's the one who brought your dad."

"He smells." Christina pursed her lips to let the words slip out the side of her mouth. Kate acknowledged the odor with a subtle twitch of her nostrils.

The judge's chamber door swung open. A clean-cut

deputy stepped out. "All arise, the fourth circuit court is now in session! The honorable Judge Demick presiding." Everyone stood. The judge, dressed in his black robes, a scowl on his broad face, carried in his hands a file folder, which he laid on the bench as he took his seat. "You may be seated."

After several appropriately dramatic moments, he cracked open the file and flipped through its pages. His full head of silver-gray hair was meticulously combed back, trimmed off his ears and collar, eyebrows groomed, shirt heavily starched and pressed, robe purposefully zipped down to show off his expensive silk tie and gold clip. Don turned and smiled back at Christina.

"Now let's see....Mr. Rodriguez, it seems you wanted to argue with me last time we were here." Judge Demick's manner was at once arrogant and stern. He peered over his half-glasses as he spoke—as if no one else in the courtroom mattered but him. Don clenched his teeth and resisted the urge to curse.

"Yes, sir," Don started to say.

Dee gave Don a nudge as he rose from his seat to address the court. Don stood too and struggled to gain a calm voice. "I'd like to apologize for that, your honor."

"So, why are we back in my court room today?"

This time Dee came to the rescue. "Your Honor, Mr. Rodriguez has successfully completed an alcohol rehabilitation program, he's been a model prisoner, and has served 30 days of the 90-day sentence at the county jail."

"I can see that." The judge again shuffled the papers. "Is there anything else?"

"We would like to petition the court to release him early so that he might find a job and care for his 12-year-old daughter Christina. We have reason to believe his ex-wife has recently relocated to Europe, leaving her in the care of her aunt." Dee turned on his heels and gestured toward the girl.

The judge tucked his chin and glanced down. "And what's wrong with her staying there until Mr. Rodriguez finishes his sentence?"

"Your honor, the punishment was harsh. Mr.

Rodriguez has learned a valuable lesson and wants to take responsibility for his daughter."

Judge Demick's penetrating gaze again rested on Christina. His face softened. "What do you think, Mr. Sands?" he said, nodding toward the prosecuting attorney, who, in turn, rose to his feet.

"Your honor, I've reviewed the file and consulted with Mr. Brady. I think it's in the best interest of the court to release Mr. Rodriguez and review his progress after 30 days. At that time, if he has found permanent work and is providing a stable home environment, I feel that we should suspend the balance of his sentence."

Judge Demick reluctantly seemed to agree. "Mr. Brady, do you have anything further?"

Don started to rise, but Dee reached over to stop him. They spoke quietly. Then Dee stood up. "Yes, your Honor. Mr. Rodriguez wishes to petition for reinstatement of his driving privileges. After all, he was not driving under the influence."

"I am aware that Mr. Rodriguez was not, by law, intoxicated," intoned the judge. "He was, however, close to the limit. It was his lack of insurance that brought him in front of this court to begin with. He's a professional driver. Therefore, his knowledge of the law makes him even more accountable than the general public. I will not review reinstatement of his driving privileges until he returns in 30 days."

Don, now seething with anger, lurched from his chair. "Your honor, how do you expect me to get to work and–?"

"Mr. Rodriguez!" the judge interrupted. "I suggest you sit down and stifle yourself before you say anything that might jeopardize your return to society and the return of your daughter."

"*I need you.*" At hearing the words echo once more through his mind, he forced himself down into his seat.

"Mr. Rodriguez, it was not your lack of insurance that landed you in jail. It was your temper—and lack of respect for my court."

Don nodded, his eyes on the polished floor.

"It is the decision of this court to release Mr. Rodriguez

on his own recognizance, pending a hearing in 30 days." The judge looked up from the open file and finished his sermon. "Furthermore, Mr. Rodriguez, I hope you've learned you cannot solve your problems unless you guard your temper. If the court learns that you do anything during your probation that reflects a lack of self-control, you *will* finish your time—and more."

Don half stood. "Yes, your Honor."

The judge jerked to his feet and brought the gavel down on his desk. "All rise," the bailiff called out. Demick, head and shoulders erect, shook his robes aside and withdrew from the room, closing his chamber door behind him.

"The fourth circuit court is now in recess."

Christina had studied the bailiff's face as he made his announcement. "I think he likes to do that," she whispered to her aunt.

Don turned and scowled at his attorney. But before he could open his mouth in protest, Dee cut him off short, commending the way he'd held his tongue. Christina made her way to the gate which separated them and excitedly greeted her father.

"You're welcome to stay with us until you get back on your feet," Kate offered. "Besides, everything you own is in a box in my garage."

Don hesitated. His first response was to turn her down. But having been evicted from his apartment during his jail stay, he had no place else to go.

"Thanks. We won't stay long."

The yellow caution sign was still planted on the hall floor when they approached the guard station. Christina spoke up. "I need to stop at the restroom again."

Dee leaned against the nearest wall to wait with his client. He was a regular at the courthouse and seemed to know everyone. The scuttle over the manhunt from the night before had already made its rounds.

"So what's the latest, Tony?" he asked the guard.

"Sounds like Bingham might be suspended for ordering his officer to shoot. Chief Anderson wasn't happy about it. Also heard he was pissed about Bingham having the whole neighborhood out on the manhunt. Someone could have been hurt..."

A muffled scream reverberated from the women's restroom.

"That's Chrissy!" Don bolted toward the door just as Christina emerged, her face blanketed in terror.

"There's a big rat in the heater!" she whimpered. "It growled at me."

The two security guards hurried over. "A rat?"

"Yeah! B-big red eyes...it growled, then ran away."

The guards warily pushed the door open. Christina pointed at the heat register at the base of the far wall. "It was behind the heater cover."

After calling out to make sure no one else was inside, they all entered and moved cautiously toward the vent.

"Are you sure it was a rat?" Don asked.

"Yes, Daddy, I'm sure!"

"Have you ever seen a rat before?"

"Not for real." She could tell by their doubtful glances that they didn't believe her.

"We'll get a rat trap." Tony slapped the second guard on the back.

Outside, a balding janitor reached over and shut the utility room door. Then he silently lifted the "Wet Floor" sign, placed it on his cart, and limped off down the corridor.

"Tony, do rats growl?" asked the guard after Don and Christina had walked away.

"Nope. Never heard one growl before."

FOUR

SNUGGED UP TO THE KITCHEN BAR, the younger children devoured their second bowls of cold cereal while the older ones hurried off for school. Resting on an acre lot, with nine bathrooms, eight bedrooms, a three-car garage, two stories rising atop a full basement, Kate's spacious though tastefully decorated home looked out over the valley. The addition of Don and Christina had hardly made a dent, with seven children of her own. Christina had chosen to sleep on a bunk in one of the girl's rooms, while Don stayed in the guest room. The decidedly upper-class neighborhood had left him slightly jealous—but he'd survive. It was kind of Kate to have taken them in.

In earlier years, Kate had been as beautiful as her sister Monica. Tall, blonde, round cheeks, full lips always turned up in a smile, and slow to anger. And although she was still attractive, the 20-odd pounds she had put on while pregnant with her two-year-old had been hard to shake. And over the years she had shortened her long, flowing tresses. Like her late mother, she was a graceful woman, born to a religious household, filled with compassion. She and Alan likewise had raised their family "in the gospel."

Kate, the oldest of nine children, had always tried to mother Monica, sixth in line. Maybe it was because they were such opposites. Monica had always been the rebellious, promiscuous teenager. She stopped going to church at fourteen, experimented with illegal drugs, wore revealing clothes, flaunted her body (which was ravishing), and constantly fought with her parents. By age 16, she was pregnant with Christina, which ended any hopes she had for a modeling career.

"Jake, come back!" called Kate to her 16-year-old just as Don appeared at the base of the stairs leading to the kitchen.

Jake turned, clearly irritated. "What?" Then he caught sight of his uncle and regretted the rebellious tone he'd used. Then he flashed a sheepish grin. "Oh, hi Uncle Don." Don smiled back, still a little sleepy.

"You forgot your backpack, honey."

"Thanks, Mom." Jake grabbed his pack, slung it over his shoulder, and slipped out the back door to catch the bus.

"He's a straight 'A' student with an attitude," Kate smiled.

Don smiled and nodded. "I don't know a thing about straight 'A's,' but I can relate to the attitude."

"How did you sleep?"

One of the smaller children interrupted their small-talk. "Mommy! I want more milk."

"The bed was much better than the county jail," Don replied. "Thanks again for letting us stay."

"You know you're always welcome."

"Mommy, I want more milk!!"

Kate spoke back over her shoulder as she took the milk carton from the fridge. "You can stay as long as you need to."

Christina, seated at the table, looked at Don with pleading eyes. "Daddy," she asked for at least the sixth time that week, "can't I go back to my old school?"

Don looked on helplessly. "We talked about this last night, 'Tina," he answered impatiently. "I'll walk you to school on my way to look for a job."

Christina sighed and propped her chin on her hands.

"More, please," piped up the two-year-old.

Kate poured more cereal and milk into the child's bowl, eliciting a "Tank you" from the little one.

"You are *so* polite," Kate praised. "Okay, kids, almost time to leave for school. Jenny's mom's walking with you today."

The neighborhood, unwilling to take any chances since the recent abductions, had organized a security patrol to accompany the younger children to and from school.

Don hurriedly gulped down a bowl of cereal, then showered and dressed. "Ready?" he asked Christina.

"I'm waiting for you, Daddy." They were headed for the door when Christina noticed the 14-year-old, still home, seated at the computer in his father's study. "Danny, why haven't you left for school yet?"

"I've got it!" he said triumphantly as he typed away, barely acknowledging Christina's question. Alan had asked Danny to test his new computer security system. Danny had been at it three full days, almost every waking moment. He seemed to have been born with a gift for computers. Kate and Alan encouraged it every chance they could, though they kept a watchful eye out when the kids were online.

Danny was an oxymoron—an admitted computer geek *and* a star athlete. On the outside he could be tough, but inside, he was a softie. His dishwater-blonde hair, personable disposition and deep-set hazel-green eyes attracted endless phone calls from aggressive 8th grade girls hoping to win his affection. "Dang!" Danny sighed, slumping back onto the chair. "So close."

"Missed your bus again?" Christina teased. "Kate's going to charge you." Her voice raised a decibel or two, the better for her aunt to hear. Kate had warned that she'd charge her children a dollar each time they missed the bus and she had to take them to school (though she rarely cashed in on the threat).

In the three weeks since Christina had moved in, she and Danny had become fast friends. There was a chemistry between them, something that balanced them out. Danny had demonstrated more than enough I.Q. for both. Yet Christina seemed to have stockpiled all the emotional maturity, love of life, spirit and spontaneity. In concert, they made a fearless duo.

Meanwhile, Don and Christina had reached the midpoint of their 15 minute walk to Brookside School. Christina looked forward to the times she could be alone with her dad so they could talk. She hadn't told him everything she wanted to the night before. Now was her chance.

"Daddy, why were you in jail?"

Don exhaled and bit his bottom lip. "Last time I saw you, your mother and I were arguing about the house. Well, I took off, had a few beers, and got pulled over on my way home."

"Mom called the cops...told them you were drunk," replied Christina, her eyes straight ahead. "She was really mad."

Don's voice raised in anger. "She called the cops?"

"Yeah, she did." Too late, she realized what she'd done; she'd just made trouble for her mother. For so much of her life she'd worked to keep the peace between them, and now, in this instance, she'd blown it. But Don, sensing her dilemma, shrugged and let it pass.

"I wasn't drunk. I only had two, maybe three beers."

"I know. So why did you go to jail?"

"The cop that pulled me over checked my reflexes, gave me a sobriety test, lectured me about domestic violence. I didn't take it too well—mouthed off at him. When they found out I wasn't drunk, they still wanted to get me for something so they checked my insurance. It was a lousy week late. If I'd just paid it, I wouldn't have gone anywhere."

"Dad!"

"Yeah, it was kind of stupid. I know."

Christina reached over and squeezed his hand. "I love you, Daddy."

Two blocks from the school they stepped out into the street around a moving van, backed over the sidewalk in front of a unkept painted-brick home. In the window hung a "For Rent" sign.

"Look, Dad. Let's go see." Christina towed him down the driveway. A man in his early fifties limped up from a side stairway that led to a basement unit. His wiry body seemed stiff and frail. His eyes were sunken back into his skull, accentuating his gaunt, thin-lipped face. Parachute-like ears billowed out on each side of his head.

Smiling, he approached, trying woefully at pleasantries.

"Good morning," he croaked, his protruding Adam's Apple bobbing up and down his skinny neck.

"You have the apartment for rent?" Don asked.

"Sorry, I forgot to take down the sign," he replied, peering back over his shoulder. He rotated the mug he held in his hand in a tight circle, twirling the ice cubes that swam in his drink. Then when he figured they no longer held any particular fascination, he looked up and added, "I do have other properties that may be available. What are you looking for?"

"This was close to my daughter's school," replied Don. "But we won't be ready to move in for a few weeks."

After another abbreviated twirl of the ice, the man said, "I think I might have just the place. Why don't you leave your name and number and I'll call you if it comes available."

"Nah. We'll stop by again." Don took Christina's hand as they turned to leave.

"You sure you don't want to leave your number?" the man called after them.

"That's okay," Don muttered over his shoulder.

The man turned and started up the ramp to the back of the truck, where a young couple was sorting boxes. "Well folks, I have the contract for you to sign." He transferred the mug to his left hand and brought a paper from the pocket of his striped shirt, buttoned to the top.

The young man reached into his pants pocket and got out his wallet. "Here's our deposit and first month's rent."

"So, you been married how long?" he asked the couple, one eyebrow raised, his head chocked awkwardly to the left as he squinted at the check the handsome young man had given him.

"Three weeks," the young bride answered, fondly touching her husband's arm.

The newlyweds turned to a nearby stack of boxes and unfolded the contract. Several minutes of silence passed as they scanned the document, then they signed, folded and returned it to their new landlord.

"Well let's see if we can get you unloaded." The land-lord returned the contract to his pocket and gave it a smug pat.

"Oh, you don't need to help, Mr. Briggs," the couple insisted.

"No, no. Glad to help." He set the mug down. "And please, call me Melvin." He glanced at a box; "Nancy," it read. Hefting it up onto his concave chest, he headed for the apartment. With an amused chuckle, the couple each snatched up boxes marked "kitchen" and followed him into the house.

"I think we'll like it here, Nance," Paul observed. She nodded slowly, then flipped her long dark hair up out of her eyes.

Melvin toted his cargo into the bedroom. He took a deep breath and cocked his head once more. He was alone. Noiselessly, he reached down and slid open the box flaps and pawed through its contents. Seconds later, hearing voices, he quickly closed the box and glanced up at the ceiling as if he'd heard someone stirring above. Then he returned to the truck, his thoughts on the young girl; he remembered seeing her and her father somewhere before. But where?

Don and Christina came to a stop at the steps of the school. She swivelled and gave her father a hug and a kiss on the cheek. "Bye, Daddy."

"Bye, love. I'll see you after school," Don said. With that, Christina turned and skipped away toward a group of girls. Don was pleased. For several minutes he stood there outside the schoolyard, watching his beautiful daughter greet her friends.

FIVE

EXOTIC animal heads, dead trinkets, trophies of beasts from far-distant jungles-slaughtered, mounted on finely-carved wooden plaques, dates and countries scrolled on brass tags beneath the great hunter's name; glass eyes staring down at fine, hand-carved furniture and costly souvenirs. It was a home that belonged to someone with money—lots of money.

Two men sat alone in the darkened room, ringed by the silhouettes of the slain beasts. They conversed in heated voices.

"You're screwing things up, Peck," the smaller of the two spat. "I've worked hard here, and I'm not about to tolerate your insubordinate attitude." His arm rose as if to give his words emphasis. "I talked my butt off for you this time, and—"

"To hell with you!" Peck growled. "I'm fed up with this little town."

The others' voice turned mean. "You get your act together and keep it that way 'til we're finished, or I'll put a bullet between your eyes and mount your fat, bloody head on my wall with all the other brainless animals."

"You—! You're trying to tell me how to keep it together, after the Mexican girl?"

The conversation had turned more than nasty; they were getting nowhere, and, besides, they'd gone over it all before. Both knew the nature of the sordid craft that fed their extravagant lifestyle. And both knew they couldn't last much longer in the small town.

Peck leaned back in his chair, crossed his massive legs at the ankles and pulled his cigarettes from his jacket

35

pocket. He slapped the pack against the palm of his hand and shook out a single smoke. Then, putting it to his lips, he asked, "So when do we move?"

The smaller man stood. "You and the men report to General Abdusala at Ijaw in five weeks. Seems Sawa's son is making trouble for the government. Take the pen; you won't be back." He pulled an ash tray from the coffee table drawer, slid it across the polished hardwood, and returned to his seat.

"And you?" Peck flicked his lighter and drew the flame to his face. As he lit his cigarette, the warm light bounced from his stone cold eyes—eyes, like those mirrored in the dead beasts overhead.

"Haven't decided yet. You'll stop in Barbados a week, pick up your orders, get your papers clean, then enter the country through Niger. That bimbo of yours can wait there 'til you're finished. Don't turn young Sawa into a martyr this time."

Peck forced the smoke downward from his flared nostrils like an angry bull pawing at the dirt, anxious to enter the ring and stamp the matador to death. But it was all allusion; no matador awaited—only lambs, awaiting slaughter by the ravenous wolves of a brutal military regime.

SIX

DON MADE HIS WAY TOWARD the business district. The morning chill lay like a blanket over the still-sleepy city, masking the sunlight filtering upward from behind the snow-capped mountains to the east. His body tingled with exhilaration. His newly-won freedom, the fresh air in his nostrils—he was alive again.

Still, finding a job that would pay enough for food and rent wouldn't be easy, especially without his commercial drivers license. The cement plant he'd worked for wouldn't even consider rehiring him until his driving privileges were restored. Besides, he'd be back on the bottom rung, no seniority, no extra benefits. Yes, a new opportunity would be his best option.

At lunchtime he stopped by the job center and began filling out the pile of applications he was given. He didn't have the money for lunch, and returning to Kate's house was out of the question.

He read down the row of questions. *Have you ever been convicted of a felony?*

Don fidgeted and filled in "Yes."

A bit further down the page: *Do you have a current driver's license?*

"No." It seemed all but hopeless. He stood, gathered up the papers, turned on his heels and strode out the door.

From behind a chain link fence halfway down the block, a red and blue sign, its lettering bordered in white, caught his attention. "Cobblecrete International, Inc." it read.

He remembered pouring the foundation for their new

building six or seven years earlier. In fact, he'd poured and worked concrete for them ten or 15 times over the years, back when they were still a small, struggling outfit. He'd watched them grow from a three-man service company to a large manufacturing plant.

He doubted the owner would remember him. But with nothing to lose, he pulled open the front door and stepped inside. No one was behind the counter—though a remote camera kept watch from a corner location to his right.

"Hello!" Don called out through the doorway that led into the back.

"We're back here!" a pleasant voice replied.

Don worked his way toward the sound of the voice, past a copy room to where a woman in her mid-twenties sat. She wore a headset phone. Lights blinked on the switchboard in front of her. "Hold on, I'll connect you." She pushed a button and paused long enough to pop her gum. Then before reaching out to punch another of the flashing lights, glanced up, smiled, and mouthed the words, "Be right with you."

Don smiled back. She seemed nice enough. Obviously a go-getter. Cute, but not necessarily sexy.

Don scanned the office. It appeared she was the only woman there. A dozen or so men, most with phones stuck to their ears, sat at other desks scattered about the room, taking orders and answering questions.

"He's not in. Would you like his voice mail?" the woman asked. "One moment, I'll connect you." She transferred the call and turned to face Don—when the switchboard lit up again. She lifted her hand as if to say "enough already!"

"Hi, how are you?" she grinned. "Sorry you had to wait. We're kind of shorthanded around here."

Don shrugged. "I'm looking for a job, anything available?"

She opened her desk drawer and pulled out an application. "Here, fill this out and I'll ask the boss."

Don had heard the same line all day. He was tired, with at least an hour walk to get home. It was a few minutes past five.

"I'll fill it out and bring it back tomorrow." Once more the phone rang, and the secretary picked it up as Don turned to leave.

"Cobblecrete...one moment, I'll connect you." She hit the hold button. "Wait!" she called after him as he disappeared around the corner. Don stopped and stepped back into the room. She connected the call. "I mean it. Sit down and fill it out." She tossed him a pen. "It's okay. He won't be back today."

Don looked over the application. *Name...address ...phone number*—all the usual.

Education. "High school."

Previous employers. Don penned in the most recent: "Ashrock, Inc. May 97–Feb. 99."

"Cecily, I'm off." A man in his mid-fifties, skin tanned and leathery from years of outdoor work, stepped out of the corner office. He glanced over at Don seated at the desk and, a bit surprised to see someone there, gave a cursory greeting.

"Hi, Ralph," Don replied.

The man squinted his eyes. "I know you...but I don't remember you," he said to Don as he rentered his office. Cecily winked.

Once inside, Ralph motioned to a seat, then reached for the application in Don's hand. "Let me see that." He began to read. In less than a minute he looked up. "If you drove for Ashrock, you have a CDL, the commercial driver's license."

"Actually, I don't." Don, briefly explained his situation.

Ralph exhaled. Then after a phone call to Ashrock, he said, "I've got a job. It's hot and dirty, pays seven-fifty an hour. We start at eight."

"I'll take it."

"Good, get the paperwork from Cecily on your way out. Good to have you aboard."

Back outside Ralph's office, Cecily, herself about ready to leave, was in a teasing mood. "I told you all you needed to do was fill out the papers." This time her smile melted away a little of the heartache Don had built up over the past months. She turned, opened her drawer, removed a folder, and handed him an employment packet.

It was nearing five-thirty as Don trudged down the long road leading from the plant. If he hustled, he'd make it home by six-fifteen.

Constructed in a heavy industrial area between the interstate and the railroad tracks, Cobblecrete's main building was backed by several smaller businesses zig-zagging their way to the freeway. Don kept his head down. The road was hard-packed base, so each time a car drove past, the dust billowed up, filling his mouth and nose.

Just as he reached the main road leading into town, another car—another dust-launcher!—pulled up from behind. Don stepped aside. Then "honk!" The driver hit the horn.

He swung around, about ready to clobber the jerk...Then he stopped short. There behind the wheel of a black, dust-coated Jeep sat Cecily.

"Scared you!" she laughed as she pulled alongside him.

"Nah," he muttered.

"Yes, I did!" chirped her singsong voice. "Saw you jump." It was almost a childlike tease, the way she hunched her shoulders and tipped her head back. "Say I did and I'll give you a ride to make things better," she pressed.

"Okay, you startled me." Casting a last glance down the long, dusty road, Don climbed in. Then the Jeep, its doors off, its soft-top on, let out a roar. He buckled his seatbelt as its tires spun in the loose gravel, making tracks for the main road.

Cecily reached down and turned up the radio. "Do you always drive like this?" he shouted over the din.

"No. I'm taking it easy so I won't scare you." She flashed her seemingly constant grin and swatted at her short, blonde hair as it whipped about her well-tanned face. Slightly crooked teeth glinted white between full lips, high cheekbones and softly-tapered nose and chin.

She was endowed with below-average-size breasts, and her hips and thighs were a little ample for Don's taste.

Don, a little defensive, sat sullenly for most of the ride. He couldn't help but press his foot to the floor when they screeched to a stop at an upcoming red light. Cecily broke the silence. "Where do you live?"

"Mapleton, Third and Apple."

"The tree streets," she yelled over the blast of the radio. But Don had long since decided not to compete with the noise.

They passed Christina's school. As they sped past the apartment with the skinny landlord, Don noticed the moving van was gone.

Minutes later, they turned onto Apple. "Third house on the left," Don said, pointing. Cecily pulled up to the opposite curb and turned off the ignition. The music stopped.

Don unbuckled his seatbelt and hopped out. "Thanks for the ride."

"Anytime."

He could have left it at that—actually wanted it left there. But his curiosity got the best of him. "Why did you offer me a ride?" he blurted out.

Cecily's reply was equally direct. "Because you needed one."

"No. I mean, I'm a stranger and you offered me a ride. Why?"

"You're not a stranger. You work for Ralph, he's a really good judge of character. See you in the morning, seven-forty-five?" She started the Jeep.

"Seven-forty-five? I thought work started at eight?"

"It does. We need to leave here by quarter 'til to be on time."

With that, the Jeep lurched from the curb. Don shook his head, amused. She'd just offered him a ride. And he didn't have much say in it. Still, he was home early. It was only five-fifty, and he'd just been given some precious extra minutes to spend with his daughter.

Supper was ready when he walked in the door. Kate

was incredible. It was a mystery how she managed to tend to her children, keep house, and still have time for a few hobbies. Her family was her life. "Someone needs to set the table," she hollered.

Don smiled. "I'll get it."

Passing the study on his way to the dining room, Don could see that Danny was at the computer, still hard at it. He popped his head through the doorway. "Any luck?"

"It's tough, but I think I almost have it."

In the kitchen Don began to open cupboard doors, looking for the plates. "Left of the sink," Kate called out without looking up from the salad she was making. A minute later, though, she drew near where Don was sorting silverware. "I got a call from the assistant principal at Brookside today," she said. "You and Christina need to have a talk after supper. It's nothing serious; something about a boy stealing the ball from her."

Don nodded. "Thanks, I'll do that."

Just then Don heard the garage door open and a car pull in. It was Alan, home from work. Don drew in a breath. He never felt as though Alan approved of him, though he was always cordial. A big man, light brown hair, heavy around the middle, Alan had never said anything to make Don believe he disliked him; it was just Alan's general tone. Kind of standoffish. Once a bishop in his church, he strictly adhered to his religious beliefs; Don didn't. Alan had made a lot of money; Don hadn't. Don knew Kate wanted him and Christina in her home— and that Alan didn't.

Kate's voice derailed Don's rather circuitous train of thought. "By the way, how was the job hunt?"

Don smiled and shared what had happened at Cobblecrete. She was delighted, of course. But he hoped she wouldn't say anything to Alan. Seven-and-a-half bucks was barely more than minimum wage. Alan made 20 times that amount.

"Shiz," Danny's muffled voice came from the other room.

"I won't hear that kind of talk in this home!" Alan yelled back.

Danny hadn't known his father was home. "Sorry."

"What's for supper?" Alan asked. "Smells great."

"Sour cream potatoes and teriyaki chicken." Kate never used recipes, but seemed to always get things right.

Suddenly from the study came a yelp. "Woohoo! I got in!" Don made a move toward the room, but then deferred to Alan, whose face instantly had taken on a serious expression, one registering complete and utter disbelief.

Minutes later, gathered round the supper table, the conversation mostly centered around Danny's successful security breach. Alan, still in shock, told how he'd recently paid tens of thousands of dollars to upgrade his system after the company had had problems with industrial espionage. Now he was eager to put the blame on the new system.

In contrast, more than anything, Danny just longed for his father's approval.

Supper dishes finished, Don asked Christina if she'd like to take a walk. He wanted to get out of the house, spend some one-on-one time with her.

"Watch out for that maniac," Kate cautioned as they wandered out the door and up the street, retracing their steps from that morning.

The last thing Don was worried about was someone hurting him or his daughter. No one could protect her like he could. Monica surely couldn't. She had won custody during the divorce, even though she wasn't a fit mother anymore. The only reason she kept Christina was for the child support. Then when Don went to jail, the support dried up. From what Kate knew, Don didn't need to worry about Christina being taken back. At least not until he made a better living.

Don put his hand on his daughter's shoulder. "Tell me about the trouble at school."

"Oops, I was hoping you wouldn't hear."

"Well?"

"My friends and I were playing foursquare and this boy, Tommy, kept taking the ball. I warned him three times, then when he did it again I went berserk. I—I chased him across the playground and...kinda beat him up. It was so embarrassing; he's almost twice my size."

"You beat him up?" Don half smiled—then his brow furrowed in worry that his daughter might have inherited her temper from him.

"Yeah...I made his lip bleed."

"Did you ever stop to think that maybe he likes you?"

"That's what my friends told me..." Then she gazed up at the western sky and hurriedly changed the subject. "Look, Daddy," she said, pointing at the sunset. "It's beautiful."

True, the sky was aglow in brilliant hues of orange, purple and red, with a blaze of sun rays stretching upward from a slender bank of clouds that hovered on the horizon. "A lady named Dr. Wendy came into our class today," continued Christina. "She told us that Ashley is coming back and how we should treat her and stuff. I have another friend named Amber whose big brother and his dog saved her."

Don tried to mirror her enthusiasm. "That sounds real neat....Just don't beat up any more boys, got it?"

"Got it."

Passing the newly rented apartment, they glanced over and through the window. There at the kitchen table sat the young couple, seemingly content. Lights on, all the blinds open, they could see the husband reading his newspaper, now and again pausing to speak to his wife.

The newspaper headlines still focused on the manhunt. But the young couple had moved to town from out of state and hadn't heard of the all the commotion—just yet, that is.

As they moved on down the sidewalk, Don couldn't help but ponder how distinct the upper-floor apartment was from that in the basement. How odd: every blind on the upper windows was shut, each drape drawn.

"He's still at large," Paul told his wife. "Seems the captain was nearly suspended without pay after the city council's emergency meeting....The department sent the blood sample they found to Salt Lake for testing. It'll take days to get back the results."

The young bride was more concerned with things domestic. "How did you like the meal?" she asked.

"Real good...." he muttered. "....They found her on Fir—just a few blocks from here."

Nancy lifted an ear toward the ceiling and listened. Someone was stirring around up there.

Paul didn't seem to notice. When she brought it to his attention, he shrugged and said, "I don't think this house has much insulation between floors."

Seconds later, Nancy let out a soft sob. "I think I burned the corn."

Again, Paul didn't catch what she'd said.

"Did you notice?"

"It was good."

At that, Nancy rose up, slid back her chair and cried, "You're not even listening!" then stomped from the room.

Paul looked up from his paper, his face suddenly registering what he'd done. Here they were, finally in their own home after living with his parents for a few weeks, awaiting their move to Utah, and he'd all but ignored his new wife. And this had been the first meal she'd cooked for him alone.

"Nancy," he called after her, following her into the bedroom, "I'm sorry, dear...."

SEVEN

DON'S CLOCK READ SIX-THIRTY when he heard Alan get up and begin his morning ritual-shuffling from room to room, waking children, shaking cobwebs from their sleepy heads. Don knew the house would be a hornets' nest before long. If he hurried, maybe he could grab a hot shower before the run on the bathrooms started.

A half hour later he ate breakfast and helped wipe down the kitchen as the children started for the bus, packs on their backs, sack lunches in hand. Danny was still in full swagger as he left for school.

Christina was one of the last to leave. "Bye, Daddy," she said, picking up her lunch and planting a kiss on Don's cheek.

"See you after work, Hon." Don smiled as he watched her race toward the front door. Just then came a honk. "That must be my ride," he breathed to himself, drying his hands on the towel hung by the sink. He turned to leave. "Thanks for everything, Kate." Then he turned back a moment and gave her an affectionate pat on the arm. He really did appreciate all her help.

"Don't forget your lunch," she said, pushing the last bag across the counter.

"Thanks again!" He was a little surprised. He'd figured to go hungry a few days until he got a check.

Cecily honked the horn again as Don stepped out the front door. "No time to waste. Don't wanna be late your first day," she yelled over the blast of the radio. Don climbed into the Jeep.

What with the radio blaring, and wind, and traffic

whizzing past—or, rather, Cecily whizzing *past* traffic— there wasn't much talk until they pulled into Cobblecrete's parking lot. Cecily gestured toward the back of the building. "We've never had a man last more than a few weeks in the powder shed," she said. "We'll see what you're made of."

"I've got it," he said, a bit testily.

"Yeah, we'll see!" She reached for the lunch bag in his hand, but caught part bag, part hand. She held on tightly. "If you'll let go of your sack, I'll put it in the fridge for you."

In the lunch room she swiped her time card through the clock. "You'll have to get a card from Parker later today. 'Til then, write your hours on this exception sheet," she said, drumming her fingers on a sheet taped next to the time clock. "I'll take you out and introduce you to Jeff, the plant manager." She opened the door and waited for Don to finish writing the time on the sheet.

A rack of dirty safety glasses lined the wall just outside the plant door. "Better put some on. Shop rules."

The clunky plastic lenses looked out of place on Cecily's tanned face. The plant itself was a beehive of activity. Inside a glassed-in area off to one side, an older man was cutting with a saw. Cecily tapped him on the shoulder and cupped the other hand to her mouth to ward off the racket. "Rex, meet Don Rodriguez, our new powder man." Rex shut off the saw, raised his bushy arms, and removed a set of ear plugs from beneath a dusty mop of white hair.

"What'd you say?" he replied, slapping dust from his pants and hands.

"This is Don. He's our new powder man," she repeated.

Rex made one last sweep of his hand, then stuck it out at Don. "Nice to meet you, Don." His handshake was firm yet sincere.

Don knew who Rex was—and hoped he hadn't been recognized. "You too, Rex."

"New powder man?" A sturdy, clean-cut man in his late twenties sauntered into the room.

"Yup, and ready to go to work," Cecily said, swiveling back and forth on her heels. A subtle grimace formed on Don's face; here she was, speaking for him like he was a little kid or something.

"I'm Jeff Hardy." The man shook hands vigorously.

With one parting shot, Cecily said, "Jeff's the plant boss. Well, see you at lunch," and she headed for the office.

Jeff motioned toward an open bay door that led outside. "Come with me." They made their way to another, smaller building at the south end of the complex. Don noticed its overhead door was crooked and bent. The building itself was an arched steel structure, probably a World War II quonset hut. Its small warehouse was cluttered and disorganized. A layer of dust hugged every surface. "In the summer it's at least a hundred and ten degrees in here," Jeff said. "A real sweat box. So you'll probably want to start as early as you can."

A large mixing machine sat in the back corner, accompanied by a mishmash of pallets stacked chest-high with bags of concrete mix. Empty buckets lined the west wall, and an army of broken pallets leaned more or less at attention along the back. A thermometer on the wall registered a comfortable sixty-five degrees. Don couldn't imagine being in such a place on a blistering-hot day.

Jeff took another 15 minutes to instruct Don in how to operate the equipment. Don listened patiently, though a little practice was all he really needed. Then before leaving, Jeff handed over a respirator, a coarse, red-colored apron, and a clipboard, and flashed his new employee a sympathetic grin. "Here are the orders that need to be filled by noon."

Don worked all morning, hoisting hundred-pound bags from pallets and dumping them into the mixer. He checked his watch occasionally to see how he was doing for time. The thermometer on the wall continued to rise as the morning passed.

"Rex Brandon," Don thought as he muddled through the names of the employees he'd met. "I hope he never remembers who *I* am."

Meanwhile, Paul and Nancy sat down to a late break-fast. They'd spent nearly the entire morning "making up" from their squabble the night before. His first class at the college didn't start until noon. Besides, they were newly-weds. Sleeping in was something they hadn't been able to enjoy at his parents' home. It just didn't feel right— "doing it" there in the bed of his youth. They'd both waited to have sex until they were married. Adherence to their religious beliefs had kept them "pure" for each other. They'd spent the last three weeks figuring it all out.

After breakfast Paul headed out for class. "If you need the car, you can drive me," he said, giving her an affec-tionate kiss.

"No, I'll finish unpacking and take you tomorrow." She reached behind him and squeezed a handful of his buttocks.

Paul winked as he turned to climb the few steps lead-ing up to the door. Nancy stood in the doorway watch-ing him drive away.

"Good morning!" their landlord's shrill voice startled her. "Off to a late start I see." He raised a brow and looked her up and down.

Nancy, still dressed in a sheer nightgown, stepped back out of range of his gaze. She wondered how long he'd been there. "Good morning to you, too," she mut-tered as she closed the door. He was a creepy little guy. He seemed nice enough, but she wasn't sure she could trust him.

By noon, Don was eat-a-horse hungry and drop-dead weary. He removed his breathing mask and toweled the sweat from his brow. The thermometer on the wall read a bit over eighty degrees. Jeff wasn't kidding about it being a sweat-box.

He stepped outside and ambled toward the main building. His clothing was soaked with sweat. The cool breeze felt good on his skin. The man at the shipping desk looked up as he passed. "You must be the new salesman," he taunted.

"I'm the powder guy."

The shipper chuckled and shook his head. Don continued toward the restrooms. Plastered in powdered pigment, it was obvious he was the grunt worker.

Further down the hall, another employee picked up the banter. "You must be the powder guy...." he snorted. This time Don merely nodded.

When he reached the office door, Cecily stepped out. Seeing him, she, too, began to laugh. "Nice color," she managed between giggles. "You're decorated to the hilt!"

Don, in an attempt to elude her, reached for the door as Cecily regained her composure and stepped in his way. "You can't go in the office like that," she said firmly. "You need to use the shop restroom."

Back behind a row of shelves, Don found the restroom door. His first gaze into the mirror surprised him. He was covered from head to foot with a rust-colored soot. No wonder everyone laughed, he thought to himself as he washed up.

Semi-clean—and by now ravenous—he found his way to the lunch room. "Everyone, listen up. This is Don Rodriguez," announced Cecily after he'd retrieved his lunch and was about to take a seat. A small sea of faces turned in his direction.

"Hi," Don nodded. "In case you're wondering, I'm the new vice president of marketing." The stab at himself succeeded in breaking the ice. Then he added, "I just haven't been promoted yet"—and he found himself laughing along with them.

"Sit down and enjoy your lunch, Mr. Big Shot," snorted Cecily. She slid out a chair next to her. Soon everyone was introduced. He did his best to remember names and faces.

"So where'd you work before?" Ryan, the shipper, asked.

"Ashrock...."

Rex sat quietly off to one side, slowly chewing his lunch, which consisted of a couple of peanut butter sandwiches and a banana. At sixty-five, he was Cobblecrete's oldest employee. Had worked for Ralph more than 20 years. Now a bread-crumb smile creased his lips. Eyeing

Don, he said, "I knew I'd seen you before. Used to work for Grangers, right?"

Don cringed. "I was hoping you didn't recognize me."

"Why not?" replied Rex. "You were a good driver." Don sensed that Rex wasn't just talking to him, but carefully directed his remarks to everyone at the adjoining tables. "It was in the early days of the company. You always got out of the truck cab to help us, especially when we fell behind schedule. Your dad worked for the same outfit." Don smiled over at Rex, but inside he felt a stab of pain—even though Rex hadn't said a word about the accident.

Don shifted uncomfortably in his seat. Maybe he forgot about it.

"How's your dad these days?"

"He retired and moved to Idaho a few years ago," Don replied. "He has cancer, you know."

"No, I didn't. Sorry."

The next few minutes brought a smattering of small talk. Rex finished eating and stood to leave. "Glad to have you with us, Don." Then he pivoted on one foot and walked from the room, a slight limp in his step. Hardly enough to notice, thought Don.

Cecily caught his attention just as the last few stragglers left the room. "What was that all about?"

Don hoped to dodge her question. "Nothing."

"Come on, Don Rodriguez. I won't tell anyone. What didn't you tell us?" Cecily reached out and fastened onto his forearm.

An earlier victim of her vice-like grip, Don caved in. "Okay, okay. Did you notice his limp?"

"Yeah. He got hurt on the job several years—"

Don finished her sentence. "And it was me who ran over him!" He stared down at the table top, his fingernail scratching at the fake wood grain. He then slumped slightly forward and took in a breath. "It was my first week on the job. I was only eighteen, just two days out of training. Rex and the rest of Ralph's crew were pouring the foundation of a home. Rex was kneeling on the ground, his back to me. I didn't even see him. Drove my truck right onto his foot. It took a few seconds to figure out why everyone was yelling at me to back up. When I did, he was in serious pain. But he didn't put the blame on me—in fact, he was more concerned about finishing the job. Even told the police that it was his fault for being in the way."

"That sounds like Rex."

"Well, the guys teased me for months. Whenever I showed up on the job they'd say, 'Watch your feet!' but Rex never once spoke badly about me."

"We love the old man. He keeps telling Ralph he wants to retire. Ralph won't let him—figures he wouldn't live long. His wife died of cancer....three, four years ago. They'd been married since they were seventeen. Broke Rex's heart. We're Rex's family now. His daughter lives in Florida, he only sees her once or twice a year. Keeps to himself pretty much, but I'm sure if you ever wanted to talk to him about your dad, he'd be a great listener."

Don nodded. I just might do that, he thought.

Cecily stood. "I better get back to work."

"Me, too. If I'm going to train for that V. P. job, I can't be caught slacking."

The thermometer registered ninety by the time he reached the powder shed. Don wasn't sure if he could stand the heat and dirt. He'd rather be driving.

By four-thirty Don had filled all the orders, each stacked neatly in rows on pallets. He reported to Jeff, who shook his head. "You're kidding. Are you sure?.... You finished the Northland order?" he quizzed, clearly pleased.

"Yes, and the three for Classic, too," Don said, pointing them out on the list.

"You're kidding," Jeff repeated. "Do you know that you've done nearly twice the amount anyone else has done in a day? Oh, by the way, I was only joking when I said they had to be finished by noon."

Jeff gave him a pat on the back. "Why don't you clean up and take it easy 'til quitting time?"

Don went to the back restroom. The shop was dark and empty, except for the mold room where Rex was still working.

Don stopped to visit. "Where is everyone?" he asked.

Rex glanced up. "They start at seven and quit by four."

"What time do you start?"

"I usually get in before seven." Rex, head down, kept at his work.

"Then why are you still working?"

"Guess I lost track of time," he said modestly. He'd made it a lifelong habit to work harder and longer than anyone else. And anyway, he didn't enjoy going home to an empty house, eating supper alone.

Don decided to get it over with; get it off his chest once and for all. "You remember what I did to you, don't you?"

"Yeah," Rex replied, lifting his face from his work, "but that happened more than ten years ago. It was an accident and you were young. I know you didn't do it on purpose."

"I see you still limp a bit. Does it hurt?"

"Not much. Only a little arthritis now and then." Then Rex, satisfied that the subject was laid to rest, said, "Tell me about your dad."

"The doctors think he has a week or two. His wife doesn't think he'll last more than a few days. Says he seems to have given up." Don's words made it sound as if he'd come to grips with the imminent loss of his father. Rex knew better. Losing a loved one wasn't easy, no matter how prepared you were.

"Is he on medication?"

"They let him have his own morphine drip. At this stage the doctors don't worry about addiction."

Don hadn't been close to his father when he was young. His parents had divorced when he was five. Afterwards, he went to live with his mom. Then when he turned 18, his dad got him his first job driving a truck. He was the youngest driver in the fleet. The accident with Rex could have cost him his job. He always thought it was because of his dad that he was able to keep it. Little did he know that Rex had called the owner of the batch plant and asked him not to punish the boy.

"I know, my wife died of cancer four years ago last month," Rex said solemnly.

"Cecily told me. I'm sorry." Don wasn't sure what else to say.

Cecily poked her head in the doorway, the characteristic grin seemingly etched across her mouth. "Ready to go?"

Don glanced up at the clock. Five, already? The last minutes had passed quickly. Rex seemed like such a mild-mannered person. Don realized he could learn a lot from the old man, if given the chance.

On the drive home, Cecily left the radio off. "I saw you talkin' to Rex. Nice guy, isn't he?"

"He is. Sure is a mild-mannered sort. I seem to be just the opposite."

Don knew when he let the part about his own personality slip that it would be a long ride home. Sure enough, Cecily began to pry.

For his part, Don tried not to say much. Instead, he let his mind review the past. Years of wild living; a temper that could heat up and boil over in an instant, just like his father's. Then the questions hit him: Would his own life, like that of his dad's, end early? Would anger be the cause of his death? Or would he be able to reign in his emotions in time? Maybe Rex could help. Don knew that if something didn't change, if he kept going the way he was, he not only might snap, but he wouldn't be able to keep his daughter.

Before he knew it, Cecily had pulled over to the curb. "See you tomorrow, Don Rodriguez."

"Oh," he said, surprised by her abruptness, "Thanks." He got out.

He went through the garage door and removed his shoes before entering the house. Kate hardly recognized him as he came through the doorway. "Kate, I don't know if you want me in the house with all this crud on me."

She just smiled. "I *do* have seven children, Don. Tip-toe in the laundry room and put your dirty clothes in the empty washer. You can use Alan's robe that's folded on the dryer."

"Thanks." Don shuffled across the floor, leaving a trail of sock prints on the tile leading to the laundry room. He put on the robe and was headed toward the stairs, when the door clicked open from the garage and in stepped Alan.

Crap! Don froze. "Oh, hi, Alan," he said sheepishly.

"Hi, Don," Alan muttered dryly, his eyes unable to tear away from what Don was wearing.

Moments later, Kate, a wash rag in her hand, traipsed into where they stood. "Hi, sweetheart," she greeted. He turned to her, stone-faced and tight-lipped, as Don plodded on up to his room.

Alan waited until he thought Don was out of earshot. "Why's he in my robe?" he grumbled tersely.

"He was covered with dust," explained Kate. "I had him change in the laundry room so he wouldn't get the house dirty. It's no big deal. I'll wash it again tomorrow."

Don stood just inside the bedroom door, straining to hear what was being said. Alan's muffled voice, however, could not hide its intent. "How long will he be here?" he groused.

"Only a week or two more." Kate was getting a little impatient with Alan's complaints. "You could treat him a little kinder, you know."

"I don't like the example he's setting for the children."

Kate's tone turned defensive. "He hasn't done anything even remotely improper," she snapped.

Suddenly the back door swung open. The arrival of children ended the conversation.

Don showered, thinking how important it was to find a place for them to live. He felt guilty for having to mooch off his ex-wife's family, though he helped around the house as much as he could.

After the supper dishes were finished, Don and Christina went for their usual evening walk. He couldn't dislodge from his mind the argument he'd overheard. He needed to find a place, now more than ever. But how he could afford the rent, much less pay a deposit and hook up utilities, he didn't know.

"Ashley came back to school today," Christina reported. "She seemed okay. She doesn't say much, but she must have been pretty scared."

Ashley...the 11-year-old girl from Christina's grade school. The one who had been abducted shortly after moving with her mother from a neighboring town. Don shivered at the thought of his 'Tina getting snatched like that.

"They'll get him, won't they?" she asked.

"Sure they will," Don said confidently. "I hear they have the best police in the state, right here in Mapleton."

"I don't know if she'll ever be the same," she said sadly. "She's afraid everyone is watching her."

"How would you feel if you were in her shoes?"

"I don't know. Pretty bad, I guess."

They continued on up the street, hand in hand, talking, sharing the moment.

EIGHT

"MRS. GARDNER, I KNOW it's only been three days, but we need you to bring her back down to the station for a few more questions." Detective Kiser "Deek" Derickson's usual mellow tone was growing impatient. Middle-aged, his dark, bushy head of hair and muscular build made him look ten years younger. Only his eyes bore the likeness of those of an older man. They drooped, somewhat puffy, toward his slightly flat nose, mostly from a lack of sleep.

It was rumored that Deek was the first pick of the city council for the captain's job the year before. His 20 standout years as a police officer made him the most qualified man on the small force. So when he had hired on five years earlier—having accepted a hefty pay cut—it was with a tacit understanding he would be chosen to replace the soon-to-retire captain. The principal reason he had moved back to Utah was so that his children could be raised among those of his own religion—and to escape the precarious streets of Los Angeles. The captain had retired right on schedule but Chief Anderson, who served as council commissioner to the police force, had persuaded the counsel to hire Bingham instead.

Deek, still in homicide, slumped at his desk, exhausted from the hours he spent on his cases. "Look, we need every bit of information we can get...I know it might upset her again. I'll do the best I can...You don't want this to happen to someone else's daughter do you? Good. I'll see you at six then. Thank you, Mrs. Gardner."

He succeeded in loosening the top button of his cotton shirt and pulled the tattered tie side to side to slacken it as he hung up the phone.

Captain Bingham was listening from his office. "She'll come in?"

"Reluctantly."

"Good," Bingham grunted. "You don't mind if I sit in, do you?" His deep, no-nonsense voice reverberated from around the corner. Captain Bingham didn't take no for an answer. Bingham, his desk facing Deek's on the other side of the office window, leaned back in his chair and brushed his long, stringy hair over his thick balding skull with his fingers in a vain effort to hide the aging effects of years of military violence. His face was hard, as if carved from granite; a chiseled scar lay deep in the cheek bone below his left eye—one of many trophies of war.

"Fine." Deek didn't want to make an issue of it. Besides, the captain had never worked on a police force in his life. A retired military man, Bingham had moved here from back east about a year ago. Now Bingham tried to run the force like the hard-nosed veteran he was, barking orders, demanding immediate action from his subordinates. However, the council had recently grown impatient with his methods. Several on the squad had already made their complaints known to Chief Anderson.

"Hold on a moment," the dispatch secretary said into her mouth piece.

"Captain Bingham, line one." Maryann served as both part-time secretary and night-time dispatch.

"Captain Bingham here." Anger flooded his face upon hearing the voice. Without another word, he placed the phone on the desk and stood to close his office door.

Deek glanced up to see what Bingham was doing. Through the window he recognized the first few words the captain said: "I told you not to call me here." Then he turned his back to the window.

"4/9 5:42." Deek noted the call on a scratch pad. He began to scroll through the data on the five abductions. What were they missing? They were no closer to catching the guy than they'd been months earlier.

"Deek, Mrs. Gardner and Ashley are here to see you," Maryann said, approaching him. Deek twitched. Ashley and her mom stood only a few feet behind her. Ashley was a beautiful girl, with dark eyes, long brown hair, and symmetrical features, her pubescent figure just starting to mature.

"Please come take a seat," he motioned.

Deek again glanced through the window that separated him and Bingham. The captain, his back to the window, was still on the phone, rocking forward and back in his chair. Maybe Bingham needn't be involved. He swivelled to face the mother and daughter and spoke soothingly. "How are you, Ashley?"

"I'm fine. Is Sig here?"

"He's working tonight with Officer Stacey."

Ashley seemed distracted. "I like Sig," she spoke, her eyes flitting from object to object on Deek's desk. "Do you think they'll be coming in here tonight?"

"He might. Do you think you'd feel safer if he were here?" Ashley nodded. "Just a minute and I'll call him."

Deek took his radio from the desk drawer and keyed up the microphone. "One nineteen to one thirty-nine....Stace?"

"One thirty-nine. Go ahead, Deek."

"Stace, I have a young girl who'd love to see Sig–his biggest fan. Can you come in?"

"Affirmative. See you in five."

Deek put the radio back in the drawer and slid it shut.

Just then the door to Captain Bingham's office swung open and Bingham stepped out. "I'll see you tomorrow, Detective Derickson," he said, his hat in hand. He hardly acknowledged the girl and woman in the office, just shuffled over to the coat rack, put on his expensive mohair overcoat, and left the building.

"Will all the other men be here this time?" Ashley asked, a little more at ease.

"No. It'll just be you, your mom, me, Officer Stacey and Sig. How does that sound?"

"That'll be a lot better." She rolled her eyes. "I couldn't even think those other times. There were too many people."

"Did it help to talk to the doctor? Let's see, what was

her name?" Deek wanted to see if she remembered.

"Dr. Wendy," Ashley informed him. "She was really nice. She asked questions about my friends, uncles, the people my mom works with. I'm not even sure what she wanted to know. I finally told her I was tired and wanted to go home to bed. I'm supposed to see her again tomorrow." Ashley turned to her mom to see if she was right.

"Yes, we are," Mrs. Gardner said quietly.

"Mrs. Gardner," Deek said, leaning forward, "I know this isn't easy for you and Ashley. Lieutenant Barker keeps his officers running special patrols in your area each day. We don't think he'll be back. I don't know how many more times we'll have to talk to Ashley before we're through."

The beam from Stacey's headlights shone through the glass doors at the rear of the office, then turned off. Stacey and the dog could be seen as silhouettes against the lights in the parking lot.

"Maryann," Deek called out, "will you open the back door for Stace?"

The door buzzed and Stacey pulled it open.

"Come," he commanded, slapping his leg.

Sig paused outside the door. He was usually not allowed inside.

Ashley sprang from her seat to greet her canine friend. "Go," Stacey signaled. In one leap Sig bounded in front of Ashley, wagging his tail and licking her face, hands and arms with his long, rough tongue.

Mrs. Gardner was disgusted, but refrained from reprimanding her daughter.

"There's no doubt he likes you," Stacey said. "How've you been, Ashley?"

"Good. I went back to school today. Everyone was real nice. The kids said Dr. Wendy talked to them about me yesterday." Ashley held tightly to Sig's collar as they walked back to Deek's desk.

"What did she talk about?" Deek asked, scooting a third chair up to his desk.

"Sit, boy," Ashley commanded. Stacey flashed a subtle hand signal and Sig sat down next to the girl.

Deek could tell she wanted to talk to Stacey. Making eye contact and giving a slight nod of his head, Deek indicated to Stacey that he needed his help. "So Dr. Wendy talked to your friends?" Stacey repeated.

"Yes. She told them not to worry, that you guys wouldn't let anything happen to them. They said she talked to them about me, too. You know, the kind of questions not to ask me and stuff." Ashley rolled her eyes.

"How do you feel about that?"

"Oh, it's okay. Some things I don't want to talk about. It's too scary."

"That's only natural," said Stacey. "Are you willing to tell me and Sig?"

"I can tell you anything. Sig saved me, you know." Sig perked up each time Ashley spoke his name. "And your sister is in my class. She says you're the best cop in the whole state."

Stacey tousled Sig's head. His big tail thumped at the leg of the chair. "Thanks. Little sisters are kind of partial."

"Maybe so," she agreed.

"Can you talk with us about what happened the other night?"

Ashley started to withdraw. "Too scary," she said in a quiet voice.

Stacey knew he needed to be a little less direct. "Sig hasn't learned to talk yet or he'd tell me. What does Sig know, but can't tell me? Did he see the man?" Stacey patted Sig on the head again.

"No! He ran off before Sig got there. I could hear the police sirens and all the voices. I kept kicking and fighting the best I could. That's what my mom taught me." Ashley paused. "I think I kicked him in the mouth."

"Why do you think that?" Stacey questioned.

"Cause I heard him swear; the "'F-word,' you know." Ashley glanced at her mother to see if she disapproved.

Stacey reassured her. "That's okay. We know which word it is....What did his voice sound like?"

"Well, not as deep as yours. Kind of high and scratchy, I think."

"How tall do you think he was?" Stacey stood and put his hand out to the side of his dark sideburns. "Was he as tall as me?" Ashley thought about the question. Slowly she began to shake her head.

"No, not nearly that tall."

Stacey began to lower his hand as Ashley looked on. Each time he would stop, she would shake her head. Finally, she stood up next to Stacey. "I think about this tall," she said, reaching to about the middle of his chest.

"So he's kind of short?" Stacey sawed at his chest, as if memorizing its height. "Mrs. Gardner, would you stand next to me a moment?" The woman stood, and Stacey moved close. She was about the height of Ashley's mark. Then his probe continued. "Do you think he was about as tall as your mother?" Ashley, her cheeks drawn up in a pained grimace, looked at the two of them standing next to each other.

"Yes only...skinny." Again she looked at her mother to see if she'd offended her. "And very strong."

"Mrs. Gardner, how tall are you?" Deek asked.

"Five-four."

So far Stacey and Deek had uncovered more information about the killer than any other investigation team. The county was involved in the investigation, along with the FBI and three other area cities. Evidence had been painstakingly examined, reexamined, sent to the labs, but to no avail. They had one DNA sample of skin taken from under a victim's nails which matched that from the blood sample recovered from the shooting. Information from each of the incidents had been plugged into the FBI's computer system to cross link the data.

Deek continued taking notes. The other teams had already questioned Ashley several times. As far as they knew, the killer never spoke. Now, out of the blue, Ashley remembered the swear word.

Stacey resumed his questioning. "Can you tell me what he was wearing?"

"Everything was black."

"What did his clothes feel like?"

"They were kind of slick."

"How did he smell?"

"I don't know...normal, I guess, except his breath. It smelled like rotten meat."

Stacey and Deek exchanged a puzzled glance.

"Do you think it was from something he ate?"

Ashley shrugged her shoulders. "I don't know."

Deek broke in to ask a question. "Did you feel any rings on his fingers?"

Ashley hesitated and looked to Stacey for assurance.

"Don't worry," said the younger officer. "He's here to help. You can answer him."

Still, Ashley directed her remarks to Stacey. "I didn't feel any."

After another 20 minutes of questions, Stacey asked, "Ashley, is there anything else you can think of that might help us?"

Ashley thought for a minute. Finally she said, "I don't think it was the "F" word...I think it was a different language. I can't remember anything else."

Stacey nodded. "Will you do your best to remember and come back again to talk to me?"

"Yes, if you bring Sig." She reached down with both hands and rubbed the sides of his body. His big tail thumped the chair again as it swept the floor. Mrs. Gardner stood. Deek shook her hand and thanked her again for coming in. Stacey and Sig walked them to the car. He told Ashley how proud he was of her for being so brave. "Now, if you need us for anything, you call me anytime, day or night," he added. He took a card from his pocket and wrote his phone numbers on it. "That's my cell number if I'm not at work. Will you call me?" Ashley nodded and bent to give Sig one last hug. Sig's tongue came out. "One last lick for the road," Stacey chuckled. "He likes you maybe more than he does me."

When the officers returned to the building, Maryann asked Stacey, "Well, how did it go?"

"Good, really good," he hurriedly replied, wanting to get together with Deek to confirm his feelings about the case. "We may have a better idea of his height and build...a small break in the case."

Deek was busy typing in the data he'd noted in the interview when Stacey entered the office. Stacey stopped to read over his shoulder. When Deek had finished e-mailing the new information to every other interested agency along with a request for a meeting, he turned to Stacey. "You did great, Stace. And you too, Sig." Sig lay patiently at the side of the desk. "It's not a whole lot, but more than anyone else has."

Stacey pulled himself to his feet. "Well I'm on overtime. Think we'll head for home." He slapped his leg. Sig jumped to go. "Good night, Deek. Maryann."

Stacey backed the patrol car into the driveway of his apartment. The council had approved the use of police cars twenty-four hours a day, reasoning that the more cars seen in the city, the bigger the force appeared. Stacey didn't use it much except for work. He preferred his truck, as did Sig, who loved riding in the bed. They lived in the upper apartment of an older home. He used the small back yard to do most of Sig's training. A short chain link fence ran around the front of the yard.

Stacey stepped out of the car and opened the back door for Sig, who hit the ground on the run. With a single, graceful bound he leapt easily over the fence. Stacey closed the door and, with a two-step flurry, also cleared the fence. He loved being a cop. He'd spent the previous four years preparing to join the force. He sent applications all over the state, but wanted to work in his hometown until he had a little experience under his belt.

His year on the force, of course, wasn't without its problems. Captain Bingham could be a hard, demanding cuss. The night shift hours were sometimes long and boring. Day work often brought him in contact with friends and neighbors. He once pulled over his first grade school teacher, Mrs. Tait, who had run a red light while going only 15 miles an hour. She had spent 28 years teaching and mothering and wiping up after first graders, and even ten years after retirement she still remembered his name. She wasn't happy that little Ricky Stacey had given her a ticket. Unfortunately, it was her fifth in under a year. Stacey had to stand in front of Judge Benson—also a former first grade student of Mrs. Tait—and watch her lose her license. They both suffered the wrath of a seasoned, old-fashioned teacher. Judge Benson would have fined her for contempt if it had been anyone else.

Sig was a bonus to the force. Stacey was only allowed to bring him to work after three months of proof he'd be a valuable asset. He wasn't paid extra for his "partner." Only the month before, Sig had nailed the biggest heroin bust in the state's history. A van driver had stopped for a burger on his way through town. Coincidentally, Stacey had pulled up to park right next to him. That's when Sig reacted. The driver, hearing Sig, was more than a little nervous. Stacey turned Sig loose to see what was the matter. Realizing he was about to see some serious trouble, the driver set out on foot. Thirty seconds later, he found himself face down on the asphalt, his hands cuffed at his back.

A rumor had gone around that they were going to honor both him and Sig for the great work they'd done in saving Ashley. Even the FBI was impressed.

Stacey wasn't married. At twenty-four, he wasn't concerned about it, although his status certainly wasn't from lack of effort or opportunity. He was well-known to Mapleton's available young women.

His dog and his work were his passion. Each time he and Sig did well, it opened up other possibilities to them. The state had offered him a job at the airport. The pay was good, but the work wouldn't be nearly as rewarding. So he'd just wait until the right job came along.

Stacey opened the front door to his apartment. "Seek!" he commanded. He didn't really need Sig to search his disordered apartment, but it was good practice. Sig made a quick round and reported back to Stacey, who produced a treat from his uniform pocket.

It hadn't been easy to obtain all the drugs necessary for Sig's training. His father had to post a bond in order to legally use and return the minuscule amounts of illegal substances needed. Stacey had purchased Sig as a pup three years earlier. In the beginning of training, he used a stuffed gorilla as a decoy. It wasn't long before Sig could find the toy hidden any place in his dad's house. Stacey slowly introduced the drugs inside the toy. Sig learned to find whatever it was his master wanted him to find. Now he was as smart and disciplined as any profession-ally trained K-9 in the country.

Stacey had moved into his own place after being hired by the force. It was quiet. His half-Italian mother wasn't around to keep the place clean, but since he didn't often entertain guests, it was no big deal. The apartment had a small kitchen, full bath, a living room, and two small bed-rooms. He shared the larger bedroom with Sig and kept a small office in the other, where he worked on police files at home.

Stacey flipped on the computer on his way to the kitchen to find something to eat. There wasn't much to choose from. He opened a couple of cans of dog food and dumped them in Sig's dish. Sig sat patiently, waiting for a signal to eat. Stacey opened the refrigerator and rifled through the cupboards. Nope, not much! Sig still sat qui-etly, his mouth watering.

"Okay, lunch!" Stacey called. Sig lunged forward. Stacey picked up the phone and dialed. "Hey, Jimmy the pizza man! It's Stace calling. Think you could send me the regular?"..."By the way, how's business?"..."Good, you deserve it after all these years."

Hanging up the phone, he returned to the computer and began calling up cases that even came close to the current one. Thousands of missing and dead girls; this was not going to be easy. Sig settled down next to the computer desk and promptly fell asleep. He would be wide awake, though, by the time the pizza man arrived. It wasn't that he liked pizza; it was the empty box that he enjoyed.

NINE

IN THE DISTANCE, down the dark, dusty country road, an old beat-up sedan, steam belching from beneath its hood, pulled over onto the shoulder. Its single occupant took one last drag from his cigarette, flicked it out the window, pulled a baseball cap down to cover his brow, and opened the door.

Dressed in black, he zipped his jacket around his large torso and walked toward two men standing at the edge of a newly-planted barley field. Two cars were parked along the opposite side of the road. The crescent moon shed just enough light to cast an eery fluorescence on one man's starch-white shirt and a fine shadow on the freshly tilled ground.

"I want out," grumbled the man in the white shirt in a well-rehearsed demand. He seemed educated, business-like—yet scared, unsure as to how his request would be received.

"When we started, I told you you'd be in it to the end," muttered the other man in a deep voice. "I know of only two ends. One, when the project's finished; the other, when flowers are placed on your grave."

The big man in black kept his back turned to the moon. The man in the white shirt was a banker at the local branch. He had never seen either of the other men's faces. He only knew they meant business.

"I know. I know. That was then. Now you have three million, seven. If I take nothing, you're almost as well off as if we finished moving the entire amount." Was he convincing enough?

Now the big man in black moved in. "Mr. Penrod,"

he growled, giving the banker a poke in the chest with his gloved hand, "your wife is a beautiful woman, your children worship you, and you go to church every Sunday. We wouldn't want any of that to change, now would we?"

Mr. Penrod answered in a low whine. "No, but it gets more risky every day."

"But you didn't think it was so risky sleeping with the teller, did you?" he sneered. "You've got two weeks to get it done. We clear the accounts every night, then the money's moved twice by the following morning. The Swiss bank account is only a number. Your money is already in your account. By the time your kids are old enough to go to college, you'll have enough to educate three more bankers just like you, and still live like a king. And there's no chance you'll be caught. When you're finished and we're gone, it'll look like the teller was the only one. You'll get reprimanded for not watching close enough, but you'll be in the clear." The man gave the banker one last, threatening poke.

Without another word, the black-clad man lumbered over to his car. The door squeaked open on its rusty hinges—its interior light failing to illuminate—and the old car groaned as its driver settled back onto the tattered seat. Riding on no more than half of its eight cylinders, the engine sputtered and turned over, sending a cloud of smoke from its exhaust. As the heap pulled away and rattled off down the dusty road, the banker noticed the license plates were missing.

"You can go, now," the smaller man said. "She'll be watching you."

The banker shook his head as he climbed into his car. "I don't look forward to it."

Paul and Nancy were ready for bed. "I'm not sure I like it here," Nancy, seated on the bed, announced as she brushed her long dark hair.

Paul made a few more passes with his toothbrush and spit what was left of the foamy paste into the sink. "What?...Why not?" They hadn't even finished unpacking.

Nancy's hairbrush dropped to her lap. "This morning as you pulled away, I was standing in the doorway. Mr. Briggs was there...at the corner...watching me."

Paul rinsed his toothbrush, banged it on the edge of the sink, and put it in the cup on the counter top. "I didn't see him."

"*I* did. He gives me the creeps."

"He seems like an okay guy." Paul replied, stepping into the bedroom. "He helped us unpack."

"I know, but even that was weird. Didn't you notice? He only picked up the boxes that went to our bedroom, even if we needed to move something else first." Nancy tossed the brush on the nightstand. "It seemed like everywhere I went in the house today, he was directly above me. I could hear him walking around upstairs the whole time."

"It's probably nothing. I haven't heard a thing all evening." He turned to face the door to the hall and noticed headlights flash across the living room curtains. "Maybe that's him coming home now."

Nancy stood and leaned to look down the hall. The car's engine shut off, just outside their kitchen window. They could faintly hear the door to the upstairs open and close. Nancy flipped off the light switch, and the two of them quietly slipped under the covers, listening for any sound from above.

"I don't hear a thing," Paul whispered.

Nancy rolled out of bed again and reached up to slide open the window. "Think I'll let in some night air." Then with a gasp, she jumped back away from the window. "Someone's looking in!"

Paul pounced to his feet and parted the curtain. "I can't see anyone."

"I saw him," Nancy whimpered. "A shadow against the street light." She started to cry. Paul pulled her close.

"Your imagination just got away from you, talking about spooky things and all."

Nancy jerked away from him, climbed back into bed, her back to him, and wept silently.

"What! Now what's wrong?" Paul breathed out three

short bursts of air. Then he climbed into bed beside his wife. I don't understand her, he thought as he pulled the covers up.

Deek finished his report and asked Maryann if she'd like him to walk her to her car.

"Sure. That would be nice. Just let me switch the calls to county." She dialed in the necessary numbers and gathered up her sweater and purse. They weaved their way through the well-lit parking lot. "Thanks again," she said. "I've never felt like I needed an escort until the last few weeks."

Maryann was known around town as a man-hunter—loose, like her red curly hair, single, always searching to "bag" the next trophy, and rarely intimidated, even by the most ravenous male—if he had money, that is.

Deek, married and middle-aged, had made it abundantly clear that he wasn't interested. "This is crazy," he sighed, opening her door. "We're not any closer now than when this whole thing started."

She could only shrug her sexy shoulder as she climbed in behind the wheel. "Well, goodnight, Deek."

"Yeah, see you tomorrow."

Deek angled back toward the building and climbed into his five-year-old Taurus. It belonged to the department, and—if you didn't count the dull spots where the paint had worn off—was the only unmarked car in the fleet, except the new Pontiac Grand Am the captain drove. Whenever any of the other officers needed to go plain-clothed, they borrowed Deek's car.

Just as he pulled out of his space, he gave the impound yard a sidelong glance. He lurched to a stop; someone was in there! A thin column of steam wafted up from the hood of the old Chevy they'd impounded on a DUI the week before. He squinted at the gate. Its lock was gone, the chain hanging from wire. He grabbed the radio. "One-nineteen, one-twenty-one...Mitch?" he said in a whisper.

"One-twenty-one, go ahead, Deek."

"What's your twenty?"

"I'm at thirteen hundred, East Canyon Road. What's up?"

Deek was short of breath. "I think we've got a break-in at the city impound. How soon can you back me up?"

"ETA is four minutes. Hold on, we'll go in together."

Deek slid his service revolver from the holster beneath his jacket. He slipped from the car. Remembering the bulletproof vest he kept hanging next to his desk, he almost started in the direction of the building. But something propelled him instead over to the impound gate, where he crouched to wait for Mitch. His mind raced. The battered Chevy belonged to Howard Reid, a harmless old drunk. Probably had gotten nabbed while out getting himself a new bottle.

He peered around the gate post, his heart about to burst. He was kind of rusty since his days in L.A.

Suddenly a flash burst from the direction of the Chevy, followed by the distinct report of gunfire. A searing pain shot through Deek's side. The dark world spun all around him. He managed to raise his head in the direction of the lot, and saw the figure of a large man rush past and disappear into the shadows. *Something seemed familiar*, Deek thought, before slipping into unconsciousness.

TEN

SLEEPING IN WASN'T PART of the routine that following morning, though he could have used the rest. Paul had spent the first two hours of the night reviewing what he'd said, another several hours dreaming of how he could have handled it better, and the rest rehearsing what he'd say to make things better. Nancy had quietly cried herself to sleep, and no matter what Paul said, she wouldn't talk. He got up before dawn, showered, dressed, and shaved. Then it came to him—breakfast in bed. Pancakes, bacon, eggs, the whole nine yards.

Opening the fridge, he examined its contents. Cold cereal and orange juice would have to do.

Don's mornings were becoming predictable. Up by six-thirty, breakfast, help Kate with the dishes, and off to work. This day Cecily didn't show up until eight. Don waited impatiently on the front porch.

"Sorry I'm late," she apologized as she pulled away from the curb.

Don spoke above the radio. "Ralph won't fire me unless he fires you too."

Cecily giggled. "He'd never fire me. I'm too important to the company."

"Me, too. He can't fire a good powder man."

Cecily turned a bit serious. "Do you know how many of our people started off in the powder shed?"

"From what I hear, no one ever lasts." And now Don, smiling, knew why.

She grinned back. "Jeff hired on as powder man when

he was finishing up his last year in college. Ryan, the shipper? Did powders just before shipping. Rex mixed powders ten or 12 years ago. And Ralph invented the formula almost 20 years ago. The powder shed is kind of like a testing ground to see how badly people want to work." Cecily had made her point.

"So what you're telling me is, that if I do a good job in powders, I'll be the new V.P."

"What I'm saying is, Ralph was impressed by your work."

At last they pulled into the lot. "I'll take your lunch," Cecily offered. Don handed it over and set out to find Jeff. It was going to be a hot one today, he thought.

Jeff was on the forklift outside the shipping door. He glanced up as Don approached, glanced at his watch, then looked back up. "We start at eight."

"I know. It won't happen again....What's on the docket today?"

Jeff's reply was terse. "A few orders, then work on inventory." Don had already tied on his apron and headed for the shed, embarrassed by his tardiness.

Deek awoke from surgery and blinked hard several times. A few people were milling about the room, waiting expectantly, each with a different reason for speaking with him. His eyes took several seconds to adjust, and his thoughts were still vague and distant.

"Hi, honey," said Deek's wife Dianne, gently stroking his arm. "How do you feel?"

A frazzled woman in her early forties, her dark brown hair with wisps of mounting grey was curled under in a bit of an old-fashioned look. Cut short like it was, it revealed both unpierced earlobes. She wore faded blue jeans, thin at the knees, a cotton shirt—wrinkled from the sleepless night—and house slippers. Her face bore the countenance of a loving mother, less concerned with the things of the world, more set on sacrifice. Each shallow wrinkle, connected to the others, much like the family tree of children she nurtured in her small home.

Deek rotated his head to the side. The question echoed in his ears, sounding far off. Each person in the room waited anxiously as he spoke.

"I don't know," he croaked, his lips sticking together as if painted with a pasty glue. "My mouth is dry."

Captain Bingham pressed forward. "Do you feel like talking?"

Dianne turned away, saying, "The doctor said you could have a little ice."

As she brought it around the opposite side of the bed, Bingham bulldozed ahead. "Officer Derickson," he said in his most official, urgent voice, "we need to talk. I need every bit of information I can get as soon as you can give it to me."

The memories of the night before were just starting to return. He'd been shot; he could remember the burning pain as he went down; he'd drifted in and out of consciousness during the minutes after it happened. He recalled hearing that "an officer is down." And he'd opened his eyes as the paramedics lifted him onto a gurney, and Bingham's voice asking him questions. The last thing he remembered was seeing the IV hanging above him during the ambulance ride.

"How bad was I hit?"

Dianne, having gone to get the nurse, returned. She maneuvered around Bingham. "Excuse me," she said, the irritation in her voice and brusque manner reflecting her dislike of the man. Deek often spoke of him in less-than-friendly terms. She, too, felt that Deek should have gotten the captain's job. Bingham stepped aside.

"You lost a lot of blood," she said kindly, now addressing her husband. "The bullet and a piece of the bone nicked your artery. It was a good thing Mitch was close or you would have bled to death."

Deek scanned the other faces in the room. Mitch was standing in a corner. "Thanks, Mitch. I should have waited in the car." Deek tried to motion with his arm as he spoke. The pain made it difficult. "I didn't think Howard would hurt anyone."

The captain leaned forward. "Is that who it was?

Howard Reid?"

"I'm not sure," Deek struggled to say. "Didn't get a clear view."

"What happened?" This time the captain was unremitting.

"I made sure Maryann was safely in her car, then I got in mine....As I started for the street, I thought I saw someone in the impound." Deek paused to take in a breath. "I took a second look and saw steam coming from the old Chevy's hood. You know, the one we took in on DUI from Howard." Deek stopped again to rest.

Bingham shook his head, obviously confused. "The records indicate it was driven almost a hundred miles since we brought it in. Two bottles of whiskey from the impound inventory list were not in the vehicle, either." He then waited for Deek to continue.

"When I looked at the gate, I could see the lock was missing....That's when I called Mitch for backup. Then I got out and crouched down by the side of the gate. I didn't expect to see anyone. Figured they were long gone. And if they were still inside, I didn't want them to escape...." Deek's strength was nearly spent.

Just then a short man, egg-bald, dressed in casual slacks and shirt, came into the room. "This man was seriously injured," he said in disgust. "I want everyone out but the immediate family."

"I'm Captain Bingham of the Mapleton—"

"I don't care who you are," interrupted the doctor, "this man is my patient and he needs rest." His point made, he picked up Deek's chart and began to browse through it. Mitch and several of the other visitors, already outside the door, waited to see how the captain would react. Despite his six-foot-one, 290-pound frame, he hadn't remotely intimidated the doctor. He swallowed hard, then turned sharply and followed the others out of the room.

"Nurse, why did you allow those people in? I left strict instructions this man was to be left alone." The doctor didn't give time for an answer before he reopened the chart and asked Deek how he felt.

"I've been better," he whispered, his lips sticking together.

The doctor braced himself as if he were lecturing in front of a class. "You're a lucky man. The bullet entered your abdomen, perforated the lower intestine in six different places, struck and broke the number five transverse process of your lumbar vertebrae. A small fragment of the vertebra ricocheted off the bullet and nicked your ileal artery. Five minutes longer and you would have bled to death. You may lose the feeling and movement in your legs for a day or two, but I'm confident it won't be permanent. The spinal cord was bruised from the blow, but it doesn't appear to be seriously damaged." Deek struggled to stay awake. "I'll check back in a few hours, after you've had a good rest. We'll check your reflexes then."

He hung the chart back on the hook at the foot of the bed and left the room. Deek drifted back to sleep.

Paul carried the breakfast tray—that looked suspiciously like a cookie sheet covered with a dish towel—to the bedroom. On it was a small, carefully arranged bouquet of flowers, picked from in front of the apartment.

"Nancy," he cooed, "how'd you like some breakfast?"

She stirred but didn't answer.

"Nance...Nancy." He placed one side of the tray on the edge of the bed and reached out to awaken her. Startled by his touch, she sat up swinging. The sudden tug of the blanket catapulted the tray off the bed and onto the carpet. Orange juice, milk and fragments of Raisin Bran were also slopped on the corner of the bed.

Nancy scowled wearily. "What was that?"

Paul smiled sheepishly. "Breakfast *on* bed?"

"What?...I was having a dream."

Paul bent down to rescue the bouquet of flowers. He brought it up, dripping with milk and orange juice, then picked a piece of cereal off one of the petals and popped it in his mouth. "I wanted to tell you I'm sorry for last night."

Nancy's scowl faded as she gave them a guarded sniff.

"They smell really nice." She cupped her hands under the blossoms to catch the dripping liquid. "Mmm, just like orange pansies."

They both smiled. Then she patted the side of the bed, and said, "Sit down a minute....Paul, let me explain why I was so upset last night." She went on to explain that she needed a little compassion and understanding when she was trying to express her feelings. She didn't want Paul to defend Melvin—or anyone else who might have been outside. Nor did she need to hear that what she was thinking or feeling was "probably nothing." What she *did* need to hear were the words, "I'm sorry," or "How can I help?" or "Can I hold you?" Paul needed a little tutoring in how to treat his new bride.

"I'll speak to Melvin, if it'll make you feel better," he told her.

"No, maybe it was my imagination."

"Just as I thought." The words had formed themselves in his mouth and worked their way out in the blink of an eye. Immediately he'd opened his mouth and inserted both feet.

"You didn't hear a word I just said!" screamed Nancy, rolling off the bed, stomping into the bathroom and locking the door behind her. Paul blotted up the mess on the floor, took the tray to the kitchen and returned to scrub the carpet. It took only a minute to remove the bed covers, which he dragged to the furnace room and stuffed in the washer. The water coursing through the pipes as Nancy showered, vibrated through the apartment.

Paul glanced at his watch. It was nine-thirty. If he left for class now, he'd have time to pick up his books for tomorrow's classes. He scribbled a note and left it on the table:

Dear Nancy,

I'm sorry I stuck my big foot in my mouth—again. Stick with me, I'm a slow learner. I'll be back from classes by three. I put the bedding in the washer. Please start it when you get a chance.

Love & Kisses, Paul

He was halfway out the door when Melvin greeted him, his voice like a squeaky hinge. "Good morning. I was just coming down to tell you I need to fix the leaky water heater in the furnace room, if that's okay."

Paul was caught off guard. "I'll—I'll tell Nancy." He went back inside and shut the door.

"Nance?" Paul rapped on the bathroom door and tried to enter. Locked. He could hear the shower still running. She must be unable to hear him over the sound of water on her shower cap, he thought. He went to the kitchen and wrote.

P.S. Melvin will be coming in today to fix the water heater, and the phone will be installed this afternoon.

No sooner had Paul driven away than Melvin, a small toolbox in his hand, returned to the apartment, bounding down the stairs two at a time like a teenager. He knocked lightly on the door, took the keys hanging from the chain at his side and pulled them from the spring coil. He knew by heart which key it was that unlocked the door. He let go of the keys and they recoiled, jingling as they came to a stop at his belt. Entering the kitchen, he read the note. The water was still running in the bathroom on the other side of the thin wall as Melvin entered the utility room. With a few quick turns of the wrench, the leak appeared to stop—then he settled down to *watch*.

ELEVEN

THE CRAMPED SQUAD ROOM was filled with officers from every agency in the state. Captain Bingham stood at the front behind a makeshift podium. He raised his hands for quiet.

"Okay, quiet! I need your attention." The years of military rule commanded consideration from the crowd. Everyone stopped talking and turned their attention toward the front of the room. Even when the room was hushed, Bingham paused for a few more moments of dramatic silence. Then he began. "We can't assume that the events of last night are related to the assaults. We don't have enough information. We've asked you to come and help us on this case so we can protect our children. The safety of the young girls in this town—and every neighboring town in the state— should be our first priority. We'll continue to look into last night's shooting from within the department. The information that Detective Derickson and Officer Stacey gathered could be the most important thing we have yet. I'll ask Officer Stacey to explain the details." The captain stepped away from the podium.

Stacey stepped up to speak, rocking self-consciously on his heels.

"Before Deek was shot, we'd planned on having you come in to share the new information we have. Last night, Ashley Gardner came in for another interview, Deek called me in to help. Ashley opened up like she's never done before. I'll let Dr. Wendy Brown, the state's criminal psychiatrist assigned to this case, explain."

A woman in her mid-fifties stepped up next to Stacey. She was attractive for her years, with a calm and pleasant demeanor. "Ashley has formed an emotional bond to Officer Stacey's dog. He represents the savior that chased away the one that was going to harm her. In the psychiatric field we call this 'transference of gratitude.' Officer Stacey is on the same plane as Sig, just not quite as high." A few of the men in the room chuckled.

"After Officer Stacey explains what he learned last evening, I'll give you a profile of the perpetrator," the doctor continued.

Stacey again moved closer to the podium and spoke. "As you read in the e-mail, Ashley believes the man is approximately five-foot-four inches to five-foot-six inches tall. She told us he was very strong yet slim. She couldn't identify any other physical features except that he has a high, raspy voice. She said he was wearing slick, dark clothing. This information is consistent with the fibers we recovered at the scene of the crime. We believe he was grazed by one of Mitchell's bullets, and it was his blood we found on Ashley. The DNA results verify, and they match up with the skin samples we found under the second victim's nails." Stacey paused and leaned his slender frame forward, rocking on his toes.

One of the men in the room raised his hand. Stacey pointed and instructed him to state his name and jurisdiction.

The man stood up. "I'm detective Dierpont from Lehi. Is it true that none of these girls have been sexually molested?"

"Yes."

"So the attacker could be anyone?" Dozens of hands shot in the air.

"I'll let Dr. Brown answer that." Stacey motioned to the doctor.

"The answer to your question is yes and no," she explained. "All the victims except Ashley were possibly molested. There's no evidence to suggest copulation took place. We think they may have been fondled, but haven't any physical evidence to prove it. He may be impotent, which is part of our profile of the attacker. We believe he's between forty and fifty-five years old. The wind pipe or esophagus of each murder victim was crushed in a manner consistent with someone trained in certain military procedures, or possibly self-taught. I found information on the Internet about this sort of kill, apparently common during the Vietnam War, used by enemy soldiers. We also believe this man was severely abused as a child. The consistent age of the victims may give us some clue as to his age at the time of his abuse. I'll prepare my report and make it available through proper channels." Dr. Brown turned back to Captain Bingham.

Several hands went up and the questions went back to the subject of Detective Derickson.

Nancy stood under the shower until the hot water was gone. She turned off the water and dried herself with a towel. The hum of the washing machine coming from the furnace room seemed to calm her heart. Paul had probably put the soiled bed covers in the wash.

She brushed her teeth and combed out her long, dark hair. After using her towel to wipe the steam from the mirror, she put on her makeup, wrapped the towel loosely around her body to keep warm and padded into the bedroom.

Simultaneously, Melvin silently picked up his tool box and stepped out from the furnace room. Nancy's eyes took a moment to adjust to the bright filtered light that blazed in through the open curtains of the windows. Setting out to close them, she realized Melvin stood next to her, and shrank back.

Her heart leapt to her throat. Frantic, she screamed, "What are you doing here!"

Melvin backed away several more steps. "Didn't your husband tell you?"

Nancy partially regained her composure, her courage bolstered. She hugged the towel tightly around her body as she retreated to the bathroom, then readied to slam the door shut if he came near.

"I told him I needed to fix the leak on the water heater," Melvin droned on. "He said it would be okay."

Nancy didn't answer—just shook her head.

"I knocked, but no one answered. If it's a bad time,

I'll come back later."

Nancy exhaled. "I think that would be best."

The landlord took two steps toward the door, then turned around. Nancy pushed the bathroom door closed a little more. "It'll only take a few more minutes."

Nancy was almost in tears. "No. No. Please...later."

Melvin turned once more, opened the front door and closed it behind him. After a few seconds' wait, she rushed to the door to lock it, backed into the corner, sank down, and began to sob.

Lunchtime approached. Don had completed 228 units for the inventory, cleaned up—nearly filling a dumpster with garbage and excess powder—and finished the four small orders on his board. The building was already 92 degrees. He was proud of himself. Jeff had checked on him an hour earlier to let him know he wouldn't be mixing that afternoon. He was completely caught up.

He brushed the dust from his clothes and headed for the main building for lunch. Passing the shipping area, he noticed Ryan, struggling to shrink wrap a large package.

"Here," Don offered, "let me give you a hand with that."

When the task was completed, Don, after cleaning the worst of the dirt from his face and hands, proceeded to the break room.

"Ralph wants to see you after you finish," Cecily said as she handed him his lunch bag. "What took you so long?"

"Just lots of dirt to clean off." Don wondered what Ralph wanted. He was eating his dinosaur fruit snacks when Ryan entered.

"Thanks for the help, man."

Don grinned. "Any time."

"Jeff told me I could have the afternoon off if I got everything on the first pickup. The truck came just as you left. Thanks again." Ryan picked up his things from his locker and headed out the door.

Don went back to digging the last of the little dinosaur fruit snacks out of their snug wrapper, which read: *No artificial colors or preservatives. One hundred percent natural.* He shook his head. "My ex-sister-in-law made lunch for me along with all the other children," he sighed. "Too bad I didn't marry her instead of her younger sister." He tucked the empty wrapper in the bag and drank the last of his "all natural" fruit drink from the pouch. Gotta go, he thought to himself. I've got an important meeting with Ralph.

"Come in," Ralph called without looking up. "Hi, Don. Close the door and take a seat." Ralph caught himself as he looked up. "On second thought," he said, eyeing the man up and down, "maybe you shouldn't."

Ralph put down his pen, leaned back in his chair and cleared his throat. "Jeff tells me you've done one heck of a job in the powder department."

"I've done my best."

"We've been considering hiring a new part-time salesperson for the front desk. If you did powders early in the morning, showered and changed in the men's room, you could sell in the afternoons." Ralph clasped his hands behind his head. "You're already familiar with what we do from watching us all these years."

Don nodded in agreement.

"After you're trained, you'll need to travel, train others and help at the trade shows," added Ralph. "If you do a good job, we'll pull you out of powders so you can sell full-time. Salespeople make a straight five-percent commission. Our top salesman rakes in about eighty thousand a year."

Don whistled under his breath. He'd never made more than thirty-five, even with tons of overtime and ten years' experience.

"You'll have to get your driver's license back before you get a company car. I don't allow anyone near a vehicle if they're convicted of a DUI."

"I wasn't—" Don started to explain.

"I know," Ralph broke in. "I took the liberty of pulling a copy of your record." Then he asked frankly, "Well, what do you think?"

"What can I say? I'm ready!" Don laughed, slightly overcome. "When do I start?" A company car...five percent commission...travel...not to mention a chance at eighty thousand a year. He'd never even been on a plane before. The farthest he'd ever traveled from home was Moscow— that is Moscow, *Idaho*!

"Clean off the dirt, sit with Dave this afternoon to get a feel for what he sells. You might also wander around the plant and familiarize yourself with our product line."

Paul, returning from his classes around three fifteen, nearly stumbled over Nancy's two suitcases as he entered the front door. "Nancy?"

"I'm in the bedroom." A thick layer of anger blanketed the apartment. Paul could feel its smothering effects.

He stepped over the luggage, a confused expression on his face. "What're you doing?"

"After you left today," Nancy spat, "our dear Mr. Briggs came in, claiming he was here to fix the water heater!"

Paul raised his eye to the ceiling. "He asked me if it would be okay. Didn't you read my note?"

"I didn't have time to read it. He was already in here when I got out of the shower." Nancy jammed the last of her things in the bag. "And I'm not spending another night in this place. I'll stay with Aunt Beverly...or whoever else."

She bent down to zip up the bag, jamming the zipper halfway. "You can take me, or I'll take the car, you pick," she hissed, yanking the half-zipped suitcase off the bed and marching toward the door.

Paul could tell by her determined voice and jerky movements that *this* discussion would go no further. The frustration she felt as a newlywed, being scared half to death with talk of the attacker, someone lurking outside the window—someone she insisted she'd seen before— and an overly friendly landlord skulking around her home, they all added up to a hysterical wife. "I'll drive you," he offered, knowing her aunt lived some eight miles away in the neighboring city of Provo and not thrilled with the idea of walking the distance to see his bride.

They drove in silence. Paul thought the whole thing was ridiculous. He couldn't understand why she was making such a big deal over such a little thing. But it would probably blow over by morning, he figured.

Fascinated by the vast product line of his new employer, Don no longer wondered why he'd been asked to sign a "Good Faith / Non-Competition Clause." This company had more potential than he'd seen in any of his past employers. They used dozens of different urethanes and plastics. Rooms were filled with diverse molds, both cast and frame. Truckloads of finished orders sat out on the loading docks. Ralph's company had grown over the years. It looked like it had a great future—and now he was part of it.

"We've got the warrant. We'll be there in five," Mitchell announced over an open channel. Captain Bingham had ordered 24-hour surveillance of the residence of Howard Reid, owner of the old Chevy sitting in the impound yard. Stacey was assigned the watch from one until four. There in the front seat of his pickup, parked a block and a half away from the Reid residence, the only movement Stacey had seen all day was when the wife left for work in the morning and when Howard wandered down to the state liquor store a few hours later.

Deek's unmarked car was in Provo to have the bullet removed from its front-left door, where it embedded after going through his gut. An expert would examine it to determine its caliber and from which type of gun it had been fired. Judge Benson was on vacation in Florida, so the city prosecutor had gone through the Fourth Circuit Court. And now, finally, they had the warrant in hand.

Mitch pulled up next to Stacey and tugged nervously at his dark moustache. Olsen sat in the passenger's seat of Mitch's car, his hair cropped so close to his scalp he almost looked bald.

"Still in there?" Olsen asked, just coming on duty.

Stacey nodded in the affirmative.

Barker and Grue eased around the corner from the other direction. Stacey started his truck.

"Stace, you and Sig take the back door," ordered Barker. "Grue will cover the south, Olsen the north. Mitch and I will go through the front. We can still see him sitting on the couch."

All five men were protected with vests. Stacey wished he had one for Sig. This was the first door-break he'd ever been involved in. He jumped the fence two houses away, Sig instinctively following his master's lead. He felt little anxiety over the entrance. Howard seemed harmless. He was a big man—all bark, no bite. Stacey was the one who pulled him over the last time he was DUI, his fourth, since the first of the year. He'd been released only two days before. Why would he break into the impound and shoot a cop? he wondered.

"He's asleep," Barker grunted under his breath. "Go in at my word."

Stacey crouched at the back door. Reaching up, he checked the knob to see if he needed to break the window for entrance. It turned easily. He eased the door open just an inch and waited for Barker to give the word.

Sig was preoccupied with the dryer vent on the other side of the back door.

"Come!" Stacey whispered.

"Go," came Barker's command.

Stacey opened the door. "Seek!" Sig bolted inside. Stacey had torn a piece of the tattered seat from the old Chevy for Sig to sniff in preparation for the raid. Sig knew just what he was looking for. Stacey followed his partner. They had a clear view of the front door. "Ka-wham!" The door tore off its hinges and landed on the floor with a crash. Howard sprang to his feet, startled by the commotion.

"Police! We have a warrant!" shouted Barker. Howard swung his body and arms frantically. Mitch was the first to attempt a take-down. Almost effortlessly, Howard hurled Mitch across the floor. Barker was next. Howard, now an enraged bull, launched him through the front window, where he landed on the porch, his mouth bleeding. Olsen paused to see if he was seriously hurt then bolted through the open doorway.

"Subdue!" Stacey commanded. Sig hesitated a split second to decide for whom the command was meant. In the meantime, Stacey saw an opportunity and charged forward from the rear, wrapping his legs and arms around the neck and body of the big man. Sig seized Howard's right arm and hung on with the fury of a wolf. Olsen went low, taking out his legs. Mitch recovered from his blow and rejoined the fight. That's when Howard went down with a mighty thud, Sig still attached to his arm.

Stacey yanked the heavy, tattooed left arm behind Howard's back. It took all of his strength. Barker staggered back in and grabbed hold of the thrashing man's head, while Grue joined Stacey in pinning the drunk's left arm behind his back. Stacey reached out with both hands to take control of the right arm from Sig.

"Release," Stacey commanded. Sig still hung tightly. "Release!" Stacey yelled again above the clamor. Sig let go, and Stacey pulled the bleeding arm behind the massive body.

The man's comparatively small mouth opened with a roar. "Get off me!" he bellowed, followed by a string of vulgarities.

Grue latched the cuffs on the huge wrists. "We'll get off as soon as you settle down."

"One twelve to medic three," Barker called out on the radio. "Come in. We've got it under control."

The ambulance team was waiting around the corner. Lights flashed and sirens blared in the street as they approached.

"I want every inch of the house searched," Bingham ordered over the radio.

Howard stopped thrashing. Stacey slowly rolled to the side and pulled himself to his feet, rubbing his wrists. He turned to Sig, now prancing back and forth in front of his defeated quarry. "Seek!"

The dog immediately began his search. He stopped briefly to sniff at nearly every object, giving every room the same thorough scrutiny. Nosing excitedly through piles of trash, reeking of alcohol, stacks of moldy newspaper, layers of dirty clothing on the floor, Sig didn't seem to mind in the least. Stacey followed behind from room to room, then down to the basement. "Nothing, boy?" Stacey kneeled, pulled the scrap of upholstery from his pocket, and held it out at Sig's level. Sig trotted over to give it another whiff. "Seek," he commanded again.

For a second time Sig initiated a routine sweep of the basement, then suddenly bolted up the stairs, through the kitchen, and out the back door, Stacey giving chase.

Stacey skidded to a stop in the kitchen, where the medics were busy working on Howard's injury. "I did nothin'—nothin'!" he repeated. "I was here, passed out on the couch last night. Ask the old lady."

Stacey glanced both ways and listened. Sig was nowhere in sight. Then he heard a scratching sound coming from outside the back door. Stacey flew out the door to find Sig frantically clawing the cover off the dryer vent.

"Off, boy!" Sig took two steps back and lowered onto his haunches.

Barker poked his head out the back door. His bloodstained chin and swollen lip looked worse than they really were. "What's he got?" he muttered, dabbing at the wounds with an ice cube wrapped in a napkin.

Stacey shook his head. "Don't know." He took a packet from his back pocket, tore it open and took out a pair of latex gloves, which he stretched over his meaty hands. He then pulled out from his shirt pocket a penlight. Carefully lifting the vent flap, he flipped the flashlight's switch and aimed the tiny beam through the opening. "What's this?" he said as he reached back almost to his elbow and pulled a bundle of loose black cloth from the pipe. Right away Stacey could tell by the feel and how it gathered at both ends that it was a pair of sweat pants.

As it was drawn out, the bundle fell open and a small revolver tumbled out onto the crumbling concrete steps below.

"Jackpot!" Barker muttered under his breath when the image registered in his mind. "Captain, we got a gun and black sweats out here," he said into his radio. "Sig sniffed 'em in the dryer vent."

Captain Bingham's voice hissed back through a gust of static. "Arrest him for the attempted murder of detective Kiser Derickson."

Stacey returned to the basement, where he'd spotted an old pair of bolt cutters resting on top of a pile of newspaper. Still wearing the latex gloves, he carried the cutters to the tableful of evidence being collected above. Two empty bottles of cheap whiskey, still with police inventory numbers attached, were also among the find.

Don was in the mold shop at four-thirty. "It looks like you've been abandoned again," he said to Rex.

"Naw," he shrugged, peering over his saw, "they always leave early on Fridays and finally turn off the blasted radio. Peace and quiet do me good."

Rex had grown somewhat intolerant of the whine the radio made. He'd lost some of his range of hearing in the service, which had also taken from him his love of music, particularly the Big Band songs.

Don wanted to get to know the old fellow better. "What can I do to help?"

"Well...see that dish of oil over there?" Rex pointed to a dirty whipped cream container. "Put on some gloves and start wiping down the mold with the rag in the dish."

Don did as he was told, dipping an oily rag in the container, wiping it over a new mold—and listening to his new friend.

After awhile, Don glanced at the clock. "I gotta go, Rex. My ride leaves at five." He snapped the latex gloves from his wrists and tossed them in the trash barrel.

Suddenly Dave came storming through the quiet shop, howling, "I've got a flat on my car! Now I'll be late to my mother's birthday party." He let out a muffled "Grrrr!" and headed to the phone to call his wife.

Don retreated into the front office. Seeing him, Cecily stopped typing, looked up with a smile and said, "I'll be five more minutes, okay?"

"Sure," replied Don.

He walked out front to wait for his ride. Noticing the open trunk of Dave's car, he hurriedly removed the spare from the back and began jacking up the car. This is a piece of cake compared to a cement truck, he thought. He had the flat tire off and the mini spare halfway back on by the time Dave returned.

"How did you do that so fast?"

"I've had plenty of practice," Don answered as he tightened the last lug nut, "with the kind of cars I've driven over the years....I'll let down the jack and you put the flat in the trunk. We'll get you to your party on time."

Don put the jack away, shut the trunk and rubbed his hands. "See you Monday. Have a good weekend."

"I will." Dave smiled as he drove away.

Cecily had been standing at the gate, watching the last few minutes of Don's good deed. "You better be careful" she needled, "or you'll get promoted to sainthood."

Don shook his head. "Far from it," he said modestly.

They climbed into the open Jeep and buckled in. This time Cecily didn't turn on the radio—or drive like a maniac. "You did well today," she commented. Don was watching her short blond hair fluttering in the wind. She was pleasing to look at. He felt a slight attraction toward her, even if she did get his goat at times.

He stretched his back against the seat, closed his eyes and breathed in. "It must be time for a change. Seems I've always gotten the raw end of the deal. This is the first time I've ever felt really useful."

He was starting to sound a little soft. Just as he started to change the subject, he swivelled his head to glance down 4th Street, which ran through an old section of town. "Wow, did you see that?" he blurted out. "There were cop cars, television crews, an ambulance." He pointed to the next street up. "Go around the block."

Cecily followed his instructions. When they rounded the corner, a large man was being escorted from a run-down house to a squad car. The crews were filming as he went. All three of the major stations were there, satellite dishes pointed toward the sky, cameras rolling. Cecily craned her neck to get a better look. "We'll have to watch the news to see what's going on." She put her Jeep in reverse and began to back away from the crowd.

"Captain Bingham, is he the one who shot Detective Derickson?" An aggressive reporter had stuck a microphone under the captain's chin. He turned from the camera, lifted his large calloused hand, and nudged the microphone aside.

"Off the record, only," he whispered.

She motioned to the camera man to kill the footage. "Okay, off the record."

"We found a weapon. The gun seems to match the caliber used in the Derickson case. That's all I can say right now."

She took a card from her purse, insisting he contact her, *anytime*, with any newsworthy information he could give. After scribbling her cell number above her name, she pressed the card into his hand.

Cecily pulled up to the curb and turned off the Jeep's motor. Christina came running from the house to meet her Dad. Bright and bubbly, she called out, "Can I go with Danny and Jake down to the river? We want to work on Jake's tree house."

"What about supper?"

"I'll go ask Aunt Kate." Christina disappeared around the house.

Cecily picked up their conversation where it had left off. "If you do well in sales, you can make a lot of money, you know?" It was clear she wanted to talk.

Don didn't mind the chat either. In addition, he needed to broach the subject of getting to work late.

"I'd like to try sales, if the concrete business wasn't so chauvinistic—"

"What do you mean 'chauvinistic'?"

"I know as much about Ralph's business as any of his salesmen, but when the customers call in, they won't give me the time of day—'cause I'm a woman....I take that back. They don't mind talking, just not about concrete. I'm propositioned almost every day." She added the latter comment with a mixture of disgust and pleasure in her voice.

Christina reappeared from around the corner of the house, out of breath from her little run. "Aunt Kate said supper is almost ready. She expects Uncle Alan home any minute. She said if Cecily wants, she can stay and eat with us."

"I'd love to!" Cecily gushed before Don had time to react. He stole a glance at Cecily, whose lips had softened into a delicate smile. He couldn't help notice that Christina had assumed the same girlish grin.

"Aunt Kate said to hurry and clean up," Christina said between breaths.

"Yeah, you're filthy!" Cecily gave Don a teasing poke as he stepped from the Jeep. He peeled off the cheap plastic cover they used to protect the seat, shook his head, and strolled to the house, wondering if he'd just been suckered into a dinner date. He didn't mind a bit. As a matter of fact, he'd been contemplating asking Cecily out on his own—he just hadn't known how to go about it.

TWELVE

KATE CAUGHT UP on the daily happenings of her children during dinnertime. It was her favorite part of the day. She always took time to ask each how their day went and what projects they were working on in school. Alan seemed quiet. He usually didn't say much. Don wondered how he was so successful in sales without talking.

After a blessing on the food, Jake started out by telling all about the neat gadgets his friend's dad owned. The man was in the excavation business. He'd let Jake and his son Bryce drive some equipment, but only in the construction yard. Jake, always curious, loved anything mechanical.

"So, Don, how's work?" Kate asked when the children had finished.

"Pretty good," he answered nonchalantly.

Cecily glanced over at Don, then gave him a little nudge. "*Tell* 'em."

Christina took it from there. "Tell us what, Daddy? Come on."

"It's nothing much."

Cecily tried to stifle a laugh. "I'll tell, then!" she muttered. "He got a raise and a promotion today. You're lookin' at the company's newest salesman. The boss was so impressed by his work...." Her voice tailed off; she'd spilled the important parts, at least.

Don sat in mute embarrassment as the family expressed their best wishes. Kate said it didn't surprise her at all. Alan even made a few congratulatory remarks.

After supper the children headed for the river. "You

be careful, and stick together," Kate exclaimed as they bolted for the door.

"And be back before sundown," Alan added as the door slammed behind them.

Don helped with the dishes and Cecily followed suit. As she cleaned up, Kate peppered Cecily with friendly questions.

"Where are you from?"

"Denver. I moved here five years ago, to go to school."

"What did you study?"

"Mostly worked on my general education. I dropped out about three years ago when I couldn't afford to continue. My grades weren't that great, anyway."

"So, have you worked at Cobblecrete ever since?"

"Ralph and my dad were good friends a long time ago. I was supposed to get married, but two weeks before the wedding my fiancé backed out. The wedding invitations were sent and everything. I had to call all the guests and tell them not to come. That's when I talked to Ralph for the first time. Didn't know him well, but he told me to call him if I ever needed a job."

Within half an hour, Don knew more about Cecily than he'd learned in the three days at work. She came from a large family—five boys, two girls—and she was the oldest....Her father was only able to help with tuition a few semesters. Soon she was working summers and nights to support herself in school....After the wedding thing, she'd dropped out altogether. She made a decent living working for Ralph, but wanted to try something more exciting—just hadn't gotten around to it yet.

Don walked her to the Jeep. Enroute, she asked him where the tree house was. Christina had pointed it out on one of their walks. "Somewhere near the dead end of Sixth and Fir," Don told her.

"Come on," she enthused, "let's go see it." She grabbed Don by the hand and pulled him toward the Jeep. He hesitated a moment, then joined in the chase, though he felt a little like a school boy.

Cecily rumbled down the dirt road at the end of Fir. The dust shot up and hung in the air around them as they got out of the Jeep. "Isn't this where they found that girl?" Cecily inquired, her thoughts a bit uneasy.

"I'm not sure." Don hadn't kept up on the events of the city when he was in jail. "I'm not that good at current events," he added as they pressed toward the river. The sun sagged low on the horizon and the shade from the big ash trees made the evening air cool. The sound of the rushing water off in the distance made for a soothing stroll. They traversed through the undergrowth in silence, each pondering their blooming friendship.

As they drew closer to the river, swarms of mosquitoes were there to greet them. The sound of hammering could be heard in the distance as they plodded through the greenery.

"I think they're over there." Don pointed toward the sound.

The ground under their feet was wet. The mosquitoes were almost intolerable. Cecily angled back and forth, tiptoeing across the more marshy spots. "I think we're in a swamp. My feet are getting wet." She took several steps back, vainly trying to escape the green water now seeping up the sides of her white canvas shoes. "Let's walk along the bank of the river; it seems higher." She took Don's hand and guided him eastward.

Switchbacking down the steep sides of the river bank to a deer trail that ran parallel to the gushing stream, the going got easier. Even the mosquitoes seemed to let up their steady assault as they headed south. Cecily didn't let go of Don's hand, even when they crested the bank to listen for where the children were. The rushing water still drowned out the hammering sound they'd heard earlier. But as they made their way through the rocks and brush, once more they picked up the sounds of construction. A few more steps and Don could make out the rough-built shape of a shack, perched in the branches of a tall ash.

"Daddy!" Don let go of Cecily's hand and peered up to see his daughter, standing atop the roof of the flimsy structure, some 30 feet in the air. Don's heart did a somersault.

"Chrissy! Get down from there!" In his mind he could

see her tumbling off the roof and landing in a heap on the rocks below.

"It's okay, Dad," she reassured, "I've got a safety rope on." A closer look proved her right. A climbing harness was fastened around his daughter's waist, linked to a rope which was tied off on a thick limb.

Don chuckled, now interested in checking the place out himself. "How'd you get up there?"

"I'll lower the ladder!" Jake called back, his head poking from the window on the side where they stood. A trap door on the bottom of the tree house dropped open and a sturdy rope-and-board ladder rolled down the massive trunk of the old ash.

Don stepped back to stay clear of the plunging apparatus. The last rung made one last flop as it stopped two feet short of the ground. "I want to go up first," Cecily begged.

Don stepped to the side. "After you."

Cecily seized the third rung of the ladder, stepped up, and began twisting partway around. Don grabbed her by the waist to keep her from smacking against the tree. "Be careful," grinned Jake from above. "It's not like climbing a normal ladder.... You have to lean against the tree or you'll tip to the side." Danny watched from the hole in the floor above. "Girls always fall the first time."

At the slight, Cecily shot him a look, then regained her balance and ascended the ladder. Reluctantly, Don let go of her. As she cautiously scaled the rope above him, he couldn't help but notice her shapely figure. Almost halfway up, Don decided to badger her a bit by jiggling the rope from below. She stopped climbing and reached out to cling onto a nearby branch. Danny again took the opportunity for some friendly taunting.

"Stop it, guys. It's scary the first time." Christina turned and slapped the nearest shoulder in protest.

Danny pulled his arm back as if it hurt. "Stop, guys. It's scary," he mimicked.

Jake came to the defense of the woman hovering below. "Okay, guys, that's enough."

Cecily let go of the limb, and scaled the remaining

few yards. "That wasn't a bit scary," she said, pulling herself onto the platform. Then, turning to Danny, she made a fist. "I'm gonna get you," she said in mock anger. "And when that big fella comes up, he'll be next!" She obviously had learned from her younger brothers how to keep them in line.

The ceiling of the house was too low for them to stand up straight. They had to bend or kneel to keep from hitting their heads. Don started up the ladder. The boards creaked as the load of his weight pulled at the structure. "You're gonna break it, Daddy," a concerned voice cautioned.

"Naw," Jake countered,"my dad's been up lots of times, and he's bigger than Uncle Don."

Christina removed her harness as she eased herself down off the roof. Don complimented them on the job they'd done building the house. Cecily leaned back and listened. She observed the way he made them feel good about themselves by praising their frail structure, pieced together with leftover scraps from nearby construction projects. She didn't think much of the workmanship— but then, she was "just a girl".

"What a beautiful sunset," remarked Christina. Everyone turned to look out the window opening to the west. The sky was a blaze of orange and yellow.

"We're late," Jake announced. "We'd better get going."

Christina was first down the ladder. Cecily was next, followed by Don. Danny, however, climbed to the roof. Just as Don was halfway down, a rope flew past him through the air, Danny attached to the end. He arched downward, taking a slight upward turn when he approached the ground. Letting go, he landed softly.

The moment Don dismounted, Jake began to pull the ladder up through the trap door, rolling it with exactness for its next dramatic descent. "Come on, Jake. We're going to be late," Danny called anxiously. He knew what a stickler their dad was for being on time.

"I can give you a ride, if you want," Cecily offered.

"Okay. You, Christina, and Uncle Don can start back

and we'll catch up in a minute. Besides, it's a secret how we get back up there, without a ladder to climb."

The three were twenty yards down-river when Jake's whoop rang through the forest. Don turned back in time to see him rapelling to the ground below.

"I know the secret," Christina said proudly. "I snuck up one day and saw how they do it. You see they have this...."

Her dad stopped her. "Maybe you'd better keep it a secret."

"You're right," Christina sighed.

After only a few minutes, the boys caught up with them.

Not far from the Jeep, the boys pulled their skate boards from the tall grass where they were stashed, and Christina retrieved her old Stingray bike, which she'd camouflaged behind some bushes. By the time Don and Cecily arrived, the boards, bike and backpacks had been loaded in the space behind the rear seat.

As Cecily drove, the conversation drifted to the man-hunt and Ashley's subsequent rescue in the woods. Christina made sure everyone knew she was her good friend, adding for good measure, "Officer Stacey's sister Emily is also in our class."

Once in the driveway the boys got out, unloaded the gear, and headed inside.

"You're coming with us to work on the tree house tomorrow, aren't you?" Christina asked Cecily.

"Wouldn't miss it," she smiled. Don was surprised by the offer—and more so by the subsequent answer. "That is," Cecily countered, "unless your daddy doesn't want me to."

"No. No, that's not it...." Don paused. "I'm just won-dering who'll pack lunch. I got kind of hungry up there."

"Christina and I will." Cecily revved up the Jeep.

Dusk set in as Don and Christina watched her pull away. "She likes you a lot," Christina said, poking her dad in the ribs in the exact same spot where Cecily had earlier.

THIRTEEN

THREE HOURS AND 48 STITCHES later, Howard was brought to the station, chained both hand and foot. Barker and Olsen escorted him down the stairs to a cell.

"Your attorney'll be here soon," said Barker as he unlocked the chains.

Howard, who—in his opinion, at least—had up to that point held himself in check, now let his filthy mouth fly. He didn't need an attorney, except to sue them for false arrest, and he'd better be out of there by that evening! He had important business to take care of!

"Stay and watch him 'til the public defender arrives," Barker told Olsen once Howard was safely behind bars.

"I told you, I was on the couch passed out!—" Howard's voice rang down the corridor as Barker escaped back upstairs. Just as he reached the top, Stacey came in the back door with Sig.

"Is he back?"

The senior officer nodded.

"How's his arm?"

"He's had so much whiskey—hasn't had time to feel the pain yet."

Bingham and two of the part-time city prosecutors stepped out of the captain's office. "Great job, Stacey," one of them said. "You too, Sig."

Sig took three quick steps toward captain Bingham and pawed at his shoe.

"Get this stinkin' dog out of the office," the captain snarled, instinctively giving Sig a little kick in the snout.

Feeling threatened—and snubbed, to boot—Sig latched his teeth tightly to the offending foot's olive-gray pant leg, sending the captain off balance and to the floor.

"Off!" Stacey commanded, at which Sig let go, took two steps back, and sat down.

Captain Bingham, pulling himself up and away from the nasty set of jaws, flew into an obscenity-laced tirade, demanding that the dog be removed.

"I don't know what got into him," Stacey apologized. "Come, Sig." He slapped his thigh and they both headed for the door.

"That damn dog is off the job until further notice!" yelled Bingham. "And you better get him locked up!"

Clear of the office, Stacey knelt down. "What's the matter, boy?" he said, sandwiching Sig's head between his hands. Sig struggled free, crouched to sniff at Stacey's front right pocket, then nibbled at it with his front teeth. Stacey reached inside to find the scrap of seat from the old Chevy.

Simultaneously, the captain was checking out the six-inch tear in his pant leg. "I knew that dog would cause trouble," he muttered. "I should never have let the s.o.b. on the force."

Maryann poked her head inside the door. "Captain Bingham, Judge Demick's office called to say that Mr. Sands was appointed to be the public defender on this case."

"That high-and-mighty Demick!" came the captain's gruff reply. "Always gettin' in the way." Then he suddenly realized that his mouth was still in gear without his brain being attached; he was rambling, perhaps recovering from the scare hidden deep beneath his words. And there, peering from behind Maryann, were the two city prosecutors, speechless.

"He's here to see his client," she finished. Grimacing as one would after accidentally dropping a baby on the floor, she stepped back and bustled away to avoid the conflict.

The sarcasm in Mr. Sands' voice was unmistakable. "The Honorable Judge Demick would be interested to know what you think of him, I'm sure."

"Good evening to you, too, Sands," the captain retorted, trying to regain his composure. "He's downstairs." Sands swung his briefcase around and huffed out of sight.

Meanwhile, Stacey and Sig headed for home. He'd already been off duty more than an hour and was mad at himself for having gone back to the station. More than anything, though, he was puzzled. Why had Sig identified the captain? Had Bingham somehow gotten in the car and contaminated the crime scene? Or was Sig confused? Stacey had too many unanswered questions. On his way, he decided to drop by the hospital to see how Deek was feeling.

"You can go now. Please close the door as you go up." Sands waited until the door slammed shut before he spoke to Howard, the only prisoner in the small, three-cell jail. "My name is George Sands," he began, sticking out his hand. "I've been appointed as your Public Defender. Are you coherent enough to discuss your case?"

"What I am is ready to sue the pants off these people for false arrest."

"What were you falsely arrested for?" Sands asked.

"They say I broke into their impound lot and shot a cop."

"Did you?"

Howard bellowed out a few choice words, then, just as abruptly, stopped. "I was passed out on the couch all night," he explained. "Just ask my old lady." Howard coughed and hacked, then leaned over to spit a mouthful of thick brown saliva at the open floor drain, half the foul ooze dripping through, the other half clinging to the edge.

Sands shuddered, then turned his attention to his briefcase. "I already did."

"Did what?" the drunk asked.

"Asked your wife," Sands said matter-of-factly, reviewing his notes. "She said she pulled a double shift at work and didn't get home until after midnight. The detective was shot at eleven-thirty. Your house is only six blocks from the station. You could have easily been home by twelve."

"She's a lying bag a' wind!" Howard coughed again.

"According to her, she got rid of all your brew when you were in the county lock up. When you got out you were all upset. She didn't bring her check home until late that night. You beat her until she gave you twenty dollars, then you went out and bought two bottles."

"I didn't beat her....She gave me the 20 bucks before she left for work."

"Where'd she get the black eye then?"

"Probably fell or somethin'. She's always doin' that." Howard leaned over again and spit. "Sounds like you already got me convicted."

Stacey made his way to Deek's room while Sig waited in the car. He cautiously poked his head into the room, crowded with visitors.

Deek spied his fellow officer almost immediately. "Stace, come in."

"I better come another time when you're not so well-liked," he said, smiling at Deek's wife, Dianne, and their children.

Dianne greeted him warmly. "No, come in Rick. The kids and I were just leaving. It's past their bed time, anyway." She began herding the children toward the door. "See you in the morning, dear."

"Bye, daddy," two of the children called out.

"It's time for us to go, too," an older woman, standing by her husband, said.

"Stace, these are my parents." Deek motioned to the older couple. "Mom, Dad, this is Officer Stacey."

"Oh, yes, Deek's told us so much about you and your dog. It's a pleasure to meet you." The woman leaned over and kissed Deek.

The old gentleman turned and waved to Stacey before opening the door for his wife. "Keep up the good work."

"Nice to have met you, too." The room became quiet. "So how are you doing, Deek?"

"Better than this morning. My reflexes are even better than the doc hoped. He thinks I'll be out of here in less than a week."

"Sounds like good news."

Deek's spirits were up; he wanted to talk. "I heard you busted old man Howard for the shoot." Mitchell stopped by when they came in to get Howard stitched up, Deek explained. "So how do you feel about the bust, Stace?"

Stacey could tell that Deek had his doubts. He stared down at the crystal-clear water in the cup that sat on Deek's bed tray. Unlike the water, his mind was muddled. "Something's not right."

"Why?"

"I don't know for sure." He paused again as he thought. "I've never seen Sig so confused. He should have identified everything in the house, including Howard. He didn't find a thing inside. Before we went in, he was messing with the dryer vent. I called him off for the entrance. He went back after we started a second sweep. Then a few minutes ago down at the station he hit on the captain's shoe. Bingham took a kick at him before Sig took him down."

"What did Bingham do?" Deek asked, now very interested.

"Don't know. Took him off the job, though. Told me to lock him up."

"Where was the captain during the Howard bust?" Deek seemed to know the answer before he asked.

"I don't know. He didn't show up 'til we were through. Why?"

"Just as I thought." Deek gave a weak grin and leaned back on his pillow.

"Deek, what's up?" Stacey asked, a bit impatiently.

"I thought I recognized the shooter as he high-tailed it out of the impound. I thought I was dreaming—until now." Deek paused. "It was the captain! I heard his radio echo my call to Mitch."

Stacey shook his head. "Come on, Deek. Howard's wife confirmed the whiskey was gone, and Howard had it. I think Bingham climbed in the car and contaminated the scene." Stacey refused to think their leader was to blame for shooting a fellow officer. "Besides, why would

Bingham be out driving that old clunker?"

Deek countered, "Why would old man Howard bring the Chevy back to the lot after taking a hundred-mile joy ride? Then shoot a cop? Howard's never been violent before," he pointed out.

"He was violent this afternoon. You should see Barker's face, and the house."

"You woke the old fool from a drunken stupor. What did you think he was going to do?"

"Yeah, you're right. So why would the captain use the car and cut the lock?"

Deek gave a shrug; he was showing signs of tiring. His eyes flickered in memory. "Just before we interviewed Ashley, Bingham got a call. He wasn't very happy about it and closed the door to talk. He'd told me earlier he wanted to be in on the interview, then, right after the call, he took off. We were the only ones there at the time. Did you notice the gate or car when you left?"

"I came and went out the other way." Stacey was growing more interested with each passing moment.

Deek slowly drew himself up on his elbows, his face now white as the hospital sheet. "Sig was confused," he ventured, "because the car smelled like a week-old drunk, but the *seat* smelled like a day-old captain. Bingham knew Sig would hit on him, so he stayed away from the bust."

Stacey pondered Deek's theory. "So why's Howard's wife lying?"

Deek lifted an index finger in response and leaned toward Stacey, supporting his weight on his left elbow. "Suppose Bingham saw her coming home at the same time he was there to plant the gun. So he went around back, shoved the gun and sweats up the vent, then confronted her on the porch and told her how she could be rid of the wife-beater once and for all. She wasn't sure, so he smacked her around a little to help make up her mind. Getting smacked around by the police captain—a big ol' ugly one, to boot—is worse than the drunken husband. So she agreed to put the old drunk away." Deek sank back on the mattress.

"Great theory, Deek. How do we prove it?"

Deek paused to take in several deep breaths. "Go see Howard's wife tomorrow. Tell her the captain sent you to verify what kind of whiskey her husband was drinking. Ask her which hand he smacked her with, in case she gets interviewed again. See how she reacts."

"I'll do it, buddy. Now you get some rest." He stood to leave.

Deek's head came back up off the mattress, his face a pasty white. "Stace, keep this between you and me. We don't have a clue what's going on." Then suddenly he reached for the basin at the side of his bed and shot a stream of vomit in one side of the basin and out the other, covering the floor.

"You okay Deek?" Stacey turned and darted out into the hall, shouting, "Nurse, we need some help down here!"

Don sat on the back deck, watching the stars and recovering from the constant commotion of the children. A cool breeze rolled down from the hillside and through the orchard behind the home. Don was about to go inside for a jacket when the back door slid open and Christina came out. "Daddy, I've been looking for you." She sat down next to Don.

"I'm just here looking up at the sky and wondering what's out there."

"Alan seems to know. Ask him," Christina volunteered. She'd been included in the family's morning scripture study and prayers. Don, too, had been invited, but hadn't felt comfortable joining in. What's more, he'd never thought God would have a place for him, what with his volatile temper and criminal record.

Don sighed. "I talked to Pauline tonight on the phone. Your grandpa isn't doing too well." Don wanted to help Christina prepare for his death.

"I know," she said. She folded her arms and shivered from the cold. "We talk about that, too." In a way, Christina seemed better prepared than he was.

He reached out and pulled his daughter close. "Here, sit with me. We'll keep each other warm." He engulfed her thin body in his strong arms and held her tight.

A few minutes passed in silence. Then Don and Christina got up and stepped back into the house to escape the night air. The late news had just started, the arrest of the alleged cop-shooter the lead story. They caught, mid-sentence, the well-modulated voice of an on-the-scene reporter: "...with the arrest of Howard Reid of Mapleton, the prime suspect in the shooting of Detective Kiser Derickson. After throwing an officer through the front window of his home, Reid, allegedly drunk, was subdued by Sig, the local K-9 hero belonging to Officer Rick Stacey. Police sources tell us a gun matching the caliber which shot the officer was found on the scene. The suspect has been arrested more than fifteen times over the last five years on charges ranging from spousal abuse to disorderly conduct..."

Accompanying the story was footage of Mrs. Reid leaving the rest home where she worked, attempting to hide from the camera a large black eye and swollen cheek.

"I went past there tonight on my way home from work," Don interrupted. "The place was a mad house."

Christina shushed him. "Dad, we want to hear."

Don headed upstairs to bed. It had been a long, exhausting day.

Stacey returned home, his mind racing with questions—in marked contrast to Deek, who seemed to have it all figured out. He flipped on the computer and accessed the National Crime Information Computer, or N.C.I.C. After entering his code and password, he stopped to think. Let's see, where was Captain Bingham from? Stacey rapped the desk with his fingers, trying to remember. Deciding that the parameters of the case were too wide, he shut down the system and picked up the phone. "Hi, Jimmy! Stacey, here. Put pepperoni on it tonight....Half an hour? Sounds good. Did you lose anything on the game? Oh....Later."

Ambling into the kitchen, he opened two cans of dog food for Sig and scooped them into the dog dish, in hopes that this time it would keep the smart aleck from carrying on about the pizza box.

FOURTEEN

DON ROSE BEFORE THE SUN DID. He had plenty to do before Cecily arrived. Since Monica, he'd never been out with a woman, and was quite unsure of himself. The house was quiet. Alan let the children sleep in on Saturdays, at least until nine.

The lawn needed its first trim of the season. Don found the mower buried in the garage, cleaned the filter, replaced the gas and oil, gathered up the bikes and boards from off the grass and started mowing. Before long, the entire household was awake. The children started in on their chores as Don finished edging.

By ten he was showered and ready to go. Cecily was late, so Christina and the boys decided to start out ahead. Christina placed the small cooler that held their lunch next to the one Don had borrowed from Kate.

Alan exited the house to survey the yard. He seemed pleased by the freshly mowed lawn. Don spoke first. "Alan, do you think there's a bike around here I could use to ride to work?"

Alan smiled. "Sure, I don't use mine much. You can borrow it."

Was this the same Alan who was so upset about his robe? Don thanked him as Cecily drove up. She turned off the Jeep and hopped out.

"Have a fun time," Alan called out as he disappeared around the corner of the house.

"The kids decided to go on ahead," explained Don.

"Let's walk!" Cecily suggested, anxious to be on their way.

Don didn't need any persuading. He bent down and

picked up the coolers while Cecily took a blanket from the back seat. Then they started out on foot.

Alan, the inspection of the lawn complete, strolled inside. Kate was busy finishing the dishes from the late-waking children. Most of them had scattered to different places in the house and yard.

"Don asked me if he could borrow a bike to get to work," Alan told his wife.

"What did you tell him?"

"That he could use mine."

Kate's expression took on a puzzled look. "Why the change of heart?"

"He's done his best to help around here. He does dishes, helps keep the place clean, and this morning he did the yard. He must be growing up."

"He's always been responsible, honey," Kate replied. "You've just had a hard time seeing past the rough edges."

"Maybe you're right."

The walk, the weather, and most of all the company was pleasant. Don and Cecily chatted and laughed as they walked along. They also savored the silence. He thought of taking her hand, but, carrying both coolers, figured it was too awkward. Cecily had decided to allow Don to take the lead in their relationship, at least for the day. Out of habit, he walked the way of his and Christina's nightly strolls. A moving van was parked in the drive-way of the apartment they had stopped to see earlier.

"That's odd," Don commented.

"What?"

"These people just moved in a few days ago. I wonder if they're moving out or moving more stuff in." Don turned and watched as they continued on down the side-walk. The distraction made him step slightly to one side and his foot slipped off the curb. The downward jolt knocked one of the coolers from his hand and it bounced on the asphalt. "You'd think I was drunk," he laughed, embarrassed.

"You drink?" Clearly she was taken aback by his off-handed admission, as her strict religious belief crept to the surface.

Don searched her eyes. Was her question on the level, or was she just messing around? Maybe it was best to let her know what to expect of him right up front. He shrugged. "On occasion I have a few beers."

"Is that why you lost your license?"

Don wasn't in the mood to have to defend himself. "Not really."

Cecily didn't take the hint—and wasn't about to drop the subject. She was starting to like him and wanted to have an idea of who she might be involved with. "So how *did* you lose it?" she pried.

Don took in a deep breath, blew it out, and launched into the story. He finished with the day he stepped into her office—having skipped the lurid details of the county lock up. He had included, however, the part about needing a place to live within a few more weeks.

"How old were you when you married Monica?"

"Seventeen."

Cecily began to compute his age in her head. "So you must be about thirty."

"Twenty-nine, to be exact." He could tell by her look the years didn't add up.

"Oh, Monica was eight months pregnant when we got married. Her parents put a lot of pressure on her to put the baby up for adoption and not get married, since she was only sixteen. I was young and stupid; my brain was run by other forces, mostly her gorgeous body. I would have killed for her. She was always mad at me for ruining her chances to be a professional model. She already had an agent. Her parents always tried to use her desire to model to keep her away from me."

"How long were you married?"

"Up until three months ago."

Cecily seemed surprised it had been such a short time since their divorce.

"At least that's when the divorce became final," Don added. "We were apart a lot longer than that."

Stacey spent the morning of his day off trying to "Sig-proof" the yard. For over three months he'd had no reason to leave the dog at home, and now he was even smarter than he was before. Stacey first closed the gate and told Sig goodbye. By the time he reached his pickup, however, Sig had already jumped the fence, torn around the other way, and was sitting in the bed of the truck, ready to go. Stacey didn't want to keep Sig inside for fear he'd be bored, nor was he willing to test, literally, the captain's orders "to lock him up," so his preference was to leave him in the back yard. Sig could tell something was up and didn't want to be left behind.

"You can't go, boy." Sig tilted his head to the side and stopped panting to hear what his master had to say. "Come, Sig," Stacey commanded.

Sig bounded out of the truck and followed Stacey to the back, through the open door and into the garage. "Enter," Stacey pointed.

Sig instantly obeyed, then turned around to look as Stacey closed the door on him. "It hurts me as much as it does you." As he walked away, Stacey turned to see his partner peering out the small, dirty window that stood about four feet off the ground.

"See you in a couple of hours, boy."

Stacey climbed into the oldest car on the force. Being the youngest officer, that's the way it'd be until he got some seniority. Revving up the old Chrysler, he headed for the Reid place.

Don and Cecily reached the edge of the wooded area. Cecily noticed a large log laying in the shade of the trees. "We have all morning," she said, laying out the blanket. "Now I'm ready to hear the whole thing."

Don relented. "We'd been married about three years when Monica became restless. I was working from sun up 'til sun down driving for Granger Rock. Monica loved to dance—the best dancer I ever saw. Of course, I was exhausted by the time I got off work and only wanted to go out on weekends. But not her. She would leave Christina at Kate's and slip away with her friends. I'd pick up little 'Tina after work and go home, cook supper, do the dishes, put her to bed...I was both father and mother. At first it only happened once in a while. I'd get after Monica and accuse her of seeing other guys. She always denied it. I got tired of it, we'd have a big argument, and she'd stop for a while.

"Finally we were able to afford a house. They weren't near as expensive then as they are now. For a few years everything was better, then it started all over again. One night I decided to see where she was going. I followed her and her friends down to Lamar's. When I went in, there she was, dancing way too friendly with some cowboy, rubbing up against him....I should have walked out right then and filed for divorce...." Don paused to get a drink from the cooler.

Cecily, who had hung on every word, asked, "What happened?"

"Instead, I walked out on the dance floor and yanked her away. The cowboy had no idea she was married to me, so we got into it. Before the police cuffed me, I broke one jaw, smashed out some teeth, clobbered three cowboys and a bouncer. I got three days in jail for it."

Cecily winced.

"We made up and things got better for a while. Then a few months later she started going out again, and before long she was leaving for two, three days at a time. I didn't have a clue where she was going until one of my buddies told me they saw her at a dance hall in Salt Lake. So one night I decided to take a ride and see if she was there. I saw her friend's car. I thought it would be smart to wait outside so I could confront her alone, and everything would be fine—until she came out with a cowboy, his hands all over her. I lost it again and beat the guy to a pulp. Got two weeks for assault and battery. Things went downhill from there. I suspected she was doing drugs—she couldn't explain where our money was going, things like that. But again she apologized and promised she'd change. I caught her twice more before two years went by. I wasn't much better—arrested twice more for assault. I just didn't want to let her go."

Don's voice softened. The pain was still etched in his face. Cecily remained quiet.

"The beginning of the end was one afternoon when I dropped by the house. I was pouring concrete at a house nearby and stopped to grab a sandwich. A brand new Dodge pickup was parked in my drive. I crept into the house and heard them in the bedroom." He stopped and took a sip of his pop.

Officer Stacey knocked on the door of the Reid home and waited. The front window had been boarded up. Small shards of glass lay on the porch, glittering in the sun.

Mrs. Reid's gruff voice came from inside. "It's nailed shut. You gotta come 'round the back."

Stacey stepped off the porch and walked around the back. When he reached the top of the stairs Mrs. Reid opened the door. The skin around her eye was violet, the swelling mostly gone. Her lip was still swollen and cracked.

"Good morning, Mrs. Reid. I'm Officer Stacey."

"Yeah, the one with the dog. I know who you are." The distaste in her tone was filled with bitterness. "I ain't supposed to talk to nobody about nothin'."

Stacey swallowed and dove in. "The captain wants me to make sure you know what you should say if you're questioned again," he insisted, trying to sound like he was in on the scheme.

The woman fairly spat out the words. "How many times does he gotta tell me? You gonna smack me too?"

"No, no," Stacey reassured her. "Just review with me one more time what you're supposed to say."

She rolled her eyes. "If it'll make you happy—and make you go away! Okay. I didn't get off work 'til midnight....It was twelve-thirty when I got here....Howard was drinkin' the whiskey he took from the Chevy—the capt'n told me to say that....He woke up about six in the morning and beat twenty bucks outta me for more whiskey....Is that good enough?" Her last question was sarcastic to the bone.

Stacey gave a subtle nod. "And what're you supposed to say about the clothes and the gun we found in the vent?"

"He ain't said nothin' about 'em."

"We'll let you know what to say."

She watched him turn to leave. All the way to his car and as he drove away, she watched, the contempt spilling from her eyes.

"I can't believe she'd bring a man into your home, into your own bed." Cecily was appalled at what she'd heard. "What'd you do?"

Don put down the drink and went on. "I was half broken, half angry. I couldn't go in the bedroom without killing them both, so I went back out to my cement truck and—and almost cried. Probably would have if I hadn't already known she'd been sleeping around. Sitting there in my truck, the only thing I could think to do was to dump my load right through the window of that shiny green pickup."

Cecily's eyes grew big. "You didn't!"

"I did. Poured it all in—all I had in the drum. All four tires blew out, the back window broke and the bed filled up. A '97, full-size pickup can hold about five and a half yards before the doors blow off." The corners of Don's mouth turned upward. "The time I got for destruction of private property was the easiest two weeks I ever did. Almost a pleasure!"

Don's face turned serious again. "The plant's insurance paid for my sweet revenge, but I was fired. Nine years on the job, then, poof!, nothing."

"I can't believe you did that." Cecily's smile had returned, her fingers flirting with her hair, in turns curling and uncurling the ends.

"I can't either, but it sure felt good. She's the one that filed for divorce. I fought for 'Tina for over a year. But because of my record, I lost the most important thing in my life. I paid alimony and child support and saw her every other weekend. Got a job at Ashrock trying to put my life back together. A month and a half ago I learned

113

Monica had lost the house. She hadn't made a single payment since I left. It was so far behind I could never have caught it up."

"That is so sad."

"I confronted her about the house the night I got pulled over." He stood up and rubbed his backside. "What time is it?"

Cecily glanced at her watch. "Yikes! Almost twelve. I'll bet the kids are hungry." She stood and gathered her things.

Stacey swung by the hospital on his way to the station. Deek looked better than he did the night before. He glanced up from talking with his children. "Hey, Stace, how'd it go?"

Stacey nodded. "Good, real good." Deek was anxious to hear what he had to say but couldn't talk in front of his wife and kids.

"Dianne," he said, "Stace and I have some things we need to talk over. Would you mind going and getting me some decent lunch—you know, burger, fries? This hospital food's killing me." Smiling, blowing a kiss and ushering the children out the door, she pulled it closed behind her. Deek was anxious to get up to speed. "So, what'd you find?"

"Hate to say it, but you were right. Bingham *did* smack her around. I think I asked too many questions when I talked about the clothes and gun. She said he hadn't said anything about them."

Deek was thinking. "Somehow we've got to get a sample of the fiber from the captain's car and get the sweats into the lab in Provo and have them analyzed to see if they match. I'm sure Bingham didn't have time to get rid of them before he left the impound area. He probably split in his vehicle, took off the dark sweats, then came back before they brought me here." Deek's face was squinched up, his mind in fifth gear. "I don't think the captain was trying to kill me; he's too good a shot. I think he just wanted to get out of the impound. I don't think killing would be a problem for him if he got shoved in a corner, though. He's told me he killed dozens in Vietnam."

Stacey was trying to figure out a way to move the sweats from the evidence room to the Provo lab without Bingham's knowledge, and how to get hold of his keys so he could take a fiber sample.

Don and Cecily made their way along the river bank toward the tree house. Cecily felt bad for Don and the troubles he'd been through, and wondered how she would fit into his life. He seemed like such a nice guy. "How's your dad?"

"Not so well. I called last night. I don't think he'll live much longer. My mom and dad were divorced when I was five, and I don't know my dad's new wife too well. She seems to be doing okay." He paused. "I thought Christina would have a hard time. She loves her grandpa, but seems to be doing better than I am. She says Alan's been helping her understand, for whatever that's worth."

Cecily took Don's lead. "Do you believe in God?"

"I guess so. I just didn't ever do anything with it."

"It?" Cecily asked. "Don, God's not an 'it.'"

"No, I didn't mean God; I meant church," Don explained.

Cecily pondered what she'd heard, and Don figured a personal example might help. "See, my dad's from Argentina. He came here when he was 18 and joined the Mormon Church for a girl he'd met. She'd been a missionary and converted him to her faith. He was a Catholic but never believed the religion had anything for him. He didn't stay with the Mormons for the same reason, and because he and the girl broke up."

"My mom moved here from Portugal when she was 16. She belongs to the Catholic Church and always wanted us kids to go with her. By the time my mom and dad divorced, I refused to go to church at all. They never could agree on the subject of religion. You should have heard them fight. Mom yelling in Portuguese and Dad in Spanish. I never was quite sure what they were saying...."

"So you don't speak either language?"

"Not a word. I understand a few things, but—"

Soon they were in sight of the tree house. The sound of pounding rang out over the rush of the river, rising higher each day from the spring run off.

"Hey, Uncle Don, watch this." Jake, hanging above them, pushed off from the edge of the treehouse's roof and glided down the rappelling rope, practically free falling. When he neared the ground, he braked with one hand to slow himself for a smooth landing.

"I don't know if I'll ever get used to them doing that," groaned Cecily. "That tree house is too high for me."

Jake unhooked his safety gear and headed back up the ladder. "You hook the lunchboxes on to the rope and I'll pull 'em up."

After a delicious lunch, the boys started in on a few repairs. Danny began pounding a nail. "Shiz!" he screamed, having pounded his thumb instead.

Now it was Cecily's turn to rub it in. "Here," she grinned, "I'll teach you how to use that." She snatched the hammer from his hand and, in three graceful strokes, drove the nail home.

"Whoa!" marveled Jake. "How'd you do that?"

"Lots of practice," she gloated. "My dad's a carpenter. I used to work for him in the summer. Here I'll teach you."

Soon Cecily had instructed them in the fine art of swinging a hammer to deliver the most forceful, accurate blow. Afterwards, she spoke to Danny. She hadn't meant to show him up, and wanted to restore his confidence. "You make my heart half stop when you go down that rope. How did you get your father to let you do that?"

Danny brightened. "Jake's a certified instructor, and I'm a certified lead climber."

Jake broke in. "You've *got* to try it, Cecily! It's such a rush."

"Not me," she answered, putting up her palms in a "stop-right-there" pose.

Don, adding his persuasive powers, slowly made her hands rise higher in the air in surrender.

"Okay, but just once." She struggled into the harness and climbed to the top of the roof. Danny went down first and "belayed"—held tight to the safety rope. Don tied himself in without a harness and steadied the rope. Christina looked on from the roof, where she, too, was securely tied.

Jake gave Cecily her final instructions and checked the harness. "You can go any time you're ready."

Cecily gritted her teeth. Her heart pounded in her chest. "No! I can't do it!" she finally said, pulling herself back in.

"Girls!" Danny teased from below.

Don sidled up next to her. "You *can* do it," he said, patting her arm. "Just let the fear out first."

I'm not a quitter, Cecily thought to herself. *Besides if these boys can do it, so can I.*

She inched back into position. Summoning up every ounce of courage, she let go and pushed away, but her natural instincts kicked in and suddenly she clutched at the rope, sending herself spinning head over heels until she was dangling upside down.

Danny swallowed hard. "You've got to let go of the rope," he called. "I've got you."

Jake peered out over the edge of the treehouse and burst out laughing. Then, still grinning, he said, "Just reach back up and pull yourself around with your left hand."

Her entire life passing before her eyes, Cecily did as she was told.

"Okay. Now slowly release with your right hand and you'll start to go down." Sure enough, as her grip eased up its pressure, she slowly began sliding down the rope and within seconds her feet met up with beloved earth.

"I'm never doing that again!" she insisted, shaking her head. And her head was not the only part of her anatomy that was shaking. Her knees were so weak beneath her, she could hardly stand.

"Isn't that a rush?" Danny asked.

Cecily could hardly answer under her breath. "A rush to your death!"

Don and Christina descended the ladder. Christina put her arm around Cecily as they sat on a nearby rock. "That's why I won't do it," Christina murmured, comforting her new friend.

Cecily refrained from mentioning to anyone that she was afraid of heights.

FIFTEEN

THE AFTERNOON SHADOWS grew long as Don and Cecily headed home, taking the same route back they'd walked that morning. Christina on her bike and Danny on his board rode a few houses ahead. Jake had left them behind to spend his Saturday evening with "the dudes"—his group of friends.

A moving truck pulled out of the driveway a few houses farther down. Christina made a half circle in a nearby driveway and anxiously rode back to meet her dad. "Dad, the apartment's for rent again. Can we look around?" She brought her bike to an abrupt stop to keep from running him down. Danny, now a block or two ahead, boarded back to see what was holding up his cousin.

"I don't think so, 'Tina. I haven't even been paid a single check yet. How can we afford it?"

"Come on, let's go see it anyway," Cecily suggested, pulling Don toward the apartment.

As they approached, the owner stepped out the basement door. "Hi, folks," he chortled as he limped up the short flight of stairs. "I remember you; aren't you the ones that stopped by the other day?"

"Right," answered Don. "Is the place for rent again?"

"As a matter of fact it is. I just put the sign back up. But I saw you coming, so I left the door open." He looked down at the drink in his hand and gave it a little swirl.

Cecily followed the children inside. "How come the other people moved out?" Don asked.

"Well, the young lady found out she's allergic to the bloom of the junipers," he lied. "Come on in and check it out."

The living room was small but adequate, the kitchen in full view just across a counter. It was obvious upon entering that a fresh coat of paint would help brighten it up. Holes adorned the walls and ceilings where previous renters had hung pictures and swag lamps. The kitchen cupboards were blanketed with several coats of paint, much of which encroached onto the edges of the glass panes. Old floral contact paper lined the shelves, and the pattern on the formica counter top was well worn from many years of use. A small table surrounded by four chairs looked as if they'd come with the original construction.

"My name's Melvin Briggs." He offered his hand. Don reached out and shook firmly, his calloused, dinner plate-size hand engulfing the smaller man's.

"Don Rodriguez."

Christina returned from the recesses of the apartment. "It's just right, Daddy," she said excitedly. "Two bedrooms and everything."

"Is this your beautiful daughter?"

"She is. 'Tina, this is Mr. Briggs."

"Hi. Nice to meet you Mr. Briggs," she answered cordially.

"What beautiful dark hair you have. You must have gotten it from your father."

"I guess so; thank you very much."

"My daughter has hair like yours. She got it from her mother." Don began to look around the apartment.

Christina, trying to be polite, asked, "How old is she?"

Melvin stopped to think. "Let's see, she'll be 17 next month."

"I look forward to meeting her."

Melvin shook his head. "Oh, that won't be possible. She doesn't live here."

Don interrupted their chitchat. "How much is it?"

"Four-fifty a month, plus a five-hundred dollar deposit. I pay the utilities because we only have one meter."

"Let's get it, Daddy," pleaded Christina.

Cecily had returned to the room. "It's a nice place for a start," she said.

"And this must be your wife?" Melvin asked.

Cecily was quick to set the record straight. "Oh, no. Just friends. Don and I work for the same company."

"His loss."

"Let's get it," Christina repeated, careful not to interrupt.

"I don't think we can, 'Tina. We can't come up with the money right now." Don knew he was disappointing her.

Cecily came forward. "Ralph will give you an advance, one time. He does it for all new employees, if they ask him."

"I don't know...."

"I'll tell you what. I'll waive the first month's rent if you can come up with the deposit," Melvin offered. "It's better than letting it sit a month."

"We'll see....Mr. Briggs, do you think you could hold it until Monday so I can ask my boss?"

"If your references check out, I'll be glad to. And call me Melvin." He turned and opened a nearby door, one that looked like a closet. A narrow flight of stairs led upward. "I'll go up and get an application," he said.

Christina was delighted. "Can we get it?" she asked when Melvin was out of sight.

"We'll see."

The house was built during the sixties, remodeled once or twice. Trees and bushes spread across the front of the home, screening off from the street the concrete stairway leading to the apartment. The bushes had been trimmed from in front of each window to let in light. The exterior brick looked more like cinder block than brick. A dirty gray color of paint had been applied, coat upon coat.

A concrete driveway ran down the left side of the home, leading to a detached garage. Peering out the kitchen window, Don noticed its overhead door was propped open on one side with a two-by-four. Shelves lined the back of the garage, housing old cans of lawn fertilizer and bug poison. A few boxes were stacked on the shelves, but it appeared nothing of value warranted locking the structure. The drive widened in the back, where steps on the side and rear of the home led to the upper part of the house.

An additional parking spot was added to the driveway out by the street to allow room for a tenant's car. None of the other homes in the neighborhood had a built-in apartment.

Inside, a family room had been pegged onto the rear of the apartment. Danny and Christina entered by walking past a door leading upstairs. The room's floor was covered with green shag carpet, the walls trimmed in cheap, dark-stained paneling. Green curtains hung down above the stubby windows. On the far left wall above the fireplace protruded an indirect light built of the same ugly paneling as the walls. Soot marked the brick above the fireplace, evidence of its usefulness. A built-in bookcase extended along the wall to the left of the dirty sandstone hearth, which ran from wall to wall below the fireplace.

Christina and Danny were "tight-rope walking" back and forth on the hearth, when Danny hopped off and inadvertently jostled against the bookcase.

"Look, Chrissy, it moved!" Christina jumped from the hearth, pushed on the far right side, and the bookcase slowly began to swivel into the next room. "Cool," said Danny, pushing harder and disappearing behind a wet bar that swung from a shallow room. "This can be our secret hiding place," he grinned. "Let's not tell anyone."

The tiny room behind the bookcase consisted of a recessed area with stairs leading upward. It took a few moments for their eyes to adjust to the darkness. The only light in the room came from the crack that ran around the sides of the bookcase. The floor was damp and cold, the room musty and unfinished. Cobwebs filled the corners. Cables and connections covered the wall, all attached to a sheet of plywood anchored securely to the studs. What seemed like hundreds of phone lines ran vertically up the corner, where they connected to terminals and boxes. "Wow!" Danny was first to say. "I wonder what all this stuff's for."

Suddenly they heard footsteps above their heads.

"Let's get out before anyone comes," Christina suggested. They again pushed on the bookcase. The heavy frame took almost all their strength to push into its original position. When it was back in place, they stood and smiled at each other.

Danny and Christina turned to see Melvin come through the doorway of the family room, heading for the kitchen. "I used this room as a TV room when my daughter still lived with me," he told the children. "I don't need the space any more." He carried several papers in his hand.

Alone once more, Christina and Danny ambled around the corner and opened the door to above. The stairs were directly at their feet. Christina started up the stairs, with Danny following a few steps behind. A closed door stood at the top stair. Christina reached to open it.

"Stay out of there!" yelled Melvin from the bottom of the stairs. Then he realized he'd maybe spoken harshly. "That's not part of the apartment," he gently explained.

Just then, Don and Cecily came around the corner and looked past Melvin. "Christina Marie!" scolded her father. "Come down!"

"Yes, Daddy," she replied. She and Danny trudged back down the stairs.

"This door leads to my part of the house," Melvin briefed them. "The upper door has a lock on it, as does this door." He rubbed his hand along the door jamb to where the deadbolt stuck out. "I'll give you keys to both. That way if we want to talk to one another we don't need to go out and around....I didn't want to take out the doors when I put in the apartment, in case I ever wanted to use the basement again. ...You see, this used to be one house."

Christina and Danny were roaming the other rooms for a second time. Melvin closed the door and locked the deadbolt above the knob, his keys at his belt. "Let's go into the kitchen."

Cecily flitted about, opening and closing the drawers and cupboards. "It could use some cleaning," she noted.

"I know," Melvin answered. "They didn't do a very good job. I felt bad they had to move, but I still gave them back their deposit."

Again, Melvin was lying, and began to swirl the ice in the drink he'd brought back with him from upstairs. It appeared to be some sort of a cola—but it was stronger than a soft drink, much stronger.

Christina and Danny opened the first door down the hall. Two water heaters sat directly to the right. One dripped periodically, leaving a slimy build-up of minerals and rust below it. Water trickling from the ooze flowed into a nearby drain. Two furnaces, shaped like deformed dinosaurs, rested in each corner. The space at the far end of the room was occupied by a washing machine. Gunk-caked galvanized pipes, hose bibs at the end, ran down its back.

With Don and Cecily busy with the application, Melvin looked on as the children explored the room. He pointed toward the open door. "Both water heaters and furnaces are in there. I'll need to get down here and fix the leaking water heater as soon as I get a chance."

Don glanced up briefly, then once again turned his attention to the form. "A washer and dryer are included?" Cecily asked.

"Yeah, but the dryer's in the bathroom."

Cecily nodded. "I saw it earlier, but didn't see the washer...."

Meanwhile, Christina, finding little of interest in the room, swung the door closed behind her as she left. Danny stayed inside. Picking up a yardstick that had been lodged at the side of one of the furnaces, he began to poke at the pile of slime under the water heater. Through the thin walls, he could hear Christina enter the room next to him, the bathroom. Danny stuck his face up to a hole in the wall near the side of the dryer. There she was, walking right past him, within striking distance. He readied his yardstick and jabbed the stick through the hole.

"Grrrrrr!" he growled, poking her in the side.

Christina, startled, flinched and screamed. It only took a moment for her to realize it was just her cousin, playing one of his tricks. "Danny!"

His muffled laughter easily penetrated the wall that

separated them. She grabbed the yardstick, still dripping with slime, and pulled. Then, feeling the gook on it, she quickly let go. Danny released the short end of the stick at the same time, sending it to the floor. When it hit the hard tile, it bounced and flipped up—just right—flinging the balance of the ooze up the front of Christina's pants, shirt and face.

"Oh, yuck...yuck! Danny, I'm gonna kill you!"

Danny, his eye still glued to the wall, shook with bursts of laughter.

Don finished filling out the form and went to see what all the noise was about.

"What's all the ruckus?"

"Daddy, look what Danny did to me." Christina scowled down at her clothes.

"What's that on your face, 'Tina?" he said, trying to hold back a smile.

"I don't know, but it's all over everything," she grumbled. "Danny poked it through the wall."

Melvin and Cecily walked in on the mess. "Don't worry, I'll clean it up," Melvin offered.

"Let's go home and get you cleaned up," muttered Cecily. She seemed to be the only one taking Christina's plight seriously. In fact, Don's smile turned into a full-blown chuckle when he spied Danny at the doorway of the bathroom, his eyes and cheeks still wet from laughter.

Christina looked at herself in the bathroom mirror. A tiny trickle of ooze still slithered down the side of her nose. Realizing she wasn't hurt, the sour look on her face slowly transformed into a reluctant grin.

Cecily wiped off the worst of the mess with her fingers and rinsed it off in the sink. Then everyone made their way to the door to leave. As they climbed the stairs, Don turned to Melvin. "I'll call you Monday and let you know."

Melvin nodded.

Don, Cecily and the children walked close together on their way home. Christina knew she wasn't safe alone; Danny made out like he was tough, but stayed close by, just the same.

When they reached the house, Danny scooted up the drive and tossed his board on the back lawn. His 11-year-old Rottweiler, her hips failing her, struggled to stand and greet him. "Hey, Mitsy! How are you feeling?" He reached down and gently caressed the sides of her jowls. The veterinarian had given him pills for her discomfort, but they didn't seem to help much. "What am I going to do with you, you old mutt?" he teased. "Dad thinks we need to take you to the vet and put you to sleep, so you won't have to suffer anymore." Danny, though, wasn't so sure he was ready to let her go just yet. She'd been part of the family from before he could remember. She was getting gray around her ears and nose, but didn't have a mean bone in her body. Kate said it was because they loved her so much as a pup.

Danny fed her her supper and changed the water in the bucket. She was the smartest dog in the neighborhood. He gave her one last tickle behind the ears before he walked away.

At the front of the house, Cecily was about to leave for home. Don placed her cooler in the passenger seat of the Jeep, trying to think of something smooth to say before she left. Again, she beat him to it. "I had a real nice time today."

"Me, too," he replied. "Oh, I almost forgot. You don't need to pick me up Monday."

"Why?"

Don didn't want to sound unappreciative. "I'm going to ride Alan's bike to work so I can get an early start in the powder shed. As you know, it gets hot in there. But if you don't mind, I'd love to put the bike in and get a ride home."

Cecily nodded her approval.

Don didn't want to appear too forward. "It's all up hill back home, you know," he stammered.

Cecily watched his mouth move. "I know," she said, only half listening. *Why doesn't he kiss me?* she thought.

Don gazed into her eyes, glistening in the evening shadows, her face soft and inviting. He could feel his heart begin to race—wanting to kiss her, making idle conversation while trying to figure out how to approach it. He felt like a school kid again.

The cool of the night made Cecily shiver. "I'm gettin' a little cold," she said, rubbing her arms with her hands. Then her eyes rested upon the blanket hanging over the side of the Jeep. This time Don took the hint.

"Here, let me cover you." He picked it up and shook it loose, then reached around Cecily and placed the blanket around her shoulders. She turned her face toward him, expecting he'd take her cue. Don let the moment slip away.

"Oh, what the heck!" Cecily muttered, opening the blanket and wrapping her arms around his neck. She placed her soft lips against his and gently kissed him.

Don reached around under the blanket and pulled her close. She felt good. It had been a long time since he'd felt the butterflies of infatuation; even longer since he'd kissed a woman.

Stacey typed away at the N.C.I.C. connection. He'd searched for hours for something, anything that might help find the killer. Information on the captain would have to wait.

"Unsolved homicides." He typed in *1993-1999*.

The cursor flashed. "Processing."

76,376.

He hit the keys again. "Advanced Search....Female."

59,515.

"Advanced Search," he pressed again. "Age."

"9-14," he entered.

12,113.

Stacey knew the FBI and every other agency had pored over the records dozens of times. They hadn't found a thing. *I'm going through these records one at a time if it takes all weekend*, he resolved. He began the search.

SIXTEEN

DON WENT TO BED happy. He'd never kissed another girl, aside from Monica.

The kiss tonight felt different. Cecily's kiss was warm and gentle. She seemed to enjoy him as much as he did her. Although he'd been hit on countless times, he had always stayed true to his marriage vows. His dad had taught him that—

A picture of his dad, back in his better days, crashed through his brain. Just as suddenly, it was replaced by another, of him gaunt and wasted away. *Who will I go to when I need to talk? Why did you get cancer? I'm going to miss you....*Don drifted off to sleep.

At just after four in the morning, Stacey finally finished reviewing almost four hundred cases, one at a time. He could no longer prop his eyes open. He flopped down to rest for a moment on the easy chair. Soon he was sound asleep, breathing deeply, his dog at his side.

Sunday mornings in the Jensen home were not the same as week days. Alan would get up earlier than usual and cook breakfast. The smallest children enjoyed the dinosaur pancakes he made.

"Don?" Alan's voice was heard outside his door.

Don hesitantly answered. "Yes?"

"Breakfast is ready. Come and get it if you like it hot." Don rolled out of bed and quickly dressed. He entered the kitchen to find the older children looking much like he did, just out of bed, hair flying every which way. In contrast, Alan was already shaved, showered and dressed in a white shirt and tie, a tattered apron strung around him to cover up the better part of his Sunday clothes. The children were seating themselves around the kitchen bar.

Alan glanced in turn at each of the children. "Let's see, whose turn is it to pray?"

The towheaded four-year-old raised her hand. "Me! Me!"

"I think you're right, Kinley. Go ahead," Alan encouraged.

She folded her arms and looked around to be sure everyone was ready and watching her. Then she bowed her head and spoke a child's prayer: simple, sincere, to the point. "Dear Heavenwe Fader, tank dee for our day and our food and house. Bess us with da tings we need and bess Don's daddy he will be okay. Bess Don to feel good, in the name of Jesus Christ, Amen." She unfolded her arms and waited for the others to do the same.

"Good job, Kinley. All by yourself, too," Kate praised.

Don turned and withdrew from the room, a lump in his throat so big he could hardly breathe. How was it those simple words seemed to melt his heart? If she knew to pray for his dad, that meant the rest of the family had made him a part of their prayers, too.

Retreating to his room, Don sat on the bed, wiping the tears from his face, asking how such a small child could speak to God as if she knew him, when he himself felt so estranged, so far away. He took a few minutes to regain his composure before rejoining the family, slipping back into the kitchen in time to claim his share of bacon and eggs.

Only scraps of food remaining on the platters, the home transformed into a mass of helping hands as older children helped the younger children bathe, dress and get ready for church. Don again retired to his room to avoid the mad scramble.

"Daddy." Christina knocked on his door.

"Come in." She entered, dressed for church. "You look beautiful."

"Are you coming with us?"

"No...I don't think so."

Stacey awoke to the sight of Sig, hovering above him, panting in his face.

"Dog breath!" Sig licked him on the mouth.

"I wish you wouldn't do that first thing in the morning," he groaned. He extricated himself from the recliner, wobbled to the kitchen and opened a couple of cans of dog food. Sig wolfed them down before Stacey could return to his computer. "Let's see, where was I?" he mumbled.

The house was eerily quiet. Don flipped on the TV. No cable...Sunday morning...in Utah. He clicked it off again and glanced around for something to read. Piles of church magazines lined the sofa table. "No."

He found himself in front of the fridge. *I'm not even hungry*, he thought, shutting the door. The family had left in such a hurry that they'd left the dishes piled on the counter, so he unloaded both dishwashers, filled one with dishes and silverware, the other with pots and pans. Alan was a good cook, but he sure made a mess of the place. He wiped down the plastic tablecloth.

Looking again for something to read, he opened a drawer near the television. It was filled with scriptures and hymnals. He shook his head and started to close the drawer, when something familiar caught his eye. A Bible, its cover worn, was tucked among the other books. Don picked it up. The book had belonged to his father. Christina must have borrowed it from him. He sat down, opened the cover, and read.

November 11th, 1957

Dear Gerardo,

I am pleased you have shown such a great interest in me. You're a wonderful man. I admire your courage coming to this country and working so hard. You have a great love for God. I want you to have this Bible to help you keep in touch with your Savior. I know you had hoped I would marry you, but my parents are old fashioned and won't allow me to continue seeing you. I love you. The color of your skin makes no difference to me. Christ said, "Come unto me."

May God bless you. I'll always remember you.
Love, Anna

Melvin pulled into the empty stall marked "Sheriff" and shut off his car. The county courthouse parking lot was empty. He preferred working weekends—only occasionally did anyone come in on Sundays. With a swipe of his card, the rear entrance doors clicked. He pulled the glass door open and passed unimpeded—no security guards, no police, no metal detector.

He was required to work at least 20 hours a week. His previous military security clearance had been helpful in obtaining his part-time job as a janitor, his main responsibility to keep the private offices clean. His supervisor preferred him to come in before work or after everyone was gone. Lately, however, he'd been appearing during working hours.

Retrieving his cart of cleaning supplies, he took the elevator to the second floor, the wheels of his cart clicking on the granite tile, echoing down the empty corridor. He stopped outside the office of "The Honorable Judge Roland G. Demick." Melvin extended the wad of keys from his side, unlocked the door, propped it open with his cart, emptied the garbage cans, made a quick pass around the room with a portable vacuum cleaner, and completed what little dusting needed to be done. Then he reached under the desk and turned on the master switch for the judge's computer. The hard drive spun as the main screen appeared.

Password, the cursor flashed.

"Court order," he typed. It had taken him a week to catch the judge's clerk entering the password. He knew his way around the judge's computer, and after a moment had access to the fourth circuit records.

Name, the cursor flashed. Melvin took the rental application from his pocket. "Donald J. Rodriguez, DOB 10/12/69." The hard drive spun again as the screen lit up.

Rodriguez, Donald Jorel

Address: 700 North 6th West, Provo, UT

DL: UT 900BR173942 Class A Current status: Suspended

Weight: 235 Eyes: BRO

Birth Date 10/12/1969, Place of birth: American Fork, Utah

Height: 6'2" Sex: M Hair: Black

Donor: Yes

Father: Rodriguez, Gerardo De La Cruz

Mother: Maria Lopez

Prior Arrests/Citations: 03/03/99 Driving without Insurance

Notes: Domestic incident. Wife called to report DUI. Apprehended 1300 South Main. Alcohol level: .02. No arrest. Cited for no insurance. Officer Rick Stacey, Mapleton, Utah.

Current status: Appeared before Judge Roland G. Demick, Fourth Circuit Court, 03/15/99. Cited for contempt. Sentenced to 90 days. Reviewed: 04/05/99. Out on own recog. Any violence, must finish sentence. Scheduled to appear 05/10/99. Driving privileges to be reviewed at hearing. Action pending. Any alleged parole violations, report directly to Judge Roland Demick's clerk.

Case # 4809281 Fourth Circuit Court

6/22/97: Arrested, wanton destruction of personal property. Posted bond.

Notes: Domestic incident. Owner Phillip R. Mendenhall reported his pickup truck was filled with cement. Rodriguez admitted filling truck from Granger Redi Mix Truck. Wife apparently sleeping with Mendenhull. Officer Fred Peterson, Provo, Utah.

Appeared before Judge Roland G. Demick, Fourth Circuit Court, 9/12/97. Convicted of destruction of Personal Property. Sentenced two weeks in county jail. Fined $5,000.00

Current Status: Time served, released 11/4/97-11/17/97.

Case # 3672092, Fourth Circuit Court

12/24/96: Cited Disorderly Conduct, Provo, Utah
Call from "The Palace." Fight in parking lot. Officers Dewit and Cowley arrived on scene 11:55 p.m. Rodriguez and other male fighting. Husband claim's wife is sleeping with victim. Wife denies accusations. No arrest made. Appeared before Judge Max Nielsen, 12/30/96. Fined $500.00; paid 1/30/97. Case closed.
Case # 459821, Third District Court

1/1/96: Warning Issued, Lehi, Utah
Call from "Cal's Bar," 335 West Main, 2:05 a.m. Fighting in parking area. Angry domestic dispute. No arrest. Officers Bukers & Wilson.
Case # 38562, Lehi, P.D.

8/2/94: Arrested, Assault and Battery, SLC, UT
Call from "Durango's Bar & Grill." Assaulted wife's boyfriend. Boyfriend transported to LDS Hospital, SLC. Bail posted. Appeared 9/7/94 before Judge Ralph Parker. One-week Davis County Jail, $2,000 fine. Officer's Goodrich & Flack.
Case # 4098361893, First District Court

7/14/93: Arrested, Assault and Battery, Resisting Arrest, Provo, UT
Call from "Lamar's," 225 West Center, 1:02 a.m. Fight in dance hall, angry husband. Officers Dewit and Macfey accosted suspect, were also assaulted. Suspect claims he found his wife with other man. Wife denies claim—said she was dancing. Appeared before Judge Hardy, 9/2/93. Released on O.R. 9/3/93. Fine at $1000.00 and 40 hr. comm. serv. Paid fine 9/4/93. Case closed.
Case # 3817456, Fourth Circuit Court

Juvenile records closed:

"Perfect," Melvin murmured. "Just perfect."

Stacey resumed his search, one name at a time. The work was tedious. He tried to *not* think of each case as a person just another number. When he took time to reflect on these poor girls' parents and grandparents, friends and siblings, he felt bad. *How much suffering has to happen in the world?* he thought.

SEVENTEEN

DON GOT UP, showered and dressed before the rest of the family had roused. He wasn't sure how long it would take to bike to work. He slipped into the kitchen to make his lunch as the rest of the weary troupe was joining Alan for prayer in the family room. Christina looked longingly toward her father, hoping he'd join them.

He waved through the doorway. "See you all later." He slung on his small backpack and walked out the door.

Christina ran to catch him. "Daddy, you forgot to kiss me goodbye," she hollered. Don wheeled the bike around. "Are you going to ask your boss for some money?"

"I think so." He gave her a peck on the cheek.

"I love you, Daddy." She watched as he peddled away.

The ride didn't take as long as expected. Don was waiting at the front gate when Jeff arrived at ten minutes to seven. "Morning," he greeted.

"You're here bright and early." Jeff unlocked the gate, and the two of them headed toward the building.

Don was feeling good. *Today will be better*, he thought. *I'll do powders until noon, then move to sales.*

Almost one thousand missing persons' reports, each painstakingly reviewed—*pain* being the operative word, here. Stacey pushed away from the computer and massaged the back of his stiff neck, rolling his head side to side, front to back. He pulled himself up out of the chair and staggered to the bedroom to get ready for work. The phone rang. "Stacey, here."

"Stace, Deek. I remembered something that might

help." He paused a moment, then plunged ahead. "The night I was shot and the captain got a call, I was able to read his lips before he turned his back to me. He told the caller not to call him at work. I thought it was strange, and wrote the time and date on a note pad and put it in my desk. He left the office in a hurry."

"Good work, Deek," Stacey replied. "I'll see what I can find."

"Maryann can look up the call and find out where it originated. Tell her it was a call to me—that way she won't wonder why we're checking out the captain. How're you going to get the sweats out of the evidence room?"

"I'm not sure. If I check them out, Bingham'll know what's going on." Stacey shook his head and frowned. "If I don't sign them out, it won't be by the book—and we may lose the evidence in court...."

"You have to do it by the book," Deek told him. "Just don't give a clear explanation of why you need them tested. Make sure the captain doesn't know you're matching fibers from his car, either."

"Bingham's handling your shooting personally, you know. He'll flip if he finds out I went over his head."

"Barker's straight as an arrow. He can get them out for you. Just ask him to keep it quiet. He doesn't need to know you're investigating our illustrious captain." Deek didn't have to tell him about Barker; he was Stacey's best friend. The guy was always trying to set Stacey up with someone to date, considering it his sacred duty to help him get married.

"I don't know how in the world I'll get the fibers without out Bingham's knowledge. He's a stickler about locking his car."

"I think the maintenance garage keeps a set of keys on file for every vehicle in the fleet," Deek said. "Ask Cartwright if he'll lend you the captain's keys. Tell him I sent you down—and that he needs to keep it quiet. He owes me one....When you take the evidence to Provo, tell Saunders in the crime lab to call me directly with the results. We don't want any of this getting back to Bingham."

"Sounds good. How're you feeling?"

"Better. The doctors think I might get out of here earlier than expected. I do therapy three times a day—just about kills me. I'd rather be at work, believe me."

"I do....Well, I've got a lot to do; best get to it." He hung up the phone. Deek was everything Stacey wanted to be.

Stacey finished dressing, then led Sig to the garage, stopping at the faucet to fill a five-gallon bucket with water. "Come, Sig," he commanded.

Sig followed at his human partner's heel, his tail down. He didn't want to spend the day in the garage again.

"I know boy, I wouldn't want to stay in here either," he sympathized. "But I have no choice."

After locking Sig in, Stacey climbed into his patrol car and headed for the city garage. "One-thirty-nine, dispatch."

"Morning, Stacey," Maryann's familiar voice responded.

"I'm on duty. Would you log me in?"

"Sure thing."

"I'll be running patrol for about an hour. Let me know if you need anything."

"Ten-four." The radio went quiet. The drive into town was almost uneventful. Stacey pulled over and ticketed an 18-year-old male tooling through a school zone at 20 mph over the limit.

Back in the car, Stacey lifted the radio. "One-thirty-nine, one-twelve."

"One-twelve, go ahead," Barker answered.

"What's your twenty?"

"I'm in the office. What is it?"

"I need to see you in about 20 minutes. Will you still be in?" Stacey asked.

"Ten four, I'm following up on the leads for Deek," he answered.

Stacey pulled up to the city garage. It wasn't a big place. Various city vehicles and equipment were parked around the building. He knew most of the people who worked there. "Where's Cartwright?" he asked the shop foreman.

"He's working on the vac truck." He pointed toward a big, yellow street cleaner, feet protruding out from under the rig.

"Cartwright, is that you?"

"Sure is." He scooted out from under the beast. His pocked face and unkempt hair belied the heart of gold that beat beneath his grease-stained "John" insignia.

"Deek needs a favor."

"How's he doing?" he asked, wiping his hands.

"We spoke this morning. They've got him in therapy three times a day. Thinks he'll be out soon."

"Good. He gave us all a scare."

"I need to borrow the keys to car one-eighteen; can you keep it quiet?"

A hesitant scowl formed on the man's protruding lower jaw. "What do you need with the captain's car?"

"It's better left unsaid."

"I can loan them without saying a word, but I've gotta log it in. I'd lose my job if anyone found out, you know. I'll do it for Deek if you need me to." Cartwright finished wiping his hands and started for the office.

"How often do the logs get checked?"

"I ain't never seen anyone check 'em, unless something's missin'. Or we're gettin' audited."

"I don't see a reason not to log it in then." Stacey didn't want the guy to lose his job, but what were the chances of the captain checking?

Cartwright opened the drawer, retrieved the large envelope marked #S118, and removed the keys, handing them to Stacey. Glancing up at the clock on the wall, he jotted down the date and time. "You have to initial here." He pointed to the line.

Stacey drew a pen from his uniform pocket and wrote *R. Stacey* next to the date. "I'll have them back in a few hours," he said.

"You tell Deek next time you see him that we've been praying for him," Cartwright exclaimed as he put the envelope back in the drawer and slid it shut.

"I will," answered Stacey. *I hope this doesn't backfire on me*, he thought as he drove off toward the station.

Melvin booted up his computer, bypassing numerous security checks. He scrolled through his files, made notes, logged on the Internet, and verified information. This wasn't so different from most other days. Between his job at the county building and his part-time evening work at the bank, he had a lot of spare time at home. He'd retired from a special task force five years earlier, where he'd served as a communications expert. Surveillance was his speciality.

He, his wife and daughter had bought the house only a few months later. They had used both the upstairs and downstairs sections—until his daughter disappeared. The house was too big without her. He made a few changes by adding the laundry downstairs. He'd rented the place out off and on through the years. Once in a while he even found renters who actually liked him. Sometimes it was a pain, but the extra income, tucked away for a rainy day, came in handy.

Logged off the net, he picked up the phone, removed the application from his pocket and made a call.

"Cobblecrete, how may I direct your call?" a pleasant voice answered.

"I'd like to speak to Don Rodriguez."

"I'm sorry, he can't be reached until lunch time. Can I take a message and have him return your call?"

"This is Melvin Briggs."

"Oh, hi, Melvin. This is Cecily. I was the one with Don the other day."

"Yes, you're the pretty little blonde. Will you tell him he can have the place if he can come up with the deposit? He checked out real good."

"I'll tell him when I see him. I'm sure he'll call you this evening."

"Good, thanks, Cecily." Melvin hung up the phone.

Stacey warily drove into the station's parking lot. Bingham's car sat in its assigned spot. Stacey pulled up alongside, opened his door, glanced around, quickly unlocked the door, and returned the key to his pocket. His eyes furtively darting in both directions, he casually opened the door and reached in, jerking a few fibers from the seat. The fabric was tight, making it difficult to get a sample. He tucked the fibers into a small plastic bag, locked the door, and closed it behind him.

That wasn't so bad, he thought. *I should've been a detective.* He strode to the back door and entered the squad room. Everyone was busy with their own problems. His clandestine actions had probably gone unnoticed.

Barker was at his desk on the phone, the receiver pressed tightly to his ear, a mask-like look of impatience and fatigue on his face. "Thank you, ma'am, we'll follow up on that." He hung up the phone, then glanced over at Stacey. "Everybody thinks noises in the night are peeping-toms, these days," he smirked. His voice sounded tired. Way too much overtime. "We need real leads, the kind that can help us solve this case. The captain says we don't have the budget for any more help. I'm supposed to do my own work and Deek's, too."

"How's it going, anyway?" Stacey asked.

"No progress. Nothing new." He shuffled the notes piled on his desk. "With Deek out and me in here, we're one less officer on the force."

"Has Howard confessed?"

He emitted a sarcastic chuckle. "Yeah, right. His attorney won't let us get close to him. We moved him to county 'cause we don't have the manpower to watch him."

"Think we should get the gun, clothing and bolt cutters over to the Provo lab and check them out?"

"Yeah. Soon as I finish the million other calls I need to follow up on...."

Stacey gave the corner of Barker's desk a thump with his fist. "I'll give you a hand. I could run them over now."

Barker dragged the keys from his pocket and tossed them to Stacey. "Get the bag from lockup and bring it back for my signature."

"Aren't two of us supposed to do it?" Stacey questioned.

Barker shrugged. "I've got a lot to do," he insisted.

"You grab it and I'll sign it with you."

Stacey decided not to make a big deal out of the minor breach in policy; such things were done all the time. He took the keys, unlocked the evidence room, and looked around for the bag. Seventy-six kilos of cocaine sat on the shelf from his drug bust only a week before, a reminder that he would soon be testifying against the guy. Resting on a lower shelf lay the gun and the bag of clothing. Sticking a new seal on the bag next to the one applied when it was brought in, he signed the log file and started with it to Barker's desk. He turned to lock the door behind him.

"What's up, Stacey?" The captain's gruff voice boomed from the end of the hall as he approached with the lumbering gait of a bear.

Stacey flinched, but kept his cool. His heart began to race. "Lieutenant Barker asked me to take these down to the Provo lab," he stuttered. "Guess he's been real busy."

"He did?" Both men stood facing one another, two gunfighters staring each other down. "Here, I'll sign with you." Bingham took the bag from Stacey and scrawled his initials on the seal. "That ought to do it," he said, handing it back. "Oh, is your dog locked up?"

"In the garage."

"I don't suspect we'll need to keep him there too long. Just keep an eye on him a few more days and we'll let him come back to work. But keep him out of the office."

Stacey was relieved. The captain hadn't seemed overly concerned by the thought of the evidence going to the lab. *Piece of cake*, he mused, returning the keys to Barker.

"Here," Barker said, extending his hand to sign the bag.

"The captain already got it."

"Did he sign you out of the evidence room, too?"

"No, I got that."

"I'll slip back in when I get down here and sign the other line," Barker said. "Now get that over to the lab and let's see if we have a match."

Don finished all the orders by eleven and washed up for lunch. He changed his clothes and stopped to see Cecily on his way up front. The phone pressed to her ear, she gave him a wink. Don couldn't help but smile in return.

"One moment, I'll connect you." Cecily pressed a button and sent the call to another phone. "Oh, Melvin called. He said you've got the apartment if you can come up with the deposit. Ralph'll be back after lunch; you can ask him then." The phone rang again, and Cecily went back to her work.

Melvin limped down the basement stairs, intent on fulfilling his promise to clean the place before his new tenants moved in. He made a quick pass around the kitchen, gathering up a few crumbs left behind. He opened the door to the furnace room and glared down at the slimy puddle under the water heater. "That'll have to wait for another day," he muttered, closing the door behind him.

A scruffy-looking old fellow wearing a crumpled lab coat sat working at a bench. His tousled hair flowed down onto his collar. A pair of wire-rimmed glasses hung at his neck. The light shining from an apparatus that perched on his head cast a luminous glow on an object he held with tweezers between his gloved fingers. A sea of small vials of liquid and strips of colored paper hovered in rows on a shelf to his right.

Stacey cleared his throat. "Is Saunders in?"

"Yeah." The man, concentrating on his task, didn't look up.

Stacey paused, then asked, "Can you tell me where I can find him?"

"Yeah." But the man kept at his work, seemingly oblivious to his visitor.

"What do you mean 'yeah'? Where is he?" The irritation that had crept into Stacey's voice was palpable.

"You're looking at him." The old fellow now stopped what he was doing and peered up over the miniature binoculars connected to the hood. He hadn't taken offense at Stacey's impatience. Why should he? Everyone treated him the same.

"Deek asked me to talk to you about the gun, sweats and bolt cutters found at the Reid home. He's wondering if you'll call him at the hospital with the results just as soon as you get anything."

"Sure thing." He'd already turned back to his work.

Saunders signed the required papers and checked the seal like it was second nature. Stacey wondered if he'd heard a word he'd said. Still he pressed forward. Removing the small zip-lock bag from his shirt pocket, he nonchalantly placed it on the table. "We also need you to see if the fibers on the clothing match the fibers in this bag."

"No problem." Saunders took the bag and laid it atop the other one Stacey had brought.

Stacey gave a little shrug. "Please, make sure you call Deek directly with the results, okay?"

The man gave Stacey another cursory glance and nodded.

Several routine traffic stops later, he returned to the station, arriving around two. Barker, still on the phone, his tired eyes staring off into space, was at his desk. The pile of phone messages had only slightly diminished. "How's it going? Can you use some help?"

He nodded, picked up a pile of messages and handed them to Stacey. "Yes, I know...." he spoke into the receiver. "We're doing our best....We'll call if anything turns up." He hung up the phone. "All we get is a bunch of junk," he spat, his frustration mounting. "Yeah, you can give me a hand with these calls. At the rate I'm going, I'll be here all night. Now I wish the media hadn't asked for help. Here," he added, extending his hand to retrieve the messages, "you concentrate on the Ashley case, sort out the Derickson shooting, and I'll give those calls to the captain."

Ignoring Barker's change of mind, Stacey sat down and began sorting through the light yellow slips of paper. Most seemed insignificant. Those he shuffled into one stack, while any good leads went into another. He continued rifling through the notes, leads sent in by over-enthusiastic callers. *An old Chevy stopped by the Levan Hotel Thursday night for about half an hour,* read one. Stacey pulled it aside from the rest. "Barker, isn't Levan about 50 miles away?"

"I think so. Why?"

"I just couldn't remember." He took another look at the message. *Call the owner at 555-1121, Levan, UT....*He slid the message into his top desk drawer and began calling on the first message from the "useful" pile.

EIGHTEEN

HAVING PUT IN AN eight-hour shift by three-thirty, Don hung around the front desk until four. He stepped out in the shipping area, where Ryan was frantically trying to get ready for UPS pick up.

"Give you a hand?" Don asked.

"Sure could use it."

In less than half an hour, Don and Ryan had cleared the board of orders. The UPS driver pulled up as they were filling out the final form. Don helped load the pile of buckets and packages onto the truck. Then it disappeared out the gate and down the dirt lane.

"That's two I owe you," Ryan said.

"No. Just trying to pass the time." Don wandered back to see how Rex was doing. The old guy was a talented mold maker and moved with a steady pace. It was fascinating to watch him work.

Five o' clock was at hand. "I've got to go ask Ralph for an advance before I go home," he told Rex.

Rex nodded and held up a warning hand. "He'll give it to you one time. Just don't ask again."

Don mustered up the courage to step into the office. "Ralph, can I talk to you a sec?"

"Sure. What can I do for you?"

"I found a place to live, but I don't have any money for a deposit and was wondering—"

Ralph cut in. "How much do you need?"

"Six hundred will pay the deposit and put some food in the fridge 'til payday."

"I have a one-time policy. I figure if you can't manage your financial affairs with one advance you'll *never* be able to manage them. We can take it out of your next three or four checks so you can survive." He pressed his phone's intercom button. "Cecily?"

When Cecily had come and gone, Ralph leaned back in his chair. He looked right past Don as he reminisced. "Cecily....She's one of the best hands I've ever had around here. I knew her dad when we were young; worked on the same construction crew. He couldn't afford to stay in school because he was helping support his mother and siblings back in Colorado. That was almost thirty years ago, but it seems like yesterday."

Cecily stuck her head back into the office. "Here's the check."

He waved her off. "Go ahead and sign it for me."

Don stood to leave. "Thanks, Ralph."

By five-thirty Stacey and Barker had finished with the messages. Stacey decided to start on the last eight hundred names he had yet to review on the N.C.I.C. Barker began straightening his desk. "I'm beat," he announced. "I need to go home, see my family, get some rest before I kill someone." Stacey silently agreed.

Barker was usually soft-spoken, laid-back. He had four children, two older girls from his wife Debbie's first marriage and two young boys together. Debbie was an attractive woman with dishwater blond hair cut to shoulder length. Frequently beaten by her first husband, she'd gotten out of the relationship after three years. Barker married her a year later; he treated the girls like they were his own. Debbie kept trying to line up Stacey with her little sister, though he always refused.

"I think I'll stay and go through these records for a while." In actuality, it was an above-average excuse to stay late so he could search through the captain's files.

Soon the office was empty, except for the captain working in his office. Maryann was taking calls up front, behind the security glass. Stacey recalled the parameters he'd been working on from home and picked up where he'd left off. He clicked through file after file, combing for details: city, state, age, mode of death, hair color, family. So far nothing rang any bells. These girls' deaths were all of the same pattern: death by strangulation. If the killer had struck before, it probably would fit the pattern. One at a time...one more.

"What are you working on?"

Stacey almost toppled from his seat. He'd been concentrating so intensely he hadn't heard Bingham come up behind him.

"I've been going through the N.C.I.C. the last few days, looking at all the unsolved cases."

"You're wasting your time," the captain said matter-of-factly. "The best criminologists in the country have been through those cases—haven't found a thing. Go home, get some rest. We need to be ready if it happens again."

"If you don't mind, Captain, I'm off the clock and it makes me feel better doing something."

"Your time....See you tomorrow."

Stacey watched him exit the station and drive away. When he felt it was safe, he went to Deek's desk and opened his top drawer. Notes and Post-its were strewn everywhere. "How in the world does he keep track of these?" he mumbled to himself, sifting through the mess. He noticed that each note was short and to the point. No one but Deek would have a clue as to what they meant.

"Let's see," he continued. "The shooting was on the ninth....Sometime before eleven o'clock."

The back door clicked. Stacey, startled, turned to see the captain stalk back in the room.

Don and the Jensen family were just finishing their meal, amid an avalanche of chatter. Jake spoke excitedly of the new track-hoe Bryce's father had bought; Danny was explaining to his father one of the myriad of ways he could stop outsiders from accessing the files on his server; and school was Christina's favored topic.

"How was your first day in sales?" Kate asked Don, who hadn't spoken a word all meal long.

"It was good. I haven't got a clue how to work the computer system, though."

"Maybe Danny could help you."

"Sure, Uncle Don!" Danny's head bounced as he spoke. "I'll have you computer-literate in no time."

Don hesitated, but spoke anyway. "I think I may rent the apartment we looked at Saturday." He was enjoying the time he spent with Kate, Alan, and their kids. But he and Christina needed a place of their own.

His mind wandered to his own boyhood years. It was as if the words to a sad song came flooding into his mind. His mother had been borderline manic-depressive, abusive—almost impossible to live with. Nothing anyone ever did was good enough—damned if he did, beaten if he didn't. She practically pecked his father to death, until they separated. She never would give him a divorce. He sued her for three years until the courts granted his request.

Amid this marital discord, Don's childhood had been filled with grief. And Christina hadn't had it much better in his home when Monica was around. This would be his chance to do better.

"We'll miss you," Kate was the first to say. Alan nodded in agreement. The children let out a moan. "How soon do you think you'll move?"

"Maybe tomorrow."

Kate asked, "Is it furnished?"

"It has a washer and dryer, kitchen table, chairs," he answered. "I figure we can camp out on the floor a few weeks."

"We might have a few things in the attic you can use," Alan offered.

"You've already done so much..." he began.

"I insist. We don't need it anyway. You can use my bike until you get your car back. By the way, where's your truck?"

"Impounded for expired registration. Left it parked in the street the day I went to court. I'll get it out as soon as I can afford it." Don felt surprisingly little resentment when he pondered his situation. After all, he'd come out ahead, in the long run. "You know, I was telling my story to Rex, this old guy at work, whose wife died a few years ago from cancer...." Don's thoughts momentarily turned to his father. "He pointed out that it was because of losing my job and the money drying up that Monica left. Maybe it was meant to be, so 'Tina and I can be together again."

"That sounds like a blessing," Alan agreed.

Just then Christina came back into the kitchen. "Daddy, Cecily's here."

Don glanced at his watch. "I didn't realize it was so late." He began to pick up the dishes.

"Leave them for me," Kate said, shooing him out the door.

Before hurrying from the room, Don turned back. "I want you to know how much I appreciate both of you. Christina's a wonderful, well-mannered girl because of the time she has spent with you all these years."

Kate returned the compliment. "You're a great father. She's lucky to have you....Now hurry, you don't want to keep that pretty friend of yours waiting."

"I forgot my coat," said the captain, dryly. He shifted his ample bulk side to side, an uneasy, odd look in his eye.

Stacey wasn't sure what to do.

Bingham glanced down at the open drawer. He spoke gruffly, accusingly. "What're you doing in Deek's desk?"

"He asked me to look for a note he put in here the night he was shot. I can't seem to find it in this mess."

"What's the note say?" the captain insisted.

"Something about a call earlier that evening."

"Good luck." Bingham unhooked his coat from the rack, then walked over and closed and locked his office door. Stacey turned to watch him leave, his prized mohair overcoat draped over his arm. Bingham claimed the hand-woven garment was a gift from a Nigerian tribal chief. Stacey watched him pace across the parking lot and out the back drive entrance to his car, parked on the street in the shadows. No wonder he hadn't heard him drive back in, and now he'd sneaked up on Stacey for a second time. And how long, Stacey wondered, had the man been spying on him through the glass?

Stacey returned to his search. There it was: *4/9 5:42 p.m.*, it read. Peeling it away from the two notes stuck to it, he turned to see the captain pull from the curb. Stacey went up front, where Maryann sat at her desk, polishing her nails.

"Maryann, I need a favor. Deek got a call the night he was shot. Can you look it up and see what number it originated from?"

She plugged the polish brush back in its bottle. "What was the day and time?" she asked, changing the screen on her computer.

"April ninth, at five forty-two."

The cursor flashed, and the calls for that day flashed up on the screen. Stacey peered over her shoulder as she scrolled down through them. Maryann was first to locate it. "Looks like it was a cell number. US Sprint. Doesn't have a name. Does Deek know who it is?"

"I think so," Stacey lied. "Thanks, Maryann, I'll let him know."

She looked at him, then peered out the window into the fading evening. "How much longer will you be here?"

"An hour or two, I guess."

"I get off at eight. I was wondering if you'll be here to walk me to my car?"

"Sure. I thought you worked until eleven."

"No, Captain Bingham thinks it's better if I don't stay so late, at least 'til things calm down around here. But it's not going to be easy to make ends meet without the extra income."

Maryann was a single parent with two teenage boys who'd come close to the law several times. Because their mom was the part-time dispatch, they hadn't been hauled in. She didn't know how to handle them—so she didn't. Her husband had moved to Washington after the divorce. He'd walked out on her after meeting up with his old sweetheart—at his high school reunion, no less. The woman he left Maryann for had been married five times before, and dropped him as soon as his divorce was final. So he'd ended up marrying some other woman—

"on the rebound," according to Maryann. It seemed he never sent any child support or alimony. Stacey avoided asking how things were going at home, because if he did she'd inevitably launch into the whole sordid soap opera all over again.

"Thanks, Maryann." He'd have to wait until morning to call the phone company. Returning to his desk, he found the note about the hotel in Levan and dialed the number. He'd wait until Maryann was gone to look through the files on the captain.

"Motel Levan," the clerk answered.

"This is Officer Rick Stacey. You called the Mapleton police department earlier today."

"It was Friday when I called," the man said testily. "I thought you folks could've used a little help catching the cop shooter."

"I'm sorry we didn't get back sooner. We're short-handed—"

"It's probably all the same. You caught him without my help."

"Caught who?"

"The big guy that came in here to meet his 'knock-out' woman the other night," the clerk clarified.

Stacey's hopes soared. "Did you get a good enough look at him to identify him?"

"Nah. He stayed out by the cars. She came in and paid. Have you talked to her yet?"

"Can you describe the two vehicles?" Stacey knew he'd dig up more information by peppering the man with question after relentless question.

"Well, let's see. He was in a dark, broken-down, full-size Chevy. Had to fill the radiator with water before he left. She was driving some sporty little foreign job. They all look alike to me. The foxiest little thing we've seen here in a long time....No, honey, I'm talking about the car, not the woman," the muffled voice was heard to say. "Sorry. My wife thinks I've been pining over the woman the last several days. Let's see, where was I?"

"Can you describe the woman?"

"I'd love to, in every detail—but I might get in trouble

with the Missus," he said in his country accent.

"Try to keep it clean, and you'll do fine."

"She's probably five-foot-ten, a hundred and ten pounds..." Stacey heard someone's voice in the background. "The Missus says one hundred twenty-five to one hundred thirty-five pounds. Blond hair..." He paused again. "Weren't her real color, though. Wife says the breasts weren't real either....She was wearin' this tight little blue dress that showed her legs all the way up, and everything else all the way down." Stacey could hear the man put his hand to the phone. "No, honey, I wasn't lookin' at 'em *all* the time."

"Is there anything else you think might help?" queried Stacey.

"Nah, they were here about an hour and then they left. Paid in advance. Cash. Gave me a tip when she said she didn't have a credit card."

"I'll be in touch in a few days. You've been a big help." Stacey could hardly wait to share the new information with Deek.

Cecily pulled up in front of the apartment. She, Don and Christina got out and started for the door. Before they were halfway up the drive, Melvin sauntered around the corner, drink in hand, flashing a sheepish grin.

"Evening, folks," he greeted in his characteristic whine. "All set to move in?"

"I think so. We'd like to look the place over one more time, if you don't mind."

"Sure thing," Melvin said. He turned and hobbled down the steps. He drew out the group of keys on the return chain attached to his belt and unlocked the door. "It's all yours." He stepped aside to let them pass. "I cleaned the kitchen and vacuumed the carpets. Saw no need to shampoo, since the other folks weren't here long enough to get them dirty."

"They look fine." The three of them made a quick pass. Nothing had changed. In less than a minute they were in the kitchen. Melvin sat at the table, slumping to one side, sipping from his mug.

"I have the contract right here." He produced a folded document from his shirt pocket. "You can review it if you want."

Don slid out a chair and started to read.

"So where do you go to school, Christina?" Melvin had remembered her name.

"Brookside. I'm in sixth grade."

"That's nice. What's your favorite subject?"

"Reading, I guess—and English."

Don interrupted. "This says it's a one-year contract?" Cecily, who'd been reading over his shoulder, paused to hear what Melvin had to say.

"Don't worry, it's the only contract I've got. I never hold anyone to it." He swirled his drink as he spoke. Don and Cecily returned to their reading, while Melvin's eyes returned to Christina.

"Reading was one of my daughter's favorite subjects, too. I read to her every night when she was little," he reminisced.

"You must miss her a lot."

Don interrupted again. "It says here we need to do a walk-through inspection."

Melvin's voice rose an octave; he was becoming agitated. He'd never had anyone review the contract so carefully. "Like I said, it's the only thing I've got. It came from an apartment complex where I lived a long time ago. The only thing that really matters is the space where we put in the monthly amount. If you decide you don't want to stay, let me know and you can go. After the place is clean, you get your deposit back."

"Sounds good," Don said. Anyway, he'd grown tired of trying to read the dingy document, a sixth- or seventh-generation copy. "Where do I sign?"

Melvin pointed to the blurred "x" on the back side. "That'll be five hundred dollars, then."

Don extracted a roll of bills from his pocket, counted off the twenty-dollar bills one at a time, and slid them across the table toward his new landlord. Melvin folded them in half and tucked them in his shirt pocket. "I'll get a copy of the contract for your receipt." He picked up the copy from the table. "You can move in anytime you like." He reached in his pocket and removed two keys and held them out. "These are for you. I look forward to having you here." With that, he returned upstairs.

Don and the girls lingered. "Do you have any furniture?" Cecily asked.

"Not much. Kate and Alan said they have a few extra pieces we can use."

Before they left, Don locked the apartment door, tossed the key in the air, caught it, and, in a final flourish, plopped it into his shirt pocket. The other key he offered to his daughter, who went through the same routine, mimicking her dad.

Stacey phoned Deek, speaking softly so Maryann wouldn't hear. He could ill afford another mistake.

"You've got to find the owner of that phone," said Deek. "I'll bet it belongs to the blonde. What'd Saunders have to say about the gun and sweats?"

"I'm not sure he heard a word I said. He hardly looked up."

"That's Saunders," Deek reassured. "His brain goes a hundred miles an hour, but he's the best lab tech in the state."

"Will he keep us covered on the fiber match? We don't want the information getting to the wrong ears."

"I'll call him first thing in the morning."

Stacey returned to his search, but found it hard to concentrate, his thoughts now preoccupied with the Bingham "jigsaw puzzle." There were still a few pieces to find and put in place, but the overall picture was slowly coming together.

Before long, Maryann appeared, putting on her sweater. "Will you walk me to my car?" Stacey stopped his search and accompanied her out to the parking lot. "How's Sig doing home alone?" she asked as she fumbled through her purse for her keys.

"I almost forgot, he's locked in the garage...." After seeing off Maryann, Stacey returned to the office and shut down the computer. "This'll have to wait. Sig's hungry and probably going crazy by now."

The drive home gave him a few quiet minutes to reflect. "I just need a single piece of solid evidence and I'll have him," he thought. Suddenly wracked by hunger, he dialed up his cell phone. "Jimmy...Stace. Send me the regular?"

Don and Cecily sat in the Jeep in front of Kate's home. The sun had already set. The sky to the west glowed several layered shades of blue, while the eastern horizon resembled the backdrop on a Broadway stage; a backlit silhouette of the mountains sliced through the top quarter of a bright, slowly-rising full moon. Cecily slipped low in her seat and gazed up at the stars, just coming out of hiding.

"I'd love to be able to see into the deepest parts of space all the worlds God's created," she let out a contented sigh, her mind lingering on the thought. "My favorite place to be is in the mountains, at night, away from city lights. Makes the stars seem so much brighter."

Don gave a "hmm" in agreement.

"Where do you think God lives?" she asked.

"I don't know. Guess I've never really thought about it. He doesn't live in that apartment, that's for sure!" he muttered a bit caustically.

"I disagree. He lives anywhere you *invite* him to live."

"Maybe we can invite him over to dinner." Don figured his flippant, borderline sacrilegious remark might succeed in closing down the subject. He wasn't willing to talk about God right then.

Cecily sensed that something was bothering him. "Why do you feel like God's abandoned you?"

Her pointed question struck a nerve. Don remained quiet for several long moments, thinking. Then he, too, leaned back in his seat. "Right now I have the best of my life to look forward to and the worst of my life to look forward to," he said tentatively.

"What do you mean?"

"For the first time in my life it seems that maybe I

can make something of myself. I have a good job, an opportunity to start over again...my daughter all to my- self...." His voice lowered. "But if I start making a good living, Monica will come back and take her away....My dad's about to die, and when he does he's gone forever."

Cecily withdrew her eyes from her stargazing and looked over at Don. Her voice smacked of cynicism. "Maybe we should just give up, not even bother to try. Maybe God put us here to live and breathe and die...and that's it."

He turned to her with a puzzled look. "That's not what you believe, is it?"

"No, it's not. I'm wondering what you believe."

"I guess I need to think about it." He reached over, put his arm around her neck, pulled her close and gave her a kiss on the cheek. "See you tomorrow." Then he climbed out of the Jeep.

Cecily sat there for a minute after he'd gone inside. *He needs the support of a family he doesn't have*, she thought to herself.

NINETEEN

STACEY WAS AWAKE by five-thirty a.m. With almost two thousand names to go, and only two hours before he left for work, he had no time to waste.

"Virginia," he typed.

Case #AV87047. He reviewed the file of a girl named Amy Grenny, age 14, the victim of a hit-and-run driver in Alexandria. Cause of death: massive head trauma. He hit enter, and the next case flashed up.

Case #AV39787. Again he glanced through the record. Arlington...5'2" female...Stacey paused, Sig sat close, begging for his breakfast.

"Next," he entered.

Case #RV23771. The girl was from Richmond, killed in a drive-by shooting, the bullet perforated her aorta.

Stacey, unable to stand the dog-breath any longer, relented. "Okay, okay, let's get you something to eat." He went to the kitchen and opened the regular two cans of dog food, shoveled them into the dish, but didn't give the usual command to eat. Sig sat patiently, waiting for the signal. "Let's see if you remember," Stacey told him, walking out of the room. Sig looked on expectantly as Stacey returned to his work.

Case #WV32976, Woodbridge, the cursor flashed. *Female 4'11". Age: 13. Name: Flora Sueldo. Found: Wooded area near Potomac River. Date: 3/17/94. Mother reported her missing. Cause of death: Asphyxiation by strangulation. Father suspected, cannot be located. Contact: Woodbridge P.D. Detective Oswald. Photo available.*

Stacey perused the record a second time. "This is closer than anything else I've found.

Woodbridge...Woodbridge. The captain's from Virginia. That's right. He served at the Pentagon." He went to his bookshelf and dug out a stack of magazines. "It's got to be here somewhere," he mumbled. He began flipping through the dog-eared magazines, one by one. "Here— found it!"

Returning to the desk, he opened a road atlas, thumbing through the section on Virginia. "*Virginia ... Virginia,*" he said over and over, almost as a mantra. Finally, he located the page. "Let's see. The Pentagon's in Arlington...." His index finger took on a zigzagging motion, searching for surrounding cities. "*Woodbridge ...Woodbridge. ...* His finger stopped. "There you are, just south of Arlington. Maybe 20 miles."

"This is weird," he continued. "Suppose the murders *are* related. The captain isn't the girl-killer. He doesn't meet the profile, or the description Ashley gave."

"Advanced search," Stacey keyed in.

Soon he had the number for the Woodbridge Police Department and the photo of the girl. Soft, graceful facial features; dark skin; beautiful, long black hair. Stacey dialed the number. The wrong-number tone sounded. "The area code you have dialed has been changed. The new area code is..." Stacey made a note and re-dialed.

"Woodbridge City," a voice answered.

"Would you connect me with Detective Oswald?"

"I'm sorry. He's no longer with the city. Would you like me to connect you with that department?"

"Yes, pl—" She cut him off before the words were even out of his mouth. He waited, the phone line clicking repeatedly as he listened.

Another voice came on the line. "Police Department."

"This is Officer Rick Stacey from the Mapleton, Utah P.D. I have some questions about an unsolved homicide you have posted on the N.C.I.C. case number WV32976. Happened on March 17, 1994. Detective Oswald was handling the case. Can you tell me who's taken it over?"

"Just a moment." The phone began to click again. A minute later the voice came back on the line. "That would be Officer Green. He isn't in right now. Want me to have him call you when he returns?"

"Yes, please. It's important."

After the dispatcher had taken down the pertinent information and Stacey had hung up, he leaned back in his chair. *This case probably has nothing to do with ours*, he mused, trying to keep his hopes in check, *but it's worth a try*.

He glanced around the room for Sig. It'd been 45 minutes since he'd put the food in his dish. "Sig!" Then it hit him. He shot up from his chair and turned the corner to the kitchen. There was Sig, sitting in the exact spot as before, a four-inch-wide puddle of saliva on the floor in the space between his front paws and the dish. The moist dog food had darkened around the edges. "Okay, lunch!" came the command, followed by the praise, "Good boy! You may not have appreciated the wait now, but some day that same obedience might save your life." Then his voice softened, as a flicker of guilt washed over him. "Sorry, Sig," he whispered.

Captain Bingham eased his Pontiac to the curb near the Reid home. The sun was just stretching its rays above the peaks to the east.

At seven-fifteen he spied Mrs. Reid leaving the house, heading to work on foot. He stayed put, watching her, until she turned to cross the junk-filled vacant lot at the corner of the old Swenson subdivision. He put the car in gear and crept along the curb, pulling into a cul-de-sac that intersected the well-traveled path she was on that led to Main Street. It was there, at that secluded spot, that he pulled his car up alongside her and rolled down the window. "What do *you* want?" her weary voice was heard.

"We may want to bring you back in for questioning," he told her. "I want to review your testimony."

"Your young officer already went through it." She started to walk away.

The captain's brow crinkled. He gunned the engine and pulled forward, blocking her path, then lurched from the car. "What do you mean he went through it?" he demanded.

"Like I told you," she exclaimed, cowering away from the man, "he went over everything the other day after you arrested my old man."

"Which officer was it?"

"You ought to know! The one with the dog."

"What'd you tell him?" His voice was breathy, insistent.

"Same thing you told me." She took a step back, out of reach.

The muscles of his jaw drew taut. "Damn!" He stomped back into the car and squealed away.

Stacey dressed, rummaging through the pockets of his pants from the day before. The key he'd borrowed from the police garage was wedged in the small change pocket. "Oh no! How'd I forget to return it? I'd better take it back after I pay Saunders a visit." He ordered Sig into the garage. The bucket of water was almost half empty and Sig seemed more reluctant than ever to go in. After the door was closed, Stacey headed for the cruiser.

He started the engine. "One thirty-nine, dispatch."

"Morning Stace, you ready to roll?" Maryann's voice was heard.

"Ten-four, log me in."

"Sure thing."

Typically, Stacey would patrol an hour or two before heading into the station. He hoped Officer Green from the Woodbridge Police would return his call. He'd left his mobile number so the call wouldn't end up in the wrong hands. He knew if he went down to the school zone, he could write at least ten citations in an hour. The captain was big on the cash flow the citations generated.

Maryann had just gotten off the radio with Stacey when the captain strode up to her desk.

"The other day Officer Stacey was looking for a phone number for Detective Derickson. Did you help him look up the number?"

Maryann nodded timidly at the hulk of a man looming over her. "Yes, sir, I did." His harsh voice and huge frame made her uncomfortable. And today she could tell he was in an especially foul mood. She flipped through the options on her computer screen, remembering the time and date of the call. Suddenly a call came in, and the screen automatically changed to "incoming caller" mode.

"Mapleton Police, is this an emergency?" she asked. "Oh, hi, Dianne." The captain shuffled around the desk and leaned forward next to Maryann so he could get a look at the screen. It read:

Incoming call: 7:55 a.m. Tuesday, April 13, 1999. Utah Valley Medical Center.

"Oh, dear, do the doctors think he'll be okay? Do they know what caused it?...I'm so sorry. I'll let everyone know....Okay, you hang in there. Bye." Maryann's face now registered distress. "Deek's in the operating room—he went into a coma last night. They think his intestine ruptured, contaminating his blood stream. They'll know more in a few hours."

Bingham's mind took in the news. "That's too bad...." His concern rang hollow. "Did you find that number?"

Once more she changed screens. "Here it is."

The captain didn't write it down—or even repeat it. He just stared at it a second, then walked off.

Barker sat at his desk in the squad room, reviewing his files and notes, when Bingham approached. "Is Officer Stacey working on any cases with you?" he asked.

"No, sir," Barker replied.

The captain plodded past and into his own office, closed the door, then picked up the phone. "Get me the lab. This is Captain Bingham from Mapleton....Do you have the results of the Reid home worked up yet?"

"Hold on. I'll check." The phone went on hold.

A new voice answered. "We found the bullet to be a definite match. And the fibers you brought in, a positive match."

"Were the fibers labeled?"

"Who's this?"

"Captain Bingham. Who's this?"

"Saunders. Sorry, captain, I thought you were Officer Stacey. He asked me to match a small sample of fibers he brought in with the gun and sweats."

"Thanks." He hung up the phone and took his radio out from under his jacket.

"One-ten, one thirty-nine."

"One thirty-nine, go ahead, captain." Stacey was stunned. The captain never called him on the radio; orders always came from Barker. And Bingham was calling him on channel two, normally reserved for private conversations.

"Officer Stacey, I need you to run to Vegas. We've got a lead that might be helpful in solving Ashley Gardner's kidnapping. I want you to personally interview the informant. The guy won't even reveal his name until we get there. Stop at the phone booth in the lobby of the MGM Grand and dial room 21022. He'll find you when you make the call. I'll call the Vegas P.D. and have them back you up, in case something's out of line. I need you to leave right away; gotta be there by one."

"Ten-four, captain."

"Stop here and get the files before you go. You may need to reference them."

Vegas was six hours away going the speed limit. Stacey'd have to move smartly to make it on time. But something didn't feel right. He decided to call Deek and make sure he had covered the Reid evidence with Saunders. "Room 312."

"One moment. I'll connect you." The phone rang several times before he hung up. Deek was probably in therapy. He decided to call back in an hour.

Entering the station, Stacey found the captain waiting for him near the lobby, a file box in his arms. "Open your trunk and I'll put it in back." Stacey did as he was told and the captain shut the trunk.

"I'll clear you a code in case you need to use the lights," he said, more than a touch of urgency in his voice. "Now hurry, this might be the break we've been looking for."

Don finished the powder orders by ten. He wondered why everyone smiled at him funny when he saw them. It was almost as if they were talking about him behind his back.

He quickly showered and reported to the front desk. Jeff and Dave were talking when he came in. Suddenly they quit their conversation. Both had the same guilty look on their face. "What's up guys?' he asked casually.

Dave answered as Jeff began to walk back to the plant. "Nothing. Ready to get to work?"

Don settled into his job as Cecily came through the front door with a box. It was the kind of box a cake or donuts would come in. Don wondered if they were going to have a party. Several customers followed Cecily into the front office, and for the next hour everyone went about their work, helping customers and answering phones.

The ringing of his cell phone brought Stacey back from the mindless trance induced by the freeway passing beneath his cruiser. "Stacey here," he answered.

"Officer Stacey," a quiet voice said. "This is Ashley Gardner. I remembered something that's really important that I need to talk to you and Sig about."

Stacey heard the phone signal growing weak. "Ashley, my phone's giving me trouble. Can I call you as soon as I get back in town?" Then the signal went dead.

Stacey cast a disparaging scowl at the signal bar and tried to make another call. "Room 312."

"One moment. I'll connect you."

This time he let the phone ring. He figured maybe a nurse would pick up and have Deek call when he got back from therapy. The mountains from Nephi to Beaver often didn't allow the phone signals through. The connection grew fuzzy.

"Room 312, Nurse Hatch."

"Is Detective Derickson in?" The static grew worse.

"I'm sorry. He's..." The connection was lost again.

"All employees report to the lunch room please! All employees to the lunch room!" Cecily's voice could be heard over the intercom.

Don looked around. What could it be? He didn't want to be put on the spot. Dave finished what he was doing and stood. "Let's go see what's up."

"It must be someone's birthday," said Rex, as they met and walked together.

"Birthday?" Don questioned.

"Yeah, we go through this every few weeks."

A row of cupcakes ran down the center of each table. Cecily was busy lighting the candles that poked from the white and blue icing. When all had gathered, Cecily led out. "Let's sing Happy Birthday to Morty. On three: one, two, three...."

It was, without a doubt, the worst rendition of "Happy Birthday" Don had ever heard. Not a single person sang on key; it was as if they were doing it on purpose. An angry cat could have done as well!

Morty, a first-year employee, blushed in embarrassment. He'd seen others sung to before, but had hoped they'd forget it was his turn.

"So who's the next birthday boy?" someone asked as they scarfed down the cupcakes.

"Rod—early next month," Cecily replied.

"The big 55!" Rod crowed.

The party was a good break, but too quickly over. Cecily was right—this company did seem like family.

Captain Bingham left the station, went to a corner phone booth and dialed out. "We've got some problems. I think I can handle it, but we've got to hurry this thing along....I know it will. No, we don't leave until we finish. Let her know. I want to be out in eight days....Yeah, I'll take care of the flight reservations. You talk to the banker to see if Rick Stacey has an account there. If he does, wire twenty thousand from one of our offshore accounts into his. Deposit twenty more, cash, and make sure she postdates the record for two days ago....Oh, and call our man in Vegas and have him handle Stacey. You know the drill. I think that should take care of everything until we finish."

He hung up the phone and made a second call. "I'm sorry, the customer you are trying to reach is either unavailable or has traveled outside the coverage area. Please try again later." He hung up the phone and returned to his car.

Working at his computer, Melvin logged in his entries. He sent the digital recording into his file titled "Captain."

"One twelve, one thirty-nine." The captain waited a minute. "One twelve, one thirty-nine," he repeated. No answer. "One twelve, dispatch."

"Dispatch, go ahead, captain."

"Have you heard from Officer Stacey yet?"

"No, sir, not since he logged in this morning. Do you want me to try him on his mobile?"

"No, I'll try later. I'll be in in a few minutes."

He pulled into the parking lot and went to his office. Opening his file cabinet drawer, he removed a folder and reviewed the file, jotting a note in the margin. "Lieutenant Barker," he called.

Barker stopped what he was doing. "Yes, captain."

"We go to hearing on the cocaine case next week. We need to review the file and verify the evidence. I can't locate Officer Stacey. Will you and Olsen check the evidence room? I seem to have a discrepancy in my notes. My log files show 75 kilos of cocaine; the arrest files show 76. After you count them, check the case files and see what the official documents show."

"Sure." Olsen and Barker headed to the evidence room. They both knew it was 76, since it had been in all the papers and on the nightly news as one of the biggest busts in the state.

Meanwhile, Stacey checked his phone for a signal. He had to talk to Deek. Something was wrong—out of place. The assignment to go to Vegas, the captain's orders, the whole thing. He decided to stop in Beaver to try again. "Beaver, ten miles," the sign read.

Entering the evidence room, both officers signed in. Barker then noticed the empty space he was supposed to have signed when Stacey took the gun to the lab. "Oops, forgot to sign Stace out," he said, slightly embarrassed at the procedural oversight. He bent and filled in the blank.

"The labels show 76," Olsen confirmed.

"The captain said to count them. You start on the lower shelf and I'll start here." He reached above the sign-out table and pulled a pair of latex gloves from the box. Olsen did the same. They both began to count, each whispering as they went. Olsen finished first and waited for Barker.

"Thirty-six," Olsen said.

"Thirty-eight."

The men stared at each other a moment as they added the two numbers in their heads. Barker was first to speak. "That's only 74!"

Olsen nodded. "We better count again."

The two men began the count again, this time giving each bag an attentive pat. Barker finished first. "Thirty-eight," he said.

"Thirty-six," Olsen repeated. "We better find out which two are missing. Let's sort and re-stack them by number."

Minutes later, the count was finished. "It appears numbers ten and 31 are missing," Barker concluded as they placed them back on the shelf. The two officers didn't want to jump to any conclusions, so they went from shelf to shelf, searching the entire room for the missing bags. Nothing turned up.

"Now what?" Olsen asked.

"I guess we tell the captain." He'd been reflecting on the events of the past few days. He'd just signed for Stacey; in fact, Olsen had watched him log an improper date and time. This was the first time in the eight years Barker had been on the force that anything had turned up missing from the evidence room. They'd hardly ever kept anything of value in there.

"What do you want me to say about the entry you

just made?" Olsen asked.

Barker swallowed and subconsciously bit his lower lip. "You'd better say exactly what you saw." He knew they were about to hang Stacey out to dry.

"Did he do it?"

"I can't believe he would."

Olsen knew the possible repercussions. "Who, then?"

"I don't know. The captain and I carry the only two keys to the evidence room...."

TWENTY

STACEY PULLED INTO the Texaco station, picked up the receiver from the pay phone and dialed the authorization number from the back of his VISA Card.

"Please enter your pin number now." The phone began to ring. Stacey was beginning to wonder if anyone would pick up.

"Hello," a female voice answered after several rings.

"Can I speak to Detective Derickson?" There was a long silence.

"Are you a family member?"

"No, I work with him," Stacey replied. "Is he in?"

"No, he isn't. Can I take a message?"

"Is Dianne in?" he persisted.

"Can you hold a moment? Let me see if I can transfer you."

Barker and Olsen strode to the captain's office. "We have a problem, captain," Barker said. "We're missing some evidence."

"What do you mean, *missing*?" He seemed irritated by the lack of information.

"We made a count like you asked. We're missing bags ten and 31."

"Who signed them out?"

"That's the problem, sir. No one signed them out," Barker said, contritely.

"Olsen, would you step out? I need to talk to the lieutenant a minute."

Officer Olsen sidled out and pulled the door closed behind him.

Stacey was growing impatient. Finally someone answered. "Surgery waiting room."

"Is Mrs. Derickson in?" he asked.

"Mrs. Derickson?" The voice could be heard asking the others in the room. "Mrs. Derickson," he heard again. "I'm sorry, no one answers by that name."

"Can you connect me back to room 312?"

"I'm sorry, but I'm just a visitor here. I don't know how."

Stacey hung up the phone and started again. The operator answered. "Can you connect me with the nurses' station on the third floor?"

"Station three, Nurse Powell."

"This is Officer Stacey, and it's very important I talk to Detective Derickson or his wife. Will you connect me, please?" Stacey's tone left no room for argument.

"Let me see if I can locate Mrs. Derickson. Can you hold a moment?"

"I'll wait." He glanced at his watch. He could never make Vegas by one now.

"I saw Stacey coming out of the evidence room yesterday, alone. Did you lend him your key?" Bingham wore a very serious expression on his face.

"Yes, sir." Barker had known better.

"I didn't think anything of it until now. Was he the last one in the room before you and Officer Olsen logged in?"

"Yeah, according to the log. I promised him I'd sign him out as soon as I got a chance," Barker explained. "I forgot completely about it until I saw the blank space just a minute ago. I signed for him when Olsen and I went in."

"Did Olsen see you sign him out?"

"Yes, sir, he did."

Bingham pointed toward the room, his instructions emphatic. "You and Olsen go back and tear that room apart. I can't believe Officer Stacey would have anything to do with this."

"Officer Stacey, I've located her. I'll try to connect you now," the nurse said. The phone rang twice and was picked up. Stacey didn't recognize the solemn voice that answered.

"I'm looking for Mrs. Derickson." A sickening feeling had begun to turn his stomach to knots.

"This is the hospital social worker. Can I tell her who's calling?"

Stacey knew now that something was terribly wrong. He could hear sobbing in the background. "Yes. This is Rick Stacey. I'm a close friend of the family."

"One moment. I'll see if she can talk to you."

Listening to soft voices, too quiet to hear, he waited before she spoke.

"Rick. Something's happened," Dianne said. Her voice cracked as she spoke. "Deek passed away on the operating room table a few minutes ago." The sobbing resumed.

Stacey was stunned. How could that be? He'd talked to Deek less than a day ago. He was doing well. "What happened?"

Dianne tried to regain her composure but couldn't stop crying long enough to get out a sentence. He heard her finally say, "Would...you...tell him?" The social worker got back on the line and quietly explained the details.

"Last night Detective Derickson started to run a high fever, which the doctors couldn't seem to control. His blood was found to contain an elevated white count, indicating an infection. Several more tests were taken. But before they could get him into surgery to see if there was a problem with the sutures, he slipped into a coma. During the operation, he went into full cardiac arrest, and passed away less than half an hour ago. Mrs. Derickson hasn't even told her own family yet. Several of her children are here with her."

Stacey, in utter shock, hung up the phone. This complicated an already worsened situation. It was too unreal. The captain would be up for murder charges if he could prove Deek's theory. Now it'd be almost impossible. And what would happen to Deek's family? He glanced at his watch again. He had about an hour and a half to travel two hundred miles. Even if he sped he could never make it. He decided to call the captain and tell him he wouldn't be on time, and to inform the office of the terrible news.

"Mapleton City Police. Is this an emergency?"

"Maryann, this is Stace. Is the captain in?"

"He is, but something's wrong. He's in the evidence room. He, Barker and Olsen are tearing the place apart. Where are you? The screen says Beaver."

"I am. The captain sent me to Vegas to interview a potential witness."

"That's odd," she said under her breath. "He's been trying to reach you on the radio."

Something was wrong; the captain knew exactly where he was. "Maryann, listen. Deek's dead. I just talked to Dianne at the hospital. Don't tell the captain I called unless you're asked. I don't have time to explain." Stacey hung up the phone before Maryann could reply. He returned to the car to think. What was Bingham up to? *The box in the trunk,* he thought. Opening it, he carefully lifted the lid from the box. Several empty file folders covered the main contents of the box—which, he discovered, was a kilo of cocaine. He realized then, in disbelief, that he'd been set up. How could it have happened? *Deek's dead, and now no one has a clue I've been investigating Bingham for the shooting.* He was in serious trouble. *How much does the captain know? Why does he want me in Vegas? I've got to figure it out.*

Back at the station, Maryann wasn't sure she had heard Stacey right. How would he know Deek was dead? Why was he in Beaver? She needed to find out about Deek first. She called the hospital while the captain and the two other officers exhausted their search of the evidence room. Two kilos were definitely missing.

"Lieutenant, we need to locate Officer Stacey. It seems we have a few questions for him," the captain said calmly.

"I'll go by his place and see if he's there," Barker offered.

"No, I think I'll drop by and see for myself. If he's there, I need to talk to him."

Maryann had little success finding Dianne. She, too, was transferred from one place to another. Several nurse stations later, she had no more information than when she'd started.

Stacey returned to the phone, removed the small notepad from his shirt pocket, and dialed the number.

"Provo Crime Lab."

"Saunders, please."

"This is Saunders," chirped a monotone voice.

"Saunders, this is Officer Stacey. How did the test results turn out on the Derickson evidence?"

"Like I told your Captain Bingham this morning, we have a positive match on the gun and the fibers. No prints were found on the gun."

"What time did he call?"

"Must've been first thing."

Stacey hung up the phone. *Bingham must have talked to Mrs. Reid, too,* he mused as he picked up the phone and dialed the station.

"Mapleton Police."

"Maryann, Stace, here. Did the captain ask you about the call you looked up for me?"

"Yes, he did. What's this all about?"

"I can't explain now. Is he in?"

"No, I think he's gone to your house to see if you're there."

"Is Barker in?"

"I think so. Want to talk to him?"

"Yes, please...."

"Lieutenant Barker."

"Barker, Stace—"

"Where are you?"

"I'm in Beaver on my way to Vegas. The captain sent me down to interview a witness. I'll bet you're missing a kilo of cocaine."

"Two; we're missing two kilos. You were the last

one in the evidence room with *my* key. What're you up to?"

"Listen, Bingham's trying to frame me. He put one of them in my car this morning. I think I'm in serious trouble. I can't explain it now. I need your help."

Barker sounded resigned. "I don't know if I can help you much. You'd better come in."

"I can't. I know too much and not enough at the same time. I'll talk to you when I can. Why the sudden interest in the cocaine?"

"Bingham asked me to count it."

"Why would he ask such a question. We all know we took 76 kilos in the bust."

"I've been asking myself the same question," replied Barker.

"Tell the captain I'm late getting to Vegas. I'll bet he puts an APB out on me—or worse. You know me. I didn't steal any of the stuff. And Deek's dead. That turns the shooting into murder."

Stacey hung up, leaving Barker in a state of confusion. He didn't have a clue what Stacey was talking about. Maryann had told everyone Deek was in surgery. He walked up front and asked, "Where did Stace call from?"

"Beaver. What in the world's going on?"

"I don't know, but I've got to find out. He told me Deek's dead."

"I've been trying to find out about that, too. I can't get through."

"Keep trying. I'll run over to the hospital." He left the room. "One twelve, one ten."

"One ten, go ahead, lieutenant," the captain responded.

"Captain, we got a call from Stacey. He said something about being late." Barker was careful with his words.

"Where did he call from?"

"He said he was south."

"Dispatch, can you give me a location?"

"The call came in from a pay phone in Beaver."

The captain's breathing could be heard above the

radio's static. "Did he say anything else?"

"No." Barker played along. "He seemed to be in a hurry."

"Maryann, contact the Utah Highway Patrol and have them bring in Officer Stacey. Tell them he's somewhere between Beaver and Las Vegas. We need to talk to him about two missing kilos of cocaine," he commanded as he pulled up in front of Stacey's apartment.

Stacey drove west on State Road 153. He'd been through the area once with his father many years before. He could go north to Delta, then double back south to Holden. Grandma still lived in Fillmore. He could leave his squad car hidden there and borrow her car. She didn't drive much anymore. Traveling the old state roads would be the long way around, but no one would be looking for him there. And anyway, he hadn't seen his grandma for almost a year, and she'd be happy to see him. She'd keep his visit a secret, if he asked her to—he was sure of it.

The captain, now wearing latex gloves, opened the car door and made his way to the apartment. Finding the front door locked, he took a pick set from his pocket. Being a little rusty, it took him almost a full minute to get in. Sig was barking furiously from inside the garage. Bingham glanced around and quickly walked the rooms to find a most likely hiding spot. Nothing seemed to stand out. He entered the kitchen, opening the cupboards one at a time. In one he found a sealed plastic dish. Taking the wrapped and sealed bag out from under his shirt, he carried both to the bathroom. With a stroke of his knife, he slit open the bag and emptied half its contents in the toilet, then flushed it down. Next he folded the bag and stuffed it in the container, before putting on the lid. Hurrying back to the kitchen, he jammed the container in the back of the cupboard and closed the door. In less than four minutes he'd entered, deposited the evidence, and left the premises. All the while Sig was barking like crazy. He could see the dog's face in the window of the garage as he drove away.

Barker arrived at the hospital and went straight to Deek's room. He noticed the bed was missing. He proceeded to the nurses' station and spoke with the first nurse he saw. "I'm Lieutenant Barker from the Mapleton Police Department. Can you tell me where I can find Detective Derickson?"

She looked at him, then back at an older woman who sat at the desk. The woman stood and introduced herself. "I'm the head nurse on this unit," she said calmly. "Can I help you?"

"I need to know the condition of Detective Derickson," he insisted again.

"I'm sorry, lieutenant. I don't think I can tell you at this time—" she tried to say.

"Listen. I'm in the middle of a possible murder," he snapped, "and I won't tolerate you sidestepping my questions. Is he alive?"

"No, he's not. He passed away an hour ago on the operating table. His family is still being notified."

Barker fairly blew his stack. "He was shot in the line of duty," he roared, "so we should have been informed immediately!" Then, calming slightly, he asked, "Where's his wife?"

"She's probably with a social worker in one of our counseling rooms on the second floor." This time she readily provided the information. Barker could hardly believe it. In the history of the city police department they'd never had an officer killed.

"I'll have Nurse Sorenson show you the way," the head nurse said. Barker nodded and the two of them walked toward the elevator.

Don and Cecily stopped for lunch. Several of the employees Don hadn't even met seemed to smile in a friendly way. There was nothing special in the brown bag, but he wasn't very hungry anyway. Besides, lunch didn't seem as good when he prepared it himself. The conversations were light, though everyone still seemed to know something Don didn't.

Stacey raced toward Delta, having made the turn onto Highway 257 some 20 minutes earlier. While passing through Milford he devised a plan that might get him home without a hitch. Dealing with the other problems, though, wouldn't be so easy. His father used to take him to the lava fields when he was young, so he knew they were just outside Fillmore. A number of miles outside town was a cave large enough in which to hide the car. It was a remote region, yet was within walking distance of his grandma's house. He could be there before dark, if all went well.

The flood of information—and misinformation—kept playing in his head. He needed not only to prove the captain was dirty but, at the same time, stop the abductor of the girls. Contacting Officer Green in Virginia was important, too, but using his calling card was now out of the question. And there were other hurdles to overcome. The captain wanted him out of the picture, and he believed Bingham would go to any length to dispose of him. In fact, now he was sure of it.

Barker paused outside the door of the counseling room. He could hear the sniffles of the children coming from within. He and Deek's family were close. It wasn't going to be easy to see them in their grief.

Barker eased the door open. Deek's five-year-old was standing in the middle of the room, looking up at his siblings and mother. Dianne was on the phone. Her eyes were swollen and red. The little redheaded son, Austin, only two, sat slumped in her lap, in total confusion. Dianne seemed to be somewhat under control as she informed the person on the other end about the terrible events of the past few hours. She glanced up as Barker entered, and her expression changed as she abruptly ended the call and hung up the phone.

"That was Maryann, I just called the station to let everyone know." Barker approached and opened his arms. She seemed so alone. Both her family and Deek's were from out of state. His parents had visited a few days earlier and then returned home when he seemed to be doing so well.

"I'm so sorry," Barker told her. The children watched them.

"Stace told me fifteen minutes ago. I came as soon as I heard," he said. She began to sob again. The children added to the tears. Barker just held her as she trembled with grief.

The captain returned to the station and placed a call to the prosecuting attorney. " ...We think we have enough evidence to sustain a search warrant....I'd never have believed it myself. He's been an exemplary officer....No, he hasn't been in all day. We think he may be on his way to Las Vegas....No, we don't have enough on him to make an arrest, that's why we want the warrant....See what you can do. We have the highway patrol looking for him now." He concluded his call. Bingham wanted the evidence and dog taken care of as soon as possible.

Stacey made good time. He didn't travel so fast as to draw attention to his speed, neither did he travel the speed limit. He made the turn outside of Delta and traveled south on Highway 50 toward Holden. The next ten or 12 miles, until he reached Fillmore, would be the most risky. He guessed that by now every trooper in the state would be on the lookout, though he hadn't picked up anything on the police scanner. He felt like a criminal on the run. What's more, his car stuck out like a sore thumb. But with any luck, no one would pay attention.

It didn't take long for a "halo zone" to form around him—a ring of cautious, light-footed drivers that naturally forms around a police or highway patrol vehicle. A few brave drivers had enough courage to go around him, just creeping past at a little over the 75-mph limit.

At last, the exit was in sight. Stacey turned off the interstate and drove west to the lava fields. The area was pockmarked and littered with jagged, weird-shaped rocks. It looked more like the surface of the moon. Giant craters and huge boulders were scattered among the debris. He wondered if he could find the caves, it having been over ten years since his last visit. Only a very few of the locals knew the caves even existed.

After nearly an hour, he finally stumbled across the large, shallow cave he best remembered. For hundreds of years sand had blown off the dusty fields from the west, creating maneuverable paths down to its entrance, which was big enough to park a semi truck. Pulling the car into the shadows at the far end of the cave, he took the sawed-off shotgun from the console, opened the trunk and removed the file box, into which he placed the keys to the cruiser. He then carried the box to an adjacent cave some 50 yards farther west. Once inside the smaller cave, he located an offshoot that ran at an angle down into the rock, hid the box and gun under several pounds of loose rock and began the eight-or nine-mile walk to the child-hood home of his father.

TWENTY-ONE

AT FIVE O' CLOCK everyone punched out and headed for the parking lot. For Don, the day's work was behind him. Now he needed to gather up his and Christina's few belongings and move into the empty apartment.

"Ready to go?" Cecily asked as she swiped their cards and walked to the Jeep. Like all the other employees that day, she seemed to be giving him some rather strange looks. Don didn't bother asking about it.

Cecily turned to him as they drove off. "Do you want to move?"

"I guess so."

Soon they were at Kate's house and had the Jeep loaded with boxes and a few pieces of luggage. It took less than an hour.

Don clapped his hands together, as if brushing off dust. "That's it. Not much, is it?"

"We have enough, Daddy," Christina offered.

Kate came out as Don, Christina, and Cecily were getting in the Jeep. "I have some mattress pads for you to use until you get some beds of your own."

"Thanks. I think we have room for them," said Don. Returning to the house, they retrieved the pads and carried them to the vehicle. It wasn't easy, but they found a way to stuff them in.

Kate gave them a wave and an encouraging smile. "Okay, see you later."

As Cecily turned the corner and neared the apartment, Don could see cars and company trucks in the driveway. "What's going on?" People were moving furniture. What were they doing, and how did they know where he was moving to? He turned to Cecily to see if she had any answers. She tried to match his confused look. "I don't know...." Then, unable to contain herself any longer, her straight-faced expression changed to a smile. "A few of the employees got together when they found out you needed some furniture. Several of them said they had odds and ends around that they didn't need, so they decided to throw you a house warming party." Don got out of the Jeep and went inside.

"Hey, Don, not a bad place. Not bad at all." Ryan was unloading a twin bed. Don could see that almost everyone from work was there, all smiling ear-to-ear. "Don, welcome home," said another. "Glad to help...." An old couch sat along a living room wall next to a side table sporting a lamp without a shade. In the family room someone had left a console TV.

Don and Christina could hardly believe what they were seeing. The fridge was stocked with food, a few dishes were on the shelves, and Melvin was in the family room placing cushions on a green hide-a-bed that seemed to match the curtains. "When I saw what your friends were doing, I thought I'd help out, too. It's not much, and you can leave it behind when you leave, but it's better than the mantle to sit on. I was actually getting rid of it. It'll give me more space upstairs."

Don walked down the hall and found Rex putting together the twin bed that Ryan had lugged in. An antique dresser, a few scratches running across its top, sat next to the bed. Don glanced into the adjoining room, where he saw a box spring and mattress on the floor, along with another, smaller dresser. Don just stood there in amazement. No one had ever done anything like this for him before. "I don't know what to say, guys," he finally blurted out.

"You don't need to say anything," Rex replied. "Your face says it all." He finished tightening the final bolts on the twin bed and walked into the other room. By the time Don returned to the front room, everything that had been in the Jeep was now in the apartment.

People began filtering out. "See you tomorrow," they said. "Later...." "Great place. ..."

When the last of them had gone, Cecily and Don plopped down on the couch. It had all happened so fast. He still wasn't sure what to do. Cecily put her hands on his shoulder and planted a kiss on his cheek. "I told you we're like family around here."

Christina let out a shriek from the other room and raced into where they sat, holding a box. "Look what they left!"

"What is it?"

"Oh, Dad, it's a Nintendo 64!" She said it as if he should know. "Ralph gave it to you. His children grew out of it," Cecily added. "It has some pretty cool games."

Danny pulled up on his bike and trotted down the stairs. "Wow! Where'd all the stuff come from?"

"My dad's friends from work brought all this stuff for us. Look, and we even have an N64! See if you can get it to work," she prodded. The two of them disappeared into the other room.

"Why'd they do all this?" Don asked, a bewildered look on his face.

"Well, let's see. You help Rex after work; Ryan was behind a few times and you pitched in; Dave had a flat tire....Should I go on?"

"No....I just don't know how to repay them."

Stacey plodded across the dusty fields, doing his best to stay out of sight of the country roads. The ranchers had already put their cattle on the ranges. He watched the young calves cavort with one another in the warm southern breeze. He figured he had at least five more miles before he'd reach Fillmore, so he'd be traveling by the cover of nightfall by the time he reached the outskirts. He occasionally picked up bits and pieces of radio noise on his hand-held unit. From what he was able to tell, he was the subject of a statewide manhunt. He decided he might as well turn it off and save the battery. It might come in handy later.

Captain Bingham's nerves were frayed. His "contacts" in Vegas hadn't reported seeing Stacey, the highway patrol hadn't stopped him, and the prosecuting attorney couldn't come up with a warrant, so Bingham had decided to turn up the heat. Stopping at a pay phone, he deposited the required change. "Did you make the deposit?"

"Forty thousand—just like you said," was the response. He hung up and dropped in additional change, took a card from his pocket and called the number written in pen above the name.

"This is Captain Bingham, Mapleton Police Department. I have some information that may be of interest to you. It must be kept confidential. We have reason to believe that our Officer Rick Stacey has stolen a substantial amount of cocaine from our evidence room. We also think he's somewhere between here and Las Vegas. We've been trying to obtain warrants to search his home and financial records. One of our informants told us he made a large deposit to his account in the last 24 hours. We also suspect him in the murder of Detective Kiser Derickson." He listened a moment. "He passed away this morning....No, that information still has not been released. At this point the evidence from the murder also implicates Officer Rick Stacey. We think he planted the gun and clothing in the vent of the Reid home. He used the car for his drug deals and met an unknown buyer in Levan. The County Attorney's office refuses to issue the warrant, or we'd know the answer to that, too. That's all I can tell you." He hung up the phone.

He knew the reporter's aggressive nature would move her to find out more. By morning everything would hit the fan. All he needed was three or four more days.

Cecily lay face down on the sofa. She and Don had scrubbed down the bathrooms, arranged furniture and gotten everything put away. Danny's main task had been to install the Nintendo in the family room, and now he and Christina, joysticks in hand, were busily blasting away at each other. Don, watching their fun, strolled back into the living room. "You must be pooped," he grinned.

Cecily smiled. "Mmmhmm."

He sat down next to her on the edge of the couch; she scooted back to give him room. "Thanks for all your help," he said, reaching down to rub her back. She gave another "Mmmm" as his hands eased up to her shoulders and neck, kneading her tight muscles with his strong hands. He worked his way down each arm to her hands, then back up to her shoulders and down her spine. He'd given Monica many such massages over the years. He had magic hands, she claimed.

He proceeded to work other areas, the therapy seeming to put Cecily into a trance-like state. She purred her approval. He heard someone rustling around upstairs, but didn't pay much attention; his mind was more occupied by his physical desires as his hands drifted down to the sides of her breasts. Suddenly Cecily raised up on her elbows. "I'm uncomfortable with your hands there," she stated bluntly.

Don pulled away. "I—I'm sorry," he stuttered. "I just thought..." He didn't understand. He knew Cecily's morals were high, but thought she'd given him enough signals to move forward with their relationship.

"Excuse me." The voice came from a handsome young man, standing at the open doorway. "Do you know if Melvin's home? No one answers his door."

Don and Cecily were both taken aback by the intrusion. They'd been enjoying the cool night air that wafted into the warm apartment and hadn't thought to close the door.

"I don't know," Don answered. "Did you see his car in the drive?"

"No, I didn't."

Don recognized his face from somewhere, but was anxious to resolve the conflict he'd just created with Cecily. The young man turned to leave, then did an about-face.

"Do you folks live here?" he asked.

"I do," Don answered. Cecily sat mutely, her arms folded across her chest.

"My wife and I just moved out," he said.

Don nodded. "Yeah, I thought I knew you."

"We've been trying to get our deposit back since we left," he explained, desperation in his voice. "He keeps putting us off. The last time he told me I better take a close look at my contract. My wife and I can't afford another place until he pays us."

Don and Cecily shot each other a worried glance. They remembered how Melvin had sidestepped the contract issue and said he'd already given the newlyweds their deposit back. Cecily's mind was trying to recall what Melvin had said concerning their departure. "How are your wife's allergies?" she asked.

He gave them a puzzled look. "She doesn't have any allergies."

"Melvin told us you moved because of her allergies," she reaffirmed.

"We moved because Melvin was in our apartment as my wife came out of the shower in a towel. We think he was here the entire time she was showering. I thought she was crazy at first. Then she asked me why I'd turned on the washer after asking her to start it in a note I wrote. I didn't start it, which leads me to believe Melvin must have." The young man displayed several bursts of anger as he spoke.

"Do you think he was snooping around?" Cecily asked.

"My wife thinks he was watching her. Do you mind if I take a quick look in the furnace room?"

Don stood and gestured for the young man to come in. "By the way, my name's Paul," he said. Introductions made, they walked down the hall and opened the door. Paul stepped in and turned on the light. There was the hole in the wall where Danny had poked Christina with the stick. He bent down and put his eye up to it.

"It's too dark to see."

Cecily went around, turned on the lights and stood at the bathroom mirror. She could see Paul's eye through the hole. "Turn off the light in there and close the door," she instructed.

Don closed the door and gave the pull chain a yank. Again Paul put his eye up to the hole, this time from a few inches back.

"Are you looking?"

"Can't you see me?" Paul asked.

Cecily moved from spot to spot. Although Paul's eye was invisible to her, he could clearly see her. By the time they'd finished their deliberations, everyone was convinced that Melvin was indeed a Peeping Tom.

Stacey was within a few blocks of Grandma Stacey's home. He knew she'd be surprised to see him, but he wasn't quite sure what to tell her. Walking down the last street, he could see that the kitchen lights were on. Grandma was a strong old woman, from pioneer stock. She always wore a checkered apron with a dishtowel hung through a loop at the front. Her long silver hair was kept rolled into a tight bun that hugged the back of her head. Her husband had died almost ten years earlier— keeled over from a massive heart attack while farming the land he loved so much. Nowadays she leased the farm to a local man, but insisted on staying in the home. She couldn't see very well, which made it difficult to do her needlepoint.

Stacey marched up the steps to the kitchen door and knocked, setting off an almost voiceless barking alarm from her old German shepherd, Track—short for "Tractor." The dog had become quite a burden to her, but she loved him and he kept her company. As a boy, he'd come to appreciate the shepherd breed from smart ol' Track.

The back porch light flickered on. Grandma Stacey pulled the curtain aside and put her face up to the glass. Her puzzled look turned to joy as she identified the visitor. With some effort she opened the door.

"Ricky, how nice to see you!" she warbled. The two of them took a moment to embrace. Stacey towered above her frail, stooped frame, even while standing one step below.

"How are you, Grandma?"

"I'm doing fine. But I think you're in a heap'a trouble."

Stacey stepped into the front room, where the ten o'clock news was on. The Channel Five reporter, live on the scene, was projecting to her audience, telling all about the missing Officer Rick Stacey—about two reports that he had large amounts of money in his bank account, about "inside" sources' claims that he was connected to the murder of Officer Derickson. The camera showed a clip of the grieving family leaving the hospital. Stacey's high school photo flashed on the screen as the reporter did her best to taint his reputation.

Stacey stood in shock. How had Bingham moved so quickly?

The lead story continued, this time with footage of the outside of Stacey's apartment. Stacey could see Sig's eyes reflecting the lights of the camera as it panned the garage windows. According to the reporter, the county prosecutor would not comment on the case, nor would he issue a warrant at this time.

A tenant a few doors down from Stacey's apartment came on the screen. "No, I haven't seen him all day," he answered in reply to the reporter's question.

"Of course not, you work all day, just like I do," muttered Stacey.

The report concluded with the fact that the story was an exclusive; they were the first to report all the facts. Grandma switched off the small television set and turned to her grandson, now seated on the couch. "Now dear, what can I do to help?" she asked with total sincerity in her voice.

He summed it up in a single sentence. "I'm being set up by a crooked police captain." He looked back at the blank TV screen and shook his head in disbelief.

His relationship with his grandma was close. He'd spent many summers working on the farm with his grandpa and had come back to help her run it in the months following his death, until they both realized it would be way too much for her to handle. Track, lay at the old woman's feet. Stacey smiled. "He's getting old, isn't he?"

She nodded. "How's Sig?"

"Like you saw, locked in the garage because he bit the captain."

"He knows, too, doesn't he?" she said matter-of-factly. "Now, how are you going to prove it, Officer Stacey?" She asked the question as if she had no doubt he was innocent. She knew him inside and out. He wouldn't lie to her, even if he thought he was going to get in the most serious trouble.

"I'm not sure," he sighed. "It's worse than I thought. The detective who was helping me through this investigation died just last night."

"Detective Derickson?" she exclaimed. "They talked about him on the early news. Six children left behind! You'd better get on the stick and stop moping around if you're going to put the one responsible behind bars," she encouraged. "I think I still have a box or two of your grandpa's old things around. Why don't we see if they're still any good?"

Before long Stacey was in a pair of his grandpa's old coveralls and boots. The plaid shirts were too small. Grandpa was a pretty large man in his early days, but had lost considerable bulk the last few years of his life. Stacey took off his uniform shirt; the undershirt would have to do. Emptying his pockets, he found the key to the captain's car, which he tucked in the top pocket of the coveralls. On a nightstand in the spare bedroom, he noticed an old love note he'd written to his granddad almost twenty years before. It was signed "Bup," a nickname his grandpa had given him when he was little. Grandpa was the only one who ever used the name, and Stacey always used to feel special as "Bup" working side by side with the wizened old man.

Having dug out an old hat she used occasionally when she went out in the sun, grandma returned to the room. The elastic head band stretched and moaned as Stacey put it on his head.

"Take a look at you now," she said. "You don't look like an officer any more." Stacey looked at his reflection. True, he didn't look the same—and even felt a little silly. "You reminded me of your granddad for a moment.

Tall...strong. Now you let that beard alone a few days and Sig won't even know you." She chuckled. "I've got a few dollars. You can use the old Mercury in the shed. I haven't driven it for a few months, but it never gives me a bit of trouble. Have you had anything to eat?"

"Not since last night." He felt like a kid when he was with her. Being in her kitchen after an exhausting day reminded him of his youth.

"Let's see if we can take care of that." She bustled over to the counter and began to prepare one of her delicious meals.

Paul spoke as they heard Melvin's car pull into the drive. Don didn't hear what he said. His mind was on Melvin, picturing him taking a peek at his daughter through that hole. He stepped out the front door and stormed up the stairs, definitely not in the mood for conversation. Melvin had lied to them. He was planning on keeping their deposit, just like he did Paul's. Don remembered seeing Melvin talk to Christina the day they filled out the application. It was true: Melvin had seemed a bit too friendly with his daughter.

"Melvin! I need a word with you," he growled.

Melvin's head jerked up. There was Don, face red, about ready to blow a gasket, with Cecily, Paul, Christina and Danny still flooding up the stairs behind him. "What can I do for you?" he cackled, staying safely behind his car, a silly grin plastered on his face.

"You remember Paul," he glowered, his words filled with bitterness and hate. "His wife's the one with *allergies* that moved out a few days ago?" Don started around the car toward him. "He told us about you being in the apartment when his wife was in the shower. We've seen your little peep hole. I think I'll break your scrawny neck."

Melvin backed away, keeping the car between them. "I don't have a clue to what you're talking about," he retorted. "But I'm sure Judge Demick would be glad to talk about this little visit you're having with me," he jeered.

Christina was the first to try to calm the storm.

"Daddy, come back inside."

A pointed scowl now set the stage for his hair-trigger temper as he fairly erupted at the landlord's comment. "First I'm going to squash this little pervert's head." He stalked around the car to try to get closer.

"I'll just head back to Aunt Kate's," Christina hollered as she climbed on her bike. "I might as well pack my things." Don then fathomed the meaning behind his daughter's subtle message. If he even touched Melvin, he'd be answering to Judge Demick again. He backed off his assault and turned to his daughter, his arms upraised in surrender.

"Okay," he said. Then turning back to Melvin, he spat out his final threat. "I think we'll be moving in a few days—just as soon as you get us our deposit back."

Melvin merely turned and slipped up the steps to his back door.

Stacey had gorged himself on his grandma's biscuits and gravy. Now she was filling a sack with assorted fruits and pastries from the fridge. "You're a smart boy. You make sure you ask God for his help and he'll see you through this, you know." She had always taught him to pray. "I'll be praying for you, too. Now you better go get that friend of yours out of the garage before they get that warrant and take him to the pound."

Stacey stood and looked down at his grandma. She was a smart lady. He hadn't even thought about the possibility they'd take Sig away. "You'll have the cover of the night," she added, smiling. "You make sure you use it like an old raccoon." She practically herded him out the door, just like she did when he was young and he thought he was too tired to keep working. "I love you, Ricky. You bring honor back to our good name." She reached up and, clasping her hands around the back of his neck, pulled him down where she could put her cheek next to his.

"I love you too, Grandma. Thank you."

She tucked a roll of cash in his hand and turned to flip the porch light off. As she watched him strike out into the shadows, heading for the shed, her phone rang. She backed over to the wall and answered it. "Hi, son. Yes, I saw it on the news....Nope, don't believe a word of it. He's too good a boy. And he's smart. He'll be just fine—I have it on good authority." She watched her own flesh and blood pull out down the gravel driveway and out onto the road to take on the most dangerous task of his life. She wouldn't reveal his whereabouts to anyone, even her own son. The boy needed every advantage he could get.

Paul left Don's apartment slightly stunned by the confrontation he'd witnessed. He was hoping gentle persuasion would get Melvin to give back the cash; now he dismally resigned himself to never seeing his money again.

Cecily, too, was surprised at Don's actions. His countenance had gone beyond intimidating or frightful—it was downright vicious. She was glad she hadn't been on the receiving end of Don's anger. Needing to escape, she coldly said goodnight and started for the Jeep, thinking maybe she'd misjudged his friendly, easy-going manner. Her headlights flashed across Jake as he cruised down the walk on his skateboard and slid in front of Danny, who was just climbing on his bike to leave.

"Mom told me...to come and get you, Uncle Don," Jake wheezed, a sense of urgency in his voice. "Pauline called. You need to call her right away....We'll stay here with Christina and you take Danny's bike." Don resisted asking any questions. All he could do was hop on the half-sized bike and peddle toward Kate's, imagining the worst, hoping for the best.

Jake, Danny and Christina went back inside to play Nintendo. Jake challenged Danny to a match, boasting, "I'll have you beat in ten minutes."

"Not a chance," Danny scoffed. "I just killed Christina five times in a row and she had ten armor points. I didn't have any."

"Yeah, but she's a girl. No offense, Chrissy."

"None taken." Being a novice, she didn't mind losing. Soon the two of them were deep in a trance, playing to the attack-and-parry rhythms of the game.

"Guys, I'm going to get my bike and bring it in," Christina announced.

"Okay," one of the boys said distractedly.

Don reached Kate's and sprinted in to make the call. "Did she say anything?" He asked as he entered.

"Your dad's not doing very well. You'd better call." Don dialed the number.

"Pauline? Don. How is he?"

"The doctor just left. He's going downhill fast. We're not sure he'll make it through the night."

"He's got to. I have to say goodbye. You tell him to hang on. I'm going to catch the first bus I can and come up."

"I'll tell him, but I don't think he'll hear me."

Don hung up the phone and dug the phone book out of the drawer. "When does the next bus go to Boise?" he asked, still out of breath. "Any seats left? Good I'll be right down."

Christina gingerly climbed the steps and looked around to see if Melvin was anywhere in sight. Since she heard Paul's story, the very thought of their new landlord gave her the creeps. The coast was clear. She darted out and snatched up the bike. Just as she'd lifted it off the ground, she saw Melvin's feet, situated squarely on the grass between her and the front door. She slowly looked up, hoping it was someone else.

"I'll scream if you touch me!" she warned. She swung to the other side of the bike for safety.

"I'm not going to touch you. I was just out here looking at the half moon. Isn't it beautiful?" He was wearing a black knit cap over his balding head. His dark clothes helped him blend into the shadows. "Besides, those boys have the volume turned up so loud they couldn't even hear you if you did scream. That's why I'm out here. It's too loud for me inside."

Christina took a few steps back. He closed the gap. "I love the night. The stars twinkle and the cold night air sucks the noise right out of everything." He looked up.

Christina took a few more steps backward, taking her farther and farther away from the front door. If she could just get a small head start on him she could ride faster than he could run. She took another step, then flung herself onto the bike and raced off down the street, looking back over her shoulder as she went. Melvin was nowhere to be seen. He'd slipped into the darkness by the side of the house.

Don asked Kate if she'd mind driving him to the bus station. "It leaves in ten minutes. Can 'Tina stay with you a few more days?"

"Of course. Don't you want to get a few things before you go?"

"I don't have time. Tell her I'll call in the morning." They went to the garage and drove to the bus stop. Don rushed in to purchase his ticket. "Tell her I love her," he shouted to Kate as he climbed onto the bus.

TWENTY-TWO

THE OLD MERCURY ROARED up the interstate. Behind the wheel of the vintage car, Stacey no longer felt like a fugitive, but rather a farmer out on an errand. Traffic thinned out several miles outside of town. If his apartment was clear, he'd have time to get in, take a minute or two to gather up anything he might need to finish his investigation, and be back in Fillmore by midnight.

Christina stopped peddling at the corner, breathing hard—yet hardly breathing—waiting, her eyes darting wildly in every direction, her heart thumping at her ribs. Melvin didn't seem to be following her. She cautiously looked back, trying to decide if it was safe to return.

Then she spied him, darting behind a tree, moving toward her in the darkness. An inferno of terror burst through her, jolting her thoughts, dulling her instincts. There she was, at Sixth and Fir, only a few blocks from where her friend Ashley had been taken. Kate's house was located at least ten blocks in the other direction, with the figure in between, shadowing her every move. Ashley had said how strong and fast he was.

She glanced around, desperately seeking a solution. The houses along the street were dark. She thought about knocking on a door and screaming for help, but realized she didn't have time. The figure seemed to glide silently through the blackness. The only direction that led away from danger was toward the woods, further from home. Christina peddled away as fast as she could.

Jake finished his blasting as Danny's side of the screen turned red with blood. "I won!" He raised his arms triumphantly in the air. "Chrissy, I restored your honor," he whooped as he looked around. No answer.

"*Chrissy?*" Danny yelled a bit louder.

They both got up to see where she'd gone. "She said something about her bike, remember?" Danny said. "She was going to bring it in."

They dashed for the door and climbed the steps. No Christina; no bike. "Maybe she went to our house," Jake offered hopefully.

"No way. We didn't tell you what happened earlier. Uncle Don was about to beat the crap out of Melvin for spying on the people that used to live here." Danny's mind began to race. "We better find her quick."

Jake mounted his skateboard and started off. "You wait here and I'll go home and see if she's there." Just then Kate pulled around the corner. Seeing the panicked looks on her sons' faces and no Christina in sight, she rolled down the window and asked in a frenzied voice, "Where's Christina?"

Danny shook his head. "We don't know. She said she was coming out to get her bike and now she's not here."

Kate's brow furrowed deeper. "How long ago?"

Danny shrugged his shoulders. "We were playing Nintendo. I think it's been ten or fifteen minutes. Maybe she went to our house."

Kate took her cell phone from her purse and dialed. "Hurry, Alan. Hurry," she pled as she waited for him to pick up...."Is Christina home?"

"I haven't seen her. What's the matter?" Alan immediately recognized the fear in her voice. It was the same tone as when one of the children couldn't be found. It usually turned out they were asleep under the bed or at a friend's house, but this time it was different. Some lunatic had shot and killed a local police detective; two children had been abducted, one narrowly escaping after being saved by the dog that belonged to the officer accused of the killing. Yeah, she had a right to worry. "Where are you?"

"I'm at Don's apartment. Drive this direction while I call the police."

"I'm on my way." Alan raced to the garage and climbed in his car. Most of the children were asleep. He didn't stop to explain to them where he was going.

"Central Dispatch. Is this an emergency?"

"Yes, my niece is missing."

"Where did you see her last?" Kate gave the address. "Please stay on the line while I get an officer." She was gone a few seconds.

"Mapleton one-twenty-one responding," Mitchell said as he spun his vehicle around. "We're really short here. We could use all the backup units you can find."

"Can you give me a description of the girl?" dispatch asked as she typed in a coded response in the computer. Kate breathed in. "She's about four-and-a-half feet tall, long dark hair, part Hispanic."

"How old is she?"

"Twelve." Kate could see Alan's car rounding the corner.

"Please hold on, ma'am."

Mitch and Olsen were the only officers on duty. Olsen was assigned stakeout at Stacey's house. He started his engine and sped off. He hadn't felt comfortable with the assignment anyway. Not in a million years did he believe Stacey had stolen the drugs, much less killed Deek.

Christina raced through the dark on her bike. *The tree house!* she thought. *I'll hide in the tree house.* She turned down Fir's dark, dead-end lane. Her bike was hard to control in the swampy grass. Suddenly the front wheel went out from under her. Down she went, crashing to the wet ground. Small insects buzzed around her; water seeped through her clothing. She lay still, listening, watching in the dim moonlight. She could hardly hear over the pounding of her heart. She turned her head and scanned the landscape to see if she was still being followed. There he was—just at the edge of the woods. He was wearing something on his head. It flashed in the moonlight.

Picking up the bike, she climbed back on. She knew

her way to the tree house, even in the dark. She raced toward the safety she thought it could offer, her wet hands clinging to the handlebar grips, her chest about to burst.

Pulling alongside the large ash, she leaned her bike against it and looked up at the ladder-pull. She jumped to reach the cord and missed. Never having pulled it before, she didn't realize it was so far off the ground. She jumped again, still short of the mark. She was too short.

Crouching behind the tree, she peered out into the darkness. Beads of sweat dripped down her face and stung her eyes. Was he still out there? Creeping back to her bike, Christina wheeled it beneath the pull cord. *I can do this*, she repeated in her mind. *I can*. She clenched her shaking, sweat-soaked hands. Slowly and carefully she stood up on the frame of the bike and seized the rope. The door flopped open and the ladder started to uncoil down the tree trunk, making a terrible ruckus as it fell.

The dark figure paused in his search, cocked his ear, then raced off in the direction of the noise. Christina started up the ladder, periodically glancing behind her as she scaled the wobbly rope.

The first squad car pulled to the curb only a few moments behind Alan. Alan told Officer Mitchell he hadn't seen Christina between his house and the apartment. Danny and Jake were huddled together, trembling not so much from the chill in the air as the thought of their cousin being in trouble. They stood a few feet away as Kate explained the scenario.

"Where would you go if you were in trouble?" Jake whispered to his brother.

"I'd go to the tree house."

"Me, too." Jake approached the officer as a second squad car pulled up. Mitch began to explain the situation to Olsen.

"I think I know where she went," Jake finally interrupted. Everyone stopped to listen. "We have a secret tree house in the woods. She might go there to hide. I just don't know if she knows where the ladder rope cord is."

"She does. I saw her peeking one day when we were

letting it down," Danny chimed in.

"Where is it?" Mitch asked.

Jake pointed. "In the woods at the end of Fir."

Stacey was almost through the mountains. The lights of Nephi shone off in the distance. He glanced down at his speed: 85 in a 75-mph zone. Nephi police were notorious for nabbing speeders. He hadn't seen many cars and had only passed a few slow-moving trucks on the uphill side of the mountains. He checked his gauges and mirrors.

Then, lights! He could see flashing lights in his mirror. He slowed to the speed limit, hoping beyond hope that he hadn't gone through a trap. In no time at all the lights closed the gap, two cars pulling up behind him. Stacey applied his brakes and began to move over. He knew the old Merc was powerful, but it could never endure a high-speed chase. Grandma had only put fifteen thousand miles on it in the twelve years she'd owned it. And she'd probably never taken it up above 60.

With room to pass, the two highway patrol cars raced by him, going much faster than they should, even on a code. He decided to turn on his radio and see if he could tell what was happening.

"One twenty-one, central."

"Go, one twenty-one."

"We think she may be in the vicinity of Fir." Mitch's voice could be heard. "Call Lieutenant Barker."

"Ten-four. One twenty-one, we have every available unit in the county on the way."

"Dispatch, we have two male juveniles, cousins to the girl, that think she may have tried to flee to a tree house in the woods."

Christina, inside the playhouse, struggled to pull the ladder up the tree. She'd seen the boys do it so easily and didn't realize its weight. Using every ounce of strength she had, she grasped onto the top rung, pulled and reached for the second. Soon the third rung was within reach. She stretched down and grabbed onto it, locking it in the joint of her arm. Tugging upward, Christina felt a sudden jerk. Pulled off balance, she tumbled headfirst out the trapdoor, scraping her right side from her elbow to her ankle. With her arm tangled in the rope above the third rung, her weight jerked her to a stop, leaving her suspended nearly 30 feet above the ground. Then she felt the ladder vibrate, as someone from below began pulling themselves upward. Her arm throbbed, her side burned with pain, and she felt dazed and confused from the fall. Screaming, she scrambled to find the ladder with her feet. The wrenching movements of the approaching figure below her again threw her off balance, but finally she recovered.

Just then she felt a hand wrap around her ankle. She wrestled to pull free of the vise-like grip, but it was no use. She could feel him using her leg for support, pulling himself up. Braced with both arms, the shooting pains almost unbearable, she inched her left foot off the step and kicked as hard as she could. Her foot connected. The grip released. Something bounced off the tree's branches and hit the ground.

Christina pulled herself up onto the floor of the hut and slammed the trap door. It bounced with a dull thud, striking her attacker as it closed. A grunt and a faint moan was heard. She turned the lock. The powerful banging on the door motivated her to move upward. She dragged herself to the window and, using her left arm, pulled herself up onto the roof. The banging intensified.

Danny and Jake had climbed in the front seat of Mitch's police car to point the way. Alan and Kate followed close behind Olsen, who raced up Fir's dusty, rutted surface. To Mitch it felt like he was caught up in a rerun of a very bad play. But this time it was worse than ever because the star had failed to show. They needed Sig.

The late news report had thrown the County Attorney's office into chaos. The captain stood in front of Demick, pleading his case for a warrant, unaware that another child was missing. And the judge, in turn, was none too happy to have been summoned to his chambers at 11 o'clock at night. He was harder than ever on the attorney.

"If you're wrong, I'll wrap you up and ship you off to Sanpete County," he threatened the attorney. "And Captain, if you're wrong, I'll recommend a disciplinary hearing in front of the Board of Justice. I don't take lightly accusing a distinguished officer of these kinds of crimes. It speaks poorly of our enforcement system. Either we honored him wrongly the first time or we're slandering him now. You better get to the bottom of this right away."

Christina knew that if the door latch broke, it would only take a minute for her assailant to reach her. She decided her only escape was the rappelling rope. Already terrified, the thought of leaping from the roof holding onto nothing but a rope was more than she could bear. Sirens whined in the distance. The boys would know where she was. But, at present, things were far from safe.

She frantically groped for the harness. Her hands trembled; her arm still throbbed with pain. The banging ended with a ripping thud. She could hear him feeling around in the darkness of the hut.

The rope lay coiled on the corner of the roof. Finding it in the shadows, she threw it off the roof. It whipped and banged against the side of the hut as it dropped to the ground. She picked it up to secure it to her harness.

Something was missing. *Figure eight*, she remembered. She didn't have a figure eight on her harness. She bent back down and felt for Danny's harness. *Where was it?* Then she felt it. Jerking it toward her, she continued to glance feverishly toward the window end of the roof. The reflection of the slender moonlight could be seen on the river. She fumbled with the carabiner, holding the figure eight. Suddenly his head appeared above the roofline. Madly she grappled to release the ring from Danny's harness. It snapped loose, and she clipped the figure eight to her biner. She needed to put the rope through first.

Holding her breath, she glanced back. The attacker

was halfway up. She unsnapped the eight and threaded the rope. "Be right!" she prayed as she clipped it on. She struggled to her feet, the braking rope in her left hand. He was so close she could smell his foul breath. He grabbed at her shirt. Her eyes closed, she stepped back allowing herself to fall from the roof. Fully expecting a free-fall, suddenly she came jerking to a stop, sending her body slamming into the side of the hut. She opened her eyes to see his head and arm hung out over the roof. He'd snatched her in mid-air.

She reached up and looked into the blackness of his empty eyes, then clawed at his face as he held her shirt, now pulled up partly over her face. Her fingers sank deep into the soft tissue of his eye, clutching and stabbing as she dug into his socket. There was a scream and he pulled back, leaving the black knit mask in her hand. Then, having turned loose of the rope to defend herself, Christina began to plunge downward, his profile providing a silhouette against the moon as she fell. She reacted in a fraction of a second to the rope grinding past her leg. Reaching behind, she grabbed the rope. It dug into her hand, burning the flesh as she came to a sudden stop. Legs bucking, she landed on the ground, squarely on her butt. She could hardly breathe, the impact having hammered the wind out of her lungs. Groaning with pain, she strained to stand up. She caught sight of the bike; it seemed a mile away. She wasn't sure she could ride it even if she reached it in time.

"*Christina!*" It was Danny's voice. It was a distant hope, a muffled faith. He was calling her; he was coming!

"Danny!" She tried to answer. Her voice cracked. She struggled to refill her lungs with precious air. Glancing up and back over her shoulder, she saw the black figure slide down the rope. She careened toward Danny's voice. Then came other voices. And finally, through the trees, there came lights! Flashlight beams filtering through the brush. On rubbery legs, she made her way toward the lights.

Stacey intently monitored the radio as he drove. He cringed at the thought of losing another girl. He felt so helpless, so alienated from it all. Several other agencies were joining in the search. Each reported into the County Central Dispatch.

"Mitch have you seen anything?" he heard Olsen ask.

"No, we're headed northeast toward the river. The boys say the tree house is only a couple hundred yards more." Stacey could hear his voice fluctuate as he ran.

Come on guys, hurry! he said to himself as he listened to the calls.

Judge Demick thrust the warrant forward. "I want to hear what you find as soon as you finish. Call me at home."

"Yes sir," the attorney said.

"I don't think you'll be disappointed, your Honor," the captain said confidently.

"You're wrong! I'll be disappointed either way." The judge stood and motioned them out the door.

Christina stumbled through the brush and fell to the ground, exhausted. Mitch's light spotlighted the disheveled figure that slumped before them, spots of blood seeping through her tattered clothes up and down her side.

"We've got her! She's alive," he shouted over the radio.

"Yes!" yelled Stacey as he slammed his hands against the Merc's steering wheel. He made the turn north at Spanish Fork and gazed out across the valley to the lights, where he knew the chase was taking place. He could drive there in ten minutes if he wanted to, but it was out of the question.

"Is she okay?" asked Olsen.

Danny was first at her side. "Chrissy, what happened?"

"Melvin almost got me," she labored to say.

"She seems beat up a bit but I think she's okay," Mitch announced as he shined his light up and down the frazzled girl's body.

Stacey breathed a sigh of relief as he pulled off the freeway. *How many times is this guy going to get away? Who is he?* This was the first time he'd attacked in the same vicinity. Maybe that would help in the search. His radio beeped—the signal his battery was running low. He glanced at the screen. The two bars remaining signaled its diminishing capacity. He hoped it would at least get him through the night.

Kate held Christina in her arms, rocking back and forth. "It's okay now. It's okay," she whispered as she swayed.

"Where's my dad?"

"He went to see your grandpa."

Mitchell knelt by the trembling girl. "Christina, you said Melvin almost got you. Who's Melvin?"

Christina raised her head from the protective bosom of her aunt, but Danny answered first. "He's the pervert landlord where she lives. I'm gonna finish the job Uncle Don was gonna do."

"Hold on now, young man. Tell me what happened," Mitch warned.

Danny began to relate the incredibly bizarre events of the past few weeks.

Stacey cautiously drove around the block past his house. He knew the entire force was on the other assignment, but he didn't want to take any chances. After his initial pass, he went three blocks south. The streets were quiet, dark. Few street lights were ever installed in the older part of town. An occasional house light was left on for security. He parked the Merc and walked down the street toward home.

"One ten, one twenty-eight."

"One twenty-eight. Go ahead, captain," Olsen answered.

"I have a warrant. Proceed to enter," Bingham ordered.

"Captain, I don't know if you've been monitoring,

but we have a serious situation here. We had a missing girl at Fir. We just found her and we're working on a sweep of the area for the perp."

"Who's on Stacey's place?"

"No one, sir. Barker, Mitch and I are here where we found the girl," he said triumphantly. "She's alive!"

"Dammit, Olsen! I told you to stay on that house!" he barked.

Olsen was shocked, along with everyone else who monitored the call. "I'm sorry, sir. Mitch and I were the only ones on duty when the call came in."

"Who do you have now?"

"We've been backed up by County, UHP, and Spanish Fork."

"Grab whoever you can find and meet me at Stacey's place," Bingham ordered.

Stacey started on a dead run toward his apartment. He knew they were only six or seven minutes away. It took him two minutes to reach the garage door. When he opened it, Sig barreled past him. "Sit!" Stacey gave the command in a whisper. "We don't have time for games." Sig obeyed his master, but had a hard time holding still. Stacey crept to the back door and unlocked it with his key. Why was the captain so anxious to search his place? He thought he knew the answer. "Seek in silence!" he whispered to Sig.

Sig bolted from his sitting position and flew through the open door. He started in the kitchen, immediately stopping at the cupboard. The house was almost pitch black. Stacey took a small flashlight from the kitchen drawer and turned it on. He checked the time. Less than four minutes. Sig quietly put his front paws up on the counter top, panting enthusiastically. Stacey carefully opened the door, checking for attachments. His beam fell on the plastic container. He slowly removed the container from the shelf and opened the lid. Just as he'd expected. "Seek in silence." Stacey whispered again.

Sig stood in front of Stacey. He knew he'd found what they were searching for, and jumped up, excitedly nip-ping at the container, knocking it out of Stacey's hand. Stacey stepped off balance and dropped the light. Its beam flashed across the ceiling as it hit the floor, the small bulb sputtering out as Stacey fell. His body hit the ground with a thud and a groan as he caught the dish, just inches from the floor.

Stacey jumped to his feet. "Seek in silence," he commanded again, this time pointing to the living room. Sig began his routine sweep, moving from room to room with the same exactness he'd done hundreds of times before.

The glow of the clock in the bedroom served as Stacey's beacon. He grabbed a dark jacket and a gym bag from the closet and stuffed a few things into the bag. The charger to his radio sat on his dresser. He quickly unplugged it and dropped it in. Sig entered the bathroom, stopped at the toilet and began to whine. Stacey checked his watch. One minute. He peeked out the side of the curtain to the front, then moved to the bathroom to see what Sig had found. It was too dark to see.

"One ten, one twenty-eight. I need backup. What's your twenty?" the captain's voice blasted out over the radio. Stacey's radio beeped twice and shut down. Once more he peeked outside. The captain's car was parked in front. Olsen pulled up behind him, followed by a county rig. He could hear the captain's muted voice. "One of you take the rear and the other come with me."

The sheriff started toward the back, Olsen followed Bingham up the walk. Stacey called urgently for Sig. "Come!" He slid open the bedroom window; Sig still sat whining in the bathroom. "Come, boy!" he said as loudly as he dared. The captain and Olsen were at the front door. Stacey slithered over the sill and stood in the side yard.

"*Wham!*" The front door flew open with a crash. Sig bolted through the hall to the bedroom and hurled himself out the window to join his master. Stacey waited until he heard the back door crash open to slide the window shut so as not to call attention to himself. Lights went on in the house. Stacey crawled over the fence as he heard the house being torn apart.

"Come boy," he coaxed. "You can do it." Sig took a few steps back, then broke into a run, ending in a graceful leap. His front legs cleared the top and his back legs dug in as he pulled himself up and over the rattling fence. The two of them eased into the night.

TWENTY-THREE

OFFICER BARKER DROVE in the direction of Melvin's apartment, backed up by a county sheriff. Either he'd find him home and be able to question him, or he'd catch him coming home from chasing Christina. Barker knew the captain's interests lay elsewhere, so if a proper investigation was to be conducted, he'd have to do it himself. And he needed to move quickly.

Mitch was coordinating the sweep of the area. So far they had located Christina's shoe, some old military-issue night vision equipment, and spotted the black ski mask hung up in the tree. The perpetrator was nowhere to be found.

They'd decided that Christina's story was strong enough to arrest Melvin if his eye was gashed, as she said it was. If no cuts were found, he planned on asking the District Attorney for a warrant.

He pulled up to the home. Everything was dark upstairs, but the basement apartment was well-lit and open. He strode up the front steps and knocked...waited...and knocked again with force. The sheriff stood in the driveway, watching the other door. A dim light flickered on inside. Barker could hear furniture being moved. Cobwebs hung in the corners of the frame; apparently the door was not used regularly. It opened a few inches and Melvin poked his face part way into the opening. "What do you need?" he squeaked.

"Are you Melvin Briggs?"

His reply was terse. "I am. What do you want?"

The lighting was poor. Barker couldn't see what the man wore, and only half of his face could be seen in the shadows. Pointing his light directly in Melvin's face, Barker saw that his eye was visibly swollen. Confident he had the right man, the officer felt an adrenaline rush. How was he going to pull Melvin through the front door? He drew his revolver and aimed it directly at Melvin's nose. "You're under arrest for the attempted kidnapping of Christina Rodriguez," he shouted. The sheriff in the driveway likewise drew his gun and pointed it in the direction of the closed door.

"Settle down, officer," Melvin said calmly. "I'll be out in a moment. I can't get past this door, but I'll come out the side by the driveway. Let's see if we can clear up this misunderstanding." He started to close the door.

"Hold it!" Barker wasn't sure how to handle the situation. If he closed the door, they wouldn't have a clue what he was doing. It didn't appear possible to force the door open, and he didn't have a warrant. Melvin opened the door and peered from the crack. "I'm not going to do anything. I just can't get past the door." Barker began to shake. He'd only drawn his revolver once before in his eight years on the force. Now he was facing a cold-blooded killer...Then Melvin struck a bargain. "Look, why don't you put your cuffs on me through the door and I'll walk out the back with my hands in the air."

Barker thought through the dilemma, deciding he had to either drag him through the four-inch crack or let him come out on his own. "Put both arms out here," Barker directed. "Is anyone else in the house?"

"No. I'm alone."

The sheriff was now standing on the porch, calling for back-up. They could hear the sirens approaching. Melvin worked both of his spindly wrists through the small opening. Barker, in turn, holstered his pistol, took the cuffs from his belt and cinched them down tightly. Stepping back again, Barker once more unsheathed his revolver. "I want you out the back door in less than 20 seconds, your hands in the air."

"Settle down, I don't want to get hurt."

Barker backed down the steps. He and the sheriff quickly moved around to a position protected by the car in the driveway. In less than ten seconds Melvin had opened the back door and was standing on the porch, his cuffed arms raised high. Three more units pulled up in front. In seconds, dozens of spotlights and shotguns were trained on the darkly clothed man. "Turn around and back down the steps." Melvin did exactly as he was told. "Lie face down, hands above your head, legs spread apart." Again, Melvin followed every order. As soon as he was prostrate, Barker and the sheriff rushed in, frisked him and pulled him to his feet, shoving him up against the brick wall of the house. "You have the right to remain silent...."

The tension was high; every officer on the scene was ready to shoot. "All I did was talk to her," Melvin mewled. "Where is she? The last time I saw her she was riding her bike down the street."

"She's right where you left her, you jerk: In the woods, bleeding, scared to death."

Melvin appeared shocked. "I didn't touch her. She was acting funny after her dad threatened me. I didn't even leave the place."

"How'd you hurt your eye?"

"I...I ran into the corner of the wall just a few minutes before you knocked," he stuttered in response.

Barker peppered him with questions as he was led to the patrol car. "Have you ever been in the military?"

"Yes, I'm retired army. What does that have to do with anything?"

Barker opened the back door to his car and pushed Melvin's head down and into the vehicle. "You s.o.b.! You'll get the death penalty for what you've done."

Bingham ripped through the house like a tornado, demolishing everything in his path. No bag of drugs. He wandered to the bedroom, slipped something from his pocket, unwrapped the contents and dropped the small object behind the dresser. Leaning against the wall, he focused his light beam on the object. "Sheriff, come give me a hand moving this dresser!" he called into the other room. "I think we might have something here."

The two of them slid the dresser away from the wall. On the floor lay a single bullet casing. The captain took a pen from his pocket, balanced the shell, and guided it into a small plastic bag. "Where's the dog?" He hadn't noticed the silence until then. "I want bank records, phone records, e-mail....anything else we can find," he demanded. "And check the garage for the damn dog," he told Olsen, too afraid to do it himself.

Bingham's fear of dogs went way back. He often bragged of his stories of hand-to-hand combat in 'Nam, nerves steady and cold. He'd been wounded three times on his tour—but had never told anyone of the tiny Chihuahua that had bit his leg at the age of five.

After leaving the clothes bag in the Merc, Stacey, having donned his dark jacket, returned and watched the scene from behind a maple, two houses away. He didn't have much time. He needed evidence, and the captain's car held it. Clenching the silent dog whistle between his lips, he gave three short puffs. Sig obediently sat. Stacey crept along the darkened street to the vehicle, took the key from the pocket of his coveralls, and unlocked the driver's door. When he cautiously swung open the door, the car's interior lights came on. He closed it again; it seemed to illuminate the entire neighborhood.

Stacey decided to enter as quickly as possible. Peering over the side through the windows, he quickly opened the door and pressed the unlock button to the others. Then he crawled to the back door and slipped in, pulling the door far enough closed to turn off the interior lights. He glanced up to see Olsen walk from the kitchen to the garage. Instinctively he ducked.

Olsen stepped through the already open doorway and felt for the light. He wasn't afraid of Sig; they were buddies. He'd been more than surprised to hear that the dog had bitten the captain. He noticed a large piece of red meat on the floor inside the door. On the other side of it was a ten-inch puddle of water. *Odd*, he thought. The only other things in the room were a few garden tools. He switched off the light and started back toward the kitchen. "The dog's not there," he announced.

Bingham let out a snort. "Did you search it?"

"Not much to search. Nothing there but an empty bucket of water and a bloody piece of meat."

"That's it?" Bingham started for the garage.

"Well, no sir, it's full of dog crap too," he responded sarcastically.

Stacey had alternately maneuvered his large frame back and forth as he worked in the back seat, making sure he was out of sight of the officers inside the house. Using his knees, he pressed forward at the base of the back seat. The right side was easy, the left more difficult. He popped the other hook loose and raised it up. Then with a pocket knife, he cut a strip of fabric from the upholstery under the seat.

Olsen and the captain crossed from the house to the garage. Bingham flipped on the light and glanced around the room. Taking a rake down from the wall, he skewered the meat, intending to move it. White powder fell from within. "What's that?" Olsen frowned.

"No idea." The captain unfastened his keys from his belt and handed them to Olsen. "Go get an evidence bag from my car."

"I've been kept awake by you people half the night. What's going on?" Bingham strutted out from the garage to see who had spoken to Olsen.

"Who're you?" Olsen asked.

"I live downstairs." The captain recognized him from the television report. He wouldn't have much to say.

"Here, I'll get the bags myself." He reached for the keys and started for the car. Stacey ducked down.

Christina lay in the ambulance. She had stopped crying and looked on as a paramedic tended to her rope-burned hand. "I'd like to take her in for a few x-rays— make sure there are no other injuries," the paramedic told Kate.

Mitch approached the ambulance door. Melvin was in custody, he told them, "arrested for attempted kidnapping. His eye was swollen, just like you told us."

Television reporters and camera crews had begun descending on the scene. One approached Mitch as the camera man got a shot of Christina on the gurney through the open door. Mitch quickly closed it. "No comment," he answered when questioned whether they'd caught the murderer of the girls.

"Has the warrant of the Stacey home turned anything up?" the reporter followed up.

"No comment," he said again as he walked away. She rushed to her car and checked her notes. Her cameraman started the car and pulled away.

Stacey hunkered down on the floorboard. *I'm dead*, he thought. The captain would surely kill him, given the opportunity. Bingham started around the back of the car. Stacey lifted his legs, prepared to kick the door open and catch him off guard so he could get away. But instead Bingham stopped at the trunk and put in his key. Stacey relaxed. The trunk popped open—as did the partially latched door at Stacey's feet. On went the interior lights. Stacey reached out and pulled the door closed with the heel of his foot, which now protruded above the window. The captain pulled the trunk lid down to see the source of the flash, but saw only the dark interior of the car. He let the trunk lid back up, this time paying closer attention. Nothing changed. He fumbled through the boxes inside and closed the lid, then returned to the garage.

Stacey was once more left alone to reflect on the danger he was in. *I don't know if I can live on the other side of the law very long.* His heart pounded as he watched everyone congregate in the garage. When he felt it was safe, he opened the door, slid out, and latched it shut. Just then a car pulled around the corner. Stace crept to the front of Bingham's car and crouched in the shadow from the headlights of the oncoming vehicle. The car pulled up and stopped directly behind. A woman climbed out from the back seat. A man, leaving the headlights on, wrestled a camera from the front passenger's side and stepped out. Camera lights brought Bingham back out of the garage. The reporter walked toward him, microphone in hand. "Captain Bingham, what has your search of Officer Stacey's residence turned up?" Bingham wasn't happy to see her on the scene, especially when his prize evidence was missing. He didn't want the word out too soon that nothing had been recovered from the home.

"Off the record," he grunted. The camera lights were turned off. "We found a casing that matched the caliber of weapon Derickson was shot with. Now you two need to get out of here."

Stacey, listening to the exchange, didn't know that his bad luck was about to get worse as he crouched only a few short yards from where the captain stood. He blew one long and three short blasts on his whistle. Sig began to bark. Everyone stopped what they were doing and looked off in the direction of the sound. The captain started toward the front of his automobile. Stacey clenched his teeth and gave one short and one long blast, bringing Sig, in an aggressive stance, bolting from his hiding place and directly at the captain.

The cameraman flipped on the lights and his camera began to roll. Bingham drew his weapon, his long shadow stretching across the yard and up the neighboring house. If he missed, he wouldn't get a second chance. Stacey leapt from the front of the car to take the man down. A shot was heard as Sig's teeth sunk deep into Bingham's arm while Stacey pulled the weapon from his grasp. Stacey then pulled away, slapped his leg to call off the dog, and the two of them disappeared into the darkness. Bingham lumbered to his feet. Olsen and the sheriff ran from the home to give pursuit, but they were no match for Stacey or his dog. Bingham called for backup.

Kate, Danny and Christina returned home from the hospital around two a.m. The x-rays had proven negative and the tenderness was subsiding in her shoulder. A nasty bump had formed on her head where she'd slammed against the treehouse and her hip was scraped and bruised. Danny wanted to hear every detail. He could hardly believe Christina had jumped off the roof. Kate kissed her and tucked her in bed. It only took her a minute to fall asleep. Tomorrow would be a big day. Officer Mitchell wanted to interview her again.

Don's bus droned on through the night. Boise lay only another hour away. He hoped he could reach his father in time. He felt terrible about the way he and Cecily had parted. How could he possibly make things right between them? And now she'd seen him rear his ugly temper, which probably would scare her away for good. He pondered how good she was, musing, *Christina and Cecily are a perfect fit, too.* Don took a moment to ponder what that thought implied. Then he leaned back against the headrest and did his best to sleep.

Stacey and Sig scrambled over fences and skulked through back yards. Doubling back to the car, Stacey got in, let Sig in the back, and drove away. By the time backup arrived, he was on his way to Provo to find an open grocery store. Sig hadn't had anything to eat all day.

Though he didn't look like the Officer Stacey who was being hunted by Captain Bingham, the bib overalls and straw hat drew more attention to him than would street clothes. He needed to get back to his house and gather a few more belongings. He also needed to charge his radio battery so he would know what was going on.

Stacey reached in his pocket and took out the roll of bills his grandma had given him. Removing the rubber band, he counted out *four* one hundred dollar bills wrapped in a dollar bill. *Bless her heart!*

Parking the car, Stacey gave Sig the signal to lie on the floor in back. He didn't want to chance someone recognizing the two of them together. Ten cans of dog food and a few staples for himself came to more than twenty-five dollars. He started the car and pulled onto State Street, then made a right-hand turn toward the cemetery. Two blocks later, flashing lights appeared in his rearview mirror.

He drove slowly on, knowing he hadn't done anything illegal. *They must be going somewhere else*, he thought at first. But when the car drew up behind him, Stacey pulled over and shut off the motor. The officer cautiously stepped from his car and came forward. Stacey ordered Sig to stay down, hoping the officer wouldn't see him.

"Good morning," the officer said. He didn't appear to be anyone Stacey knew.

"Somethin' wrong, officer?" he said in his best attempt at a country drawl.

"Did you know your tail lights are out?"

"No, sir, I didn't."

"Can I see your registration and driver's license?"

"Let me see if I can find them." Stacey fumbled through the glove box and produced the registration, grateful it was in the name of his aunt, who kept the paperwork in order for his aging grandmother.

"Driver's license, too," the officer asked as he began to examine the papers.

"Sir, I don't believe I got it with me. I think I left it on the dresser when I put on my pants." He groped through his pockets. "You see, it's my grandma's car. I brought her up to see some family. She's 80-some-odd years old and we rarely leave Fillmore with this car. She wasn't feeling so good, so I came down to the store to get her some medicine. Here, let me show you." He began to fumble through the bag.

"No, I don't think that'll be necessary." He handed back the paperwork. "Just see if you can get those lights fixed for her."

"Sure thing, officer."

Stacey knew what the officer was thinking. A good percentage of the people driving at night are either drunk or up to no good. The dusty old car made his story sound authentic, but the lights would be the first thing he'd fix. To his knowledge, a warrant for his arrest hadn't yet been issued. From the news report, he'd be charged with Deek's murder, as well as the assault of Captain Bingham. Stacey couldn't afford to show his face until he accumulated enough information to put Bingham away.

He waited for the officer to pull away, then opened a can of dog food with his knife. Sig patiently waited. When finished, they headed off en route to Mapleton.

Stacey parked on a side street and they walked to his parents' home in the upper-class part of town. Still carrying a key, he slipped into the room over the garage to catch a few hours' sleep, entering through the garage so as not to disturb anyone. He wouldn't be safe staying there more than the night, so he'd be sure to be out before dawn.

TWENTY-FOUR

D ON HOBBLED from the Greyhound shortly after seven. He hoped the local transit system could get him where he needed to go. He'd seldom used public transportation. That night's bus ride was the first trip he'd ever taken without his truck. From there to his father's place was a 20-minute drive. How long it would take by bus, he didn't know. He stopped at a phone to call his father's home.

"Hi, it's Don. How's he doing?...Good. I knew he'd hang on....Oh? What happened? I'll call." He hung up the phone and hurriedly dialed again. "Collect...Don...Kate, what's going on? Yeah, she said it was urgent..." He listened, consciously resisting the urge to swear. "I'll get back as soon as I can," he said. "She said he's still hanging on. I haven't seen him yet....No, I'm still at the bus stop."

Finally he settled down enough to hear what Kate was trying to say. "'Tina's okay?...I'll call back a little later." Don was torn between anger and sadness. "I should have killed the little pervert last night," he whispered as he began to search for a bus schedule.

Stacey awoke to the all-too-familiar wet tongue on his cheek. It was later than he'd hoped. Sig needed to be let outside. The battery had charged while he slept; he plugged it into the back of his radio, unplugged the charger, and put it in his bag. Quietly, they crept down the stairs to the garage. He felt silly sneaking around in his parents' house, but the last thing he wanted to do was drag them into this mess.

Suddenly someone approached. He turned and scooted back up the stairs, waiting by the door, listening. He could tell by the gait and by the humming of a popular song, that it was his kid sister, Amber. Then all at once the footsteps started upstairs, the door opened, and in she walked. At first she was taken by surprise, then she opened her arms and ran to greet him. "Rick, we've been worried about you."

"I'm fine, Amber." Sig thumped his big tail on the wall as he waited for his share of the greeting.

She turned her brother loose and gave Sig a pat. "Why are they saying all that stuff about you?"

"I know some things about a powerful and dangerous man, things he doesn't want me to tell anyone. He'll do anything to keep me quiet."

"Why don't you go to the FBI?"

"I don't have enough evidence to put him in jail yet."

"Mom and Dad said you didn't do it. They've been worried sick. We need to go tell them you're okay."

"No. No one can know I was here. I need you to keep it a secret. Do you understand?" Amber nodded. "If he finds out I was here, you may be in danger, too."

Amber reached down to give Sig a few more pats as they talked. "My friend Christina was attacked by that killer last night. We saw her in the ambulance on the news just a few minutes ago. We saw you and Sig go after Captain Bingham—is he the one?

"I can't say. I need to go. There's lots to do. You tell Mom and Dad that I'll be fine. They taught me how to take care of myself. Besides, I've got Sig to look out for me. Now hurry back downstairs."

Amber started for the door, then turned back. "I almost forgot why I came up here. I left my pack here yesterday." She shuffled over to the window and retrieved it. "Don't worry, I won't tell *anyone*," she said slyly, as if she were already part of his undercover scheme. She reached for the door and stopped again. "What if I need to contact you to tell you something important?" she asked in earnest.

"I'll try to stay in touch. If I don't, you'll think of something, I'm sure."

"If I do, you meet me here at midnight." She was always trying to help him with his police work.

"What do you mean if you do?"

"If I think of a way to contact you, meet me here at midnight, on the dot." She was insistent.

"Midnight it is, then. I'll watch for the sign." He watched her go out the door and down the stairs. He and Sig soon followed.

Captain Bingham, bandaged and indignant, was less than thrilled with the throng of reporters waiting at his door. He practically drove over the crowd of camera- and microphone-wielding bodies to free his vehicle from the horde. Noting his reluctance, the news-hungry mob transformed into a moving assemblage of autos, trailing his unmarked Pontiac to the station.

Stacey decided the best place for him to hide was the last place anyone would be looking. Getting there without being seen would be the hardest part. He pulled into the back of the post office, commanded Sig to stay down, strolled over to the phone and dialed the number. "Stacey here....I know. I need your help. I didn't do it. You know me better than that. Give me three days. If I can't prove it, I'll turn myself in....Has a warrant been issued yet?...Good, then you won't be breaking any laws. Meet me in the parking lot of the Raintree Apartments at ten....I'll tell you what I need."

Bingham, having fought his way through the crowd, was met by the County Prosecutor himself, Mr. Jay White. Melvin had been kept in city lock-up since his arrest. He'd made one brief collect call that night.

"Demick wants us in his courtroom by eight with your prisoner," began the prosecutor. "Some bigwig, out-of-state lawyer flew in a few hours ago and set up a hearing. We better go over what you've got—and it *better* be good."

"I'll get Barker in here and see where we're at." The

captain took his radio and made the call. "One ten, one twelve."

"Go, captain."

"I need you in the office. What's your twenty?"

"I'm just pulling in, sir." Barker barreled in amid a sea of questions thrown his way. The men went into an office and closed the door.

It took Don almost an hour to arrive at his father's home. Several cars were parked in the driveway. He knocked on the door.

"Maria!" Don exclaimed. "I didn't expect to see you here."

She reached out and wrapped her arms around his waist. He was the only one with any height in the family, standing almost a foot taller than his younger sister. Don hadn't seen her for more than three years, she having moved to Oregon shortly after her marriage. Since then, he didn't even know she was on speaking terms with her father. Her eyes looked tired and bloodshot. "We drove through the night after Pauline called."

Within a few minutes' time, brother and sister were reacquainted. Then Don asked about her relationship with their dad. "We stopped here to see him the year after I got married," explained Maria. "We found he wasn't the monster Mama had made him out to be. We've been close ever since."

Don was pleasantly surprised. His dad had never talked about any of the siblings. He thought he was the only one who kept in touch.

"How's he doing?"

"This morning, a little better. He was quite sure he wasn't going to live through the night when we talked to Pauline."

Maria led Don back to their father's bedroom. Once a strong and proud man, full of fire and fight, he lay motionless, his frail body slender and still. The once-round face was sunken, bony, dispirited. Dark shadows filled the void around his eyes. Don sidled up to the bed, wishing he'd come sooner. Dad had gone downhill so fast.

Only last summer he was out on the lawn playing football with Christina. He'd retired from trucking only four years before. At that time, he still could almost whip Don in arm wrestling.

Pauline sat next to him, holding his hand. She leaned down to whisper in his ear. "Don's here. He drove through the night to see you."

The father's eyes stirred ever so slightly, then opened a fraction of an inch. He labored to turn his head, wanting to see his son. Don drew near and sat in a chair at his side. The old man raised his hand and slowly motioned Don to lean closer. *"Mi hijo..."* he whispered, his voice weak and raspy.

"I came to see you, Papa. I needed to be here."

"I am better," he said listlessly. "For now she is safe."

"Who, Papa? Who's safe?"

The old man once more sunk back into his pillow. Don looked to Pauline for help.

"He hasn't made sense all night. I think he heard me talking to Kate about Christina. How is she?"

"Kate says she's fine. A few scrapes and bruises, but she'll be fine."

Pauline nodded and smiled. "She told me the little thing fought like a wildcat. She must have a little of that fierce Rodriguez blood in her."

"I guess so."

The old man moved his hand again and struggled to open his eyes. He began to whisper. Don cocked his head and strained to hear. "Go back to her. Use your head." He stopped and closed his eyes again, his strength spent.

"What did he say?" Pauline asked.

"Something about 'go back to her, use your head.'"

"He's been asking for you off and on through the night. He seems to want to tell you something."

"Why don't we get you some breakfast and a shower? You look like you've been hit by a Mack." She stood and walked Don from the room, her private joke understood. Don and his dad had both driven heavy-duty Mack trucks to deliver their loads of concrete. When they arrived home exhausted, they always referred to the hard days' work that way.

"I'll call you when he wakes."

Don fought to hold back the tears as he left the room.

"All arise," the deputy intoned.

"Drop the formalities. Let's get this damn thing in gear." Demick was in no mood for protocol. "Mr. White, nice of you to come. This is a closed-door hearing—for reasons I can't discuss. I hope you have everything in order. Proceed."

"Your honor, we have evidence to link the defendant, Melvin Briggs, to the attempted kidnapping of Christina Rodriguez. Christina is prepared to testify that he approached her in an aggressive, threatening manner and that he chased her through the woods. She told the officers at the crime scene that she scratched at his face and eye. When he was arrested, Mr. Briggs's eye was swollen, as you can see." He gestured in Melvin's direction. "He admitted speaking to the victim shortly before the attack. The evidence in this case leads us to believe he is the same man responsible for the other murders and kidnapping over the past eight months. We'd like him bound over for trial, without bail."

Demick listened carefully. "Is that all?"

"We'd also like to request a search warrant for Mr. Briggs's residence, and permission for a DNA sample to be taken to match with the other evidence."

Demick turned to the defense attorney. "Well, what do you have to say?" He conspicuously resisted calling him by name. He didn't much care for the hotshot attorney.

The lawyer swaggered forward, eyeing the judge. "Your Honor, the evidence is purely circumstantial. Talking to a person is not a crime. Mr. Briggs walked into a doorway last night, hurting his eye, shortly before the police arrived. He's a highly trusted employee of the county. He owns property in the valley and retired as a decorated army colonel." White glanced at Bingham as the attorney droned on. "He doesn't constitute a flight risk, and thus should be released on his own recognizance. If everyone who talked to the victim last night was arrested, we'd all look pretty silly."

Demick's eyes dropped to the open file folder in front of him. What he was about to do went against his better judgment. "Mr. White, you'd better put a stronger case together, then come back to see me. Your request for DNA and a search warrant is denied. Mr. Briggs, you're free to go." Demick rapped the bench with his gavel.

"Your Honor!" White stood to protest. He could hardly believe his ears.

"My decision is final, Mr. White."

"You're going to let this lunatic back on the street?"

"You're out of order. If you don't shut up, I'll place you in contempt." Demick stood and strode from the room.

"All arise—"

"Just a minute." The bailiff was cut short again as Demick retraced his steps to the bench. "The defense may leave. Captain Bingham, you and Mr. White sit down for a moment." The two of them looked at each other. Everyone else shuffled out of the courtroom, Barker taking up the rear, when Demick barked another command. "Officer, sit down with your captain." Barker returned to the front and sat down. "Before we all go off looking like idiots, I want to know what your search turned up at Officer Stacey's residence last night."

Bingham was the only one who knew anything about it. "Your Honor, we believe we found a casing that matches the gun used in the Derickson murder. It will be sent to the Provo lab this morning," he said. "Also, as you probably already know, he attacked me last night."

"Where's Officer Stacey now?" the judge asked.

"I don't know, your Honor. He...got away."

"Don't you think it would be prudent to locate him?"

"Yes sir, we're doing everything we can to find him."

Cecily hadn't watched the morning news, and country music had been her only companion on her way in to work. So she was both disappointed and bewildered to find that Don hadn't shown up. Then it hit her–maybe he'd had to go see his dad, or had received news that he'd died.

When Jeff came up front, a concerned expression smothered his customary smile. "Did you hear from Don?"

Cecily simply shook her head.

"You didn't hear about Christina and how she was kidnapped? It was all over the news."

Cecily sat in stunned silence as Jeff filled her in on the events of the past night. Then she picked up the phone and dialed Don's number. When there was no answer, she phoned Kate. All the while she felt guilty for leaving on such bad terms the night before. After all, he was doing his best to apologize for his inappropriate behavior. But then again, for the first time in their relationship she'd witnessed his violent side.

Kate picked up. "Kate, Cecily. How's Christina?... She's okay, then?...Where's Don?..." Her face grew more grim by the second. A minute later she offered her services, said her goodbyes, and hung up the phone.

Christina slept in until eight-thirty. Kate was careful to wake the other children and get them off to school without disturbing her. When she finally did crawl out of bed, her first concern was to get to school so she could let her friends know she was all right. "I have to go, Aunt Kate...."

Kate finally relented. "Get dressed and I'll drive you."

Melvin and his attorney were escorted from the building past the bevy of reporters, who noisily spewed banal questions and thrust their microphones into the men's sullen faces. Neither spoke as they made their way through the mob. It took five deputies to keep the reporters from engulfing them. No one could believe this man, accused of the most horrid crimes imaginable, was free to leave. Soon they were in the safety of the car on their way to Mapleton.

Melvin's counsel shook his head. "It's getting complicated."

"I'll take care of the problem as soon as the opportunity arises." Melvin's voice was brazen and sure.

"Do you need any help in the matter?"

"No, this is one I need to take care of personally. I no longer have any doubt."

"Don't let it happen again," the attorney said firmly. "Do you think he suspected anything?"

"I doubt it, although he was surprised."

The men didn't speak again until Melvin was dropped off in front of his home. "Call me if you get tied up again. Otherwise use the proper channels."

"Yes, sir." The lawyer drove away. Inside and out of sight, Melvin drew his blinds and hid from the reporters.

Christina gave her aunt a kiss goodbye. Kate reminded her that she'd pick her up for the appointment a little before one.

At school, the entire class had heard every detail about the incident. But now they could all relax: Melvin was arrested and the town was safe. Only Ashley seemed uncomfortable. She wasn't completely convinced the kidnapper wasn't still out there, and Officer Stacey and his dog were no longer around to protect her. And the secret she held deep in her heart would stay locked away forever. It was as if keeping it silent would make her safe.

Soon the class was dismissed for recess. Ashley, Amber and Christina found a quiet place to talk. "It was scary, wasn't it?" Ashley asked Christina.

"The worst thing in the whole world."

"I'd probably be dead if Sig hadn't come, and now they're saying all those bad things about your brother. What's he going to do?"

"He didn't do any of the stuff they're saying. He's the best person I know."

"Maybe we should see if we can help him," Christina was first to suggest.

"How can *we* help?"

"We'll think of something," they agreed.

Stacey sat in the parking lot of the biggest apartment

complex in town, which ran parallel to the tree cover of the river. If he left the old Merc with the other cars it would be less likely to be spotted than on the street. The parking lot was within walking distance of his home. He found an old Reader's Digest in the glove box and read while he waited. Sig was bored hiding on the floor of the back seat, wanting nothing more than to sprint around the lot.

The story Stacey stumbled upon was so engrossing he didn't notice the police car pull into the parking lot and circle around in front of him. He looked up only after the squad car had pulled up within inches of his mirror.

"Must be a good story," Barker teased. Stacey bolted upright in his seat, then relaxed. His friend was right on time.

"It's a story about a dog—you know how I am." Sig seized the occasion to stand up on his hind legs and beg caresses from Barker as the two men spoke.

"I'm glad to see you got him before Bingham did," Barker said, referring to Sig. "He would have loved to see Sig locked up or dead. I think he's scared of him."

"It was close. I was in the house when they began the search. He planted half a kilo in the cupboard and another full one in the trunk of my car."

Barker's nose wrinkled. "Where's the other half?"

"I think he dumped it in the toilet."

"He made a special trip to your house to see if you were home; he must have left it then. I should have followed him."

"If he'd caught you, we'd both be in hot water," Stacey warned.

"He's going to issue a warrant for Deek's murder as soon as he gets a match on the casing he conveniently found at your place. He's issuing a warrant for the assault, as we speak."

"I heard him leak that information to the reporter last night. I was right there."

"You shouldn't have attacked him."

"He was about to step on me."

"What's he up to?"

Stacey felt sure of himself. "That's what I'm going to find out. Now you've got to get me home."

"Home?"

"I don't know of a better place to work from. It'll be the last place he'll look."

Stacey and Sig climbed into the patrol car and hunkered down in the back seat. It wasn't easy to stay hidden with the two of them in the same cramped space.

"If the warrant was issued, I'd have to arrest you, you know. It would be a snap. I'd be a hero. You're both locked in the back of my car."

Stacey chuckled. "It's a good thing I trust you. The captain might know a lot more about the murders than he's letting on. I found a murder that matches the profile in Virginia. I think it was at the same time he lived there." Stacey admitted, however, that it was only speculation. "Are you working on Deek's murder?"

"No, Bingham's decided to head it up himself. I'm working on this Briggs case."

"Is he the guy from last night?"

"Yeah, I've never seen anything like it. White looked like an amateur. Some stuffed-shirt attorney flew in and seemed to take over the whole courtroom. Demick buckled like a squashed bug."

"Demick, the stone-cold judge." Stacey lifted his head as he made the comment. "Something bigger than sex is going on around here."

"Sex?" Barker asked, backing up in Stacey's drive.

"I haven't told you? I found a clerk in the Levan Motel that saw a broken down Chevy and a blonde in a sports car. They came in for a half hour fling the night Deek was shot. He described the captain. Just didn't get a good close-up view."

"I'll see if I can check up on it," Barker said as he opened the door and acted like he was reviewing his notes. "You slip out while I distract anyone that might be watching by knocking on the front door."

He'd backed up within a few feet of the garage. The cover of the driver's door would hide them from view of the street. Barker opened the back door, then reached back inside to pick up his metal file holder.

"Don't use your phone. I'm sure Bingham'll be monitoring it to find you. Keep in touch. You've got three days before I come to get you. If he finds you first, I'm not sure I can keep you alive." Stacey and Sig slipped out from the back seat and in through the garage door.

TWENTY-FIVE

A MEAL AND A SHOWER made a world of difference in Don's outlook. But having to put on the same
dirty clothes made him wish he'd taken time to grab a
few of his things. Even in the hurry and confusion, he
also should have remembered to call his work and let
them know he wouldn't be in. He went to Pauline's phone
and dialed.

"Cobblecrete, how may I direct your call?" he heard
Cecily say.

Don's heart raced when he heard her voice. He wondered how she felt about him. "Cecily, Don—"

"Hi. I talked to Kate. You all right?"

"Yeah, I'm fine—"

"And how about your dad?"

Don could think of no way to put a positive spin on
things, so he took the candid approach. "He's dying. They
didn't think he'd live through the night. I hopped on a
bus and came straight up."

"I'm so sorry. Did you get to talk to him?"

"He's quite confused, barely conscious. I'm not sure
he even knows I'm here."

"When do you think you'll be back?"

"No idea. I need to be there to help 'Tina. But I also
need to be here with Dad....Oh, tell Jeff I'll call him later
today and let him know when I'll be back."

"I will. Can I help with anything?"

"No, thanks. I'll call later." Don hung up and went to
sit with his father.

Cecily turned on the news on the lunchroom TV. She

sat in amazement as she listened. Melvin had been released. They were talking about Judge Demick and a possible conflict of interest, in that Melvin Briggs had access to the judge's chambers. His secretary claimed they didn't know each other personally—that Melvin merely cleaned the office.

The news was followed by a local talk show, where the kidnapping was the only topic. One caller suggested blackmail as a reason the judge let him go; another wanted to hang Melvin right then and there; and the talk show host cautioned his viewers that perhaps more evidence was needed. Back and forth they argued. After broadcasting photos of Melvin's injured eye, some viewers still wondered, while others were even more convinced of his guilt.

Stacey settled in, showered, and put on some clean clothes. Careful to keep the house in the same order as when he found it, he used a new towel, folded it and put it back in the cupboard. He dried the walls and shower curtain with a washcloth, leaving it in the bottom of the tub where it was before. He couldn't chance the captain returning and seeing something out of place.

Sig would have to use the garage. Getting him back and forth worried Stacey. The renter below worked from eight to five. Stacey took special care to stay still during the day, deciding he'd only go out at night. He didn't notice Sig sniffing the concrete floor where the raw meat had been.

The next problem was the lack of a phone. Scrounging through the kitchen drawer, Stacey found a small convertible screwdriver. He took a chance and slipped out back. Sig patiently waited in the kitchen. The phone box was mounted next to the bedroom window. Opening the box, there seemed to be more wires than he remembered, but, fortunately, they were labeled with the corresponding numbers. He disconnected the two wires he believed led to his phone, then returned to the kitchen to see if his was dead. "Bingo!"

Next he carefully walked past the narrow opening

visible to the street into the garage, where he remembered seeing a small piece of wire hanging on a nail. Returning to the box, he cut two small pieces of wire and attached them to the connections that he assumed served his neighbor's phone. He closed the box and tightened the screw. Back in the kitchen, he tested his handiwork. Yes! As long as no one was home below, he'd have a phone.

Melvin, anxious to review the images of the past twelve hours, passed through the multiple security checks on his state-of-the-art computer. He started out by creating logs to document the recordings, after which he verified that they were electronically stored and filed. He was a master at his trade. His military training had prepared him well for the high-tech equipment he controlled. Each disk was meticulously coded and safeguarded. It always seemed such a pain to verify and re-verify passwords and codes, but he couldn't afford to let them fall into the wrong hands.

Melvin's safeguards were masterpieces of design. If opened improperly, a built-in program immediately erased the contents of the disk. In fact, on one occasion he'd found three of his disks empty. He could only guess who the offender was, though it was no use trying to pursue it.

Silently, he contemplated the task at hand. It was time to finish the job. Having killed before in Nam, this assignment would be like any other. But the timing would have to be perfect. If not this week, next week would do. The horrors of Nam and the pains he'd endured the last five years after the loss of his daughter, had zapped his passion for life. He was left a hollow shell, a lonely, cynical, emotionless old man.

Bingham phoned the lab. Saunders verified that the cartridge casing was a match. A microscopic burr on the pistol had left an obvious identifying mark. The evidence would be enough to make convicting Stacey a mere formality. Before the phone was back on the receiver, he was barking orders for an arrest warrant to be issued.

Kate dropped the children off at the sitter's and set out to pick up Christina from school. As she drove, photographs played through her head of the previous night and the horror her niece had endured. Actually, most of her niece's 12 years had been filled with trauma. Yet, the experiences only seemed to make her stronger. She hoped this one would not leave any serious emotional scars.

Christina was waiting just inside the door of the school, the principal at her side. Seeing Kate pull up, she pushed open the front door and raced to the car. "He said they let Melvin go!" Christina wailed, out of breath.

"I heard. The judge told them they needed more evidence."

"How much more do they *need*?"

"I don't know. I thought your statement and the mark on his eye was plenty."

Christina was becoming riled. "Why don't they go in his house and look?"

"Well, honey, they need a search warrant, and the judge wouldn't give them one."

"That's not fair," she groused, the injustice thick in her voice. "He's just going to hurt someone else. And Dad's going to go crazy when he gets back. He might kill Melvin."

"Maybe we shouldn't tell him yet. He has a lot to think about right now, anyway."

"Wouldn't that be lying?"

"No, we won't lie. I just think it would be best if we don't say anything until he has a chance to deal with the fact your grandpa's dying."

The girl's face drooped. "I'm going to miss him."

Stacey's number one priority would be to contact Officer Green in Virginia to see if he had come up with anything that might help. Second was to get caught up on the news. The 32" television in the living room had been damaged in the raid, so he picked the smaller one up off the floor of the study and turned it on while making the call.

"Police department, please. Is Officer Green

in?...Thank you." His luck was changing. He flipped through the channels as he waited. "Officer Green, this is Officer Stacey in Mapleton, Utah....I know, my service was giving me trouble....Oh? What did he have to say when you spoke to him?"

Officer Green began to explain that, unable to reach Stacey, he'd called the office. In turn, the secretary had transferred the call to Bingham. Stacey winced, but not from what he'd been told. Instead his full attention was directed at the television. He couldn't believe what he saw. The murder suspect was being released! He turned up the volume to hear what had happened.

Officer Green went on to tell him that the captain had spoken with him at length about the homicide. Then he informed Stacey he couldn't release any more information to him.

Frustrated, Stacey ended the call and turned his attention to the unfolding events of the day. He'd call back later and use a few more persuasive tactics. He changed channels and saw the same story from another viewpoint.

On the other end of the now disconnected line, Officer Green immediately put a call through to the Mapleton Police Department.

Kate and Christina were seated at Barker's desk, reviewing her story. The officer, as was his habit when it came to children, was speaking down to her. "We'd like you to talk to a nice lady doctor. Think you can do that for us?"

Christina tried to cooperate. "Do you mean Dr. Wendy?"

Suddenly Bingham's voice thundered from the next room. "We've got him! He's in his own basement. Let's go! Put on your vests and stay off the radio. He might be monitoring calls." Olsen and Mitch, who were busy filling out reports, jumped up from their desks as if they were puppets on a string and hurriedly put on their vests.

"Move, Barker! No time to waste. He's already killed one of my men, so don't take any chances. Make sure your first shot counts. We have the advantage."

Captain Bingham wrestled with the zipper of his vest. He had succeeded in convincing his officers that Stacey—"armed and dangerous"—would kill again if he had to. He'd also led them to believe that Stacey had used Reid's old car to distribute drugs, and that Deek must have come in on him as he returned from one of his deals. Stacey, he assured them, had stashed the gun and clothing in the vent the day of the search. The fact that Stacey and Sig had attacked him cinched tight the conspiracy. The men knew Stacey was a perfect marksman. Believing Bingham's story, they'd do their best to take him out.

"Sorry, Christina, but this is an emergency. We'll do this another time." Barker slapped on his vest, furiously trying to figure out how to warn his friend of the danger. "We'll each take separate vehicles!" he heard the captain call out.

At home, Stacey finished watching the news and flipped on the computer, one of the few things in the place that hadn't been destroyed by Bingham's search.

Don sidled up to his father's bedside and took him by the hand. The doctor had left the house just minutes earlier. At least for the time being, the old man was holding his own. "Mi hijo." The words fell from the old man's lips as easily as ever. As a boy, Don had refused to learn Spanish, thinking it would make him a little less Hispanic—more like his Anglo friends. Of course, he did understand a few words and phrases, but he'd pushed them back in his memory, and now they lay dormant. And, by experience, he did know that those times when his father used the endearing term *"mi hijo"*—his little son—that a serious discussion was in store.

"Yes, Papa." The fingers of his father's hand lifted ever so slightly. Don moved closer to hear what he wanted to say. It seemed that between the sleeping and the morphine drip there was not much time to talk. When his father's pain was so intense he couldn't tolerate it, he'd give himself another boost of morphine, wait a few seconds for it to kick in, and then fall back into his unconscious state.

"Cerca. Mas cerca. Nearer," he murmured, now gulping in breaths of air.

Don leaned in, his ear almost touching his father's mouth. He struggled to hear—and understand—the words he labored so hard to say. *"Mi hijo...no tienes tiempo....Regresate a la casa...de tu hija. Es peligroso....No uses la fuerza...si no tu mente primero....Vente a Cristo, mi hijo....Vente a Cristo."*

Several seconds passed before Don raised his head. His father had once more closed his eyes in slumber.

The four police cars pulled up three houses down from Stacey's apartment. Each man took down the sawed-off shotgun from the console of his car. Olsen seemed the most nervous. In fact, he was more than scared. More than anything he wanted to do his duty. Being a cop was all he'd ever dreamed of.

Bingham gathered the men close. "The apartment has one entrance." He glanced at Olsen, who'd helped in the first search. The officer nodded in agreement. "Olsen, you and I will go in; Mitch, you watch from the rear." Then, glancing at Barker, and sensing that he'd be the least likely to shoot his friend, he grunted, "Barker, take the front. Go on my signal." The four men took up their assigned posts, three ready to shoot, if necessary.

Meanwhile, in the apartment, Sig sat up at attention, ears erect, head cocked to one side. Stacey continued listening to the television reports and typing up his notes documenting the captain's activities for Barker to follow up on—at least that was his hope. Sig nervously scampered from room to room. Then he returned and nudged Stacey's arm, whining. For the first time Stacey realized something was wrong.

"Ka-wham!" Stacey heard the downstairs door explode off its hinges. He had no time to think. Instinctively, he grabbed at the gun and wad of cash on the table, then darted for the bedroom. The sound of a forced entry resounded from the apartment below. Stacey threw open the window. As he did so, the paper money slipped from his hand. Sig followed as he vaulted out of the window to the asphalt below. His feet stung as he hit.

Stacey craned his neck to see if anyone had witnessed his escape. Over the fence out front stood Barker, a shotgun in his hands. *The double crosser!* he muttered to himself. The squad cars were parked down the street. Stacey opened his fist. There among the scattered quarters lay the key to Bingham's Pontiac. Cautiously he tiptoed around the hedge and into the yard next door, Sig silently at his heels. Across the back yard they crept, then slithered over the fence. Having acted quickly, he'd managed to avoid being caught.

Off in the distance he heard Olsen shout, "He's not here!"

Through the neighboring yard they moved. When they finally reached the third house, Stacey sprinted down the driveway, straight for the captain's car, Sig close behind.

Crouching in back of the car, Stacey finally exhaled. Had Barker seen them? No one was in sight. Inching his way up to the door, he inserted the key. Turning it, the door's button popped up and he motioned Sig to join him in the front seat. The engine came to life with a roar and the car lurched from the curb.

"Captain, he's got your car!" Olsen yelled.

Stacey glanced back to see Olsen leaning outside the open window with radio in hand. Bingham, still standing upstairs near the computer, simultaneously raised his weapon and fired, sending debris flying in all directions.

Kate, at Christina's insistence, dropped her back at school. "I'll be here to pick you up after class."

"It's okay. I'll walk home with Mrs. Kelly"—the mother who was assigned the security group from the neighborhood.

"I don't know, dear. I'd feel better if you came home with me." She'd never say it out loud, but the thought kept occurring to her: What if Melvin decided to get rid of the key witness?

"It's fine, Aunt Kate. I'll have to do it sooner or later."

"Okay, then. You make sure you stay close to Mrs. Kelly."

Maria looked on as Don rose from his chair and left the room, despair evident on his face. She wondered what her father had said to him. She followed him to the kitchen. "What did he say to you?"

"I don't know. It was all in Spanish....Something about my daughter being in danger ...and about Christ..." He repeated the words back to her.

She had avoided the language as much as Don. "Sorry, can't help you."

Melvin was experiencing problems with one of his remote digital surveillance cameras. "I can't pinpoint what's wrong," he murmured, eyeing the front window to see if any reporters still lingered. The last thing he wanted to do was make repairs. Seeing no one in sight, he shut down the system, got in his car, and drove away.

School out, Christina pulled Amber and Ashley aside. With Melvin out of jail for lack of evidence, her plan was simple: "We need to help get the evidence they need to put him back in jail," she explained.

"Are you crazy?" Ashley was the first to say. "I wouldn't go near him again for a trillion bucks."

"Listen," Christina said firmly, "do you think he would've come after you if all three of us had been together that night?"

"No."

"So one thing we know is that Melvin's a coward. A peeping tom and a weaseling little worm of a coward." Christina was adamant. This was a side of her the other two had never seen. As a small child she'd learned to shut her emotions off in order to protect herself from the things her mother did to her dad. Now they'd stirred in her like the call of the wild to a caged wolf. Surely the Rodriguez blood flowed in her veins.

Ashley let out a throaty laugh. "You're nuts. I think you'd better talk to Doctor Wendy."

Seeing how reluctant her friends were to get involved, Christina's wits momentarily returned. "You're right. I guess it's a job for the police."

Ashley and Amber headed off to catch up with the group starting off down the street. "Come on," Amber called.

Christina hesitated. "My aunt's coming to pick me up," she lied.

Captain Bingham stood in front of a smoking computer, his radio in hand. "Olsen, take pursuit. We'll follow and chase by radio."

Barker bolted through the door from his position out front. "You shot the computer!" he yelled.

Bingham slapped at the air and gritted his teeth. "It was an accident, dammit!" Then, grabbing Barker by the arm, he growled, "I'll go with *you*!"

Olsen's voice crackled over the radio. "He's headed south on thirteen hundred toward the river."

The captain pondered the best course to take. A high-speed chase was not the best move, especially when the one being chased had a radio and the newest police car on the force. Stacey, at this point, actually didn't pose a serious threat, since he no longer had access to his computer and notes, nor his hand-held radio. In fact, the note pad Stacey had worked so hard on was now safely in his own pocket. "Olsen, change of plans. Back off. We'll get him another way." Then he punched the button on his radio. "Stacey," he jeered, "you're a dead cop—unless you turn yourself in."

"Captain, I think I'll do that, "Stacey's voice boomed out over the radio. "Meet me at the bridge across the river on Columbia Lane. I'll be there in fifteen minutes."

Bingham, wide-eyed, looked at Barker; Barker stared back. Neither could believe what they were hearing. "Watch for your car," Stacey added, mimicking the captain's tone, "and please don't shoot me. I'll be unarmed."

What was going on? Bingham's mind grappled for an answer. "Head for the river," he ordered Barker. Olsen and Mitch did the same.

Christina walked the five blocks from school to the

apartment. From down the street she could see that Melvin's car wasn't there. She crossed the street and walked by on the opposite side, then crossed back over to the house next door. From there she turned and made cautiously toward the gate. No one saw her enter.

Inside the yard, she unlocked the door, and walked into the apartment. Opening the door that led to the stairs above, she began her ascent. She remembered how anxious Melvin had been to stop Danny and her from climbing the stairs. What was up there he didn't want them to see? And would his door be locked? She'd just have to find out.

The stairs creaked with age. Several times she paused to find a better spot to take her next step—and to listen. It still appeared no one was home. Finally at the top stair, she reached for the door knob and turned. The door opened.

Melvin was on his way back home when he spied the three police cars parked just off the river bridge. He wasn't eager to drive past them, but decided the seven-block detour was a less desirable alternative. His surveillance target would probably return within the hour and he didn't want to cut it too close. The reporters in his front yard had been distracting.

As he crossed the bridge, all four officers stared—but not at him. Their attention was directed on something floating in their direction, several hundred yards up the swollen river.

As they waited for Stacey to show, Barker had been the first to notice the object. At first he dismissed it as a log, but as it drew closer, he recognized it as an automobile. A car, in the middle of the river! It seemed to pitch and bob with the flow of water. Every so often, as one of its tires grazed a rock on the bottom, it would spin wildly.

Looking on in disbelief, Bingham regurgitated a string of profanities, ending with, "That's my car!...He dumped my car in the river!"

As the car rocked to and fro with the current, the officers noticed that the white roof was streaked with brown. Olsen squinted to get a better look. "There's something written on it....you're going down!" he read, the bold letters scrawled in mud.

All four men, their mouths agape, stood near the railing as the car, pointed downstream, drifted under the bridge and struck one of its main beams, sending vibrations up through its steel structure. The sudden stop sent the rushing water up over the back window, over the roof, and into the air like a waterfall. In seconds, the entire car lay at the bottom, its buoyancy lost to the heavy load of water.

The four men stood, rooted to the concrete. Bingham finally regained his voice. "I'd put a bullet between his eyes right now, if I could," he mumbled.

The most complex piece of computer equipment Christina had ever seen sat amongst a clutter of disks, electronic equipment, wires and components. The largest computer was connected to a TV monitor, and they were each connected into other computers, forming a vast network. *Danny can help figure this out*, she thought. Then she heard a car pull into the driveway. "Melvin!" The awe she had experienced seconds ago now turned to fear.

Glancing around the room, she realized it would be impossible for her to get around the wall, through the kitchen and down into the stairwell before he entered the back door. The car door slammed shut. She heard footsteps coming up the rear stairway and the screen door creak open. She feverishly looked for a place to hide. Too late—someone was tramping across the kitchen floor.

The officers headed to their cars. The long lock of hair Bingham always combed forward in swirls to try to hide his balding head now hung sideways over his ear onto the collar of his sweat-soaked shirt. Barker, a line of perspiration running down his back, struggled to keep himself from smiling. *I've got to hand it to you, Stace,* he mused. *If you're going to be on the wrong side of the law, you might as well have some fun while you're doing it.* Neither Mitch nor Olsen, tired and hot, found any of it one bit amusing.

Upriver, hidden in a clump of trees, sat Stacey with Sig at his side. His tactic had gone over better than he'd hoped. "The force of the currents was with me," he reveled in his best Yoda impression.

By pulling such a stunt, Stacey was counting on unnerving Bingham just enough that he might do something stupid. Yet he was still far from gathering the evidence against the captain he needed. Leaving his notes behind had been a devastating blow. He hoped one of the other officers might have found the notebook before the captain did.

Melvin rifled through the shelves, searching for the parts he needed. Christina, jammed back against the wall underneath the computer table, her head bowed to the floor, was sure he could hear her heart pounding. The only thing between her and Melvin were the five casters on the bottom of his chair.

Melvin muttered something under his breath. It was taking much too long to find the component he was looking for. Feeling the pinch of time, he decided to check the site before he left. He pattered into the room, reached over the chair and turned on the computer. Christina thought she would die.

The chair rolled out and Melvin sat down, his legs and feet turned sideways to the desk. The machine whirred. Several beeps and clicks later, Melvin began to type. Shifting his weight, he scooted partway under the desk. Christina could feel his feet only six inches from her head. On he typed.

All at once voices started coming from the computer. It sounded like a movie—only more like people talking back and forth in a doctor's office. More typing. The sound changed. Now it was the voice of a man, talking on the phone. Melvin scooted forward again. This time the toe of his shoe grazed her arm. She closed her eyes, held her breath, and prayed.

Then Melvin pivoted his chair back and to the side, and he pronounced the words Christina most feared hearing. Even with her eyes squeezed shut, she could see her life passing before her. Yet, strangely, the tone of his voice was gentle, almost fatherly. "Come on out. It's okay."

Bingham dispatched a city tow truck to drag his car—or what was left of it—out of the churning river, doing his best to stay out of sight—and out of reach—of the reporters with their camera crews. The small-town tumult had attracted the interest of the national press. Bingham couldn't risk having his face plastered on every television set in the country.

But soon it would all be over. He'd be out of the miserable little town, out from under its petty little problems, back to the action-packed, conflict-ridden world he relished. Over the past years he'd grown anxious and unsettled. Now he thirsted for the bustle, the commotion, the thrill that his former life offered. All that was left was to see that this final enemy was exterminated. Stacey seemed to stir the roaming desire and hatred for which his soul longed.

Christina waited—but nothing happened. Forcing her eyes open, she saw a big orange cat slink out from the side of the desk and rub up against Melvin's leg. "Good Tilly," he cackled, gliding his hand down her back. All the while, the cat kept a close eye on Christina, still cowering under the desk. Melvin bent to stroke the cat under its chin. Christina could see his swollen eye as he picked up the animal and placed it on his lap. Then he went back to stroking the plastic keys of the computer. Again Christina could hear voices. They seemed faintly familiar.

Suddenly the cat jumped up and hissed, its claws digging into Melvin's legs. "Get out of here!" he screamed, standing and sweeping the creature away. The cat scurried to safety in another part of the house.

Melvin resumed his work on the keyboard. Then, several moments later, he shut the equipment down. The minute or two he remained at the desk, jotting something down on a notepad, seemed to Christina like an eternity. A prayer repeated itself over and over in her mind. "Please, God, if I get home safe, I'll never do anything bad for the rest of my life."

At last Melvin pushed away from the desk, stood and walked through the kitchen and barged out the door. Christina listened as his car started and pulled out of the drive. She waited, too scared to move, hoping he wouldn't change his mind and return.

TWENTY-SIX

KATE CONTINUED WIPING the granite counter top as she picked up the phone. "Hi, Cecily," she said, without missing a swipe. "No, I expect her any minute...I know, the poor thing...Sorry, we've been gone all day."

She put down her sponge and went out to the front door. Christina's school group was past the house and halfway in front of the next. She pressed the phone to her side. "Mrs. Kelly," she called, "did Christina come home with you?"

"No, the girls said she was waiting for you to pick her up." The same panicked expression suddenly fell over both women's faces. Mrs. Kelly rushed to the porch.

Kate craned her neck, peering up and down the street. "She told me she wanted to walk home. I wonder where she'd have gone."

"I'll stay here while you go see if she's waiting at the school," Mrs. Kelly suggested, trying to remain calm.

Kate quickly explained the problem to Cecily, who, before running to her Jeep, shouted, "I'll drive past the apartment and meet you at the school."

Danny was just skateboarding around the corner as his mother rolled through the stop sign. "Where are you going?" he hollered, grabbing hold of the door handle.

"To look for Christina!"

"I'll go with you!" He hung on, skating alongside the vehicle. Kate, startled by his action, impulsively slammed on the brakes. Unprepared for the sudden stop, Danny flew forward and hit the mirror. "Uhhh!" the blow knocked him off his board. But, being a teenager, Danny jumped right up, seemingly unfazed, picked up his board, tossed it in back of the car, and climbed aboard.

"Are you all right?"

"Fine. Where is she?"

"I don't know, she was supposed to come home with the other kids."

Christina crawled out from her hiding place. *I've gotta show this stuff to Danny*, she thought as she flew down the stairs to the apartment below and ran outside, locking the door behind her.

Soon she was skipping down the street, trying to figure out why she felt so good and so bad at the same time. She remembered Jake yammering on and on about the rush he felt rappelling from atop the tree house. Detective work gave her the same sort of rush, she decided. She'd looked Melvin in the eye—so to speak—and lived to tell about it. She'd beat him twice, in fact.

Then, as she reviewed the events of the past hour, something occurred to her: "His eyes..." she whispered to herself, "they weren't so cold and hollow." And the door in the tree house—it'd fallen and hit him on the head....Yet she'd seen no bumps or cuts. Maybe it wasn't Melvin! "I need to talk with Dr. Wendy," she said between breaths.

Stacey considered the predicament he was in. No food, no home, no money, no radio or computer, no car—and no friends. *How could Barker double cross me?* he asked himself. If he hurried to the Merc, he might beat Barker to it. He was only a few hundred yards from where he'd parked it.

He knew Bingham had to be fuming. And if the big guy acted out of spite rather than sound judgment, he could be had.

The trees provided cover as he and Sig trudged along. When he approached the parking lot, he crouched down and peered cautiously through the trees. His car was exactly where he'd left it. "Sit," he commanded, then calmly walked over to it. *So far, so good.* He opened the trunk and removed the spare. From behind it he took the plastic container and the captain's gun. If Barker crossed him, the car wasn't safe. He returned to the cover of the trees, breathing a bit easier. At the next bridge he ducked under its girders to wait until nightfall.

Kate spun around the corner in the direction of Melvin's apartment—where she met up with Christina, walking alone. "You scared us half to death! Where've you been?"

"I decided to walk home past our apartment. I needed to prove to myself I wouldn't be afraid the rest of my life."

Later, after suffering through one of Kate's "talks," helping with the supper dishes and an hour of homework, Christina coaxed Danny to his bedroom. Promising he wouldn't tell a soul, she shared with him where she'd gone, recounting the entire frightening experience. She wasn't sure he believed her— until she described the computer. He'd read in magazines about such equipment.

She also explained how the police couldn't get a warrant to search Melvin's apartment for evidence, and without evidence they couldn't put him in jail, adding, "We live there, so we don't need a warrant."

Before long, she'd sold Danny on her plan. He was a bit apprehensive, but looked forward to seeing this awesome computer network for himself. "It's settled then," said Christina, her promise to God forgotten. "We'll start tomorrow. We'll tell your mom and dad we're going to the tree house."

The second bridge was much older than the one that led onto Columbia Lane. It also rested higher off the water. Stacey had wedged himself up into one of several large cavities between the tall metal trusses. It was cramped and the roar of water was almost deafening, but there just weren't that many safe hiding places around.

Sig bristled at the contents of the container his master carried. Stacey removed the plastic bag from the container, dropped the empty dish into the river, and tucked the bag under his arm. The smell of wet concrete and rusty steel was soon forgotten as the ice cold water sent a wet chill through the air. Stacey, dressed only in jeans, a shirt and the thin jacket, sat shivering in the cold, over his head in trouble, perched above a literal stream of troubled waters.

Maria roused Don from his nap. His father was awake and wanted to speak to him again. "You must return...and keep...*tu hija* alive," the old man told him between slow, labored breaths. The effects of the drugs made it hard for him to focus. He seemed to slip in and out of consciousness. "She's still...in much danger. I can go in peace...if you will promise me...to do as I tell you."

Don strained to understand the words, some in Spanish, some in broken English. He managed to drag enough Spanish from memory to determine what his father had said. "Promise me," his father repeated. He opened his eyes and gazed into Don's face, pleading. For a brief moment Don saw behind those eyes the strong, dynamic man he once knew.

"I promise, Papa."

"Now...you must return home. There's no...time to spare." And then he repeated, word for word, the warning, all in Spanish, that he'd given before. Then again he closed his eyes. Don contemplated what his father had said. He was reluctant to leave. His dad was probably just delusional. But it was true: Christina had been in serious trouble only the night before.

After pondering the situation and discussing the matter with his sisters, Don decided he'd do as his father wished. As he went to bid his last goodbye, his father jolted awake once more. "You must go....My spirit...goes with you," he intoned. Then he drifted back to sleep. Reluctantly, Don made a call to the bus station. Maria would take him first thing in the morning.

Stacey's parents anxiously watched the news reporter rattle off the day's events. For the third day in a row, the vicious cop-killing, drug-stealing officer had slipped through the hands of the law! A clip of the captain's car sticking up out of a torrent of water was the backdrop for the newsman's fretful report. Amber, lying on the floor, offered comfort. "Mom, don't worry. He's smart. And we know he didn't do it. He wouldn't. He couldn't. He was safe this morning—" She immediately clapped her hand over her mouth, horrified. She had betrayed her brother's confidence.

"What do you mean, dear?"

"I promised I wouldn't tell."

"Tell what?"

Her father joined in. "Amber, if you know something, you have to tell us."

"Rick...he was here last night. I saw him leave this morning," she confessed. "He told me a man was trying to put the blame on him for things he didn't do. He said he was going to find enough evidence to put him away."

"Where did he say he was going?" her father asked.

"He wouldn't tell me."

Her father began to pace the floor. He had many friends at the county and state level. If he made the wrong call, he could do a great deal of damage; on the other hand, if he made the right call, he might be able to help. "Thank you, Amber. Now it's time to get to bed."

Amber sobbed into her pillow, her mother seated on the side of the bed, consoling her. In the family room at the opposite side of the house, her father had picked up the phone. The man he judged to be in the best position to help his son was his old friend Jay White. He placed the call.

Feeling like an icicle, Stacey and Sig lurked under the bridge. When night fell, they came out of hiding and made for their destination. In less than half an hour they stood at the back door of the police station. If no new prisoners had been brought in, the place would be deserted. The empty parking lot confirmed his hunch. With his keys to the building, he opened the door and disarmed the alarm. Sig hesitated before entering. Stacey assured him it was okay.

With a lock-pick set in hand and a small flashlight from Barker's drawer, he went to the captain's office, gently worked the door open and slipped inside. Sig was commanded to stay on alert outside. Stacey went through every drawer and checked every file, scattering them around the office. The captain only kept file copies; Stacey's disturbance wouldn't interfere with any legitimate police work.

For nearly a full hour he searched, turning up nothing of importance. Sig was growing impatient, but stayed at his post. Stacey checked his watch. He'd better get out of there soon. He guessed Grue was on duty, and one of the standard practices of the night officer was to drive past every few hours and check the building.

As he made preparations to leave, Stacey took the captain's mohair coat off the coat rack and put it on. He then proceeded to dump the contents of the bag, which he'd kept tucked safely under his arm, over the entire office. If this didn't give Bingham heartburn, he didn't know what would. Next he took a pencil, drove it into the keyhole of the captain's door and broke it off. A little white-out lettering on the window provided the perfect finishing touch. It read: *Match this fabric to the seat in the captain's car. The same fibers match the clothing found in the vent.* Then, using a piece of tape, he stuck the little cloth piece onto the door.

Finally, he went to his desk, removed the charger and extra battery from its place, and shoved them in the pockets of the coat. Taking the spare dog whistle from his top drawer, he looped the string over his neck. Stacey felt good—his list of assets was growing.

As he started to punch in his alarm code—likely for the last time—Stacey realized he needed a radio. The code already set, he waited for its countdown. When the digital display gave the "all clear" signal, he hurried over to Deek's desk, snatched up the vest hanging from the back of his chair, removed the captain's overcoat and put on the vest. The interior alarm began to sound. Stacey pulled the coat back on over the vest. What he was about to do was risky, but he had nothing to lose.

Exiting the building, the pair slipped behind the garbage dumpster, some 20 yards from the back door.

Bingham lived closer to the station than anyone else, yet he always seemed to be the last one on the scene. Now Stacey was staking his life on it. Quietly they waited.

Grue was first on the scene. He stayed outside the building, much more cautious than Stacey had expected. Stacey could see him through the car window, calling for backup.

It was another ten minutes before Olsen arrived, and Barker pulled up a minute later. Between the three of them, they elected to enter—to Stacey's relief. Mitch arrived after they'd secured the building.

It was odd: Bingham hadn't made his grand entrance. Perhaps he hadn't even been called. Stacey gazed on through the rear glass door as Barker removed the piece of fabric taped to Bingham's office window, then had given instructions to the other officers. Olsen argued, even as the other men nodded their agreement. Olsen slammed a chair against a desk and stomped away before finally giving in, but Stacey could tell the young, gung-ho cop wasn't at all happy.

Stacey watched as Barker took a razor blade from his desk and scraped the white-out from the window. Mitch returned with a damp cloth and wiped off any residue. Barker then picked up the phone and made a call. Stacey assumed it was to the captain.

He calculated it would take at least seven minutes for the captain to arrive. Commanding Sig to stay, Stacey crept out to the three police cars parked behind the building. Using his razor-sharp pocket knife, he pierced the sidewalls of each of the left-front tires. *The timing must be perfect. I can't put Sig in danger.*

Suddenly Deek's Ford Taurus came squealing around the corner, catching Stacey completely off guard. It was Bingham. He hit the ground, rolled, then froze, ending up in front of one of the squad cars, his legs in plain sight. Air still hissed softly from the flattened tires.

The captain, wary, stopped three car lengths from the entrance and opened the car door. Stacey, the dog whistle between his lips, blew one short blast and one long. Sig leapt from behind the dumpster. In an instant his athletic body had closed the gap between himself and the car's open door. Bingham struggled to wrest himself from the car. From his vantage point, Stacey could see his feet hit the ground.

He gave three short blasts, and Sig started to bark on the run. The sound came from deep within his chest, a deep, savage growl. While the sound was terrifying enough, it proved to be not quite as intimidating as the flashing white teeth showing from under the bared lips. Bingham, the dread in his face registering off the scale, then reached for his .38. Seeing Sig was in danger, Stacey rolled from under the car and went to his aid. But he needn't have worried. Sig instinctively lunged to the side, then bull-rushed his assailant, reflexively biting and twisting the arm with the weapon. The captain lost his footing and fell to the pavement. Stacey drew his weapon and charged forward, the muzzle of the gun pointed directly between Bingham's eyes. "Off, Sig!" Immediately the dog obeyed.

Stacey put his finger to his lips—"Shhh." After disarming the captain and jerking the radio from his belt, he glanced in the direction of the station's massive double doors. All was quiet. Apparently none of the other officers had heard the commotion. Then he turned his attention to Bingham. "I think I'll deposit your brains here in the parking lot and mingle them with the blood of my friend Kiser Derickson," he snarled, "the man you murdered just after returning from your fling with the blonde in the blue dress." He drew back the hammer on his revolver. "But first tell me what else you're up to."

Bingham sat in a puddle of urine. By the smell, Stacey figured he'd also lost control over his bowels. Bingham looked for some means of escape. There was no fear of Stacey, or his gun; he'd been in tighter spots before. It was the dog—the damn dog!

Gathering his wits about him, Bingham boldly told Stacey where he could shove his gun, and warned that he'd better kill him right then, because if he didn't, he was a dead man. Until one of them was in the grave, in all the earth there wouldn't be a safe enough place to hide.

Just then, Olsen stepped out the back door, looking for Bingham. Stacey thought about killing his adversary, then and there. It would be so easy. But then he'd miss out seeing Bingham go to jail. "Works for me," he said, lowering the gun.

Then a shot rang out. Stacey careened backward, and dropped his revolver in the captain's smelly lap. Groaning with pain, he crawled across Bingham's prone body to get to the car. As he pulled himself up behind the wheel and put the car in gear, two bullets penetrated the rear door. Olsen continued firing at the fleeing auto, one bullet shattering the rear window.

Bingham rolled over and, partially regaining his senses, raised the gun and fired off three more rounds at the fleeing car. The empty revolver clicked five more times before he realized no ammunition remained. Barker, Grue, and Mitch crashed out the rear door at the same time that Mr. Jay White, County Prosecutor, pulled up to the building. They saw the captain struggle to his feet, his foul mouth letting loose. Grue jumped in his car and started from the parking lot. He only got as far as the walk—his front tire was riding on its rim.

Mr. White placed a call from inside his automobile. Bingham released another string of vulgarities as a precursor to ordering them to make chase. Barker and Mitch stood looking down at the pitiful wreck of a man, not knowing what to do. Mr. White put down his phone and cautiously stepped from the car. Barker stepped forward to greet him.

"Give me your weapon, and the keys to your car," demanded Bingham, holding out his hand to Barker.

White shook his head, silently overriding the captain's direct order. "Let's go in and talk."

Stacey struggled to breathe, the pain warming his face. He wiped the tiny beads of sweat that had built up on his forehead, as if gathering steam for the night to come. The bullet certainly had brought his momentum to a slow crawl. Deek's vest had saved his life. When the bullet hit the vest, it had been deflected downward and to the side so that it had entered his body in the region below the armpit, though with much less force. Still, it had carried a whale of a punch. He knew of vest-wearers who'd been knocked unconscious. Thank goodness that hadn't happened. The captain would have retrieved the gun and ended it all right then.

Part of him wanted to laugh. The last picture in his memory was of the captain squinching his nose and cheeks, his face wrinkled up like a prune. The sound of the gun shot had surprised them both.

Stacey couldn't afford to take Bingham's threat lightly. He outweighed Stacey by 60-plus pounds, but Stacey's youth was on his side. The captain had been angry and careless; by contrast, Stacey had been calm and willing to fight for what was right.

Stacey maneuvered the car to the home of his friend and former mentor. A single light was on in the master bedroom when he knocked on the window. Dianne peeked out. Seeing Stacey's face, Sig at his side, she immediately slid aside the pane of glass. "Rick, what are you doing here?" As she spoke, her eyes darted randomly into the darkness. He could see she'd been crying. She looked older without her makeup; her puffy eyes and red nose made his heart ache.

"I want you to know I didn't shoot Deek," he whispered.

"I never, ever believed you did," she said between sniffles. "Deek told me about the things you two were working on. I've been at a loss as to how to help you."

"Hey, you've had enough to do." Stacey struggled with shortness of breath and dizziness, and he winced with pain as he spoke. "I don't think I can come to the funeral. I wanted to tell you how sorry I am."

"What's wrong? Are you hurt?"

"I took a bullet in the side. Olsen thought I was going to kill the captain. Luckily I was wearing Deek's vest."

At mention of the name, each gave the other an awkward glance. Neither said a word. They didn't need to.

Dianne broke the momentary trance. "You'd better come in." Then she pushed the window shut. By the time he reached the back door, she, in her bathrobe, was waiting to meet him.

Dianne had worked as a nurse before their first baby had been born almost 19 years before. She insisted he remove his coat, vest and shirt to get a closer look at the wound. "It's not my coat," Stacey said between breaths, pulling it off. "It's Captain Bingham's."

The irony of it all caused the corners of her lips to perk up ever so slightly. Struggling in pain to remove his shirt, she reached up and lifted it to reveal a hand-size bruise. Light-colored in the middle, dark rings of varying shades spread out more than six inches, forming a wavy ring of swelling flesh.

Dianne stifled a gasp. "You need to see a doctor. It might have bruised your heart."

"I don't think it would be a good idea right now. I just scared the crap out of Bingham. He'll have every agency in the state hunting me by now. It's not safe for you if I'm here. I'd better get going."

"Not before I wrap you up," she insisted. Then, tenderly, she said, "You probably have three broken ribs, too." She left the room to get her supplies. Meanwhile, Sig had seized the opportunity to sniff the Derickson's miniature collie. It was sort of a K-9 ritual every time they came to the home. Actually, he seemed more interested in the smaller dog's food dish than he did the dog itself. Dianne returned with several ace bandages and a prescription bottle. "Sig looks hungry."

"He hasn't eaten since this morning."

"You're probably both starving. Go ahead and let him eat. I'm sure Max won't mind." Stace gave the proper command and Sig, in just seconds, had licked the dish clean.

Dianne took a roll of gauze and tightly wrapped Stacey's chest. "Now, here are some pain killers. You're going to need them. I've had them around since Austin was born." She tucked them in the captain's coat as Stacey struggled to put the vest back on. Before he left, she placed a quart of orange juice and a plastic bag full of leftover pizza in another of the roomy pockets. Finally, she stepped into the living room and took a handmade afghan from the back of the worn out couch.

"Can I leave Deek's old Taurus in the garage a few days?" he asked. "I took it from the captain."

"No one will even notice it's there. Here, this'll keep you warm." She handed him the blanket. She declined to ask what he was going to do or where he was going. She knew better—as did he.

As he headed out the door, she reached out and patted his arm. "Our prayers are with you."

"Thanks. I know." Somehow she would make it without Deek. He knew she would.

TWENTY-SEVEN

B INGHAM WADDLED INSIDE to his office. He was furious at the sight.

Olsen, after fixing the flat tire, then had the dubious pleasure of driving the captain home, but not before he found a full-size garbage bag to cover the passenger seat. He'd had drunks wretch in his car, but that didn't smell nearly as bad as the captain did now.

Inside the interview room, Mr. White sat across the desk from Lieutenant Barker. "Officer Stacey's in a lot of trouble, you know?" White said.

"He's only trying to antagonize the captain."

"Well he's doing a fine job, I'd say." White fought to maintain a straight face at the thought of Bingham, a full load in his pants, sashaying around the office, trying to act dignified. "What else can you tell me?"

"He shot Stacey's computer with a shotgun this afternoon. Said it was an accident."

"Have you tried to figure out what was on it yet?"

"No, he wouldn't consider it. I think he might have missed the hard drive, though."

"Any idea of how we can reach Officer Stacey?"

"I don't have a clue. He thinks I stabbed him in the back. I don't know how Bingham knew where he was."

White's knuckles softly rapped the side of the desk. "I spoke to his father just before you called. Apparently he spent last night *there*. We've got to find him and bring him in."

Barker shook his head. "Even if I could reach him, I doubt he'd come. He doesn't know who to trust anymore."

White brusquely leaned forward and put his face up to Barker's, as if he were about to reveal some profound secret. His countenance darkened noticeably. "I'm going to take Bingham off active duty pending an investigation. You're the acting captain. You put Olsen on administrative duty until we investigate his actions. I'll assign five county deputies to your city; we'll get to the bottom of this. The county investigator will also be assigned to your projects until we hang that slippery Briggs. If Bingham is dirty, you need to get me the evidence to prove it." He stood to leave, then added, "By the way, I can keep Bingham out at most three or four days."

Barker nodded. "Stacey gave me enough to get a good start. I just hope the captain didn't cover all his tracks."

"Lieutenant Barker, if you ever tamper with evidence again and I find out about it," he groused, referring to the writing Barker had scraped off the captain's office window, "I'll personally see you convicted for it."

"Yes, sir," he said apologetically.

The two men left the room. Bingham was just returning from getting cleaned up. White approached him with the news. "Captain, I'm relieving you of active duty. I'm worried about your safety. It would appear that your Officer Stacey has a vendetta against you. You can't seem to stop him, and your force is practically immobilized because of him."

Bingham turned defiant. "You don't have the authority for such an action. I was hired by the city, and I intend to fulfill my responsibilities."

"You'd better get your information in order, captain," the prosecutor said in return. "My office can override your jurisdiction any time I feel it's necessary."

Several of the county deputies White had called in were waiting in the office. Taking exception to Bingham's tirade, they sidled up closer to White in a semi-protective posture. Bingham still wasn't ready to give up his position of authority. He'd taken Stacey's attack personally. Every other item on his agenda would go on hold until that punk was dead. No one had ever caused him such embarrassment, fear, humiliation. He drew closer in an attempt to use his stature and raw demeanor to intimidate the soft-bellied attorney. "I'll leave when you've got a court order," he scoffed, advancing on White. Two of the sheriffs moved between them.

In a well-practiced move, White lowered his chin and stuck his nose no more than an inch from Bingham's. "Captain, you can take a few days off *with* pay and enjoy your time at home, or you can spend a few days *without* pay in the county lock-up. It's up to you. But as of now, Barker's the acting captain. Now, I'll take your badge and keys." He held out his hand.

Bingham knew he couldn't win such a power play, but neither could he do-in Stacey from inside a jail cell. He relinquished his badge and office keys, then stomped out the door. The tires of his Lexus screeched on the pavement as he drove away. "How does a small-town police captain afford a fancy car like that?" White asked.

Stacey found it hard to breathe. Just walking seemed like more work than his daily three-mile run. He picked his way through the newly-planted corn fields, heading directly west, crossed the interstate and into the next field. The pain was almost unbearable; climbing fences, nearly impossible. What once was only a leap and a bound had become a painful, deliberate process.

Finally he took a pill from the bottle Dianne had given him and brought the orange juice out from the pocket of the coat. The capsule seemed to lodge in his throat and stick before he chugged down a swallow of the warm liquid.

Standing at the edge of a willow thicket, he glanced at his watch–two thirty-five. He found a secluded spot and did his best to make himself comfortable. He soon fell asleep. The pills were well on the way to keeping the pain at bay. Sig curled up at his side and sniffed at the air, which carried the fragrant blend of pizza, cow and deer dung, and everything else the great outdoors has to offer.

Bingham slouched in the privacy of a phone booth, the receiver to his ear. "Looks like I might need some help....I know. But I'm not leaving until I take care of some personal business. I don't care!" he snapped, before erupting into a barrage of obscenities. "This time he's messed with the wrong man! I need every resource we have to find him. I'll take care of the rest." He slammed the receiver down and elbowed his way out of the booth.

Melvin hung up, made his digital log and once again picked up the phone. "He's in trouble. He's demanding help. Send me some extra people....I know it's not in the budget, but send them—unless you want this thing to blow up in our faces."

Don arose early to catch the seven-fifteen bus. The old man didn't stir when, one last time, he kissed him goodbye. Already he'd lingered on two days longer than the doctors had thought possible. They hadn't given him food for several days. It only seemed to make it to his abdomen, from where they had to pump it back out.

Riding the bus through the day, he decided, was a boring way to travel. To take his mind off the monotony of the trip, he sat back to ponder the words of his father. They all came back to him, but none of it made sense. Something about Christ....

He'd have to make the trip back to Boise soon. His father had requested a *natural* burial, which meant that his body needed to be entombed within 24 hours after death. Don had never heard of such a thing. According to Pauline, the law dictates that if embalming is not performed, the burial has to occur within a one-day period. At least that was how she explained it.

Don gazed out over the desolate highway south of town. He was feeling a strange, inner peace about the impending loss, though he didn't understand why. Maybe what his father had told him had spoken peace to his subconscious. Or maybe he was finally coming to grips with the inevitable. Either way, having seen his father in such a deteriorated state now made him wish for the sweet peace death would bring.

Sig's persistent barking—not to mention his dogged

attempts to back down a big brown bull that was seeking shelter from the flies—finally roused Stacey from his drug-induced sleep. He was so stiff he wasn't sure he could sit up to find his pills. Food was the last thing on his mind. His head was spinning. Slowly and painfully he removed the coat and vest from his upper body. He took another pill from the container, then read the label: Codeine. They contained codeine! He was allergic to the painkiller. As a kid, it'd made him sick for days. With even the smallest dose he would be bedridden and willing to die rather than endure the overwhelming nausea it caused.

Sig continued to chase and bark, running circles around the angry bull, too slow and fat to even get close. Stacey, looking on, could only see a blur of objects going round and round. He laid back down and looked up. Even the trees were spinning in circles. He closed his eyes; it was no use. Endeavoring to sit up again, he crab-walked back a few feet to lean against a tree. What he would give to be in his mother's home under her vigilant care! This was going to be a very long day.

Barker was operating on three hours' sleep. His new force was ready to accept their assignments. He sent one deputy to a computer specialist with the annihilated computer tower. Another drove to Levan to obtain information from the motel clerk. And still another was ordered to bring in Howard and Mrs. Reid. With the charges filed against Stacey, old man Howard had been released. Barker guessed he and his wife wouldn't be very helpful this late in the game.

Chief Anderson reported to the station to see if he could be of assistance, willing to help pick up the slack. Actually, the city council had been considering doing away with the chief's title for years. The first city Chief of Police also held a seat on the city council, and the tradition had been maintained ever since. Over the years, the council position lost any authority in police affairs, but reported the activities and quality of work done by the force. Anderson was a likeable man. His persuasive skills were above those of any of the other members of the town council. Hence, Barker put him on the phones.

News reports exaggerated the shooting. The wounded rampaging officer was loose in the valley, they claimed. But Barker wasn't too concerned about catching him. He knew he would be turning himself in before the first of the week. Mr. White, however, in order to maintain public trust, had assigned one of the newly-recruited deputies to try to locate him.

A young man boarded the bus in Burley, Idaho. He wandered down the isle and chose the empty seat next to Don—who wasn't exactly in the mood to chat. "Hi, I'm Eric Roberts," he said, putting out his hand.

"Don Rodriguez."

"Don Rodriguez, habla Español?" The young man spoke with a very good accent. Don shook his head. "Where are you from, Don?" he persisted.

"I'm from America, okay?" he stated tersely. He'd been asked the same question at least a hundred times. Whenever anyone found out he didn't speak the language they assumed by his appearance and surname he *should* speak, they wondered where he was from.

The fellow, a tad chagrined, remained pleasant. "That's not what I meant. I wondered where in America are you from?"

"Sorry, I get the same dumb question all the time."

"I understand."

Don sighed. "Born and raised in American Fork, Utah. How about you?"

"Burley, Idaho. At least I lived there my first 19 years. Then I lived in Argentina for two years. Now I'm attending BYU." Don was well aware for what purpose this 21-year-old kid had gone to Argentina. He'd been a Mormon missionary. And it just so happened that Don didn't feel much like a religious discussion at the moment, and knew that if he got the young man started, he'd be trying to baptize him before they got to Provo.

"Where are you going?" the young man asked, trying to keep up the conversation.

"Home."

"Back to American Fork?"

"No, I live in Mapleton now with my daughter."

"How old's your daughter?"

"Twelve." What *was* this, 20 questions?

"Where are you coming from?" he continued.

"Boise."

"Family?"

"My father..." Don's voice cracked, "...lives there."

"How is he?" the incessant questions continued.

Don wondered who this kid thought he was. He was about to tell him to mind his own business, when the words slipped out. "He's dying...."

An entire hour passed by before Don realized he'd been doing all the talking. He'd told the young man about his father getting him his first job; how his dad had moved here from Argentina when he was a young man; and how, at the age of 18, he'd finally gotten to really know the man. He spoke of how strong his father had been, and of the crushing changes that had befallen him in his illness. The young man listened better than he talked. Before long, Don was petitioning his help in translating the wishes of his father. Don could hardly forget the foreign yet intimately tender words that were so earnestly whispered in his ear.

Christina plodded along with the group on their way to school. Kate was adamant, having made it crystal clear the trouble she'd be in if she didn't "stay with the group."

During first recess she pulled her friends aside to share with them the scary yet exhilarating thrill she'd felt inside Melvin's house. It almost smacked of boasting. Initially, neither Ashley nor Amber accepted her tale as truth. But after showing them the apartment key and describing the computer system Melvin was using, they believed her story.

"I'll bet there's enough data in that room to send him to prison forever," Amber was first to say. Then she had an idea: "We've got to get my brother Rick to come and help us." The others agreed. But how could they contact him? He was out there somewhere, wanted by the police for killing another cop and stealing and dealing drugs–crimes the girls were sure he would never commit.

Amber's eyes lit up as they talked. "Will you both promise not to tell anyone if I tell you a secret?" Both girls nodded. "I mean *promise*," Amber continued. "Cross your heart, hope to die, stick a needle in your eye?" Both girls went through the motions of crossing their hearts and raising their hands in the attitude of taking an oath.

Amber swallowed nervously. "I saw Rick just the other day, right after they accused him of doing all those terrible things. He slept in our room over the garage. No one else but me knew he was there. He told me that a pretty mean guy is out to hurt him; I think it's his boss. I told him that I might have to get hold of him when I dig up something that might help. He didn't think I'd be any help at all, but...."

Just then the bell rang, drowning out her words. "Anyway," she concluded, "we need to figure out a way to send him a signal or something. We'll talk at lunch...."

Things were still reeling out of control–both literally and figuratively—when Stacey awoke. One moment he'd shake and shiver until his teeth chattered, the next he'd be so hot he'd have to strip down to his shirt sleeves. Then the cycle would start all over again. The pain in his side was worse. The bruise, dark and swollen, now stretched all the way from his armpit to his waist, and from the middle of his back around to the center of his chest. Unable to breathe, he'd struggle to loosen the bandages, then try to tighten them when the pain got too intense.

Sig, bounding around the nearby fields, seemingly uncertain as to what to do with himself, would come and inspect him occasionally, but no commands fell from his master's lips. On one of his visits Sig came away with a few bites of pizza, but, crazed by hunger, he soon began to wander farther and farther away, returning less often. Stacey didn't even notice.

Amber sat at her desk, oblivious to the lesson the teacher was giving. She pondered the information about Melvin. "How could she contact Rick?" It would have to be something big enough that everyone knew about, yet insignificant enough that no one would get hurt. Her eyes absently gazed at her teacher—then at the wall behind her. "That's it!" she suddenly realized. She raised her hand high in the air.

"Yes, Amber, do you know the answer?"

Amber hadn't even realized what the question was. "No, I need to go to the restroom," she lied.

"Can't you wait 'til lunch?"

"This won't wait," she said, standing up.

"Hurry back."

Amber, a funny look on her face, scurried from the room. It was less than a minute before the fire alarm went off. Teachers immediately began organizing students and leading them out onto the playground. None of them were expecting a fire drill. The principal, Mr. Cook, didn't go to the field with everyone else. He hurried from one fire-pull to the other to see which one had been tripped. Finding the broken glass near the restroom, he waited to see who might emerge. It took less than a minute before the bathroom door cracked open.

"Come out, young lady." Amber hesitated, then slowly opened the door. "Amber Stacey, what can you tell me about the fire alarm?"

She dropped her head and issued a humble confession. "I did it."

"You wait for me in my office."

Amber walked at a snail's pace toward the principal's office while he went to the playground to call the school back in. "Why would this young girl pull the alarm?" he thought. Christina and Ashley knew.

Growing adept at herding the cattle in the adjoining field and with no particular goal in mind, Sig had rounded up over a hundred head of cattle and was pushing them toward the interstate. Once in a while one would break free, and he'd chase after it and drive it back to the herd.

The work was hard–but exhilarating. Sure, he'd seen the powerful animals on the farm in Fillmore, but he'd never been allowed to chase after them. And Stacey didn't seem to mind. As a matter of fact, Sig was rewarded once with pizza when he returned to "report in."

Soon the herd reached the corner of the field. Sig didn't know enough to realize they were at a stopping point. Fences, after all, never were a barrier to *him*. And so he continued to press, bobbing and weaving, until the tightly packed animals were cornered against the fence. Each time an animal would try to escape, a nip on its heels would head it off, forcing it back into the corner. Before long, the animals on the outside were jostling against the others to keep away from the dog's incessant pestering. Sig was growing more and more proficient at his abilities, but could not seem to move the group.

Finally the combined weight of the spooked herd started snapping the wooden fence posts. Stumbling over and tearing through the barbed wire, the cattle began to spill out onto the highway. On the move once more, the frantic herd headed off down the interstate, the corridor acting like a cattle chute for the stampeding animals. Autos swerved and honked, and the traffic soon came to a near standstill. Part of the herd split and went north, the other part went south. The commotion was more than Sig was expecting. Feeling confident that he'd successfully cleared the field, he pranced back, panting, to the grove where Stacey lay.

"False alarm at Brookside," Chief Anderson announced as he picked up another call, this one sounding more urgent. Seems a herd of cattle was raising havoc on the highway. They'd apparently trampled the fence, one witness claiming that a lone German shepherd had terrorized the herd. At first the chief dismissed the possibility of it being the famous K-9. Stacey wouldn't allow it—unless he was incapacitated or dead. Maybe the bullet did get through, or maybe it was just another trick to upset the captain. Chief Anderson would leave it be, for the time being. Finished answering calls, he slipped out of the station and down the hall to his own office, to make a call in private.

By the time they arrived in Utah, Don's new friend had successfully helped him translate his father's words. In addition to the warning his dad had given him about Christina, Don discovered that he'd promised to no longer fight—that he'd use his intellect instead of his fists to solve his conflicts. But there was more–his father had made him promise to "come to Christ" and "hear him."

He tried to rationalize his way out. *Making a promise to someone when you don't even know what you're saying isn't much of a promise.* He knew his father had returned to religion in his later years. But they'd avoided talking about such things, because Don took no interest in them.

"Sounds like good advice," nodded his young friend. Don turned his eyes to the window, where green fields of winter wheat passed by. He was trying to justify the things his father had said in his delusional state. How could *he* know Christina was in danger?

Amber sat quietly across from Mr. Cook while they waited for her parents. She'd never been in any kind of trouble before. Why now? He'd used every child psychology technique he knew to get her to reveal her thoughts, her motives, or whatever had persuaded her to pull the alarm. She wouldn't budge.

Her parents arrived, her mother still wearing the shoes she usually went walking in. Her father sported a pair of brown dress shoes. "Amber," her mother was the first to speak, "what happened?"

She remained silent.

Her father spoke in a harsher tone. "Amber, your mother asked you a question."

She slowly raised her eyes to see the flustered look on her mother's face. She could no longer contain the emotion. Tears began to flow. "I want to go home," she said between the sobs.

Melvin methodically logged in the data and saved it

to files before picking up his own phone. "We've got a lead on the cop. I need that help right away....Yeah, and see if you can get a tracking dog. He's in a remote forested area. I think it will be dark before it's safe to go in. I'll keep you posted." He hung up the phone.

Lying down didn't stop everything from moving. Stacey felt no better than before. He'd be willing at this point to turn himself in, if he knew he'd be safe. He hadn't even thought to turn on the radio and was unaware of the cattle drive taking place less than a mile away.

By and by, Sig returned to his side; he seemed tired and hot. Occasionally, Stacey would drift into a shallow sleep. He dreamed he called Barker on a secure channel and was picked up and taken to the bedroom of his teenage years. His mother was standing in the room, spooning red Jell-O into his mouth using a giant salad spoon, while Bingham held a knife to her neck and threatened that if Stacey didn't eat it all, he'd slice his mother's throat. Stacey jerked back awake.

The bus pulled up to the Provo station. Eric Roberts prepared to get off. He told Don it had been a pleasure talking with him and hoped he could find peace in the impending passing of his father. A minute later the bus moved on. Twenty minutes later Don was back in Mapleton.

TWENTY-EIGHT

HOWARD AND MRS. REID grudgingly came into the station. They'd talk, but only on one condition: If they'd help convict the person responsible for setting up Howard, the department would help pay for the damages to their house. Barker led them to the interview room to discuss the case. Mr. Weeks, the county investigator, joined them. "You both understand that you're here without counsel?" asked Barker. They both nodded. "I'm recording our conversation, so please speak loudly. Let's begin with your full names."

The Reids nervously leaned forward over the recorder and stated their names.

"We believe some of the evidence used to arrest you was tampered with. We also believe you may have been lying to us in our previous interviews. I would like to interview each of you separately. Mrs. Reid, would you please wait out in the hall?"

With an approving grunt, she complied.

"Mr. Reid—" Barker began.

"I want it on tape," Howard broke in, "that you're gonna pay for our door and window." Staring Barker down, he coolly folded his arms. "Oh, and I also want you to cover the doctor bills on my arm." He lifted up the burly arm like it was a fragile flower.

Barker turned to Weeks. The man nodded in confirmation, whereupon Howard cleared his throat. "I was out of whiskey. I came down here'n cut the lock off to get my two bottles. I was dyin' for a drink, and the old lady didn't have no money. That's all. 'Cept Captain Bingham mighta' seen me walkin' home."

"Where did your wife get the black eye?"

"I don't know, 'les I hit her when I was drunk."

"You don't know where the clothes or the gun came from?"

"Na, I ain't had a gun in 20 years. Pawned it for some cash."

"That's all. Step out, and ask your wife to come in."

The big man stood, lumbered over to the door and gestured for his wife to enter. She stayed out of his way until he was well clear of the door, then came back in and took her seat.

"Mrs. Reid," began Barker, "where did you get the black eye and cut lip the night before we arrested your husband?"

Her eyes shifted back and forth between Barker and Mr. Weeks, her lips drawn into a tight slit across her plump cheeks. "Can't say."

"Why can't you say? Are you afraid of someone?"

"If I talk to you, you talk to them, then they come and see me again."

Mr. Weeks spoke up. "Who are *they*?" Mrs. Reid staunchly shook her head. "You know, we can protect you from whoever it is you're afraid of."

"Don't think so. You can't even catch one of 'em—and the other's got too much power." She watched their faces and suddenly sensed she'd already said too much.

"Are you talking about one of our officers?" Mr. Weeks continued.

"The one with the dog. He's in it with the other one," she muttered, perhaps in the belief that if she gave up Stacey, Bingham would go easy on her.

"We can make sure Officer Stacey, the one with the dog, doesn't find out about our conversation, if you can tell us who the other one is," Barker assured the woman.

Mrs. Reid anxiously glanced from one man's face to the other; she was in over her head. "How do I know I can trust *you*?" she whined.

Barker let out a sigh. "Well, Mrs. Reid, I guess you'll have to decide that on your own." Then, looking over at

Weeks, he added, "I think we represent the law the best we can."

"If I tell, can you promise us protection?"

"We'll protect you the best we can," Barker replied.

Lowering her head and picking at the little fuzzy balls sticking to the surface of her polyester slacks, she barreled ahead. "Captain Bingham's the one that hit me. I was walking home from work...that's when I saw him kneeling down on our back porch. I always go in the back door. I guess I kinda' spooked him or something. He got up and smacked me. Said it was an accident. He was looking for two bottles of whiskey Howard stole out of the car. He made me go in and look for 'em. I found Howard passed out on the couch. Sure 'nuff, he had a couple of bottles that weren't there before I left for work. Howard wanted money before I left, but I didn't have none. I said he'd have to wait 'til morning after I got my check cashed."

"Where did Officer Stacey come in?"

"He came back the next Saturday to make sure I did what the captain said to do."

"What did he say?"

"He wanted to be sure I told about Howard takin' the whiskey."

Barker screwed up his face in thought. "Did he talk about the captain?"

"Said the captain sent him."

The two men finished up and excused the Reids. Then they went to the conference room to discuss what they'd learned. Now Barker was really confused. Why would Stacey say Bingham had sent him unless he was in on something?

"I need to report back to Mr. White," Weeks said. "He'll shuffle through all the facts and know what to do with them."

Don lit out in the direction of Kate's house. In bad need of a shower and a shave, not to mention a change of clothes, and passing just a few blocks away from the apartment, he decided to stop there first. He assumed

Melvin would still be in jail, so he wouldn't have to worry about losing it again. "Castration would be too good for him," Don muttered to himself.

Melvin's car sat in the drive. Don unlocked the basement door and went inside.

Upstairs, Melvin, hearing the sound, made for the inside door and started down the stairway to investigate.

In the meantime, Don had stripped off his shirt and had come out of the bathroom to retrieve a towel, when he heard footsteps on the stairs. He sprang out of sight, crouching directly behind the door. The door opened slowly and Melvin stuck his head through. Don immediately lunged at the door, slamming it on Melvin's neck and pinning his head in the apartment. "Well, what have we here?" Don cooed evenly, as if he'd just caught a rat in a trap.

Melvin struggled for his footing and sputtered to explain what he was doing. Don reached through the opening of the door and, seizing Melvin by the collar, pulled him in and slammed him up against the wall, his feet suspended in midair. Don drew back; Melvin tensed, bracing himself for the blow.

Pausing, his teeth clenched, his adrenaline pumping, Don struggled for self-control. Finally, he lowered his arm. *Use your head before you act,* his dad had said. The warning flashed through his brain. He'd have to deal with Melvin some other way.

Castration, he remembered. Don packed Melvin into the kitchen. "I'm going to castrate you, you little pervert," he growled.

Melvin began to squirm. Don picked him off the ground and slammed him down on the table like a slab of meat. The man didn't utter a sound. He just lay there, belly-up, his eyes wide with terror. Don took out his pocketknife and leaned his body weight down onto Melvin's chest while he opened the blade. The table groaned under the load. "I've never done it before," he snarled, squinting into the horrified man's eyes, "but I saw my friend's dad do it to some sheep once. Didn't look so hard. Made the sheep squirm a little, though." That said, he jammed the blade through Melvin's pants at the knee and slit the fabric to the crotch.

"I didn't hurt her," Melvin mewled.

Don, intent on teaching a most unforgettable lesson, wasn't listening. He raised the blade and drove it down with a thud—right into the table top between Melvin's legs. "Nah, I think I'll wait until next time," he muttered in disgust, dragging the shaken landlord off the table. Melvin, hunched and red-faced, stole a glance at the knife, its handle still wobbling, its blade buried at least a half inch into the tabletop. "Now get out of my apartment," Don warned menacingly, his pointed scowl boring through the landlord's chest. "I still have a year on my contract."

Melvin turned, scuttled for the stairs and scampered up to the safety of his own apartment.

Don felt good. He'd literally scared the pants off the little weasel, all without striking a blow. But why was Melvin out of jail? What had happened while he was in Boise? Don propped a chair under both doorknobs to make sure he'd have no more visitors. Then he took his shower.

Amber slouched in the back seat of the car next to her mother. Her father had applied the silent treatment the whole way home. Now she was convinced that she'd made a terrible mistake.

Arriving home, Amber hurried up the stairs to her bedroom, but her father called her back down to the kitchen. "We need to talk," he said under his breath, attempting to control his temper. Her mother sat down next to her, semi-protectively, while her father sat across the table in a distinct "tell-me-the-truth-or-else" posture. "I want to know what you were thinking, young lady."

Before she knew it, Amber had spilled the whole story. She'd hoped that by pulling the fire alarm she could let her brother know she needed to contact him. Then he'd meet her at midnight in the room over the garage as they'd agreed. At the time, at least, it seemed like the right thing to do.

Afterwards, Amber could hear her father in the other room, speaking quietly on the phone. "Jay, Richard Stacey. I think there might be a way we can talk to him....I know he is. I need your word that you'll come alone to hear his side of it. I'll call you if I can make the arrangements."

A few miles away, Melvin made a log and recorded the phone call. He'd been a busy man.

Seated on the fire hydrant at the edge of the playground, Don waited for the bell to ring. Soon a torrent of noisy children, carrying backpacks and lunch boxes, flooded the schoolyard. One of the mothers Don recognized was organizing children for the walk home. Christina and one of her friends, both chattering intently, joined the group. Don looked on as Christina took something from her pocket and gave it to Ashley.

"You've got to get this to Amber. It's the key to our apartment. And here's the address." She handed over the note and key. "Her brother can hide there until we have enough evidence to put Melvin back in jail." Don paused for them to start from the playground before he stood. Christina saw him. "Hey, Dad!"

He took her in his arms and gave her a squeeze. "Hi, 'Tina. I missed you. I'm so glad you're okay."

"How's Grandpa?"

Don's face turned somber. "I don't expect he'll live through the night. They took all the tubes out but the morphine drip, the one that controls the pain."

"I'm so sorry, Daddy." The two of them walked hand-in-hand down the street, Christina doing her best to bring him up to speed on everything that had transpired the last two days. She told him how scared she was in the woods and how she slid down the rope by herself. They stopped at a bus stop bench to chat.

"Did you know Melvin's out?" Don asked.

"Yeah. I didn't say anything 'cause I was afraid you'd get mad."

"I didn't know until he stuck his head in the apartment about an hour ago." Christina started to panic. She could imagine the scene: Melvin, lying dead on the floor and the police coming to arrest her dad. "Don't worry, I think I figured out how to handle him." He struggled to maintain a straight face as he told her what happened— sparing the offensive details. The two of them laughed as they started off again for the Jensen home.

"Have you really seen it done before?"

"No, but *he* didn't know that."

Now it was Christina who turned serious. "Dad, I need to ask you a favor. And you have to promise not to tell anyone what I'm going to tell you." Don agreed. Christina recounted the story told by Amber, explaining why her friend had pulled the fire alarm and that Officer Stacey probably needed a place to stay. She added that the police didn't have enough evidence to keep Melvin in jail and if Officer Stacey was in their house he could help get all the proof they needed. Don listened, fascinated by his daughter's imagination.

"So, can he come to our place and stay, Daddy?" she pleaded.

Don didn't want to dash her hopes, so he simply said that Officer Stacey was welcome anytime. "Thank you Daddy!"

Don knew better; a cop on the run would never trust his life to three grade-school girls.

Chief Anderson was once again answering phones from Deek's desk. Anderson, an independent businessman, claimed he'd made his fortune in stocks. Rumor had it he'd actually bought the election five years earlier, trouncing the three-term incumbent. With time on his hands, he spent more hours in the city building than all the other council members combined, mostly listening to angry citizens' complaints. He was active in the community and had been instrumental in blocking commercial developers from building a massive waste incinerator on the edge of town. On the heels of that victory, he'd had no trouble winning a second term. Now he even entertained thoughts of running for mayor when the revered Mayor Jenkins retired.

Barker and Weeks sat nearby, discussing the evidence

they'd gathered. Barker's man had finally broken into Stacey's damaged hard drive, recovering invaluable data. "Okay," he began, going over the case one more time, "we've got a clerk who saw a man matching Bingham's description in Levan, and a possible homicide in the precinct where he may have lived. Howard knew Bingham; he'd seen him walking away with the whiskey. The lab confirmed as a match the fabric taped to the captain's window—and we found where it had been cut from the seat in his car. Let's ask for a warrant." Barker picked up the phone.

"With all the other crap going on, you'd better be right," Weeks prodded. "I think we've got plenty, but Demick will hit the roof if we're wrong."

Chief Anderson, eavesdropping, excused himself and went into his office.

Smoke hovered above the tables in the restaurant's smoking section. Bingham puffed on his Camel Light, the fumes billowing from his nostrils giving him the appearance of an angry bull. Across the table two men listened closely to his instructions. "My contact has a shaky lead. He may be hiding where the river dumps into the lake. It's at mile marker 265. I saw him take a bullet last night. He's probably hurting. Even if he was wearing a vest, he'll still be in trouble." Bingham spoke from experience. He took another drag on his cigarette. "I want him alive. I'll take care of the details. And don't mess up my coat—it already has one hole too many in it."

Without a word, the men stood and sauntered out the door. Bingham's mobile phone rang. "I understand. Tonight or in the morning?...Tell her to leave without me. I'll meet her in Barbados next week."

The Department of Transportation workers finished repairing the fence. Not a single cow had been hit—though the entire mile-long section of asphalt was a sticky mess. Cow dung, now flattened and strewn about by the restored flow of slow-moving vehicles, peppered the highway.

The repair crew finished their work and loaded their

tools in the truck. A dark Suburban pulled to a stop nearby. Two men climbed out, eased themselves through the barbed wire fence and traipsed across the field. The cattle, only mildly disturbed, parted to let them pass.

At the opposite end of the field, Stacey repeatedly tried to pull himself to his feet. A swig of warm orange juice made him even more nauseous. His mind reeled; nothing mattered anymore.

Sig trotted over. Stacey rewarded him with the rest of the pizza. Racked with hunger, the shepherd didn't notice the two figures plodding in the direction of where his master lay.

Don shared his story around the supper table, choosing his words carefully so as not to offend anyone. Alan, fully absorbed in the story, laughed hysterically; tears coursed down his face and his body shook uncontrollably. Finally gaining his composure, he explained why he'd found the tale so funny.

It seems he'd grown up around sheep. In the spring, every day he'd go out with his grandfather to dock the newborn lambs' tails—and to castrate the young rams. He was open and free with the terms. As he spoke, Alan occasionally broke into fits of laughter. The picture of Melvin stretched out on a table, squirming like an un-cut ram, did him in. Once more gaining control, he began to formulate new ideas on how to drive Melvin crazy. The family joined in.

Kate took the younger children to bed. She wanted no part of such a scheme.

TWENTY-NINE

THE LAST THING MR. WHITE, the County Prosecutor, was going to do was call Demick back into his office after hours. The warrant would have to wait until morning. "I'll go over his head if he turns me down," he said to Weeks. "From what I'm hearing, we have more than enough evidence. See if you can find a connection between the captain and Briggs. Bingham doesn't meet our perpetrator's profile, but we just might find something."

"Looks like I might be up all night—again!" Barker despaired. "My wife and I have hardly seen each other the past two weeks. She keeps asking if we're still married."

"I'll stay the night if that's what it takes," Weeks offered.

"Why don't you take Stacey's desk and we'll access the National Crime Database." They began the search.

After dinner, Alan suggested Don ought to play a nice friendly—and loud—game of Nintendo. "Didn't Melvin say he couldn't stand noise?" he gushed. Don listened in dismay as Alan concocted a list of wild ideas to drive Melvin out. "We can't do anything illegal, immoral, or dishonest," he cautioned. Suddenly Alan's stuffy shirt was looking more like a football jersey.

As the two men strategized, the children coaxed their father into telling his "train tracks" story. Alan began: "When I was 15, we lived on the west side of Provo. One night I was going to a friend's house and needed to cross the train tracks. A train engine was idling just a few feet off the crossing. Boy, I could feel its big engines rumbling; they literally shook the ground. I stopped my bike. It wasn't moving and the lights were off, so I decided it was safe to cross. I can imagine the engineers watching me. One of them probably poked the other in the ribs and said, "Watch this!" I was halfway across when all at once the big light went on and the horn blasted. I just about died! The engineers were probably rolling around, laughing, as they watched me jump on my ten-speed and tear off.

"A few years later," he continued, "I owned a '61 Ford pickup. I'd found a huge police spotlight in a junkyard and had it mounted on top of the truck so I could hunt jackrabbits. Then I added an air tank and a diesel horn. Well, one night my friend and I backed my truck down a dark railroad crossing—and waited. My best friend's cousin was the first one to come along. He only lived a few blocks away. Just as he started across the tracks in front of us—I think he was driving his dad's Ford Falcon station wagon—we flipped on the light and hit the horn. All we could see of his face were teeth and eyeballs. After he recovered, he asked to join us. And, wouldn't you know it, the next guy to come along was one of my father's friends. He spun around in his old Dodge Dart and chased us all around the county. He couldn't catch us, and finally gave up. I don't know what he planned on doing to us if he'd caught us."

Amid his children's laughter, Alan went back to his scheming. One of his more plausible suggestions was to take the small compressor he kept in the garage to the apartment and blow pressurized air between two strips of plastic to create a horrific sound. Don chuckled, more at Alan himself than the wild pranks he proposed. After all, this was Alan, the dignified executive; Alan, the man who made his kids do everything by the rules—who now was teaching them how to drive someone crazy. He explained that, because of his standing in the community, he couldn't possibly join in the fun—directly. But, if they were careful, he would allow Danny and Jake to spend a few hours helping. He'd pick the children up around ten.

Don, Jake, Danny and Christina eagerly headed out the door. "Don't let anything happen to them," Alan called out as Don toted the small compressor out behind him.

Don grinned back. "Not a chance."

A German shepherd ambled into the opening, gazing out into the darkening shadows. The moon had not yet emerged from behind the peaks of the Wasatch Mountains. Each of the two men took a case hanging from their sides, removed a sophisticated piece of equipment and slipped it on their heads so they could see what Sig was looking at. He'd spotted a beautiful four-point buck, feeding some distance from "his" cattle.

The men waited and watched as the dog cautiously began to stalk the animal. Then they split up, each heading for the spot from which Sig had emerged. The dog alertly crept in and out of the edge of the willows, keeping close track of the animal's movements. The buck would stop, sniff the air and listen, then put its head down to feed again. The wind was in Sig's favor. He'd never seen such an animal before. The river was quieter there at its wide point of entry to the lake.

The men soon closed in on *their* quarry.

A rustle in the brush roused Stacey, who had alternately dozed off and awakened dozens of times that day. This time, however, was different—though he wasn't coherent enough to know why. He *was* aware, though, that Sig was nowhere to be seen.

He managed to pull himself to a standing position. Then he put the whistle between his lips and blew the "come" command. For the moment, his mind had drifted back to reality. He could tell he was dehydrated; his lips were parched. He took the juice from the overcoat and slowly began to drink. Leaning against the tree for balance, he held it down. Sig still hadn't returned. The brush rustled again, and suddenly Stacey was knocked to the ground. The intense pain in his side took his breath away. He could hear his attacker breathing in his ear as he crushed the breath out of him. It definitely was *not* Sig.

"Over here," the man on top of him called out.

A second man bounded from the brush and joined the first. Stacey had no strength to fight. He lay helpless, his face pressed in the dirt, his hands and arms pinned under him. He tried desperately to free one arm so as to reach the weapon in the pocket of his coat. He'd use it, too. These men definitely were not peace officers.

It was then that he heard Sig's deep, throaty growl from just beyond the edge of the trees. Both men heard it too. It took their focus from their captive as they drew their weapons and peered out in the direction of the sound. Sig's growl was joined by another. In seconds, Stacey realized Sig was involved in a full-fledged dog-fight.

One of his assailants leapt to his feet; both expected a vicious animal to come lunging out at them from the brush. The standing man gave instructions to the other to keep Stacey down, then he crept toward the dogs, his weapon drawn. By now the growls had evolved into a series of aggressive attacks.

Stacey, pretending to offer little resistance, inched his arm close enough to withdraw the captain's gun through the coat lining. The man straddling him had become more concerned with the fact that his partner had not yet returned than with keeping Stacey down.

"Frank!" he called. No one answered. "*Frank!*" his voice boomed out again, simultaneously shifting his body weight. Stacey seized the opportunity. Propelling his shoulders up with his left hand, he partially rolled to his back, sending his assailant off balance. As the man toppled to the side, his knee jammed into Stacey's broken ribs. Stacey let out a loud groan as he pulled the trigger. The man jerked sideways, then slumped down on top of him in a limp heap.

Stacey pushed him off, then quickly slipped the night-vision equipment from the man's head and put it on his own. He heard a gunshot in the distance, followed by a brief yelp. The fighting stopped. Stacey was in no condition to take an aggressive stand, so he staggered behind a tree and waited.

Don and the children walked down the steps, unlocked the door and turned on the lights. Jake was the first to fire up the Nintendo. "Dad's gone crazy," he said with a grin, turning up the volume. Danny joined him in a game as Christina went to open the window. It was a party atmosphere.

In less than five minutes Melvin stalked out to his car and drove away. Christina gave Danny the thumbs up sign.

"Uncle Don, you try it," Danny urged, waving the joystick.

"No. I'm not any good at those games..."

"Okay, you practice a few minutes with Jake while I get something to eat. I'll adjust it to an easier level."

"Now, you've got to get at least 255,000 points to beat me..." Jake began to explain. He moved over, making room for Don in front of the TV screen. In a few minutes, after Don was engrossed in the game, Danny and Christina slipped into the kitchen.

"We can't sneak upstairs—they'll see us," she said. "Let's start in the metal building out back." Flashlight in hand, the two of them slipped out the front door and around the side of the house. The small metal shed sat a ways back from the house, mostly obscured from the road. Its walls sat on a row of flat cinder blocks laid at ground level. As they approached the shed, Danny noticed a lock. Already discouraged, he was ready to return to the safety of the apartment.

Christina reached out and tugged at the plastic hasp holding the lock in place. "Danny, the bolts aren't even tight." Then she added, "You're not scared, are you?"

"I'm not scared," was his quick reply. The two of them worked at the bolts and, in less than 30 seconds, the metal door creaked open. They entered and Danny pulled it shut behind them. Christina flashed her light around the small eight by ten foot structure. Tiny rays of light shot from the cracks as the beam catapulted across the walls and floors of the shed. They were standing on a row of concrete blocks. Weeds, the kind that only seem to grow in dark places, grew on each side. But, oddly enough, one side seemed to flourish, while the other side seemed dead. A narrow row of shelves lined each side of the shed, and a half-dozen boxes rested on an old pallet at the back. The name on each box, written in black marker, read "Leah."

"Hmm!" Danny whispered. "I wonder who Leah is?"

Christina took a lid off one of the boxes. Inside were old clothes reminiscent of the fashion of five or six years before. She picked up the first item she saw, a sweater. Dust had settled in through holes cut out at the top of the box, creating thick, round spots on it. "This must have been his daughter's," she said, holding it up against her body. It was almost her size. Danny lifted up a shirt. A button fell off and bounced on the concrete blocks into the weeds.

"Shine the light down here," he whispered, crouching to find where it had gone. Christina shone the light on the floor. "There it is." He reached into the weeds and pulled. It seemed to have attached itself to something. He yanked a little harder. Christina knelt to get a better look. Earth and weeds began to lift as she realized the button Danny was pulling was sewn onto a sweater buried in the dirt. Both children turned and stared at each other. Danny turned loose of the button and jumped to his feet. Christina covered her mouth and held back a scream.

The children bolted out of the shed and slid the door shut. In silence, they crept back into the kitchen and sat down. Danny's knees were weak, banging against each other under the table. His stomach churned. Christina wiped her sweaty palms on her pants as she swallowed hard.

"Don't tell *anyone* until we decide what to do," she finally said. "This could put him away forever. Swear you won't tell." Her cousin nodded without a word. His mind raced, thinking of what—or who— lay just under the soil.

"I won!" Don shouted from the other room. "I finally beat you!"

"Next time I'll lower my handicap," Jake warned. A horn honked in front. It was Alan, there to pick them up.

Danny slowly rose from the table. Christina ran to her room to retrieve her things.

"How did it go?" Alan asked as Jake climbed in the car.

"He left just a few minutes after we started," Jake said triumphantly. "Uncle Don sucks at Bond, though."

Alan flinched at the use of the word. "*What*?"

"Sorry."

Christina started out the door with a small bag of her things. Don was right behind her. "Please come with us," she pleaded. "I don't want you to stay here by yourself. It's not safe."

"Don't worry, 'Tina. I'll be fine. I can take care of myself." He scooted her toward the car.

"Be careful, Daddy. You never know what he might do." She watched him close the door as they drove away, then stole a knowing glance at Danny.

Struggling to stay focused, Stacey hunched up against a tree, expecting the other assailant to return at any moment. The bushes rustled. Then the figure of a dog limped into the small clearing. "Sig," Stacey whispered. Sig raised his head, recognizing his master's voice. Still lying on the ground, the wounded man moaned in pain. His half-conscious stir gave Stacey hope that he wasn't dead.

Sig dragged himself over to where Stacey hid. A massive wound was gaping open like a torn paper bag from Sig's upper left side. Stacey could tell that it wasn't from a gunshot. It must have been sustained in the dog fight. Blood oozed from several spots, quickly forming in a pool on the ground beneath the dog. Stacey fought back the sickness and nausea that floundered in his stomach. It was no use. Turning his pained body to the side, he retched violently.

The pain of his broken side was almost too much. *I can't let go*, he thought, struggling to remain conscious. When he felt slightly more steady, he removed the coat and vest. Occasionally glancing around to see if anyone was coming, he slowly lifted his shirt and removed the tightly wound bandages. Without the pressure they supplied, it felt like his insides were going to fall out.

Sig lay panting on the ground. Stacey reached out and folded the flap of skin back over the wound, exposing the dog's ribs. Sig winced. Sig, turning his head weakly, licked Stacey's hand. At the "stand" command, Sig struggled to his feet and let Stacey wrap two of the three bandages around his chest.

A groan again came from the man lying on the ground. Taking a chance, and feeling compelled to help, Stacey hobbled into the clearing and turned him over, revealing both an entry wound in the abdomen and a gaping exit wound at his lower back. He removed the man's jacket. Keys and a cell phone fell from the pocket—items which Stacey slipped into his own. Then he tore the man's shirt into two pieces and placed one on his stomach and the other on his back. Spying a gun laying nearby in the dirt, Stacey picked it up and tossed it in the trees. In his sickly state, he had no use for it.

The smell of blood and bowel rose in the air like a noxious cloud, making Stacey sicker as he continued to cover and wrap the bleeding man. Several times he resisted the urge to throw up. Rolling the man side to side, he managed to tighten the bandage around his wounds. The urge now too strong, he again began to dry heave. This time, without support, the pain was unbearable. He collapsed onto the ground, unconscious.

Barker and Weeks had learned next to nothing about either Bingham or Briggs. It was almost as if their personal histories had begun when they'd moved to town. Detective Green, from Virginia, was helpful when Weeks had called him at home. He'd carefully reviewed the case and reported that Oswald was indeed the original investigating officer. Oswald had quit the force five years ago, only a few days after the father of a girl killed in his precinct was accused of molesting and murdering his own daughter. The father had been arrested and finally was now going to trial. Weeks convinced Green to help locate Oswald so he could explain the case in greater detail.

It was learned that Green had tried to call Stacey less than two hours after his initial call. Unable to reach him on his cell phone, he'd called the office. That's when Bingham had taken the call, telling him that Stacey was suspected of selling drugs from the evidence room, and that if he heard from him again not to release any information. It had been a bonus when the caller ID recorded the address and phone number to Stacey's home, so many states away. Green wanted to know if they had Stacey in custody yet.

By eleven-thirty both men were convinced that they'd hit a dead end and decided to call it a night. Barker, however, needed to do one more thing before he left. He watched Weeks drive away, then found an empty box and began the painful task of emptying Deek's desk.

Amber crept out of her bedroom and down the stairs. She still held out hope that Rick had heard of the false alarm at her school and knew what it meant. Quietly she tiptoed through the garage and up the stairs—unaware that her father was sitting on a chair behind the cars, waiting, hoping he would see his son. Inside the upstairs room, she waited in the dark.

Preparing for bed, Don decided the scare tactics he'd used on Melvin were the best defense *and* offense he'd ever used. He'd blocked the inside door that led from the upper part of the house, keeping the front door unobstructed in case he needed to exit in a hurry.

Shortly after turning out the light and settling into bed, he heard Melvin drive in. Only minutes later, footsteps and the sound of things being moved around above his bedroom jolted him from his half-conscious sleep. Then all heck broke loose—it sounded like Melvin was cutting wood above his bed or sawing a hole through the floor. The vibrations pulsed down through the ceiling. Don rolled out of bed, both out of curiosity and just in case the ceiling collapsed.

Upstairs, Melvin stood with one foot on a board, which lay on an upside-down five-gallon bucket in the middle of the room. He'd been contemplating how he could get his pesky tenants out of the apartment. Don was explosive and dangerous, and Christina posed a serious security concern. Outside his computer expertise, he recognized his ability to reason was limited. And going to the police was out of the question. The only thing he could think to do was to drive them crazy until they left.

And so there he was, leaning over a board with a rusty old handsaw, drawing it back and forth across the board, and hoping to keep Don awake—without ever again getting within his reach.

Don moved to the kitchen to get a drink of water. Melvin giggled to himself, getting a kick out of what he imagined Don was doing down below. Don swore; Melvin laughed aloud as the grating sounds resonated through the uninsulated floor.

Stacey regained consciousness to find the wounded man gone—and the night gear missing. Sig lay motionless at the edge of the clearing. He struggled to his knees to see if his police companion was alive. Sig, still breathing, ever so slightly raised his head to acknowledge Stacey's presence. Stacey checked the pocket of the overcoat and found the keys and phone where he'd left them. He draped the coat over his cold torso, staggered to his feet, and went to carry his dying dog from the brush. He knew he needed to find help before it was too late.

Stumbling from the trees, they started across the field. Tripping over a root, he fell to his knees. There sprawled in the grass before him, lay the meanest-looking Rottweiler he'd ever seen. Stacey laid Sig down and took the penlight from his pocket. The dog, motionless, had taken a bullet to the head.

Once more he lurched to his feet, Sig in his arms, and plowed toward the silhouette of a vehicle parked on the shoulder of the highway, several hundred yards ahead.

Amber, weary of waiting, soon lay peacefully in the room above the garage. Midnight came and went; Rick never showed up.

Mr. Stacey climbed the stairs to find his daughter sleeping on the bed. He drew the covers up and around her shoulders, kissed her goodnight, and retired to his own room.

THIRTY

THE PICTURE IN BARKER'S HAND was the last of Deek's personal belongings. He stared at the photo, remembering the occasion–the fourth of July less than a year ago. "Just a bunch of grown-up kids," Barker chuckled. There he stood, along with Deek, Stacey and Deek's brother-in-law, arms over shoulders, dressed in full paintball gear, each covered in blotches of paint. Deek had hoisted his shirt to reveal several nasty-looking welts on his chest and abdomen. Stacey was new on the force. It was the first party he'd come to. The brother-in-law, who often played a rambunctious game of paint ball with his sons, had wanted to have a serious shoot-out with the "cops from Mapleton."

They'd all met in an open area of fields and trees out west of Deek's house. Working as teams, Barker and Stacey had gotten the best of Deek and his brother-in-law, partly because Deek had taken an early paint ball squarely in the mask, obscuring his vision for much of the time. By the time it was over, the men had emptied their guns on each other. Barker smiled as he reminisced. The ringing of his cell phone broke the spell. "Out of area," the caller ID flashed.

"Barker here."

"Paul, Stace. I shot a guy; he's hurt pretty bad. You'll find him in the woods, west of marker 265. Look for the dead Rottweiler in the field. Last time I saw him he was about 20 yards north of the dog."

"Where are you?"

"Can't say."

"Stace, listen to me. We've got enough to take down

Bingham. You've got to come in."

"Is he in custody?"

"He will be in the morning."

"I doubt it..." Stacey, breathing hard, grimaced with pain. "These guys he sent after me...were military; they had it all."

"Are you hurt?"

"Not as bad as Sig."

"Come in, then. You've got to come in."

"You've got to pick up Bingham first...or I'm a dead man. He's up to more than just trying to kill me....You can bet on it." Stacey turned off the phone. With Sig resting in the back, he fired up the Suburban and pulled onto the highway.

Barker called central dispatch. "I need every available deputy you've got."

Don shuffled into Christina's room to try and catch some shut-eye. The battle of wits was wearing thin—and Melvin was proving to be a brutally relentless opponent. He always seemed to know where Don was. The footsteps and the sawing, echoing throughout the apartment, would move above him from room to room. Don would change rooms, the sawing would stop for a minute, followed by footsteps, then the insane cacophony would resume, directly overhead. He thought he could hear what sounded like the ultra-quiet buzzing of a remote control car, moving through the heat vents that ran overhead. Or maybe it was just his agitated imagination.

Retreating to the family room, Don picked up the remote and clicked on the television, staring aimlessly in its direction. Then—there it was! Something flickered by in the heat register that opened just over the television. It had lurched mechanically, pointed in his direction, then had done an about-face and vanished out of sight. It appeared to have two red eyes.

Suddenly the lights in the room went out. He kept his eyes on the screen, which, just seconds later, went to static, as if someone had disconnected the antenna. He played along, swearing loud enough to be heard upstairs.

Melvin's high-pitched, crazed laugh resonated through the vent. Obviously, he was relishing this little game of cat and mouse.

Don jogged to the kitchen, then stopped to listen. The buzzing and the footsteps followed. Craning his neck, he peeked through the heater vent grate. There, back in the shadows, two ever-so-faint lights could be seen.

He's getting sloppy, Don mused. Walking to the bedroom, he found a screwdriver and a clothes hanger, which he reshaped to form a long hook. Then he positioned himself under the vent, his tool ready. Carefully threading it back through the vertical holes in the grate, he twisted it sideways.

The buzzing sound intensified—as did Melvin's cursing. Holding onto the end of the hook, Don unscrewed the grate and eased his mechanical prey out of the vent. It was shaped like a rat on wheels, a tiny remote camera as its nose. Don flicked on the bedroom lights and smiled broadly directly into the lens. He wanted to make sure Melvin saw exactly what he would do next. Placing the expensive device face up on the floor, he took his heaviest pair of work boots from the closet and slipped them on his bare feet.

"No!!" Melvin shrieked as the boot came crashing down.

Ten deputies formed a line next to the fence. Spaced about ten paces apart, they began to traverse the field. One of the deputies called out: he'd spotted the dog. It took only a few more minutes to locate the site where the struggle had taken place. Deek's vest lay in the dirt beside several spatters of dried blood. "I want this area roped off. Continue to search for a body," Barker instructed. The deputies worked their way across and back, systematically scouting the area.

Stacey slowed to a stop in front of Deek's house. He staggered to Dianne's bedroom window. At the rapping sound, the bedroom light turned on and the window opened. "I need your help. Sig's bad off."

Together they carried the almost lifeless animal into the house and lay him on the kitchen table. Then Stacey let out a groan, turned to take a step, and crumpled to the floor. He didn't know how he'd made it. The waves of nausea still swept over him. "I'm allergic...to codeine," he mumbled.

Dianne took the phone book from the table, dialed, and waited. "William, I'm so sorry to wake you. This is Dianne Derickson....Thank you, I know. We miss him, too....No, I need to ask you a big favor. I have two friends who need medical attention in a terrible way. I can't...I know you don't. Do you still have your supplies? One is allergic to codeine. He's so weak he can't even stand. He also has several broken ribs. The other's lost a lot of blood and needs stitches. Please hurry." She rattled off her address and hung up the phone.

Stacey was in rough shape but his condition was not life-threatening. Sig, on the other hand, was having trouble breathing. From the rattle in his chest, Dianne guessed one of his lungs was filling with blood. She gently rolled him onto his wounded side so the weight of the choked off lung wouldn't apply pressure to the other. Sig let out a whine, but nothing more. She cut the bandage off his chest and examined the other minor cuts and abrasions. Nothing else seemed to be serious.

Sig seemed a bit more comfortable. Perhaps the collapsed lung was draining. She began to clean the other wounds as best she could. Stacey occasionally tried to sit up and see how Sig was doing. It was taking her friend forever to come.

Then there came a faint knock at the front door. A silver-haired man with white, bushy eyebrows and a tired back stood on the porch, medical bag in hand. "Come in, William. Thank you so much for coming."

The old fellow tottered slowly inside. "It took a bit to find the Phengran in my office—or should I say, my son's office. Good thing he didn't change the locks." He smiled pleasantly and looked around. "I haven't made a house call in 15...20 years. Now let's get down to business," he grumbled good-naturedly like the retired old codger he was. He yammered on as he followed Dianne into the kitchen. "Where are these two patients?—my land, it's a dog!"

"I know, William—and a very good friend. I think he has a collapsed lung. Lost a lot of blood, too." He walked around the table and saw Stacey on the floor.

"This man doesn't look so good, either." He took a small bottle of pills from his sweater pocket. "This will help." He listened to Sig's chest. "You did learn something all those years ago," he teased.

Dianne filled a glass of water and gave Stacey one of the pills. "Give him two," muttered the old doc, turning his attention to the dog. "Don't know if I've ever seen someone hit quite so hard by a painkiller before."

He and Dianne worked well together. She seemed to know exactly what he needed. She strung an IV from a cupboard door and did her best to keep track of the flow and serve as assistant. Stacey started to come around.

"Must have been one heck of a reaction, young man," William said, glancing up from his work. "Codeine works on the central nervous system as well as the nausea centers of the brain. We find that those with the worst reactions to it usually developed a sensitivity when they were young."

Stacey, though coherent, still wasn't feeling any better. "How's my dog?" he grunted through the fog, sounding a bit unappreciative.

"I think he'll make it." Stacey noticed that the old man's hand shook as he raised it up from the gash on Sig's side. However, each time his hand came back down for another stitch, he was steady and calm. A slight cackle escaped his lips. "I've never blown air into a dog's lungs before." He took another stitch. "Must be some dog for Dianne to care so much about him."

Stacey pulled himself up into a chair. He wondered how Dianne had persuaded the old doctor to come and help. "Oh, Rick, this is Doctor William Frisby. I've known him since I was a child. He was our family doctor. I also worked with him as a student nurse before I met Deek."

The old man nodded. "Nice to meet you, Officer

Stacey. You the one they're blaming for Deek's death?"

Dianne and Stacey were a tad stunned; neither one had spoken his last name. "I knew Dianne didn't believe you had anything to do with it the second I saw you," he explained. "She wouldn't have brought me here unless she trusted you."

The minutes passed. William's work on Sig was almost finished.

Stacey turned to Dianne, a hint of sadness in his weary face. "I'm sorry I missed the funeral."

"Actually, it was postponed until today," Dianne replied. "The autopsy suggested some sort of chemical poisoning. They're not sure what it is—or where it came from. The hospital's in a panic. It may have been introduced during the emergency surgery. The poison—or whatever it was—apparently was slow to act—until it got to his heart, which sent it straight to the brain. That's what killed him."

Stacey sat in silence for a minute or two, thinking. Then he said, "I wonder if there's a connection between Deek's death and the military. I think the men who attacked me and Sig were military." A minute later he went on. "Barker just told me they have enough evidence to pick Bingham up. It should happen this morning, but I don't think they'll find him. He's looking for me. Whoever found me had done their homework, and had money to spend. Their equipment was some of the best I've seen." Thinking through all the facts, he suddenly blurted out, "I'd better get out of here—and soon!"

"You're not taking your friend anywhere," said the doctor as he put the last stitch in Sig's side.

"I'll keep him in the garage, where he'll be out of sight," Dianne offered.

"Now let's take a look at those ribs, young man," the doctor groused, positioning himself in front of him like a riled-up grade-school teacher. Stacey pulled himself to his feet and removed the overcoat. It dropped to the floor, exposing the enlarged bruise, now black as coal. Dianne gasped. She'd seen a lot of injuries, but never anything like this.

The doctor raised his stethoscope up to listen. "Deep breath." Stacey did his best. "Sounds like you got some fluid in your lungs, too. Could turn into pneumonia. Heart sounds okay. I was afraid it might be bruised." He ran his fingers across the blackened tissue. "Couple of ribs out of place. I'd better see if I can put them back. I've seen bronc riders that look like this." He turned to his case and brought out several bandages. "It's not going to feel so good. You up to it?"

"Do I have a choice?"

The old fellow cleared a spot at the end of the table. "Sit here facing the wall," he said, slapping the table. "Dianne, I might need your help."

Stacey gingerly climbed onto the table. "Now, I want you to put your arm over my shoulder and do your best to relax." The old man stood on Stacey's good side and reached his arms around the officer's broad chest. "This might take the wind out of your sails. Help me catch him if he goes out, Dianne."

The old doctor began to squeeze, every few seconds shifting the position of his hands. Stacey hung on to the doctor's neck, also squeezing, not realizing he might break the poor fellow's neck. A scream broke free from deep in his gut. He managed to stifle it in his throat. The old man's strength was phenomenal. Then something popped. Stacey immediately felt light-headed. The doctor could feel Stacey's grip slacken around his neck, then came a second pop, and something gave way.

"Get ready," was the last thing Stacey heard, as everything went black. He awoke to smelling salts a few minutes later. His chest was wrapped tightly and he lay face up on the table, his feet hanging over the side. He tried to get up.

"Hold on...slowly." Stacey could feel Sig stir next to him. Turning so that their noses were only inches apart, Sig did what Stacey hoped he would. Out shot his tongue, swiping it across Stacey's mouth. Dianne's eyes filled to overflowing.

Stacey scratched Sig under the chin. "Best kiss I've had all month."

Dianne and Dr. Frisby helped Stacey up. "You only have a few hours before dawn, so you'd better get going. Sig'll be in good hands here." Dianne handed Stacey a bag of things she'd put together and helped him with his coat. "We put something other than codeine in here in case you need it."

Stacey lifted his arm to slip on the coat. The pain had subsided. He headed to the car, bag in hand. His mind was clearer now. He needed some clothes and a place to sleep. He'd stop by his parents' home one more time. If he hurried, he could be in and out before anyone knew it.

As he pulled away from the curb, another car pulled out several blocks down the street.

Barker and his deputies had not found the body. Sweep after sweep had revealed only that someone was dragged away. The search was called off until morning, and all but two of the deputies went home to bed. Beyond exhaustion, Barker followed their lead.

Too jumpy, Don still didn't get much sleep. Every sound made him flinch. Once, he thought someone was in the apartment and sat straight up in bed. Around three-thirty he finally nodded off for good.

Parking several blocks from his parents' place, Stacey took a backyard route that required little fence-climbing. He knew the yards where every dog lived, and took pains to avoid them. Soon he was at the back door and up the stairs. The closet door rattled softly as he slid it open.

"I knew you'd come," came a sleepy voice from behind him.

Stacey almost jumped out of his skin. If he'd been up to par, he'd have seen Amber lying there on the bed. He knelt down next to her. "Hey, Amber!"

"Did you hear about my signal?" she asked hopefully.

"No, I didn't."

"I set off the fire alarm at school so you'd come."

"Sorry, I wasn't in the best condition."

Amber just smiled. Then her face brightened. "My

friend has some evidence. She sneaked into that creep's house and saw a huge computer and hundreds of disks. You need to help her get them."

"I don't know if I can. I'm not safe right now."

"She gave me the key to the apartment and everything. No one's staying there. Maybe that's where you could hide. And then you could make sure he doesn't hurt someone else." Amber placed the key she was clutching in Rick's big hand.

"Who's he?" Stacey asked.

"My friend's the one that got attacked last week. She lives in his basement apartment."

Stacey hadn't kept up on the news. "Are you talking about the Briggs guy?"

"Yup. My friend Christina Rodriguez moved into the apartment under his house. That same night she was attacked. Now she has evidence, enough to put him away." The door to the bedroom suddenly opened. Stacey reached for his gun.

"Rick, I had a feeling it was you." It was Stacey's mother, her arms outstretched and coming toward him.

"Ohhh!" he cried as she hugged him.

She stepped back. "What happened! Are you hurt?"

"A couple of broken ribs. I'm doing better now."

"Where've you been? We've been worried sick."

"I can't tell you. I could be placing you all in danger." Stacey removed his coat. In the moonlight the bruise could be seen above the bandages.

"Oh, my gosh!" Amber gasped. Mrs. Stacey bit her lip.

He took a shirt from the closet and began to put it on. His mother rushed to help. Just then a dark sedan coasted past the house, its lights out. Stacey crouched by the window to watch it pass. When it reached the corner it stopped and turned left.

"I've got to leave." He grabbed a few more things from the closet and started for the door. His mother began to cry. "I'll be okay, Mom. It'll all be over in a few days." He slipped down the stairs and hurried out the door.

THIRTY-ONE

STACEY DIDN'T KNOW IF he dared use the Suburban again. He fumbled through his pockets to find something he could use to mark it to tell whether it was tampered with—revealing also if someone was on to him.

The crumpled scrap of paper wrapped around the key would do. He opened it and read the address, then tore it into six small pieces. Each piece he popped into his mouth and chewed to fashion a sticky little spit-wad. Then, rolling the balls into strings, he knelt by the side of the SUV and smashed the strings onto the bottom of each door frame, forming a miniature bridge from the running board to the door. Then he scooped some of the silt from the gutter and coated the strings, camouflaging them. He did the same to the hood and back door. Upon his return, if someone had opened any of the doors to the vehicle, the bridge would be broken and he would know not to use it.

Many questions remained to be answered. Stacey considered them as he passed through backyards and vacant lots. Where had the other attacker gone? Why hadn't he returned when he heard the shot that took down his partner? And what had happened to the wounded man? He couldn't possibly have walked away.

He was growing tired. Although he'd slept off and on over the past few days, he was still weak. Slightly disoriented, he felt the effects of the powerful medication playing tricks on his mind; he needed to sleep.

Four a.m.. A serene calm hovered over the Salt Lake

City airport. Two men, side by side, walked purposefully down Terminal B. A blonde, buxom woman sat with her back to the corridor. She'd never been to Barbados before, and was a bit on edge, wondering what she'd do on her own for a whole week.

She'd met Bingham in Africa. And now she'd grown too accustomed to his lavish lifestyle. But theirs was an enigmatic relationship. He was nervous to be seen with her in public, and he kept secrets from her. In fact, she hardly knew him.

Still, Barbados would be another exciting adventure in her life.

The click of the door made Don lurch out of the bed and grope toward the hall, blinking his eyes awake.

Halfway down the dark hall someone snatched hold of his arm and wrist. In seconds he was on the floor, face down, wrist burning. A knee dug into his back and a hand clamped over his mouth. "If you want to stay alive, be quiet," a voice barked as the hand slowly slipped away. "Who are you?"

Don was seething. "Who wants to know?"

The grip tightened, the muscles and tendons burned in his arm and shoulder. "I'm not in the mood for games! Who are you?"

"Don Rodriguez—" His teeth were grinding. If he ever got out of this death grip—and if his arm was still intact—he swore he'd kill this guy.

"Is your daughter Christina?" The voice softened.

"Yes."

"I'm sorry. I was told no one was here."

His attacker at once released his arm and stood up. Don rolled over to see a man as tall or taller than himself, slightly thinner, wearing a long overcoat.

"I'm Amber's brother," Stacey said, extending his left hand to help him up. Don, still stunned and hurting, didn't understand; this man was either a cop or an ex-cop. Finally, though, he accepted the gesture, seized the hand, thumb over fist, and pulled himself to his feet. He didn't notice the grimace on Stacey's face. And both men were too distracted to hear the quiet conversation taking place upstairs.

Melvin was beside himself. "Here? In my house?...How did he get in?...Thanks." He hung up the phone and strained to hear what was being said down below. He needed his rat! Its crushed shell lay on his kitchen table. He'd retrieved it—such as it was—after Don had tossed it out on the lawn. He planned to fix it. Shaking his head sadly, he realized he should never have gotten so emotionally involved.

Meanwhile, a man parked in a dark sedan a few blocks down the street, talked on his cell phone with Melvin.

With the approach of dawn, the airport had grown more crowded. The shapely blond was escorted from her seat and ushered out to the terminal curb. Getting into the back seat of the awaiting Suburban, she was whisked away. She would be questioned and re-questioned until she was willing to tell everything she knew.

Don and Stacey exchanged introductions as Stacey quietly explained how he'd gotten the key, and assured him he would be leaving right away. Don couldn't recall where he knew the man from.

As the two of them tried to make sense of it all, Stacey mentioned what Christina had told his sister about how she'd gathered up evidence—that she considered "hard evidence"—on Melvin. Don was aghast to learn Christina had been snooping around upstairs, and promised Stacey he'd have a talk with her.

Then it was Don's turn to share the extraordinary battle he'd been waging against Melvin: All about the landlord's peep-holes...all about his wild antics to drive them out of the apartment...and all about the mechanical rat with red eyes—the same "rat," Don was now convinced, Christina had seen in the county courthouse restroom. They speculated that if Melvin had had access to the judge's chambers, or had listened in using his mechanical sleuth, he could have something on the judge.

Don decided it wouldn't be such a bad idea for Stacey to stay there with him. The fridge was stocked with plenty of food and Christina's bed wasn't being used. He made sure to warn Stacey that Melvin had barged in unexpectedly the day before. They both laughed quietly when Don mimicked the look on Melvin's face as the knife plunged into the table between his legs.

Stacey could tell he and Don would become friends. They already were allies, sharing a common desire to see the man upstairs behind bars.

"Where's your dog I've heard so much about?" asked Don.

"Staying with a friend."

Soon the eastern sky was light. Don needed to get to work—that is, if he still had a job. Showered and shaved, he tossed a few things in a plastic bag for lunch and headed out. Christina's bike lay on the lawn. Picking it up, he straddled the seat. The tires flattened considerably under his weight as he peddled off down the street.

Stacey locked the doors. He took the extra precaution of folding two tiny pieces of paper and tucking them in between the frame and the door at both entrances. Surveying the apartment, he decided that he'd sleep behind the wet bar in the family room rather than in Christina's bed. He found an extra mattress pad in one of the closets and positioned it behind the wall, gun readied. Soon he was sound asleep.

Don needn't have worried. Jeff was ecstatic to have him back.

Before clocking in, Don asked if he could call his dad's house. Maria answered. His father was about the same, she said, somehow still holding on. He'd always been a stubborn man; death would be no exception. Eventually it would win out, but the fight wouldn't be an easy one.

Other employees offered their condolences. "How's your father?" Rex asked, genuinely concerned.

"Not well. They've taken the feeding tubes out and are watching him wind down. I wanted to stay with him but he insisted I come back to be with Christina. He hasn't spoken since." Tears welled up in Rex's eyes. Don wasn't expecting such a reaction, but then found that his own eyes had become moist. If anyone knew how he felt, this man did. Rex silently reached out and hugged the younger man. Don self-consciously returned the gesture, his hands awkwardly patting the man's back. He had often longed for such displays of affection from his father—displays of love he knew his father could never give.

"Excuse me." Cecily had come in to work early. Each man stepped from the other and drew a sleeve across his face. Don turned so Cecily wouldn't see the tears; Rex was a little less discrete. Sensing what had just happened, she quietly swiped her card and left the room.

Don retreated to the solitude of the mixing shed.

Christina pulled Danny aside. "We've got to go back and see what's in the shed."

"No way! Not if you paid me a million bucks!"

Christina, at least when it came to her cousin, had become a master manipulator. "I'll just go by myself then—if you're too *scared*."

Danny was stuck. He'd feel guilty if he didn't go, scared out of his wits if he did. But if she went alone and anyone found out he was too chicken to go with her, he'd hear about it forever. Then again, this wasn't just any old adventure. What if Melvin killed and buried them, too, just like he did with his daughter?

"Okay," he said at last. "I'll go on two conditions: we wait 'til Saturday, and we go when it's light." Then he added, "By the way, we forgot to put the bolts back in. What if he sees it's unlocked and moves the body?"

Christina pondered the possibility, suddenly very worried.

Close friends and family had come to the Derickson home, each hoping to provide a measure of comfort and support. The viewing started at ten, the funeral at eleven. The mood was solemn. The children, seemingly in a daze, were dressed in their Sunday best. The older ones had already cried until they could cry no more. Austin, the two-year-old, was confused. All he knew was that they were going to church and that his daddy wasn't home. He strolled about from room to room. Standing in front of his mom, he looked up and asked, "Daddy at?" Dianne had heard the question now dozens of times. She had tried to explain, but he was just too young to understand.

She knelt once more. "We're going to go see him in just a minute, honey," she said sadly.

His little face perked up. "Daddy come home?"

"No, dear," she sniffled, her heart in her throat. "He's in heaven. We're going to go see his body."

The little fellow wasn't sure if he was supposed to be happy or sad. "Okay, Mommy," he said, wrapping his trusting arms around her neck and burying his face in her shoulder. She always felt better when he squeezed her tight.

Sig was in the garage. He lay quietly, licking his wounds. Despite the stitches in his side, he was becoming a little more frisky.

At the police station Barker and his staff were dressed in their best. He had called Dianne to see if there was anything he or his officers could do. She'd sounded tired. She did, however, want to share with him what little information Deek had told her about Stacey's findings before he died.

After speaking with Dianne, Barker made a second call. Officer Green explained that he couldn't find any records beyond Oswald's one-year stint on the force.

It was more than an hour before the start of the viewing, so Barker decided to drop by the city offices to look through their own personnel files. Chief Anderson's door was open as he passed by, the chief sitting at his desk. "Lieutenant Barker, can I speak to you a moment?" Barker did an about face and stuck his head in the doorway. "We have a council meeting coming up next week and I'd like to keep abreast of the investigation. How's it going?"

"We'll get a warrant on Bingham later this morning. We're still working on some leads on Briggs. I think we can get enough to make it stick. It's only a matter of time."

"Keep me apprised. I feel partially responsible for Bingham's actions. I thought he was the right man for the job. And by the way, just let me know if you need any help."

"Thank you, sir."

Barker continued down the hall to the personnel office. Chief Anderson was being most helpful. Over the past five years he'd been influential in increasing the size of the force. His recommendation had been the deciding factor in Bingham getting the captain's job. He'd convinced the council that new blood would strengthen the force. And though Barker didn't like to admit it, Bingham had helped take the small-town attitude out of the men, making them more efficient—more like officers than friends of the community. As a result, crime had dropped by 22 percent.

At the personnel office he asked the secretary if he could see Bingham's file. She was more than willing to oblige, but became a mite confused when she couldn't find it in its usual place. After thumbing through the other drawers, she told Barker she'd have it sent over to his office when she located it. He doubted she'd find it.

Melvin absentmindedly played with the phone cord as he spoke, twirling it nervously and wrapping it around his fingers. "Can you get your hands on a harmonics generator?...I can't take that chance. I think I can have them both out by morning....I made a costly mistake last night—lost my rat....I can't, they want me locked up....Good, I'll pick it up around noon."

Christina's mind was far from learning about dividing fractions, the subject her teacher was discussing. Amber had said her brother accepted the key to the apartment, but probably wouldn't be staying there. She hadn't heard from her dad to see if he was okay—after sleeping in a house with a killer living upstairs. She knew she'd better return and secure the shed before Melvin found out they'd been inside. She began to devise a plan.

Dianne and the children arrived at the church at nine. She took a deep breath. *I can do this*, she repeated again in her mind. The hardest part would be seeing the tears of all her friends. She'd come to terms with the loss of her husband—and best friend—at least for the time being.

The hearse arrived. The bishop was there to direct the proceedings. They stood together and watched as the casket was wheeled up the walk and into the building. Bishop Hunt was a great source of strength to the family. He'd even offered financial help, if she needed it. Deek did have a small life insurance policy, but it could never begin to help finish raising the children or see that they made it through college.

The mortician directed the family to the viewing room, making sure a box of tissues was close at hand. Friends began arriving. Flowers were placed near the closed casket. The younger children were being escorted from the room when Austin started in again. "Daddy at?" he questioned. *"Mommy, Daddy at?"* One helpful friend tried to pick him up to take him out when he began his protest. He let his body go limp and raised his arms up to keep from being picked up.

Dianne stepped forward. She'd promised he would see his dad.

"Maybe he needs to say goodbye first," Dianne told the well-intentioned friend. "I need to keep my promise and let him see his daddy one last time." The mortician raised the lid on the casket. Dianne picked up the small boy, held him close, and carried him over. Austin watched closely as they approached.

"Daddy sleeping?" he observed.

"Yes, sweetie, Daddy's sleeping." Austin's little hands were clasped tight, knuckles white as he looked on. Suddenly he bent and catapulted his little body toward his father. He had no problem waking his father from a Sunday afternoon nap to play a game; he assumed this time would be no different. His hands landed on the cold, folded hands that crossed the body at the waist. Dianne, caught off guard, pulled him back into her arms. His little brow drew in and his chin began to quiver. His eyes filled with tears as he asked one last time, *"Daddy at?"*

Dianne could no longer hold back her own emotions. "He's not here, honey. He's gone to be with his Heavenly Daddy," she said as the small boy curled up in a ball and cried on her shoulder. Not a soul in the room could hold back the tears. Not even the seasoned mortician, who turned to adjust the flowers.

Stacey awoke after three hours' sleep, hoping the draw of the funeral would make it safe to venture out. He was willing to be seen for something so important. After checking the doors and determining no one had attempted to come in, he gingerly unwrapped the bandages. The process was slow. It would be harder to wrap it back up again.

He kept Bingham's revolver on the window sill as he bathed; he wasn't going to take any chances. Still in a great deal of pain, he dressed in the clothes from his high school days, trimmed his dark beard and donned a hat he had found among Don's things. After checking the curtains to see if it was safe to leave, he locked the door behind him and proceeded down the street. He was uncomfortable the first few blocks, but soon began to feel more at ease.

Every flag in the county was flying at half mast. The funeral was packed. The speakers lionized Deek as an extraordinarily devoted father, husband, friend and police officer. More than 70 squad cars lined the street to escort the cortege to the cemetery, a tribute to the many friends Deek had made over the years. Every local television and cable crew was on hand.

At the same time the somber congregation began to file from the church building, Stacey was on the other side of town where he'd parked the Suburban. After inspecting the little "security strings" he'd placed on each door, he was satisfied it hadn't been touched. This would be the last time he'd dare use the vehicle.

He drove to a secluded lane inside the cemetery, parked the vehicle in the shade of a giant pine and slumped down in his seat to wait.

Christina left class without her lunch. With her class about to enter the cafeteria, she told her teacher she needed to return to the room to get it. Sixth grade was the first to go to lunch, so the playground was empty when she raced across it toward the street. The old crossing guard warned her of the dangerous man living only a few blocks down.

Christina felt a rush as she neared Melvin's house. She could see from three or four houses away that his car was not in the driveway. She felt some comfort knowing she could replace the bolts without being seen. If only her older cousin had come along...

She wiped the sweat from her palms and glanced around, then veered through the gate and ran around back. Her body shuddered at the thought of what might be buried with the sweater.

Her heart was beating fast—then it skipped a beat. There, sticking out of the plastic hasp on the shed door, were four shiny new bolts. Each was secured at the head with a red epoxy, smeared around the hole it went through.

She began to run....

THIRTY-TWO

THE SHINY GRAY HEARSE inching its way down State Street seemed out of place among the long double column of police cars, lights flashing. Stacey looked on, his senses alert for any sign of danger. As the procession approached the cemetery entrance, all but ten of the cars continued on down the street. Each hit the siren as it passed the gate in honor of a fallen comrade. Stacey watched, wishing he could be present to support his friend's family. Startled by the ringing of the cell phone, he pulled it from under the seat. It rang six or seven times, then quit.

The hearse stopped near the grave site. Stacey was too far away to see faces, but recognized Dianne and her family. The cell phone rang again. This time Stacey answered it, figuring that, if traced, they would find it abandoned in the cemetery. He pressed the send button and listened.

"Stacey, is that you?" He recognized the captain's voice. "My men aren't as good as me. When I find you—and I will—you won't walk away alive." Bingham went on to describe in graphic detail a knife stuck deep in Stacey's spine.

Patiently listening until Bingham had expended his venom, Stacey calmly spoke. "Will you still smell like a dirty diaper?" He then turned off the phone. Since no one could follow a dead signal, he put it in his pocket. It might come in handy.

Stepping out of the vehicle, he walked over a slight rise, there to watch his fellow officers ceremoniously remove the flag from the casket and carefully fold it. Deek's family stood in a row as Barker presented Dianne the folded flag.

Stacey couldn't hear Barker whisper to Dianne, "Stacey wanted to be here," but saw Dianne look up to where he stood.

"He is!" she whispered in return. Barker didn't turn to look out of fear of drawing attention to the far-off, solitary figure who slipped out of sight and down the hill among the headstones and pine trees.

Don interrupted his work and returned to the office for lunch. Not in the mood to discuss the condition of his father—and fearing his emotions might creep up on him again—he'd purposely come in late. Having mentioned to Jeff that he would need to leave again soon to attend his father's funeral, Jeff had asked if he could work at least half a day the next Saturday to run an inventory of powders. Don had agreed, and looked forward to spending the second half of the day with his daughter. They hadn't done much together the last several days. Cecily showed up in the lunchroom a few minutes after Don arrived.

"Hi," Cecily said, breaking the ice.

Ill at ease, Don felt just like a teenager, wondering if they were making up or not.

"I'm sorry about your dad. How is he?" she continued.

"He hasn't spoken since I left. I don't know how he keeps holding on." He wanted to tell her everything that had happened–the promise he had made to his father without knowing what he'd committed to do, the ride on the bus, the young man who helped him understand his father's message, his encounter with Melvin and all about Stacey. Cecily was his best friend. But was he hers? He wasn't sure if he could trust his heart to her or not. Every ounce of him wanted to love her, to feel her in his arms, to kiss her. He was even willing to live by her standards, if that's what it took. He just wasn't sure if she would take to someone who seemed so unreliable. *Most good Mormon girls wouldn't marry anyone outside their faith,* he thought. How did he stand a chance?

"How much longer do they expect him to hang on?" Her voice nudged him from his thoughts.

"He can't last much longer. They've removed the feeding tubes."

"Will you go back up to the funeral?"

"I plan to. He requested a natural burial and a simple funeral," Don explained. "He doesn't want to be embalmed, so it'll take place within 24 hours after he goes."

"Would you let me drive you when it's time?"

The question took him by surprise. She'd just said the words he'd hoped to hear. She *was* still interested in him. "Okay," was his simple answer. His tongue was tied, but his heart was jumping for joy.

Cecily had been equally unsure, still wondering if he liked her or not. After all, he hadn't called her when he got back, he hadn't spoken to her at work that day, and now she'd offered to drive him to Boise for his father's funeral and all he could say was "Okay"?!

"Well, better get back to work," she said, feeling rejected.

Don's mind wrestled for something else to say. Did she really want to go with him, or had she offered just out of pity? He wanted to thank her for her friendship and concern for his daughter. In that moment, he felt a closeness to her that he had never felt before. But how could he tell her?

Cecily stood to go. As she made her way to the office door, she longed for him to call her back and tell her he'd missed her. She ached to tell him that when she heard his voice on the phone she felt butterflies. But no words were spoken, and she returned to her desk.

Don returned to the powder shed, his sandwich and chips still in hand. The two days he'd taken off had put him way behind. Working late was the only way he could possibly get caught up.

He installed the harmonics generator and ran wires to boxes at every floor vent in the house. *This equipment'll drive the bugs from the house!* he thought to himself.

Melvin's renters had long ago worn out their welcome. Now he needed his privacy. Who would have known things were going to escalate so rapidly? And with a cop around he couldn't take care of one very important item of business. The ingenuity of his set-up made him grin with delight.

The mass of people at the cemetery had nearly dispersed. Mr. White and Barker stood several yards away. "Here's your warrant," White said, handing over a folded document. "Be careful. We can't afford to lose any more of our officers."

Barker took the pages. "Demick give you any trouble?"

"No, he's just about had all he can take of this, though. State attorney general might run an investigation on the allegations the judge is being blackmailed by Melvin Briggs. Anything new with you?"

Barker gave a subtle shake of his head and stared off in the distance. "Not much. We can't find anything more on Bingham. Not surprisingly, his files have disappeared, and there're no records on file with the Driver's License Division. We've been following a lead Stacey found in Virginia. Same with that officer....It's weird. It seems like he doesn't even exist—nor ever did."

"Let's get him in county lock-up and see if he exists," White nodded. "You take as many county men as you need."

"Thanks."

"I think I'll pay my respects to Mrs. Derickson." Mr. White turned away.

Dianne had stayed at the grave site. Seeking closure to the bitterly painful events of the past several days, she wanted to be there when they lowered the casket into the concrete vault and covered it with the lid.

Stacey decided to see what he could get on Bingham. His house was situated in the river bottoms up the canyon, backed by the river. If he used the dense tree cover and the broken old fishing pole he'd found along the banks, no one would even notice him. He didn't believe Bingham would be home.

Stacey spent more than an hour pretending to fish, gradually working along the river. Finally he reached a point some 50 yards away from the house. Then he noticed three men coming his way. His heart began to race. Desperate, he glanced downstream—and saw three more men coming from the other direction! All six were clearly marked as police. Only one of them paid any attention to him; the others headed for the house. Being arrested before he broke into the captain's house hadn't been part of the plan.

"I need you to move along," the officer said gruffly, pointing down river.

Stacey nodded and *gladly* turned back in the direction he'd come. The officer, however, hadn't said anything about *how far* he should move along. So, still in sight of the house, Stacey crouched by a clump of brush to watch. He peered through the undergrowth as the officers initiated the break-and-enter. He could hear them yelling—and was glad he wasn't inside.

In less than an hour the house was empty. Stacey continued his fishing masquerade. He decided he'd wait until dark to enter.

Christina came in the door from school. Danny was in the study working on the computer. "Dad said they fixed the problem with their system. I don't think it's any better. I've already gotten part way in," he said, working at the keyboard, "And I'm just a kid...."

"I went to Melvin's house at lunch."

Danny stopped what he was doing. "What if he saw you?"

"I made sure his car was gone before I went around back."

"Sure, that would stop him from coming home!"

"Listen, he's put new bolts on the door. They have some kind of glue on them."

"Good, we can't go back," he said, knowing she was thinking of some sort of plan.

"The shed's put together with screws. We can hide behind it and take out a few, lift up the metal and crawl in. It's even better because no one will know we're inside."

"I was afraid you'd have another idea."

"I wonder if you could get into Melvin's computer and see what he's doing."

"You want me to dig in the shed for dead bodies *and* hack his equipment?"

"Well, *I* don't know how to do it."

"I do—" The words just came out!

She smiled. "Let's see how things go tomorrow. Maybe we can do both."

"Sure," Danny said, and went back to his project.

Five o'clock came and went. Cecily waited for Don to come up to the office. By five-thirty a gloom had come over her. *He's probably doing this on purpose,* she brooded. His hesitant acceptance of her offer at lunch made her begin to reconsider their relationship. *He wanted to go further than I was willing the other night. Maybe he wants sex more than a relationship. After all, he's been without a woman for a long time. He must think I'm a prude, and only accepted my offer so he didn't have to ride the bus again.*

Before long she decided she'd better just tell him that after thinking it over, she wouldn't be able to take him to Boise after all–and be done with it—and him. Maybe they could still be friends. And when the clock hit five forty-five she got in the Jeep and drove away, sure her heart was breaking.

Don finally finished all the orders. He hadn't paid attention to the time, but still hoped he could catch a ride with Cecily. Seeing the Jeep gone, he mounted the bike and started for home. She hadn't come to tell him she was leaving.

Before he got to the end of the lane, the back tire was completely flat. Climbing off, he began walking it home.

In the Jensen home, meanwhile, Jake and his friend Bryce had come up with a dozen new ideas to share with

Don on how to drive Melvin crazy. When Kate heard their scheming, she decided it was time to end this. She hadn't been very happy with Alan, what with his wild ideas from the night before. And she wasn't about to stand by and let her children get mixed up with a killer–much less provoking him!

After her no-nonsense talk with Alan, he'd come to realize that he'd made an unwise decision. He'd placed his children in harm's way, involving them in such dangerous activities, and he wouldn't hear of any more tricks.

Following his talk with the children, Danny announced that he was making headway into breaking the new security system. Alan didn't believe he could do it. His programmer had told him it would be impossible.

Nearing dinnertime, Christina asked her aunt if she'd seen or heard from her dad. Kate suggested she call Cecily to see if they were together.

"The last I knew he was workin' late," Cecily said when Christina called.

"Will you go with me to look for him?"

Cecily hesitated, then agreed. It might be a good time to tell Christina they probably wouldn't be getting together anymore.

Before long, Christina had buckled herself in the Jeep and they were whizzing along in the direction of Cobblecrete. Christina promptly broached the subject of why her dad hadn't ridden home with her.

Cecily was a woman who believed the direct route was the only route. "I don't think your Dad's interested in seeing me," she said point-blank.

"Are you kidding? He's crazy about you!"

"Why do you say that?"

"I can see it in his eyes. Can't you?"

They hadn't driven half a mile when they saw Don pushing the bike on the shoulder of the road. He glanced up and his countenance changed. He stood straighter and smiled, he even ran his hand through his hair to smooth it down. Christina laughed as they pulled over to the curb. "See, he feels better just seeing you."

"Christina was worried," Cecily called out cautiously.

"I'm afraid this bike wasn't made for a man my size."

"We'll give you a ride the rest of the way."

Don was hungry and tired. He'd been up half the night dealing with Melvin, and early that morning with Officer Stacey. He'd worked longer than usual, in temperatures at a hundred degrees. He'd ridden a bike with half-flat tires to work and walked the same bike home. It'd been almost too much for one day. A ride would be much appreciated.

But there was a problem–his clothes were covered in a powdery palette of colors that would get all over the Jeep's seats, he explained. "You can take the bike and I'll walk the rest of the way." He put the bike in the back of the Jeep.

Cecily wasn't surprised at the snub. She'd actually expected it.

"He's just very tired," Christina assured Cecily as they drove away. Neither of them had fully appreciated the magnitude of the burdens he was carrying. Cecily dropped Christina off and helped unload the bike. She was eager to leave before he got home.

"Bye, Christina. Hope I'll see you later," she said, as she drove away.

As he trudged the last few blocks to the Jensen home, Don had time to think of what he'd just done. Cecily had said nothing about her wanting to see him, only that Christina was worried. She hadn't come to see him at all; she'd come only because his daughter had called. He turned the corner—the Jeep was gone. Just like after work, she hadn't waited. Maybe it was for the best. A relationship might complicate things right now. A wave of sadness settled over him as he tried to adjust his thoughts to the loss. His brain tried to compensate for the void he felt by rationalizing: *all the flirting must have been a game. She gets the guy where she wants him and drops him. No wonder she's still single.*

Don asked Christina to see if Kate would let him make a long distance call. She could bring the mobile phone to the door so he wouldn't need to go inside. She soon returned.

"She says you don't need to ask," Christina said, handing him the phone.

The call revealed that his father's condition hadn't changed. Pressing the end button, he turned to Christina and apologized for his having to go away so quickly before, and promised that they could spend the next afternoon together after he worked the morning shift. She was pleased—both that they could be together and, more importantly, that now she'd have the chance to get away that morning and see what was in the shed.

It was dark in the river bottoms. Two steep mountainsides, rising a quarter mile on each side, blocked whatever sunlight remained.

Stacey approached the house from the rear and entered through the badly jimmied door. Indirect light from the western sky made it through the high upper windows, casting faint shadows on the empty rooms. How'd the captain move out so quickly? Then he realized the carpets didn't show any furniture marks. Mostly paper plates and cups filled the kitchen shelves. Only a bed and nightstand met the bare necessities of the upstairs bedroom, and clothes were scattered on the floor and in the closet. Not even a phone was to be seen. *No wonder the search team had been in and out so quickly. There was nothing to search.* He opened the door to the garage, but immediately saw that the place was bare. *Bingham clearly had been ready to take flight.*

Stacey opened the back door a crack and peeked out. In that instant, a dark figure ran from the trees toward the house. Leaving the door ajar, he moved his way behind an empty pantry door, drew the captain's revolver, and pointed it through the one-inch opening.

All at once something touched him on the back of the neck, sending Stacey recoiling sideways into the pantry's wall. Reflexively reaching up and slapping away at whatever it was, he discovered a pull chain to a light dangling from the ceiling. Okay, so a light bulb was directly overhead; did that mean he'd soon have a great idea?

After a breathless minute, the back door slowly

creaked open and someone walked through the kitchen, stopped a few feet from where he was hiding and began rolling the fridge from its place. Stacey could hear the man grunt as he lugged it out. He wore military head gear, which included both a heat sensor and a lamp. Stacey could see exactly what he was doing. He brought out a tool and began removing the screws from the back panel of the refrigerator. With the panel part way off, the man reached inside and pulled out a small object, placed it in his pocket and rolled the refrigerator back in place.

Having a vague idea how the headgear's heat-sensing capability worked, Stacey assumed the door was sufficient protection from his body heat. What he didn't realize was that his few minutes in the small opening was actually building a "shadow" of heat—a shadow that finally caught the intruder's eye. Not expecting anyone in the house, he walked toward the pantry door. Stacey reached up and grasped ahold of the pull chain. The very instant the door opened, Stacey yanked down on the chain. The blinding light gave him a split-second advantage. The man reached to draw his weapon, but Stacey was too fast. He caught the hand, jerked it back over the man's shoulder, and sent him sprawling to the floor, his headgear skidding onto the floor a few feet away. Still struggling to get his gun—and to catch his breath from the hard slam he'd taken—the man suddenly felt a cold barrel on the side of his head.

"Don't do that." Stacey tightened his grip. He could feel the tendons and bones stretch and strain under his grip. The man made no sound. "What did you pick up, my friend?" No answer. "I met your buddies the other night. Who are you?" Still no answer. "Well, you don't seem to know anything that can help me—maybe I should just let you go." Stacey increased the pressure to the arm; any more, he judged, would snap the bone in two. "Now give me your other arm."

The glint of agony that shone in his attacker's eyes told Stacey he'd do anything to comply, in hopes the pain would let up. Stacey also brought the man's foot up and took a shoelace from the shoe. In a moment, both arms were tied tightly together, twisted at a grotesque angle behind his back.

Using his arms as a lever, Stacey rolled the man to the side and took a gun, cell phone and a thick ballpoint pen from inside his dark jacket. There was nothing more. Putting the goods in his own pocket, he removed the almost dead phone he carried and clipped it to the back of his guest's pants, all the while questioning his captive. Still unwilling to volunteer any information, Stacey hog-tied the man's hands and feet so tightly the laces dug into his skin. "I assume you'll see my old friend Bingham, or whatever his name is. Tell him I have whatever it is in the pen you so carefully came to get. I'll keep the gun, thanks. Maybe the phone has enough battery left to call him. He just might come and bail you out. I'll turn this phone on at eleven. Tell him he can call me then." Stacey picked up the headgear and turned out the light.

"He'll kill you," the man snarled, writhing on the floor.

Stacey turned and slipped away into the darkness.

Don finished his shower and lay down to rest. He knew Melvin was home, since the car was in the drive. He wondered where Stacey had gone—

Suddenly his ears felt like they were going to burst! Covering them offered no relief as he flailed about on the bed. He tried to stand but couldn't keep his balance. Then, as abruptly as the sensation had started, it quit. Only Melvin's high-pitched laughter drifted down through the heat vents. *What's he up to?*

Then the noise—or whatever it was—started up again. His head reeled. Everything went out of focus, and he capsized onto the floor and half-crawled to the door—before it again quit, followed once more by the laughter.

Don staggered into the front room and out the door, locking it behind him. He needed to come up with a better idea than last night's party if he wanted to get any sleep. Regaining his equilibrium, he mounted Christina's bike and rode off down the street.

THIRTY-THREE

DIANNE SAID GOODBYE to the last of her friends and visitors. Only close family remained in the small home. Though exhausted both emotionally and physically, she'd held up well.

A knock came at the door. Barker stood on the porch. "I know this isn't a good time to talk, but it's important."

She stepped down off the porch to the side of the house near the garage.

"I need your help. Do you know how I can reach Stace?" She remained quiet. Barker's expression bordered on anguish as he explained, "He thinks I double-crossed him." Then, to prove his loyalty, he told her how he'd helped Stacey get back to his place, how Officer Green's call from Virginia had been forwarded to the captain, and how the next thing he knew he was trying to figure out a way to keep his friend from getting killed. How much did he need to tell her before she believed him?

Dianne bit her lip. Deek and Barker had been friends a long time. He'd been even closer to Deek than Stacey was—mainly because Stacey had been the newcomer on the force. She could trust Barker; his story matched Stacey's. "I *am* expecting to see him again," she finally offered.

Then she reached over and punched in the garage door code. To Barker's surprise, as the door slowly rolled upward and the light came on, there stood Sig, wagging his tail. Although he'd struggled to his feet and his movements were slow and deliberate, he was still willing to greet a friend. And there sat Deek's old car, too. "That sly devil," Barker grinned. "Who in the world would've guessed Stace is hiding out here?"

"He's not. He came to me after he was shot—then again after Sig was hurt."

"If I wasn't in charge, you could get in a lot of trouble for this," he teased.

"If I didn't trust you, you'd never have found out."

"Good point."

"Now let me tell you what little I know—so I can go to bed." She recounted the codeine incident, about Doc Frisby and Stacey nursing broken ribs, how he'd told Deek of his suspicions about Bingham and how Deek thought it was the captain who'd shot him.

Barker glanced up into the night sky. "I suspect someone on the force is helping Bingham. Could be Olsen. He seemed eager to see Rick out of the way. I need Stace's help. He knows more than I do. Will you tell him to call me when he comes for Sig?"

"I'll tell him. He'll be glad to know he can still trust you."

"Thanks, Dianne." He looked into her tired face. "I wish I could make Deek come back." He reached out and hugged her—more for his own good than hers.

Dianne, the last of her tears spent long ago, groaned into his shoulder, "You take good care of Rick. He believes he's up against something a lot bigger than the Mapleton police force."

"He is." Barker drew away and bent to give the police dog a reassuring pat.

Don stood outside in the darkness, gripping the bike handles, trying to decide whether or not to return to the apartment. He was, after all, dealing with a killer, one who might just be crazy enough to come after him, too. But he hated the thought of being whipped by a man half his size.

"What do you think you're doing?" Don startled at the voice, coming from behind a tree.

It was Stacey! "I was on my way home when I saw you come flying out of there. And then I tracked you up and down the street with these." He raised the sophisticated headgear, now in his hand.

Don took the equipment. "What are they?" he asked, slipping them over his head and toying with the dials. "They give distance, height...everything."

"That's not all." Stacey reached up and adjusted the zoom lens.

"That's incredible. Where'd you get them?"

"From someone who's in a lot of trouble with his boss by now." At that moment a funny thought crossed his mind. He wondered if the hog-tied man had freed himself or if he'd figured out how to phone the captain by punching up the numbers with his nose.

Stacey's brief reverie was broken by Don telling him of Melvin's shenanigans, in particular the cryptic "noise" that hurt his ears.

At hearing this, Stacey became concerned. "Melvin has the same high-tech equipment as Bingham. I don't know if you should go back inside."

"I can't go into my own apartment?"

"That's not what I'm saying. I think your landlord may be linked to the same guy I took this thing from," he said, indicating the headgear. "If so, neither of us is safe in there."

"Well, let's find out...." Don had come up with a scheme of his own.

Silently entering the apartment, Don and Stacey made ready to give Melvin the surprise of his life. Don wheeled Alan's compressor into the furnace room, cut the end off the air hose, turned off the gas valve leading to the water heater and unscrewed the flex line to the heater. Disconnecting the quick coupler from the compressor, he inserted the gas line into the end of the rubber air hose. *Two can play this game*, he thought as he completed his preparations.

Stacey, meanwhile, had slipped out to the garage and found an empty paint can. Opening the lid, he dropped the pen he'd taken from Bingham's gopher into the crusty container, replaced the lid and returned it to the shelf he'd taken it from. He then donned his headgear and waited for his cue.

Don, hearing Melvin walk across the floor above, switched on the television and raised the volume to a deafening roar. At once the reception turned to static. Don swore in mock disgust. Melvin laughed. Don went to the furnace room and began banging on pipes. Predictably, Melvin turned on his device.

The sharp pain instantly drove Don to his knees. Stacey could feel the effects all the way from the garage. Don, his equilibrium shot, reached out to turn a knob on the compressor, sending a small amount of gas through the rubber hose to the line leading to the pipe duct above. After enough gas had leaked into the ducts to give off a deceptively strong gas odor, Don turned off the valve and took the hose from the line. Again he banged on the pipes.

When he reckoned he'd gotten Melvin's attention, he plugged the air hose back into the compressor, this time sending air whistling through the hose—and echoing throughout the house. His inside mission accomplished, he ran outside, slamming the door behind him. Up the steps he bounded, two at a time, and crouched outside Melvin's back door, cigarette lighter in hand.

It took 20 seconds for the smell of gas to reach Melvin's nose, one second for its meaning to register on his face, and no more than five to sprint for the door and throw it open. Just as he began to jump off the step, Don reached out and caught hold of his ankle. Melvin tumbled halfway down the stairs before Don hauled him to his feet, flicked his lighter to life and stuck the flame in his face.

"I think I'll light your pants on fire and toss you back inside!"

Melvin, who removed protective earphones from his head, remained remarkably calm. Don, baffled by his poise, picked him up and steer-wrestled him out to the front yard—a part of the plan to allow Stacey access to Melvin's open apartment.

Melvin found himself face to face with his enraged tenant. The front of his shirt bunched up in Don's brawny paw, the flame still held aloft in the other hand. "Maybe we should call a truce."

Don was stunned by the statement. His eyes stared

past the flickering flame to meet those of his tormentor. Deep within those eyes, Don could see something good, a light he'd never seen before.

Don released his thumb from the lighter, snuffing out the flame. "What do you have in mind?"

"It's like this," said Melvin, raising a finger in a professorial manner. "I'll stay out of your way, if you let me live in peace. You'll never hear or see me, I won't talk to you or your daughter and I'll give you back your deposit—and give you ten days to find a new place to stay."

Don's heart slightly softened. Then, returning to his senses, he growled, "I don't think so! How can I trust a word you say?" Still gripping the smaller man's shirt, Don felt a chain knotted up amongst the cloth. "What's this?" he asked, pulling it out. It was a medallion of some sort, its face having been cut in half.

"A purple heart."

"Right—and I'm Colin Powell!" Don smirked.

"It's the truth," Melvin said. "Earned it in Nam. I was a communications officer—set up surveillance to spy on the enemy. I was caught behind enemy lines and got shot in the butt. Wasn't much of a wound, but the bullet had some kind of chemical on it. Almost killed me. Instead they cut out a good chunk of my rear end." He reached down and pressed against the left side of his rump. His hand tweaked at a spot where flesh should have been. "It's affected the rest of my health, too. People sometimes think I'm crazy."

"Sounds about right," Don laughed, loosening his grip. "Why's the heart cut in half?"

"Well, when my daughter was eight her mother kept threatening she was going to take her back to Nam. Leah—that's my daughter—and I were really close, as close as you are to your daughter. She was always worried it might come true, and so was I. Her mother was starting to get weird. Well, one day, to comfort Leah, I cut the heart down the middle and put a chain on each half. She made me promise her that if we ever were separated, I would find her and bring her home. Now...I haven't seen her in almost five years. Her mother claims she's safe..."

While all this was going on out front, Stacey had seized the opportunity to enter the upstairs apartment. Struggling to keep his balance from the awful noise, he slipped on the headgear and stared in awe at the vast array of computers and components. He recognized the zip and jazz disks which lined the shelves, row upon row. Most of it was for surveillance. A small, partially disassembled mechanical device sat on a desk next to one of the keyboards. He guessed it was the rat Don had told him about. He dropped a few of the disks in his pocket and initiated a quick walk-through of the dark house.

In a small room in back, Stacey found several rows of exotic plants, well-groomed and meticulously arranged on shelves against the outside wall. Below the open window, the wall itself was dirty and worn and the window sill scuffed and damaged—as if someone had regularly climbed in and out of it. A bamboo mat lay in the center of the floor. A plastic cup sat on the shelf with the plants, probably used for watering. Picking it up, careful not to leave any prints of his own, he placed it in his jacket pocket.

The adjoining bedroom was normal-looking, with the bed in disarray. His search complete, he stepped out of the house and back into the garage.

"You don't know where your daughter is?" Don asked.

"If I knew that, I'd have her here with me."

Don felt an odd kinship with this man, yet he wasn't about to let him renege on his deal. "I'll hold onto the medal until I get my deposit back and we part ways."

"I won't take it off until I find her."

Don had to hand it to him—he was a stubborn little cuss. But he had to have some collateral, otherwise the guy was going to welsh on his promises. "We call a truce while the chain is around my neck. You'll get it back when I have *my* cash, the last renter gets *his* money, and Christina and I walk away from here unharmed."

Melvin reluctantly drew the chain up over his head. "Agreed."

Don sensed that one last threat was in order. "If you don't shut off the contraption, I'll blow more than a whiff of gas into the place. I'll fill it up."

"You mean it's not gas?"

"Just enough to get your attention. The rest is compressed air." He gave Melvin a gentle shove, whereupon Melvin retreated to the presumed safety of his home.

They met around the corner to exchange information. After hearing what Don had learned, Stacey rattled off his findings. "He has some of the most sophisticated equipment I've ever seen. If he wanted to, he could probably hear what we're saying right now." Then, tapping his jacket pocket, he added, "I picked up a few of the older disks—ones he wouldn't miss. Maybe I can find someone who can read them."

"My nephew might be able to help out. He's pretty good."

Stacey wasn't thrilled at the idea. The last thing he wanted to do was get anyone else involved, especially a kid. But, with his options slim, he agreed. "You realize, don't you, that the evidence we find won't be admissible in court? As a matter of fact, everything in the apartment may be inadmissible."

Don nodded. "I want him in jail more than anyone, but from what I hear, he may have something on Judge Demick. The rat he used in the vents is probably the same one he used to spy on women in the restroom at the county building. If he's using it to blackmail the judge, we don't have a chance of using *anything* until we expose the judge himself. Maybe we can find enough to get him thrown off the case."

"The only thing we can hope to find on these will be old information," Stacey countered. "We need a warrant—and a major computer expert."

At that moment Melvin was on the phone. "Where

are they?...Good. Don't let them out of sight." He hung up and placed a second call. "...This thing's getting out of hand. We've got to wrap up and get out of town....Tomorrow night will be fine. Have you located her yet?...If you don't find her soon, someone else'll get hurt. She's out of her mind."

Two men sat across from each other, a carton of Chinese take-out on the table between them. The home was expensive, luxurious. One of the men spoke calmly to the other. "This time I plan on staying. I like it here. I'm comfortable—I make a good living. People here respect me. And I've been wanting to retire. So you go on alone. You'll find everything you need in a green Pontiac parked in long-term parking, row M-1." He slid a car key across the table. "I suggest you pull out as soon as you can. You've already made it more difficult to get out safely."

"I won't go until I'm finished with Stacey," grumbled the other man. "If I walk away now, I'll never get any respect again."

"Maybe it's time for you to retire, too. Lay on the beach. Settle down with that cute little bimbo of yours...make pretty little babies to play with."

"I've been thinking about it. No kids, though."

"Good, it's settled then. I'll have someone take you to the airport tonight."

"I'll take you up on that offer—but tomorrow, after it's finished. If I don't get my pen back, I'll be hunted by half a dozen different governments. I won't be able to find a dirty hole to hide in. Neither will you."

"I know."

"Is everything in order for the morning?"

"Yes."

"I need a shower and a place to sleep."

"You know where the guest room is. You'll find everything you need." The two men stood and cleared the table.

Stacey and Don stood talking several blocks from Kate's house. "Okay, you get your nephew to take a look at the disks; I'll work on Melvin," said Stacey. "If my hunch is right, he's connected to the men that are hunting me. It'll surprise me if he doesn't already know I've been snooping through his stuff. I'd suggest you avoid the place, too. Now, should we meet back here in a couple of hours?"

Both men looked at their watches. "One-thirty then," Don confirmed as he headed out. Stacey left in the other direction to see what kind of cover the orchard might offer.

Don stopped to talk to Jake and his friends, who were playing late-night hoops in the driveway. "Did Christina tell you about the laser?" Jake asked Don excitedly.

"What laser?" He then remembered Jake babbling about some laser they could "borrow" to use in one of the many "Melvin schemes" they'd bandied about.

"The one we've got in the garage." Jake scurried to the garage, opened the door and walked out carrying a yellow case. "You could shine the beam through Melvin's windows and—"

"Sorry guys. Melvin's out of my league—not to mention a dangerous man. We won't be playing any more tricks on him." Then he started off to find Danny.

"Dang!" Jake said. "It would have been a blast."

"We better get this thing back to my dad's business first thing in the morning," Bryce said nervously. "I didn't even tell him I was taking it. It cost him four thousand bucks."

THIRTY-FOUR

ALAN AND DANNY were in the study sitting in front of the computer when Don knocked on the door. Alan waved him in.

"I was hoping you'd still be up," Don said. "I have a few disks I need Danny's help with."

"Go ahead. He was just showing me how I can fix my security problems at work. He broke into my system—again!"

Don shrugged. "I'm not sure you want him to look at these. They're out of Melvin's house."

"Wow! Did you see his computer? It—"

"What computer's that?" Alan asked.

"Ummm...the one I heard that's in Melvin's house."

"Who told you about it?" his father persisted.

Don understood Danny's hesitation. "Just a minute. I'll call her in." He stepped out the door and called Christina, who didn't really want to drag herself away from the movie she was watching with the other children. Hearing the insistence in his voice, however, she came on the run. After directing her to a chair, he looked her in the eye and said, "I've heard from a very reliable source that you were in Melvin's house."

Christina turned to Danny with a piercing glare.

"He wasn't the one, either," added Don.

Christina was puzzled, "If Danny didn't tell, then who did?"

Don wasn't about to play games. "It doesn't matter. Now tell me what you were doing there."

Christina answered with a sigh, "I was looking for evidence. Officer Barker said that's why Melvin's not in jail—

not enough evidence. I thought maybe I could find some."

"Christina! How foolish is that? The man tried to kill you, for crying-out-loud!"

She fought to defend her motives. "And I don't want him to hurt anyone else."

Alan turned to Danny. "Were you with her?"

"I was alone," Christina mumbled.

Don resumed his lecture. "The man's dangerous. So dangerous that I'm not going to stay there myself."

Christina's mind sought out an excuse to change the subject. Pointing to the chain and medallion hanging around her father's neck, she asked, "What's that?"

Don saw right through her little ploy. "I want you to understand," he growled, determined to make his point, "That house is off limits. Is that clear!"

"Yes, I understand—completely. I won't go back in the house....Now, what is that?"

Don was still riled up. "It's some half-assed song-and-dance number Melvin gave me," he grumped. Then, embarrassed by the language he'd used, he bit his tongue. "Said the other half of his purple heart is on a chain around his daughter's neck. Said he wouldn't take it off until he finds her. I made him give it to me until we get our deposit back."

"Did he say what her name was?" Christina said anxiously.

"Leann....Linda. I can't remember."

"Oh, well."

Danny shot a glance at Christina. Knowing exactly what she was thinking, he discreetly wagged his head side to side. *I'm not going back there*, he said to himself, *no matter what she says*.

"Now that that's out of the way, let's see if I can help Don." Alan motioned the children toward the door.

"I can help!" Danny protested.

"I'm guessing what's on these disks isn't suitable even for a grownup to see." Alan ushered his son out the door and closed it behind him. Then, turning to Don, he mumbled, "I'm not the genius he is but I can open a file or two."

Don handed the disks to Alan, who realized they weren't normal floppies. "Good thing I had a zip put on this new machine." He inserted one in the drive and changed screens. A few key strokes later he shook his head. "Empty."

He tried a second disk. Again, nothing. All four disks were empty!

Danny came and poked his head through the doorway. "So what's on them?"

"Nothing. They're all empty," his father told him.

"No way!"

"Look for yourself," Alan offered, moving from behind the desk. Danny sat down and tried to browse the disk. He opened the recycle bin and asked to restore the information. The answer flashed on the screen: *unknown format*. He opened a file in "Danny's stuff" and tried again. Still no go.

"I think you dumped the menu just loading them without a password," he said accusingly. "I wish you would've let me help."

"You think something's on these?"

His tone was one of impatience. "Something *was* on them—before you tried to open them." He continued to type in commands, using resources he had tucked away in his files. "I might be able to save bits and pieces—if I'm lucky."

"Alan, can I talk to you in private?" Don asked.

They stepped into the hallway. "Melvin's become a real threat. I was wondering if I could stay here 'til I can find another place for us. Oh, and also, could I borrow your bike to get to work?"

"Of course. You and Christina are welcome to stay here as long as you need to. Actually, I've wanted to tell you something: I misjudged you before, and I apologize."

"Thanks." Don then turned away. Lately he'd had a few too many heart-to-heart chats.

Stacey walked the perimeter of the orchard behind the Jensen home. He had no idea it was so big. He stopped less than a third of the way around. It would take all night.

He turned west, cutting back through the orchard, hoping to take a shortcut. Almost halfway through, near the northern end, he came across an old farmhouse. It could have been the original pioneer home, built when the orchard was planted. Rusty farm equipment and broken crates cluttered the yard. Inside was a small living area, probably where, in later years, migrant workers stayed. Obviously abandoned, he decided it would make a good place to stay for a few days. He'd even be able to bring Sig there. He missed his friend and companion. And it was time to drag the Taurus out of Dianne's garage. He could park it in the trees. Checking his watch, he realized he would need to hurry to meet Don.

Moving briskly through the orchard, he noticed the last of the cherry blossoms were falling. They smelled fresh in the warm night air. Cloud cover hung low on the foothills, a sign that a spring storm was looming. The place was one of a kind. Not that many orchards were left in the area, what with families selling off the ground when their parents passed on. All around the area new homes had sprung up on huge tracts where only cherry and peach trees once stood.

Stacey's thoughts were halted by the hissing of some creature in the grass. A flurry of flapping wings and rushing wind caught him off guard. Practically tripping over himself, Stacey raced headlong into the night to avoid being bit by several angry geese. He'd nearly trampled the nesting mothers. His grandfather used to keep a few geese on his farm. They were fearless, especially when protecting their young or a nest. And suddenly, like finding a long-missing piece of a complex puzzle, Stacey saw how they would be a perfect addition to his plan—still in its early stages—to settle his feud with Bingham.

Stacey began counting the rows of trees he crossed. Fifteen minutes—and 82 rows later— he was standing on the gravel lane at the edge of the orchard. Using a tall electric pole as a marker, he plodded down the lane to the connecting street. Four or five blocks later, he arrived at his and Don's meeting place.

A dark sedan pulled around the corner and crept

down the street. Backing off the sidewalk and behind the cover of an old willow, Stacey spied Don coming his way. The driver pulled over and stopped, exhibiting unmistakable interest in Don. Stacey ducked down and ran to the backyard of the home. The curve of the hill took him out of visual range of the parked sedan. In a few minutes he was running uphill through the trees. His side burned with each jarring. Crawling around the house, which backed up against the orchard, he adjusted the hood of his headgear to zoom in on the sedan.

The driver looked like a kid. He was sipping a drink and occasionally raising to his eyes what appeared to be binoculars. Stacey could see Don patiently waiting at the designated spot. The young man in the car sat quietly, his window rolled down. Stacey needed a distraction—something to throw him off guard. Seeing the young man bend over as if to pick something up, Stacey made a dash for the vehicle. Across the front lawn he came, drawing his weapon as he ran. The man's head reappeared in the window, and he began to pour himself another cup from his thermos. The onrushing figure made him drop his drink and reach for his weapon. The sensation of hot coffee in his lap forced him up off the seat.

"I wouldn't try that," Stacey warned as he pushed the barrel of his gun against the young man's neck. Stacey reached through the open window and unholstered the gun from the man's side. Unlocking the back door, he then climbed into the back seat, simultaneously reaching up with the barrel of his gun and shattering the dome light.

"Put your hands at ten and two on the wheel so I can see them," he barked.

The man obliged. "I'm a federal agent," he started to explain, his voice thick. "Don't think about harming me or you'll be hunted down by every federal agent in the country."

"Do you know who I am?" Stacey asked.

"Richard Michael Stacey."

Stacey felt a little sorry for him. The guy was scared half to death, had dumped a cup of scalding hot coffee in his lap, and now a "cop killer" had a gun aimed at the back of his head.

"Why are you watching me?"

"Just following orders."

"How did you find me?"

"I was given instructions where to locate you."

"You followed me last night?"

"That was a different agent."

"What's going on?" Stacey demanded.

"I'm not privileged to that information. I'm assigned to keep tabs on you, that's all."

"So where've I been today?"

"We lost you after the funeral. We followed you from the Rodriguez residence, I lost you for the last two hours, now you're pointing a gun at my head and I'd feel a lot better if you'd put it down," he said, his voice still anxious.

Stacey lowered the weapon. "Why don't you give me a ride back to the Rodriguez residence so I can get my things." He reared back and smashed out the window of his door with his gun. Glass flew everywhere. The agent ducked as if he'd been shot.

"Why'd you do that?" the agent asked.

"There aren't any door handles back here. I can't afford to be locked in," Stacey explained. "I don't have a clue who I can trust. Before we leave, let me see your badge."

The young agent reached over to the passenger seat and lifted a small black case, raised it up and folded back the cover. "Agent Tovar, special federal agent. Yes, let's do take a drive."

Tovar started the car and pulled away. A half a block down, from the safety of a tree, Don, having heard the breaking glass, watched them pass.

"How long have you been in the field?" Stacey asked.

"Two years—and this is the first time anyone's ever pulled a gun on me." His voice now carried a curious blend of apprehension and excitement.

"Sorry, I know how you feel....Do you have a phone?"

"Yes." Stacey put his hand up over the seat as Tovar took it from his hip and handed it back.

"When we're done with our ride, you can tell your boss to call me." They drove in silence until they reached the apartment. "Park in front," Stacey demanded. "Get out and come in with me."

Agent Tovar looked back as Stacey got out of the back seat. "You're serious?"

"Very." They walked down the steps to the door, Tovar in front. "Unlock it." Stacey handed him the key.

Melvin, light sleeper that he was, heard the downstairs door open. Easing himself off the bed, he peered out the side window. The dark sedan parked at the curb out front commanded his attention. He snatched up a weapon and tiptoed to the front room for a better view. Minutes later, Stacey and Tovar emerged from the apartment and drove away.

Melvin picked up the phone. "We've got another problem."

Pulling up in front of Dianne's house, Stacey cuffed Tovar to the frame of the broken door, then went to Dianne's window. She seemed to be expecting him. "I hope this is the last time I need to wake you up," he apologized. "I've come to get Sig—if he's strong enough to leave."

"I'll meet you at the back door."

Sig was ecstatic. After a brief—and wet—reunion, Dianne spoke: "Paul came to see me."

"Does he know you've been helping me?"

Dianne nodded. "But he didn't cross you. The captain got the call from your contact in Virginia. Barker was worried about keeping you alive."

Stacey sighed with relief. "Maybe he can help."

"That's exactly what he has in mind. Only one problem, he thinks someone on the force is still helping Bingham."

"Who?"

"Doesn't know. He wants you to call him on his mobile."

"I'll do that. Will you give this to him for me? I need him to see if he can run a match on the prints." Stacey brought out the cup he'd taken from Melvin's apartment and handed it to Dianne.

"I'll be glad to."

"I also have someone here to take this car away."

Her face registered confusion. "Who?"

"There's a federal agent cuffed to his car in the front yard who'll be more than willing to drive it away. I'm sorry to do this to you, but they'll probably be back to question you. Just tell them everything you can."

"It'll do me good to get it off my chest."

Stacey picked up a bag of dog food. "Can I take this?"

"Of course."

Stacey pulled the vehicle out to the street. Returning to Tovar, he undid the cuffs and handed him the key to the Taurus. "I'll leave your weapon in the trunk of your car and the keys up the tail-pipe. When your boss calls me, I'll tell him where you can find your car." Stacey offered his hand as a gesture of goodwill. "Hey, Tovar, sorry about the coffee."

Tovar hesitated before extending his hand in return. Each man gave a stout grip, as they parted ways. Tovar was confident the man he'd just met was a good cop.

THIRTY-FIVE

DON HADN'T SLEPT WELL. He was worried about Stacey. Still he dragged himself out of bed and into the shower. He'd promised Jeff a half day's work. He decided to drop by the apartment and get a change of clothes before going in. He did his best to keep from waking the family as he walked down the stairs past the study. Danny sat at the computer, the glare of the screen reflecting on his face.

"What are you doing up?" Don whispered.

"Trying to find out what's on the disks."

"Making any headway?"

"I've been at it most of the night, and now I think I know why he destroyed the information. I've almost figured it out."

"You better get some sleep."

"In awhile."

"I'm going in to work. Tell Christina I'll see her about noon."

"Sure."

The threatened storm from the night before had just arrived. Droplets of rain pelted against his face as he mounted Alan's ten-speed. The dark, rain-heavy clouds that rolled down the mountainside cooled the valley. Don pushed off down the drive. Up the street sat the sedan that had passed him the night before. The car was empty. Glass littered the asphalt near its back door. There were no clues as to what had happened.

Climbing back on the bike, he rode toward his apartment. The cool moist air seemed to slip right through him as he peddled along.

Arriving, he made a cautious entrance. The wool overcoat and extra clothing Stacey had left were gone. He wondered if his cop friend had spent the night there—after warning *him* to stay away. Climbing into his work clothes, he grabbed a jacket and headed out. There wasn't so much as a peep from Melvin.

The light sprinkles had turned to rain, and by the time Don sloshed up to the building—the tires of the bike flicking a rooster-tail of water—he was soaked. He went straight to work, the fine powder sticking to his clothes.

Stacey completed his preparations and lay down for a few hours' sleep before the expected call from Bingham. In the vacant house deep in the orchard, the new leaves on the trees gave plenty of cover.

With the mountains to his back and the rain on his fur, Sig, too, was content. He wasn't fond of the bandage Stacey had applied, but still took the opportunity to give his master a wet kiss when he came near to apply the salve. He'd never before experienced a real dog fight. True, he'd chased away some of the neighborhood dogs, but they were nothing like the hulking animal he'd faced in the field. That brute was a trained killer.

Earlier, Stacey had spoken with Agent Buseth, Tovar's boss. The two of them talked for several moments before detailed instructions were given. The agent had seemed most interested in the fountain pen, as he suspected Bingham would be. Buseth warned Stacey not to underestimate Bingham. He also advised him of the dangerous nature of the pen and its contents. Stacey was left with the impression that as long as he was in possession of the pen, he was calling the shots. To test the theory, he'd warned Buseth that if he tried to locate him from the phone signal, he'd never see the pen. Buseth yielded to the demand. He'd cooperate and wait for further instructions.

Christina forced herself out of bed at seven a.m. A task of supreme importance was at hand. She fluffed her pillows and arranged them under the covers in the shape of what she imagined a slumbering 12-year-old looked like. It just might buy her a little more time. Most of the family stayed in bed later on Saturday mornings.

She'd been careful in choosing the words she spoke to her father the previous night. She'd said, "I won't go back *in* that house"—not once mentioning the possibility of searching the shed for more clues. Someone needed to see what was buried in there.

She crept to Danny's room, but he wasn't in his bed. Shuffling downstairs, she peeked into the study. Danny was sound asleep on Alan's desk. "Danny," she whispered. He didn't move. She gave him a shake. "Danny!" He stirred ever so slightly. "Come on, we've got to go check out the shed."

Beyond exhaustion, the boy couldn't open his eyes. Mumbling something about being back by noon, he turned his head and fell back asleep.

"I'll have to do it by myself," Christina muttered. "Melvin can't get away with what he did."

In the garage she found a small garden shovel and a screwdriver. Feeling the rain, she went back inside for her jacket. Unable to locate it anywhere, she found Jake's in the laundry room and decided to borrow it. Though much too large, it would keep her dry. Her bike was in the backyard, its tire flat. The only other one was Jake's. *He never uses it anyway*, she reasoned. *And I'll be back in just a couple of hours.*

Taking caution, she parked the bike behind some bushes down the street from the apartment. Moseying up the sidewalk, she tried to convince herself that her shortness of breath was from peddling the bike. "I'm not afraid," she chanted over and over under her breath. For a moment, she stood behind the big spruce in the yard next door, watching the house. Nothing was out of the ordinary. Melvin's orange cat sat meowing on the back step. If she could just make it into the back without being seen, she'd be in the clear!

Glancing both ways, she made a run for it. A bundle of nerves, her foot slipped on the slick concrete and she went down, sprawled across the driveway. The trowel fell from her hand, clattered across the pavement and clanked against the step, out of reach. The cat hissed and bolted for the backyard as Christina struggled to get out of sight. She shuddered, crouching beside the building.

Peeking through a crack running between the shed and the garage, she could see the back step. There came the darn cat again, crying to be let in. Then the back door creaked open, and Melvin stepped out. Christina, her heart racing, held her breath as he peered up and down the driveway. She assumed he could see the trowel she'd dropped—and in fact did walk down the steps toward it, momentarily passing out of Christina's view. Then back up the stairs and into the house he went.

Leaning up against the garage wall, she stared down at her scraped, trembling hands—and started to cry. The rain dripped off the garage roof onto the jacket. *What am I doing?! This man has tried to kill!* No one knew where she was but Danny—who was sleeping at the computer!—and here was Melvin, wide awake!

Looking down at her skinned hands, she noticed how pink and tender they still were from the rope burn. Her fear slowly transformed into anger. She thought of what he'd tried to do to her and her friend, and imagining the other girls—who knew how many—less fortunate than herself.

Drawing the screwdriver from her pocket, she brazenly began to remove the rusty screws from the metal siding, stacking them at the base of the shed in a neat pile. They were tight; the job was slow and difficult.

Finally she had taken out enough of the screws. Carefully folding and creasing the corrugated tin flap upward, she squeezed inside. Jake's coat hooked itself on the tin as she entered. She pulled it free, then waited while her eyes adjusted to the darkness. Slivers of light slipped in from joints at the corners of the structure and from around the doors. Tiny particles of dust drifted and danced in the mostly vertical rays. *Sunbeams!* she mused, *even without the sun shining!* Christina hoped that was a good omen.

Without the trowel the work would be tedious—and dirty—as now she'd have to dig with the screwdriver.

The boxes she and Danny had gone through had been resealed. She started breaking off the stringy weeds and tossing them to the side. The button on the sweater seemed to stare up at her in the darkness.

Hands trembling, she cautiously began to dig, working her way around the sweater in an attempt to extricate it first. The work was slow and painful. She would pick at the dry, crusty dirt with the screwdriver and remove it with her bare hands.

Jake had hit the snooze button twice before finally prying himself out of the sack. It was against his nature to get up so early on a Saturday. He went into the bathroom thinking he would go back to bed after he and Bryce returned the laser. As he tugged on a pair of pants, he glanced out the window. It was raining! A sweatshirt pulled down over his head quelled his shivers.

After putting on his shoes, he opened the closet to get his jacket. Oh, that's right—he'd left it in the laundry room. Another thorough search—no jacket. Where was it? He was unfazed; it'd show up sooner or later. More than likely his mother would pull it out of some obvious spot.

In the kitchen, he poured himself a glass of orange juice and sat down to wait for Bryce.

Three or four inches down, the dirt turned to a dark clay which gave off a foul, stale odor. The rotten fabric of the sweater gave way to mere strands of fiber. The name *Leah* echoed in her thoughts. The black letters written on the boxes behind her seemed to whisper that name to her.

The hole she'd been digging was now 18 inches in diameter and a good two feet deep. Her fingers were now raw from moving the dirt. The palms of her hands stung. The trembling gradually subsided as she dug to the rhythm of the rain bouncing off the shed from the garage. And for a while she propped up her courage by focusing on putting Melvin in jail. But before long her only wish was that Danny would have come with her.

Bryce rapped on the back door. Kate, just exiting her bedroom, walked across the family room to let him in. "You're up early this morning."

Jake came huffing from the kitchen. "I gotta run. Bryce and I need to take his dad's laser back. Have you seen my brown jacket?"

"It's hanging in the laundry room."

"It is not," he griped.

"So, where did you leave it?"

"I don't know."

"So wear your red one."

"Are you kidding? That's from two years ago. It makes me look like a dweeb!"

"Well, dweeb," Kate mocked in a good-humored tease, "I guess you need to take better care of your things."

He stormed back into the laundry room and pulled out his old jacket. The arms rode up several inches too far, exposing his wrists. The slam of the door as he left was his way of saying his mom was to blame for the mood he was in. She watched him out of the kitchen window as he raged like a miniature hurricane around the back-yard.

Kate smiled a sympathetic smile. *It does make him look a like a dweeb*, she thought—*whatever that is!*

Within a minute Jake stormed back inside. "Now I can't even find my bike!" he yelled. "I'll bet Danny used it because his is flat." And up the stairs he marched to bang on Danny's door. No one answered. He barged in, then, just as quickly tore out again. "Where's Danny?" he shouted over the railing into the open family room below.

"I think he's still in bed. With all this noise, though, you can bet he's not sleeping."

"He's not in bed." Two-timing it down the steps, he caught a glimpse of Danny asleep on the study desk. "Danny, where'd you leave my bike?" he yelled.

Danny jerked awake, mumbling incoherently. "—Wha-a-at?"

"Where's my bike?" Jake repeated.

"Christina probably took it," came the reply. Then he promptly plopped his tired head back on the desk.

Jake was not at all satisfied with the answer. "Why would Christina take my bike?!"

"Cause her bike has a flat and so does mine." He lifted his head and yawned.

"I'll go ask her." Jake started up the stairs.

"She's not there..." There came another yawn, and then—"...she's gone to Melvin's shed!" He sprang to his feet, a panicked look on his face. Why couldn't he control his big mouth?

Jake returned to the study—his mother close behind. "You'd better tell me what you're talking about, young man," she ordered.

Danny stuttered...then, seeing his mother's glare, began spilling the beans, jar and all. "We were in his shed the other night...and found boxes of old clothes that said *Leah* on them. Christina picked up a sweater from one of the boxes...so I picked up a shirt and the button fell off. When I looked for it I found a different one—hooked to another sweater buried in the dirt....She went back to dig it up and see if Melvin's daughter's buried there."

Kate began to yell for Alan, still lounging in bed. Jake came skipping back down the stairway. "She's not in her bed. Uncle Don's gone, too." A relieved expression came over Kate and she relaxed a bit, thinking Don and Christina were together.

Alan came racing out of the bedroom to the top of the stairs. "What in the world's going on?" he shrieked, pulling his robe the rest of the way on.

"I'm not sure! Christina's gone; so is Don."

Finally Danny piped up again. "Uncle Don's at work. Left early this morning. He told me he'd be back by noon."

Kate again flew into a panic. "You tell your dad what you told me. I'll call Cecily to see if she can pick Don up from work. Then we'll call the police if we need to." Alan looked on, dazed and confused.

The phone rang several times before a tired Cecily picked up.

"Hello."

"Cecily, this is Kate. We think Christina's missing again. Don's at work. Will you please see if you can find him? We'll meet you at the apartment."

Cecily was suddenly wide awake. She didn't have time to ask questions; Kate had already hung up. Taking a jacket from the closet, she lit out for the Jeep, still wearing her baggy sweats. No big deal: Don could care less about how she looked, anyway.

Alan didn't dress either. "Call the police!" he shouted as he and the three boys rushed to the car. The vehicle sped from the garage as Kate was patched into County Dispatch.

The clay grew slick and oily and the odor grew worse the farther down Christina dug. The pile of dirt in the middle seemed to fall back in the hole as quickly as her hands could scoop it out. She stopped digging. Was that a sound she heard from outside? A sliver of the driveway could be seen through the crack in the doors. Nothing.

She thrust her one pointed tool in the dirt. It struck something solid. She tried to pull it out, but the clay was packed too tightly around it. Something squeaked at the back of the shed. Christina glanced behind her; the tin flap seemed to move. Was it rattling in the wind? Her eyes moved back to the crack in the door, and again she listened. It was difficult to hear anything but the splashing rain and the thumping of her heart.

Sweaty and a little nauseated, she continued tugging at the screwdriver. It still refused to yield. *I've got to get out of here.* The rain-drenched jacket grew heavy. She shrugged it off and threw it on the boxes behind her. Then a shadow passed across the crack in the door. She found herself holding her breath. Did someone know she was there? The incessant rain muffled all the other sounds.

She reached down into the hole one more time, and suddenly lost her balance. Trying to catch herself, she grabbed the screwdriver. It gave way under her weight—

and there she was, half in the hole, blinking dirt from her eyes. And hanging from the end of the screwdriver was a piece of jagged bone. Around it was draped a chain with half a purple heart.

Christina opened her mouth to scream, but she could draw in no air. Her lungs filled, but not with oxygen. And she knew it was more than decaying flesh she smelled—there was gas, too.

Wrestling to gain her balance, Christina pushed her way out of the hole. Her head spinning, she crawled to the back of the shed, longing for a breath of fresh air. But the flap wouldn't budge; it was screwed shut! Someone had replaced the screws! *The noise wasn't the wind at all. It was someone closing me in!*

In the bottom corner of the shed she could vaguely hear a gentle hissing sound. Something was being fed into the shed! She struggled to her feet as the vertical shafts of light seemed to spin around and around. She stumbled toward the crack of the door, then fell back alongside the hole. Lying there, looking down at the dirty, half purple heart hanging from that jagged bone, the last horrifying thought that raced through her mind before she closed her eyes and drifted away, was, *I'm going to be buried here next to this body!*

Alan and the boys fishtailed around the corner. At the apartment, Danny was the first one out, hitting the pavement on a run before the vehicle had even stopped. Straight to the shed he flew. Seeing the hose running into the shed at its base, he ripped it out and banged against the metal side. "Chrissy! Chrissy!" he yelled. He raced around back to see if she'd gotten in. The sheet-metal panels were screwed tight.

"She's not here," he said, puzzled. Scurrying to the front door of the apartment, he jumped down into the stairwell and pushed and pulled at the knob. "It's locked!" He frantically began kicking at the door. Alan, coming up from behind, moved him aside. Backing up a few feet, he flung his shoulder against the door. The sides of the weathered jam splintered and the door collapsed, sending Alan crashing to the floor. Danny jumped over his dad and ran hollering through the apartment.

"She's not here, either!" he brooded. Darting madly back up the steps, he ran headlong into Melvin, standing in the driveway.

"What's going on here?"

"Where is she!" Danny screamed, swinging his arms. Melvin was quite adept at dodging the barrage of fists.

All at once Barker pulled up, lights flashing. As Melvin averted his attention from Danny's attack, the boy connected with a blow to the midriff. A puff of air escaped Melvin's lips. His face turned red as he dropped to his knees and crumpled to the ground on his side. Danny pressed his own knee into Melvin's shoulders and continued to punch at the dazed man.

Two feet off the ground and being held by his father and Lieutenant Barker, Danny continued swinging his arms and legs frantically, determined to finish the job. "He's got someone buried in the shed," he screamed at the top of his lungs, "and now he's got Christina!"

Alan took hold of Danny in a bear hug. "Settle down, son!"

Melvin rolled over in the wet driveway to get up.

"What are you talking about?" Barker asked.

"His daughter's buried in the shed out back. Christina and I found a sweater buried in the dirt."

Barker turned to Melvin. "Mind if we take a look?"

"This is ridiculous. No one's buried in my shed!"

"Then you won't mind if we look."

"Hi, Grandpa!" Christina ran—though it felt almost like she was floating—to meet her grandfather. Everything seemed so bright and clean. "Are you feeling better?"

"I'm feeling much better, dear. And I'm so glad to see you!"

"How'd we get here?" she asked.

"That's not important right now."

Melvin finally gave his consent; they were more than

welcome to inspect the shed. "I'll go get the keys," he said, turning toward the house.

With a roar, glass from the windows of the garage sprayed out across the open driveway, showering Melvin's car. Pieces of metal flew straight into the air. Bits of clothing shot everywhere, gently drifting to the ground. Everyone standing within 30 feet of the garage was blown off their feet, leveled by the blast.

An eerie calm then washed over the area. Besides the random thud and ping of items dropping from the sky, the only sounds that could be heard were the barks and howls of dogs throughout the neighborhood.

Moments after the explosion, Don and Cecily pulled into the driveway. They'd both felt the blast's percussion from a block away. Shards of glass covered the hood of Melvin's car; the shed's doors, which lay gnarled and black, had been smashed into the wood fence. Part of the shed had landed on the house's roof, and another metal wall lay in a twisted heap on the next door neighbor's lawn.

"It's time to go now," Grandpa said to her as he led her by the hand.

"I'm going to miss you, Grandpa."

"I know," he said softly, his words seeming to drift away into the rainy sky.

Alan raced to the spot where the shed once stood, Don and Cecily right behind. Amid the rubble, a hole and a pile of dirt was all that remained. The rain, oblivious to what had just occurred, continued to fall, unimpeded. A small torrent of water sloshed off the garage roof and began filling the hole. As the muddy water surged, Don noticed the glint of half of a purple heart undulating in the hole.

"Daddy!"

Everyone's eyes followed the sound of the voice. It was Christina! She stood in a wobbly daze on the back lawn. Her hair was scorched, her face smeared, and her clothes covered with mud and soot. Don rushed over to pick her up. "What happened? ...Are you okay...What—?"

"I think so."

"One-twelve, dispatch. I need an ambulance right away...."

Cecily waded through the debris to where Don stood, Christina enfolded in his arms. He slowly lowered Christina to the ground and peered over at Melvin, who stood in horrified dismay, staring numbly down into the hole. Don's fingers tightened into a fist, a river of hate flowed from his eyes. If it hadn't come pouring from his mouth, an onlooker would still have seen the thought pass clearly through those lethal eyes: "I'm going to kill him!"

He hurled himself at Melvin at whiplash speed. Barker was the first to be tossed from his path; Alan the second. Melvin dodged Don's initial charge, and made a dash for the back steps. That's where Don's grip closed around his leg. "This time you're dead!" he bellowed as he steer-wrestled the wild- eyed landlord and slammed him to the ground.

"No, Daddy!" Christina's voice rang out clearly, with a distinct sense grace and serenity. Don froze. "It's okay," she said, shuffling to her father's side and touching his arm. "It's okay."

Don's anger was immediately replaced by sobs of grief. His hands dropped to his side and he slumped to one knee. His daughter wrapped her arms around his neck and held him tight. This hug was different like the one he'd gotten from Rex. Don knelt among the bits of muddy gravel and scraps of cloth and fragments of glass and wood, holding his daughter, his salty tears mingling with the rain.

THIRTY-SIX

PAULINE WATCHED THE NURSE pull the sheet up over her late husband's wrinkled face. She asked Maria if she'd make the calls. The first was to Kate.

Her voice cracked as she spoke. "Hello, this is Don's sister Maria. Is he home?"

"Not right now, Maria. I'm sorry," Kate said, "Can I help you?"

"Can you get a message to him?"

"I can." She already knew what it would be.

"Our father passed away a few minutes ago."

The sound of quiet sobbing could be heard through the phone. "I'm so sorry, Maria. I'll have him call as soon as I can reach him. What can we do to help?"

"Nothing...thank you, anyway. The arrangements have all been made."

"How's Pauline?"

"I think she'll be fine. He seemed so peaceful those last few minutes. He smiled as he went. His lips moved, but nothing came out. I think he was happy to finally go."

"That's good, dear. Are you going to be all right?"

"Yes...now he doesn't have to suffer anymore." Kate could feel Maria's loss. They ended the call and Kate left for the apartment.

The ambulance arrived. Barker wasn't quite sure what to do with Melvin. There still wasn't any evidence as to who or what was buried in the backyard. Before covering the site with a piece of plastic, he'd give it a look-see. The chain with the half purple heart was partially buried in the muddy water. He walked back to the hole and stared at the heart, slowly disappearing into the mud.

Don was a sight. Each drop of rain that fell on him managed to wash away a little more of the mud that streaked down his face and arms. Christina stood by his side, holding his hand, and Alan and the boys surrounded them, offering unspoken support.

Melvin stood conspicuously alone on the back porch, as Barker had instructed. Before long, he stepped down and cautiously approached the rain-drenched cluster.

Don remained calm. He took the chain out from under his shirt and rocked it side to side like a pendulum. "It's her, isn't it?"

Melvin slowly nodded. A resigned sigh passed his lips. "Yes."

Don yanked down hard on the medallion at his throat. The chain broke, leaving behind a slender white line around his neck. He reached over, raised Melvin's hand and placed the chain in his limp fingers. It hung there draped over his fingers, glinting gold, wet and shimmering, as if suspended in time and space.

Barker listened to the brief exchange, then pulled Don aside and asked him what it was all about. After hearing Don's account, Barker decided he would make an arrest.

"Melvin Briggs, you're under arrest for the murder of your daughter, Leann Briggs..."

"Leah! Her name was Leah..." Melvin mumbled as the cuffs were placed on his wrists.

Barker led Melvin to the squad car. The broken chain had fallen from his hand and was lying on the wet ground near the hole.

"Grandpa's home," Christina whispered, still holding her father's muddy hand.

He bent to listen. "What did you say, 'Tina?"

"I saw grandpa. He's feeling better."

The paramedics helped the dazed girl to the stretcher. "Her eyes are dilated....She appears to be in shock. Let's get an IV in her," one said.

Kate arrived, distraught. "What happened? Is she all right?"

Don met her. "She appears to be in shock. And they say she may have a concussion."

Kate climbed into the back of the ambulance ahead of Don to find a place where she could hold the child's hand. She could see Melvin sitting in the back seat of a police car, parked just in front. His head hung, tears streaming down his bruised face.

Barker instructed several deputies who had arrived to rope off the area. A crowd had gathered and a few reporters were clustered together. Alan stood by the curb in a pair of wet slippers, his saturated robe trickling whirling water patterns on the cement.

Danny, already inside the police tape, slipped unnoticed in the back door of Melvin's apartment. He figured if he could get just one more disk he could unlock it without destroying the information. The rain let up as the ambulance pulled from the curb.

"I'm fine Aunt Kate," Christina said softly. "Grandpa was holding my hand."

"From the bump on her head, she might hallucinate a little," the EMT explained.

Then Kate remembered why she'd come. "Maria called just before I came...he's gone," she whispered.

Don glanced over at her. "I know."

Danny couldn't believe his eyes. Though he had no idea what everything was used for, it was a computer geek's dream come true. He was dying to sit down and play for awhile. "Danny!" he heard his father call from outside. Knowing what kind of trouble he'd be in if he were caught in Melvin's house, Danny skimmed the rows of disks and found two that were compatible with his father's PC. Dropping them in his shirt pocket, he hurried through the kitchen to the steps leading to the apartment below. Just before he reached the door, the cat darted out in front of him. It hissed and hunched its back before scurrying away. He unlocked the door and hurried down the stairs.

The tension was thick on the drive home. "I can't believe you decked him," Jake gushed. "His knees buckled, his eyes rolled back in his head."

"That was the most awesome punch," Bryce added. Alan wasn't sure he wanted his boys to revel in the violence. He had been amazed by the flurry of fight that had spewed from his son, and was even more surprised that he had taken Melvin down.

Danny, however, was rather embarrassed that he'd lost control like he did. "I feel bad for him. It's probably been eating at him forever." The car became silent again, each of them reflecting on the mental state of a man who'd kill his own daughter and bury her in the backyard.

Cecily decided to go home and make herself presentable before she went to the hospital. Poor Don. He wasn't as tough as he acted. The other day she'd seen him sobbing in Rex's arms, and now he had cried like a baby. She could remember seeing her own father cry only once.

She weighed this jumble of thoughts, mulling over their relationship. *He's been under a lot of pressure. Maybe I'd better give him the benefit of the doubt...and see what happens.* Her fear of his presumed combustible temper had been washed away by Don's tears. She showered, dressed, dried her hair and put on some makeup, then headed for the hospital.

Still in one of the emergency room recovery cubicles when she arrived, Kate, Christina and Don were discussing the impending trip to Boise. Cecily stuck her head through the curtain.

Kate flashed her a smile. "Cecily, we were just talking about you. Don said you offered to drive him up to Boise."

Cecily nodded.

"His father passed away this morning. He needs to leave this afternoon or tonight. The services are in the morning."

Cecily nodded again and asked Christina how she was feeling.

"I'm just fine," Christina said, though her face looked drawn and tired.

Don just sat there, smiling at Cecily. Kate continued.

"They said the CAT scan came back negative. She doesn't have any signs of physical trauma—just shaken up. The doctor doesn't want her to go to Idaho. Says she should stay in her bed for a day or two. We're waiting for her to be released."

The nurse drew back the curtain. "Okay, young lady, you can go. We don't want to see you back here again. You've done more than your part to put him in jail—now leave the rest up to the police." She turned a half step, then reappeared and added, "Oh, Lieutenant Barker asked me to call Dr. Wendy. I set up an appointment for Monday at four o'clock. Is that okay?"

"Fine, thank you," Kate said as they picked up their things to leave. Don and Christina didn't say much as they strolled out the emergency exit. He was still a filthy mess. Alan pulled to the curb, almost as if it had been planned.

"Daddy, you go with Cecily and get cleaned up so you'll be ready to go. I'll go with Aunt Kate and Uncle Alan. I'll see you before you leave." She was already doing better, acting more like herself.

Don walked to the parking lot with Cecily. "I'm sorry I upset you the other night," he said, getting it over with as quickly as possible.

Pleased and surprised by his apology, she said in return, "No...I shouldn't have made such a big deal out of it. I could've expressed my feelings better."

"I appreciate everything you've done for Christina and me, especially driving me to Boise."

"My pleasure. I enjoy your company. I'm sorry about your father."

Don reached over and took a small lock of her hair between his finger and thumb, fiddling with it a moment before fixing his gaze on the woman it belonged to. How beautiful she was. Cecily felt a chill on her arms and neck.

Stacey awoke to his watch alarm. He rolled over to see Sig sit up and turn his head to the side, waiting for instructions. It was the best few hours' sleep he'd had in over a week. A shake of his head called him back to reality. He had two broken ribs, his dog was still only half-way healthy, and he'd soon get a call from an enemy who wanted him dead.

The air smelled clean, as only it does after a downpour. Sig at his side, he slowly made his way through the orchard. Fifteen minutes after starting out, he reached the edge of the trees, where he would wait for the captain's call.

Bingham was already on his cell phone, shouting into the mouthpiece a choice string of adjectives followed by, "You've had all night to be ready to cross-link this call!...I don't care if he is. I want someone who can locate that phone. I've got two minutes before I call him, and you'd damn well better be ready!"

Meanwhile, Stacey leaned into the trunk of an old cherry tree and pushed the cell phone's ON button. "Batter up," he said to Sig, who celebrated the occasion by lying down to rest. The phone rang several times, then quit. Sig perked up to listen, then laid his head back down in the tall, moist grass. Stacey waited until the phone rang again, but still didn't answer. He wanted Bingham to squirm.

He answered when the phone rang for a third time. "You're not supposed to call until eleven tonight," he said before turning off the phone. "Come on, boy. That ought to give him a 20- or 30-mile radius." Stacey slapped his leg and walked back toward the old farmhouse, thinking about his pending confrontation with the captain. Arriving at the door, he instructed Sig to rest while he continued his work.

Bingham tried to call again. When he realized the phone had been shut off, he slammed his own phone on the floor, sending pieces flying everywhere.

Cecily waited in the living room for Don to shower. The place gave her the creeps, even with so many people working just outside the door. Indeed, two men in coveralls and a half dozen others—forensics experts, detectives—had gathered under a makeshift canopy, which had been erected over the spot where the shed had once stood. Huddled over the growing hole, they whisked at dirt and sifted through the fine clay. Three camera crews had positioned themselves outside the police tape, umbrellas overhead to cover their expensive equipment.

Still, this was the apartment of doom, of subterfuge, of so many memories—most of them bad—in such a short time. She remembered the newly-married young man and how he and his wife had felt so violated when they realized she'd been spied on. She remembered the antics of a lunatic landlord. And, so vivid in her mind, was that day's implausibly horrific events. She had tried to convince Don to go to Kate's house to shower, but he'd insisted it would only take a minute. Besides, all his clothes were still in the apartment. She'd already gathered most of Christina's things, now arranged in two boxes on the floor.

Finally Don walked out of the bathroom, pulling his shirt over his head and smoothing it down his torso. Cecily watched out of the corner of her eye.

"I'll pack a few things and we can get out of here," he said.

"The sooner the better. I keep thinking I'm hearing things upstairs. I'm a little spooked being here."

Don returned in a few minutes with a gym bag and a jacket. Cecily bent to lift the boxes. "Here, I'll get those," Don offered. He piled the bag and jacket on top and hoisted the boxes against his chest.

Outside, the rain had started up again.

Seeing Don, the reporters rushed to meet him. "Mr. Rodriguez?" they seemed to ask in unison, "can we..."

Don pulled himself up into the waiting Jeep and off it sped, the reporters talking and the cameramen keeping their cameras fixed and dilated until it disappeared from view.

Within minutes they were at Kate's house. Danny was at the computer. "Any progress, buddy?" Don asked. He nodded without looking up. Kate was in the kitchen preparing a special meal for Christina. Don asked if he could use the phone and called home. After discussing with Pauline the funeral arrangements and how peacefully their father had passed through the veil, he asked if there was room to bring a friend. He knew she wouldn't object. They would arrive early that evening.

Kate finished fixing a tray containing favorites of Christina's, and asked Don if he'd take it up to her. He toted the tray, burdened with an array of emotions—guilt for having left her behind; relief that Melvin was locked up; and disappointment in himself for having trusted the man's word. Standing in the doorway of the spacious room Christina shared with her two younger cousins, he watched as they bustled and fussed about like little mothers to make her comfortable. Don could see Kate's personality in them.

"Hi, Uncle Don," greeted the older of the two girls. She was about eleven, with dishwater blond hair and her mother's sparkling blue eyes.

Don smiled and gave the thumbs-up sign. "Hi, Katie."

"Oh, you can put that right here." She pointed to a small table sitting below the large dormer window that looked out over the valley. He walked to the window and took in the magnificent view. The sun was halfway hidden by low-slung clouds hovering above the lake. The rolling mountain range sat off in the distance, readying itself for one heck of a sunset, several hours away.

His gaze dropped to take in more proximate objects. The damaged sedan was no longer parked down the street. The neighbor's cat prowled across the front lawn in pursuit of a moth. Steam rose off the street as the sun poked its head from the clouds again. Don turned around. "Are you going to be okay here if I go to Boise?"

"I'll be fine, Dad."

Don knelt at the side of the bottom bunk. Katie, old enough to realize things might get personal, ushered her younger sister from the room and closed the door behind them.

"You felt him, didn't you?" Christina asked.

"I did. Pauline told me he smiled as he passed away. Now tell me—how did you get from inside the shed out on the lawn?"

The question brought a smile to Christina's lips. "He

held my hand and took me somewhere very beautiful, just for a minute. Then he said he had to take me back. He said 'I love you' as he left me."

A lump formed in Don's throat. Why couldn't his father have said these words just once to him? Christina could see her dad's eyes begin to fill with tears. Hers were also swollen.

"Daddy, Grandpa was there all along, all through the time I was in the shed and afterwards. He was there to tell you that he loves you, too. That's what you felt when I touched you: It was *love*. *He* was full of love. He got it from the place he was at, then gave it to me to give to you. When I put my hand on your arm, you felt it, didn't you!" It wasn't a question, rather, a statement.

Tears slid down his cheeks. Yes, he had felt it—and he could feel it now. It was like nothing he had ever known before. He bowed his head to hide the tears. Christina placed her warm palm under his chin and raised his face. Their eyes met. "I love you, Daddy, and so does Grandpa. And God loves you, too. That's why he let Grandpa come visit us."

"I love you, too, Christina Marie."

THIRTY-SEVEN

STACEY MADE UP for his lack of electrical expertise by using his farmyard mechanic skills. His grandpa was a master of repair and the cantankerous old man had passed a few of his practical teachings—as well as a few tricks—down to his grandson. Stacey would make good use of both in setting up his plan.

As he strung the rusty old cable through the trees, his mind wandered back 15 or so years. His father had insisted that he spend a few weeks each summer working on granddad's farm. He recalled his first experience driving a tractor, at age 12. "A man who knows how to work with his hands can do anything he wants," was one of the conservative old farmer's favorite axioms. Stacey had wanted to go swimming, play football and fish with his friends, not shovel cow manure and hoe weeds. But the experience had proven life-changing—those were summers he'd never forget.

Stacey tied the cable to the back of an ancient John Deere tractor and cranked the starter. Its long stroke motor sputtered, coughed, then fired and puffed, exhaling smoke from the throat of its rattling stack. A little engine work went a long ways.

His grandpa had put him on the old tractor his first day on the farm. He reflected on the scene. His assignment had been to disk the alfalfa field. He soon found the task to be enjoyable, with the throbbing, throaty rumble of the engine under him. Grandpa's German shepherd loved to chase the seagulls away. Grandpa knew if he could teach his grandson to enjoy work his life would be successful.

Stacey broke out in a smile as he remembered how his attention had been captured by the flight of birds fleeing from the dog. The next thing he knew he was nose down in a concrete irrigation ditch. His grandpa had warned him to watch where he was going. Shaken but unhurt, he'd looked up to see his granddad sprinting toward him. He'd turned off the tractor and was approaching the old man, head down, prepared for a scolding—a reprimand that never came.

Stacey returned to the present. The motor wound down, the erratic pop of the old magneto struggling to give its kick. Stacey offered a silent prayer that it would start when he needed it most.

Once again his mind drifted back to the field, and his dear grandpa. "Are you okay, Bup?...I was afraid you might be hurt." Stacey could still feel the old man's strong arms wrapped around his shoulders, punctuating the hug with a squeeze. "Don't worry about her," he'd muttered, gesturing toward the tractor. "She's been in worse spots than that before."

The relief had washed over him—so strongly that he could feel it even now. He'd been expecting a kick in the pants, not a firm arm to steady his quivering muscles. That boy of 12, a few dusty tears streaking down his face as he walked back to the farmhouse for lunch, had promised himself that he'd never lose sight of where he was going again. And he'd tried to keep that promise.

Stacey finished the calibrations he'd made on the old tractor's engine and, his mind tripping ahead to his next task, brushed the dirt from his hands and knees. He knew that he needed to catch Bingham off guard. If everything went as planned, the cable pulling the metal pots would distract Bingham long enough to take him without anyone getting killed.

After stopping at her place to pack her things, Don and Cecily started up the freeway. The Jeep's rag top flapped in the wind, making it impossible to carry on a conversation without shouting. Don wanted to share with her all the things he was feeling, but didn't want to yell.

At the same time, Cecily didn't quite know how to comfort Don in his loss. She interpreted his quiet mood as sullenness. She didn't feel she could just rattle on like she usually did. Occasionally she'd glance over at him and wonder what he was thinking. At times he'd look back at her and smile. His face seemed soft—warmer than usual, more at peace. She wished she could touch him, to caress the sad lines in his cheeks and forehead, and kiss his face to make the pain go away. She imagined a future with him, the two of them together, two or three children all seated around the kitchen table, laughing and talking about their day at school. She pictured helping Christina put the final touches on her prom dress, and imagined how beautiful she'd look walking down the front stairs of their home.

"Look out!" She swerved to the right onto the shoulder of the freeway to miss a deer bouncing across in front of her. Leaving the motor idling, she breathed a sigh of relief.

Don leaned his head back and looked over at Cecily. "That was close. You all right?"

"Yeah. Just day-dreamin' a bit," she stammered.

"What about?"

"How glad I am that Christina's not hurt and thinkin' how pretty she'll look at her first prom."

Don reached over and stroked her hair, sending a wave of prickly sensations up and down her arms and back. She smiled in return. He ran a finger down the side of her forehead to her ear. Her skin was soft and smooth. He reached under her hair and caressed her neck. The sun was shining and the vehicle had gotten warm. Seeing the flush of goose bumps on her arms, he thought to ask if she was cold— until she leaned gently into his hand. Then he knew what they were from.

"I'm not going to be able to concentrate on the road at all if you keep doin' that." Don saw the coquettish smile that accompanied her words of warning. For a few seconds more he continued to run his hand down her shoulder and arm. Then, feigning embarrassment, he pulled away and gave the "forward, ho!" sign with his arm.

As she pulled back into traffic, Don leaned against the roll-bar and gazed over at her. His mind drifted as they accelerated along the concrete highway. *She does have feelings*, he mused. He began to think of how life would be with her at his side. Someone to come home to, someone who'd be there with open arms, someone he could love, cherish, hold—and who felt the same toward him. They could build a life together. She would probably want children. He wished he had more. She would go to bed with him and wake up with him. The look in her eyes was one Monica never was able—

Monica! Why did she have to intrude on his fantasy? She'd inevitably come back demanding alimony and child support payments so she could buy her drugs. He'd either lose Christina outright or be in a court battle that could rage on for years. How could he put Cecily through that?

Cecily stopped for fuel at the little town of Gooding. Don pumped the gas as she went in to pay. He felt pretty stupid letting her pay for things, but right now he had ten dollars to his name—and not many hours in at work. Cecily bounced back to the Jeep, full of life, her hair dancing with her steps. In the light of the orange sky, her blond mop was like a sea of golden strands. Don tried to push the thoughts from his mind. *It couldn't possibly work without her being hurt. Marriage is just out of the question.*

"You hungry? My treat," she offered. Climbing back into the Jeep they drove a few blocks to a local café.

A sleek Lear jet landed at the Spanish Fork airport. Melvin's attorney stepped out, climbed into the white Tahoe, and ten minutes later was sitting in the chambers of an angry Judge Demick, whose clerk's voice came over the speaker phone. "Mr. White is on his way."

Demick gave the attorney a reproving glare. "This entire process is completely unacceptable," he groused. "If I release him, I won't ever be trusted to deliver justice in this town again. Every newspaper and television station in the state will use me as the butt of their jokes."

"I have a million dollars in the form of a cashier's

check here in my briefcase. Make sure the bail isn't more than that," the attorney warned.

Judge Demick's clerk poked her head in the office. "Mr. White's here."

"Show him in, then come and take notes, please."

White walked in, scowling at them disapprovingly. It was out of line for the two to have a private conference in the judge's chamber without him present, and they knew it.

"Mr. White, you remember Briggs's attorney?"

"Yes. What's going on?"

"We're here to set bail," Demick said.

White's sour expression turned to one of outrage. "You what?! I've got a forensics team that just finished digging up the remains of a young female in his backyard. And you want to set bail?...I want a new judge appointed to this case immediately. I'll go over your head, right to the governor if I have to. I want a search warrant for his house—and *I want it—*!"

"Sit down and shut up, Mr. White! If I could tell you what the hell was going on I would. I can't! I have a federal gag order right here." Demick slapped a paper on the desk. "In the meantime, I suggest you park some of your best people outside the suspect's home and make sure he doesn't leave until our hearing on Monday. Then I'll be happy to give you all the information you want." Demick picked up the phone and handed it to White. "Bail's set at one million dollars! See that he's returned to his home at once."

White snatched the receiver from the judge's hand, "If he hurts someone else, the blood'll be on *your* hands. I'm warning you—you'll be finished as a judge!"

"One more word from you, Mr. White, and I'll lock you up. So help me! You won't see daylight for a month!"

Melvin's attorney calmly opened his briefcase and took out the check. "I'll need a receipt for that," he said casually, handing it to the clerk, who stared down at the zeros, eyes wide, and shuffled from the room.

White on the phone struggled to keep his attitude in check. Barker picked up on the other end. "Demick set bail for a million dollars. It's already been posted. Mr. Briggs needs to be returned to his home right away."

Barker was astonished by the news. "I heard him say it was his daughter! Are you kidding me?"

"I wish I were, Lieutenant. I want you to coordinate five of my best deputies to keep an eye on him. I'll call the sheriff."

Barker hung up the phone, dismayed at what he'd just heard. He instructed Olsen to accompany him to lower lock-up, explaining they were going to let Melvin go. He closely observed the younger officer's reaction.

"It doesn't surprise me," Olsen said indifferently. "He must have something real good on that judge."

"I'm going to take the rest of the afternoon off," Barker added as they made their way down the stairs. "I want you to take charge in my absence. I won't have my radio on. I need some rest."

"No problem, Lieutenant," Olsen responded smugly.

Grue slouched at his desk reading a book when the two men entered. "Are we ready to move him to county?" he asked.

"No, you and Olsen are taking him home," Barker answered.

Grue stood in disbelief. "I don't understand."

"I don't either. You two wait with him in the squad car until I send a few deputies over. They'll take the first shift. We'll be on 24-hour watch until he's arraigned on Monday."

Melvin, pleased by what he'd just heard, was already on his feet, peering between the bars. "I told you I wouldn't be in here long," he gloated.

Barker walked over and leaned his face down close to Melvin's. "You won't be *out* long, either!" he threatened.

Melvin backed away from the bars. The moment Barker turned to walk away he called out defiantly, "I won't be back at all!"

Pausing mid-step, Barker pivoted on his heels, drew his night stick, raised it up and slammed it against the bars directly in front of Melvin's head.

"You may be right," Barker whispered. "You may be right."

Returning upstairs, he placed a call to the crime lab. "Is Saunders in?"

"Speaking."

"This is Lieutenant Barker. Did you get a chance to examine the cup I sent down?"

"I did. Got lots of prints—but couldn't find a match. Want me to send over the report?"

"Please, as soon as possible."

"Fax number?"

Barker gave him the number. While waiting by the fax machine, an idea came to him. His cousin worked for the office of immigration in Nebraska. As soon as the information arrived, he'd make some special inquiries.

Waiting to be served their meals, Don and Cecily took their first chance to talk without the incessant flapping of the Jeep's canvas top. "...She thinks my father helped her get out of the shed," Don said.

"What do *you* think?"

"I'm not sure. I don't know how anyone could survive a blast like that without so much as a scratch."

Cecily nodded. "Do you believe we live after we die?"

"I guess so. On my last visit, my father was saying things to me...that everyone thought were delusional. Now I believe him."

"Like what?"

"He insisted I go back to be with Christina, saying she was in danger. He made me promise I wouldn't fight anymore. I didn't even know what I promised until a guy on the bus helped me translate the words from Spanish."

"Is that why you didn't hurt Melvin? Because of your promise?"

"No. I'd completely forgotten about it. But when Christina touched my arm, every angry feeling in my body was swept away. I can't explain it. It was the most powerful yet peaceful feeling. I felt like a baby being held in my dad's arms as I knelt there holding my daughter in mine." Don breathed in deeply.

Cecily studied him. "The other day with Rex must have felt the same."

"My father..." Don exhaled, "never once told me he loved me. I knew he did, but he never said it. I've never been hugged by a man before. Rex has something about him that touched my heart."

"Do you know what it is?" Cecily asked.

"Not exactly."

"It's God's love."

Don looked down at his plate. Then he asked, "How do you get it?"

"It takes a lot of desire...study, prayer, work. You don't always feel it like you did today. Sometimes the feeling's weak, sometimes it's strong. But it changes people's hearts and minds, and helps them through life, gives them a reason to do good."

Yes. Don couldn't remember any time in his life that he'd felt comfort and peace—as he did right now. "I liked the way it felt."

Barker called his cousin Clint. "Check the records from about the time the Vietnam War ended," Barker instructed. "I'll call you later tonight." After he'd gathered his things, including his vest, and a few extra rounds of ammunition, Barker called his wife to tell her he'd be late again. He stayed on the phone longer than normal. He told her to kiss the children goodnight, and his "I love you" before he hung up came from the heart.

The forensics team was completing their investigation. The tent had been removed and the reporters had disappeared shortly after the coroner carried away the skeletal remains of Melvin's daughter. Olsen and Grue waited in the car with Melvin.

"Did you see that?" Grue asked, craning to see through the gate to the far end of the busted out fence.

"See what?"

"Someone just ran across the backyard."

"Probably a curious neighbor or a stray reporter," Olsen suggested. Melvin remained quiet. He knew very well who it was.

The first deputy arrived to begin his shift. Olsen got out of the car. "How soon do you expect the others?"

"They're on their way."

"Good. I've got some things to do. I don't want to be baby-sitting this creep all night."

"Gee, thanks. You'll leave it to us, then?"

"Just another boring night trying to stay awake," Olsen needled.

"Why do they think they need *five* of us?"

"White wants his every move covered."

"But we could take care of that with just one."

"Just make sure he stays here—and move in to arrest him if he does anything suspicious."

Two more deputies came on the scene. Grue helped Melvin out of the car and removed his cuffs. "It would sure be nice if you tried something stupid tonight," he whispered in Melvin's ear. "It'd save the taxpayers a lot of money."

"I will," Melvin whispered back.

Grue pulled away, staggered by Melvin's brazenness. "Get out of here," he said, pushing him toward the door. Melvin certainly had a way about him, a crude though clever way of rubbing emotions raw and then throwing salt on the wound. He strolled to the door and climbed the steps. Then, with nothing to lose, turned to face down the officers. Despite his small stature, he seemed an imposing foe. His contemptuous sneer combined an element of panache. *They didn't pose much of a threat! It wouldn't take much at all to elude them.*

He walked in the house and quickly set out scouring the rooms. The kitchen and living room displayed their usual, sterile appearance. But in the back bedroom he came upon a sight that sent a shiver down his spine. His cat, the one remaining thing he loved, a noose strung tightly around its neck, hung dead, from a hook in the ceiling.

Melvin turned away. Then, donning a particle mask, he carefully began collecting pollen from two of the exotic plants on the shelf. The work was exacting, the harvesting slow; the stingy plants clung to their powerful resource as if it were the most precious on earth.

Once a minute pile of the pollen lay on a white sheet of paper, he painstakingly loaded a small amount in the end of three long straws, plugging each end with a piece of tissue. Then he taped the ends to hold the tissue in place.

Returning to his computer, he reviewed the information it had been collecting while he was gone. Then he made a call, choosing his words carefully. "As far as I can tell, he's still at the previous location. This may be my last communication. I need to take care of the item of personal business we talked about earlier...My life's been destroyed....Yes, I think I know where I can find her."

The moment she stepped in the door, the thing that caught Cecily's attention was the religious atmosphere of the home. Many of the paintings that hung on the walls and the books standing on the shelves led her to believe the family shared her faith.

"You didn't tell me your father was a religious man."

"He wasn't until a few years ago. Pauline's been good for him."

Don introduced Cecily to his sister and stepmother. The women embraced. Cecily could feel their warm and gentle spirits. "I'm so sorry for your loss," she sympathized. "Don's told me what a good man he was." Pauline seemed calm as she told them again how happy her husband had been in the hours leading up to his death.

Maria took their jackets and showed them where to put their things. "Pauline's a very private person," she explained. "I've heard her sobbing in her room every night. She's suffered, but at the same time, is relieved that his suffering is over."

Pauline entered the room. "We're expecting a full house tonight," she said to Cecily. "Don's other siblings will be here for the service. I've organized the guest room for the two of you, if you don't mind sharing the space. I've set up a cot if you need it."

Cecily, blushing, looked over at Don, who returned her gaze. "I'll be happy to use the cot," he said. "Thanks,

Pauline."

"It won't bother you to stay in that room?" she asked.

"No, I loved him," Don replied. Cecily wondered what they meant. Then Don added, "Are you expecting *everyone*?"

"Everyone but Mother. She refused to come," Maria chimed in.

Barker bounded along the dirt road in his brother's four-wheel drive, making sure no one was following him. He'd pulled off the asphalt on his cross-country detour a few miles back. He parked the vehicle above the orchard. Walking in among the trees, he heard something moving in the high grass...."Sig, you old scoundrel! You gave me a scare. Where's Stace?"

"Right here," Stacey said, standing up amid a clump of sagebrush. "You would have been covered in paint— if I'd only had a gun."

"It's a good thing I trust you," Barker laughed. Striding up to his friend, he reached around his shoulders with both hands and gave him a hug.

"Ouch! Careful with the ribs."

Barker pulled away. "Dianne told me she's never seen a bruise like yours. The pain must have been unbearable when the old doc snapped you back together."

"It put me down."

"That's what she said. Told me she'd never forget seeing you and Sig lying together on that table, and Sig reaching up and giving you a big wet one across the mouth!"

Stacey grimaced. "I'm going to do two things when I get through with this mess. The first will be to teach him not to do that and the other is to find a girl who likes dogs."

"I keep telling you we need to line you up with my wife's sister."

"I'll take you up on that."

THIRTY-EIGHT

MELVIN RETURNED to the kitchen. He hadn't needed to use his warfare talents for many years. It might take a bit of trial and error to make a good homemade bomb.

After collecting a couple boxes of wooden matches, he sat down to scrape off their heads. He hated the thought of setting his own place on fire, and hoped the fire department would put out the flames before they reached his computer. He'd call in the alarm well in advance of the actual blaze, but the small-town volunteer fire department wasn't the speediest on earth.

Gathering some of the phosphate he used to fertilize the plants, Melvin added it to the brew. From the smell it gave off, he knew it was the right mixture.

From the darkness of the basement, he checked the position of the deputies and their vehicles. Two men stood in the backyard, one was parked in the driveway, and two out front. If he could get one of the men in back to leave, he could easily distract the other.

Melvin moved his explosive concoction from the back bedroom, then climbed the back stairs, where he collected several old newspapers, along with a metal trash can. Wadding up the paper, he stuffed it in the can. Finally, he attached the bomb to his small mechanical rat. His little spy was about to take its last trip. His weapon ready, he changed into his dark clothing.

Stacey and Barker talked for an hour, sharing information and going over Stacey's plan. Barker needed to start the old tractor at the precise moment, then cover his friend's back. Pulling a small radio from his pocket, he handed it to Stacey. They'd use it only if necessary. Then he made a call to his cousin. "Clint? Cousin Paul. What'd you find?" Barker's eyebrows raised as he listened. "Thanks, I owe you one...."

"I took a cup from Briggs's house and had Saunders run the prints," Barker explained once he'd hung up the phone. "He couldn't come up with anything. On a hunch, I asked my cousin, who works in the immigration office in Nebraska, to check 'em out."

"Did he find out anything?"

"The prints belong to a woman named Jau Fei Phelps; her maiden name is Wong. Married an American soldier—a guy named *Melvin* Elliot Phelps—and came home with him from Nam.

Stacey was quick to offer an assessment. "If her prints are on the cup, she's got to be living in the house—and ought to be willing to testify against Melvin for their daughter's murder. She's probably scared to death of him. I better see if the feds are ready for the fireworks to start." He made a call to Agent Buseth, not wasting any words when Buseth picked up. "I'll give you the pen as promised, if I feel comfortable that Bingham will never be a threat again. Are you sure you and your men can apprehend him when he comes?"

"You can bet your life on it, Officer Stacey. If Bingham arrives, we'll catch him, and he won't be taken alive. Once he's dead and the pen is in our hands, you can walk away."

"What's so special about the pen?"

"I'm not at liberty to say."

"Dammit! I've got my butt hanging out a mile and you won't tell me why. I just changed my mind— forget the whole thing!" Stacey punched the End button.

"What's going on, Stace?" Barker asked.

"We're about to be hunted by a killer that's sworn a blood oath against me, and the feds won't tell me what's going on." The phone rang.

"Okay, okay! The pen contains a chemical agent called 'VN twenty dash three-five-two.' We believe Bingham has already killed with it—and will kill again. I'll deny its existence or that I even told you about it if you ever quote me. Don't let Bingham get near you, or he'll kill you for it."

Stacey smiled. "I don't plan on getting killed. You just take care of Bingham." He hung up the phone. "I can't trust these federal boys. They're so concerned about the pen that they don't care about anything else."

Danny's fingers shifted from key to key. He was confident he'd broken two of the six codes required to access the disks. He downloaded another program from the Internet, an old military file. Similar programs had led him to the age and language of the disks. *Now, if I can just access it—*

Alan stuck his head in the door to inform him he could only work until midnight. "Yeah," Danny mumbled absentmindedly. Each code was getting easier to break. If things went well, he could be done by eleven. He knew the information on the disk was at least six years old. Still, it was harder to access than anything he'd ever seen.

Christina was enjoying the pampering her cousins were giving her. Kate would pop in occasionally to see how she was doing, but for the most part, the girls took care of all her needs. She had supper in bed, they combed her hair, they laid out her pajamas...

Pauline had been right—it was a houseful. Don and Cecily excused themselves and went to the bedroom to set up the cot. "I hope you won't be too ill at ease with me here," Don said. "If you are, I'll be glad to sleep in the living room with my nieces and nephews."

"I think it'll be fine. Besides, from what I've seen of them so far you'd never get any sleep."

"I promise I'll be a perfect gentleman."

"I know you will." Cecily paused in thought. "What did Pauline mean by 'minding' to sleep in here?"

"This is the room where my father slept when he became ill. The bed was his. He and Pauline slept apart the last few months. He insisted on it so she could get some sleep. Otherwise, she usually slept here in the chair." He gestured toward an old recliner sitting against the wall.

"So this was his bed?" A touch of hesitation colored her words.

Don nodded. "I'll be glad to sleep in it, if you'd prefer not to."

She nodded. "I don't mind the cot." He completely understood.

Pauline had changed the linens, and the medical supplies that had lined the walls and cluttered the dresser tops were gone. It wouldn't be much different than when he'd visited them last Thanksgiving, just after they'd found out he was sick. His father had suffered in quiet, thinking it was just another sign of old age and a life of hard work. By the time he went to see the doctor, the cancer was well advanced. That was the last time Don had seen him as a strong and vital man. He was still up and around on Don's next visit, but not in good shape. He'd rest during the day, killing time watching inane TV programs.

"Goodnight, Aunt Kate." Christina lay in bed, contemplating the day. The rain had stopped. Crickets chirped out in the yard. Her younger cousins were soon sound asleep. Feeling an overwhelming need to thank God for her blessings, she rolled from her bed and knelt on the floor. "Dear Heavenly Father, I'm glad that grandpa's with you," she whispered. "Thank you for letting him come to help me. Bless my dad that he can come to know you now. I'm happy he felt your love today. Help him to feel that love again. I forgive Mr. Briggs for what he's done and please help him to change, too. In Jesus' name, amen."

She climbed back into bed and wiped the tears from her eyes. "Oh, and help me to have good dreams." She closed her eyes and drifted off to sleep.

Stacey powered up Bingham's phone and waited for its ring. When it came, Stacey pressed ON. "Good evening."

"I want a chance at you, Stacey," Bingham threatened.

"You're about to get it. How long will it take to pin-point my location from this phone?"

"We're on it now."

"Good. I'll be waiting for you. Make sure you're alone or you'll never see your pen again."

He'd give him only five minutes.

After staying up late with his siblings, chatting and reminiscing, Don bid them goodnight. "I'll go change in the bathroom," he told Cecily, "and you can use the bed-room."

Several minutes later he went to the kitchen, had a drink of water, bade Pauline goodnight and gave her a gentle hug. His surprise that all the siblings had come was thoughtfully explained by the considerable amount of time his father had spent mending old wounds. He'd hoped everyone could get together before he died. Or at least *when* he died.

"He will be watching and smiling tomorrow at his family reunion," Pauline told him.

Don returned to the bedroom and rapped lightly on the door. The light was out and no one answered. He opened the door to find Cecily kneeling in prayer beside the cot. He closed the door most of the way and looked on in silence. Cecily knelt for several minutes, then raised her head and crawled under the covers of the cot. Don waited a few more moments before entering.

"Pauline thinks Dad was planning tomorrow as a fam-ily reunion and he'll be there to see us all together," he said.

"He probably will be. When was the last time you were all together?"

"I don't think it's been since Dad left....many years."

"Sounds like it'll be a sad day but also a joyful one. I guess that's where the term *bittersweet* came from," she commented.

The room grew quiet. Don was dying to ask another question. He finally mustered up the courage. "How do you pray?" he blurted out.

"Who, me?"

"No. If someone doesn't know how to pray and wants to, how do they do it? How do they start?"

She smiled in the semi-darkness and said, "Well, first, that person needs to call on God and thank Him for their gifts and blessings. Then he might ask for the desires of his heart—the things he needs most. When he's finished he would end in the name of Jesus Christ."

"Thanks. Goodnight," he whispered.

"Goodnight. Thank you for letting me come and share this time with you. Sweet dreams." She turned her head and closed her eyes.

Minutes later, Don closed his eyes. In the darkness he began, "Dear God..."

"They've moved out in your direction." Melvin's squeaky, high-pitched complaint sounded almost desperate. He cupped the phone's mouthpiece up to his lips. "She's not here—I haven't seen her in days. I need some help....probably after the girl. She's gone completely nuts. She even killed my cat....I know you've got your hands full; so do I. Listen!" The pitch of his voice raised a half octave as his temper bubbled up—then boiled over. "If you don't shake a couple of men loose to help me right now, it'll be too late!...screw you!...then I'll take care of her myself!" He slammed down the phone. Agent Buseth tucked his phone away, too.

Using his computer skills, Melvin electronically patched lines. When he reported the fire, dispatch would think the phone call was coming from across the street. Returning to the basement with his rat—he opened the window and directed the device down the driveway.

Melvin then ran to the back bedroom and ignited the tightly wrapped wad of paper. It should only take a minute for the officers in the backyard to see the flames through the open curtain. Scrambling back upstairs, he snatched up the remote control and, pressing his face to the front window, guided his beloved rat to a spot just behind the deputy's Bronco. Bumping it up against the tire, it made enough noise to get the officers' attention.

Turning a dial, Melvin caused the little rat to then roll onto the sidewalk toward the vehicle's open window.

"*What's that?*" the puzzled deputy asked, pointing. Just then central dispatch reported a fire in the vicinity. The deputy told her to hold on for a moment as the mechanical package rolled past. Both officers in the rear looked up to see smoke pouring from the basement window. Then the rat exploded out front.

Both men in the Bronco instinctively ducked. They glanced at each other, bewildered, slightly dazed, their ears ringing, but neither hurt. One of the officers from the rear ran to the front to investigate the blast. The other, having run over to the house to peer through the basement window, called in the fire from his radio.

Seizing the moment, Melvin slipped out the window. The deputy reached for his gun, but Melvin was quicker—and better prepared. The end of one of the straws in his mouth, he blew its contents straight into the face of the stunned deputy. Blinking his burning eyes and struggling in vain to keep his feet under him, the officer crumpled to the ground. Melvin limped away into the night.

Bingham drove up the dirt road, parked at the gate, and slipped on his headgear. A silenced automatic weapon in his hands, the bullets in its chamber would not be used to kill Stacey, they were for the dog- the one thing Stacey loved and the thing he, Bingham, most despised. He needed Stacey alive if he wanted the pen back.

In no hurry now, he carefully surveyed the area, aware that Stacey had taken several hours to make ready for his visit.

Olsen fielded the call from dispatch. Listening, the hair on his arms stood on end. He was in trouble.

He punched in a call to Mr. White. "We've got a problem...."

"I'm sending over the bomb squad and the sheriff," snapped White. "Be extremely careful. I'll meet you there."

The deputies found their fellow officer, staggering and hallucinating in the backyard. When he heard them coming, he drew his weapon and began firing wildly in the air. His bullets spent, two officers tried to subdue him; two others joined in before he was restrained. Neighbors on both sides and from across the street peeked out from their windows, not daring to venture from the safety of their homes. They'd seen more going on at the once-quiet home than they cared to know about.

The fire truck pulled up in time to see the last of the flames in the bedroom flicker and die. White and Olsen arrived. The county attorney was beside himself when he learned Barker had taken the night off. Several additional units arrived to back up the confused deputies. They began evacuating the surrounding houses in case there was a second, larger explosion.

Danny had managed to break all but the last code. Twenty minutes remained before he promised his father he'd call it quits. Desperately he tapped at the keyboard. From behind the glow of the computer screen, Danny couldn't see the black-clad figure lurking in the darkness across the street.

Bingham sensed he was not in any immediate danger as he crawled on his belly through tall spring grass. Though tedious, it was a mode of travel with which he was well acquainted. Through the years he'd seen almost every kind of man-trap imaginable, and had conquered every one. *This small-town cop is no match for me!*

Fifty yards away, Barker, not moving a muscle, crouched behind the cover of some wooden pallets, stacked six-deep on each side. From his position there was enough room for him to get a good view of the orchard. He directed his gaze down the moonlit row to where the geese lay sleeping, heads tucked under their wings, grouped together, looking like a bevy of harmless gray pillows tucked into a grassy bed. The tractor was parked close by, its steering wheel tightly chained in place for the direction it needed to travel.

Stacey lay low behind three rows of old salamander stoves, once used by fruit growers to keep the blossoms from freezing during cold spells. Sig had been commanded to lie still, 20 rows to the west.

Mr. White, Olsen and the County Sheriff stood talking several houses away from Melvin's apartment. The sheriff was experiencing a "temper problem." Upset that his men were put in such a dangerous position, he'd taken control of the operation. It took less than 15 minutes to assemble his SWAT team. They were equipped to make a quick break-in. No more second chances.

Calling Melvin out on the bull horn brought no response. The dazed deputy, still disoriented and mumbling incoherently, couldn't remember a thing. Although the men who'd been on the scene didn't believe Melvin was still in the house, they needed to take precautions. They could be entering a booby trap. Tear gas was fired into both the front and back upper windows; the basement was also gassed. Still no response from inside the house.

The bomb squad suggested they send in a robot first in case any other explosive devices lay in wait. The sheriff agreed—anything that would protect his men. A few minutes later a police van arrived, and four men hoisted the machine to the back steps. Two shotgun blasts tore open the back door, and the robot, remote camera attached, rolled in.

The men watched on the screen. Smoke cleared as the kitchen table came into view. Rotating 180 degrees, the robot revealed the door leading downstairs. It searched the kitchen, then moved down the hall. As it approached the entrance to the living room, the screen went fuzzy. "Proceed down the hall. We'll check the front room last," the sheriff ordered.

The light shone down the hall and into the bathroom, then on to the bedroom, where the ghastly sight of the dead cat dangling from the ceiling came into view. Otherwise, the bedroom was empty.

When the small contraption made its way back down

the hall to the living room, again the picture went fuzzy. The interference was too much for the short-wave signal. The technician tried to adjust for the bad reception, but to no avail. The sheriff called his men together for final instructions. Every room upstairs proved clear except the southeast corner of the house.

"Proceed with caution. The man could be armed— and we know he's dangerous. Use deadly force, if necessary." A collective murmur went through the SWAT team members as individually they pondered the tacit order to shoot on sight.

Olsen tried to explain that the front door was blocked. Paying no attention, the sheriff ordered the men to their assigned posts. On command, the two-men groups stormed the house. The screen connected to the robot showed the raid—things spraying throughout the living room and being knocked from shelves.

"Upstairs! All clear, sir!" the radio blasted.

"Basement clear!" a second voice sounded.

Feverishly Danny worked at the last code, much harder to break than the rest. Each time he thought he had it, it would elude him. "It must have some sort of time limit to it," he mumbled to himself. He clicked on to the BIOS set-up and used a command to stop the clock on the computer. Then he returned to the code.

His intensity kept him from noticing the eyes outside the study window. The old family dog raised its head from napping to let out a few half-hearted warning barks as the black figure slipped out of view, around the front porch, up the corner stones on the side of the house and onto the overhanging roof, stealing along the roof valley until standing outside the girls' upstairs bedroom window. Silently, the screen was cut from its frame.

Downstairs, with the clock off, Danny at last had broken through the code! The program opened with a jolt. Photos of dead or sick people flashed on the screen, frame after frame. Battered black bodies lay in rows, bloated from the hot sun. Bamboo shacks filled the background. The photos of those living, showed them with hopeless eyes and distended bellies. Weeping wounds covered their bodies.

Looking at the grisly images made Danny nauseous. It wasn't what he'd expected to see. If anything, Melvin would have taken photos of his female victims, or perhaps of women and girls he'd spied on through the bathroom wall or with his intricate monitoring devices. He'd hoped to find information that would lead to Melvin's victims, buried in remote locations.

He scanned the disk a second time, pleading for answers, but it was all the same. He slumped in his chair. The grandfather clock in the entryway began to chime. Determined to at least keep his promise to his dad, he disappointedly shut down the computer.

The children slept in the glow of the streetlight. On the roof someone waited, listening, watching. Inching the bedroom window open, he slipped in. A straw was brought out from under the jacket and a silent puff of fine dust sprinkled over Christina's face. She moaned softly, her peaceful face becoming a mask of dread, her pleasant dreams changing to scenes of horror. Her mouth was taped shut; her arms were taped together and her slender, limp body was lifted out onto the roof. Christina's abductor threaded his neck under her arm, tossed the rest of the body over his shoulder and cautiously climbed down from the roof.

In the hall outside his room, Danny shuddered at what he'd just witnessed. He couldn't shake the gruesome visions from his mind. Christina had made him promise to tell her what he found. He considered waiting until morning, since his cousin had already been through so much, but he felt too depressed to sleep without telling someone what was on the disks. *I've got to tell her,* he reasoned. *She always has a way of making things seem better.*

Slowly he opened Christina's door. The room felt cold. The window was ajar. Stepping to close it, he noticed the screen peeled out onto the roof. *Where'd she go?* was his first thought. He rushed back to the door to turn on the light. Christina wasn't in her bed! His younger sisters groaned from the bright light.

"Mom! Dad! Christina's missing!!!" he yelled down the hall.

Alan bolted upright out of bed. Out into the hall and up the stairs he went. Kate was right behind him, fearing that something was terribly wrong.

By the time they reached the bedroom, Danny had hopped out the window onto the roof. In the yard below, the old Rottweiler struggled to break free from her chain, bravely barking at the figure slinking across the backyard. Danny ran east along the roof of the wrap-around porch in time to see Christina's body being lifted over the wrought-iron fence.

THIRTY-NINE

THE FRUIT ORCHARD extended at least a half a mile east toward the mountain from Kate's house, and north and south almost three-quarters of a mile in each direction along the foothills, covering more than 50 acres of prime development land that had thus far been left untouched. Old roads and trails serviced the power lines running along the easterly border of the trees; homes lined the fence on the west.

One narrow dirt road, two blocks from Kate's home, accessed the interior of the property leading to the old farmhouse. A locked gate halfway up the road kept traffic from entering. With the exception of using a tractor, the old fruit-grower, who'd built a new house on the south end, still farmed the land the same way his father and grandfather had 70 years before. Migrant workers pruned the trees late in the winter and returned to pick the crop in midsummer.

The property could be accessed from dozens of backyards and from more than a mile and a half of dirt road along the foothills. Stacey had instructed Buseth and his half-dozen agents to wait east of his and Barker's location until Bingham was on site. Stacey's trap was more a backup plan, in case the feds failed in the capture.

Bingham, headgear operating, struggled to identify the heat sources in the grassy rows ahead. He approached with caution, analyzing every detail. Crawling along at a deliberate pace, he spotted a rusty cable extending in foot-high coils on top of the damp grass. *He's not very smart.....Must think I'm some kind of amateur.*

One end of the cable ran in the direction of a nearby

tree, its frayed wires stopping just short of the trunk. Following the cable with his eyes, he could see that the other end ran toward the row of trees to his back. It too stopped short of the tree. *It must have been left as a decoy*, he reasoned. He warily crossed the cable and continued up the row.

His experience in battlefield strategy gave him an enormous edge over Stacey. The chance for the rookie cop to kill him had come and gone; he should have done it then. *The kid doesn't have it in him to kill!* he thought— somewhat gratefully. *No guts—that'll be his downfall.*

Bingham was closing in. Barker watched from a distance, pondering what he was up against. *This is no game of paintball!* he reminded himself. Sure, he was a seasoned police officer with hundreds of hours of training, but thus far in his career he'd seldom needed to draw his weapon. He remembered the fear he'd felt standing on the porch with his gun aimed at Melvin Briggs's nose. The palms of his hands were moist and cold then just as now.

Barker looked on intently. Bingham was almost to the mark. What if the tractor didn't start, or if Bingham chanced to go up the wrong row of trees? How many more of Bingham's friends were lurking in the trees? Stacey was taking some big risks—too many variables in his plan.

A second gunman slipped from the passenger side of Bingham's Lexus parked at the bottom of the trees, while two more approached from above. They carried sniper rifles and headgear identical to that of Bingham's. The man from the back seat walked several rows up and started into the trees. Ten rows later he made a quiet call on his radio. "It's a trap! I repeat, it's a trap. Pull out. We've got feds in the trees." Bingham listened through his earpiece, raised his silenced rifle to his shoulder and fired a single shot.

Barker's headgear exploded, folding and collapsing backward, as a hollow-tip bullet smashed into the side of his forehead. He crumpled to the ground, a trickle of blood seeping down his temple onto the side of his nose.

Buseth and his men saw the flash through the trees. "Move! Move! Close the road and don't let him out," he ordered his men. Two vehicles pulled out across the road leading to and from the orchard. Federal agents fanned out through the orchard, cautiously examining each tree and stump in their path.

The boy jumped from the porch roof and sprawled onto the grass before springing to his feet, the 10-foot fall hardly slowing him down. Old Mitsy recognized him, and again tugged at the chain, barking.

Danny's confidence was at a high. He'd successfully taken Melvin down. Now who was this new attacker? *Or had Melvin escaped from jail?* he wondered. The anxious fear he'd felt earlier in the day returned.

The back porch light came on. Danny watched helplessly as the attacker, Christina in tow, disappeared into the trees. He and his friends had played hide-and-seek in the orchard as children, so Danny was familiar with its layout. And the kidnapper wasn't moving all that fast, what with lugging a 75-pound girl. The picture of the man scurrying away into the trees, carrying all that *dead* weight, sent a jolt through his body. What if Christina were dead? She hadn't screamed for help or moved the entire time.

Inside, Kate raced through the house, still turning on lights, now certain that her niece was no longer in the home—and equally certain that her young son was out in the orchard chasing some dangerous lunatic. A wave of lightheadedness passed over her as she thought of the possible danger. One or both of them could be killed or seriously hurt. After calling the police, both she and Alan stumbled out the back door, where Danny was just turning loose the crippled old dog.

"Where is she?" Alan yelled to his son.

Danny called out as he slipped through a hole in the rod-iron fence, "I'm going to get her!"

"No! The police are on their way!"

The sheriff and his men were at a loss as to where to

look for their cunning escapee. "Dispatch, Mapleton one twenty-eight."

"One twenty-eight, go ahead."

"You aren't going to believe this but Christina Rodriguez is missing again. Her aunt is on the line. Someone just took her from her bed and carried her into the fruit orchard behind their house."

"Pull out!" the sheriff ordered. "I've had it, I want him dead."

The men began to pour into their vehicles.

To Christina, it felt like she was being carried on horseback through a jungle. The back of the horse—or whatever it was—dug into her middle as it went. She felt sick to her stomach. She began to thrash about in a bid to break free.

Her masked, human captor, meanwhile, fought to keep a hold of the girl—and away from her feet and flailing arms and head.

The entire corps of deputies was in route from Melvin's house. The city's early Sunday morning silence was transformed into an echo of wailing sirens, every officer eager to see the last of Melvin Briggs. The windows and yards on Kate's street were alive with flashing blue and red lights.

Peering through the small opening at the top of the old salamander, oil burning in its belly, Stacey had seen the burst and heard the muffled report from Bingham's rifle. Sig, who'd been listening to Mitsy's barking, resisted the urge to leave his position. Stacey had spread out on the ground to return fire, before spotting Bingham disappearing back down the row of trees. Stacey took out the radio and called out, "Barker, you okay?... Barker!...Barker!" Then he frantically set out crawling to where his friend lay.

Christina's attacker dropped the girl to the ground and turned to ward off the vicious-sounding dog, which latched its jaws on the dark-clad figure's thigh. A scream, high-pitched and unnatural, wafted out over the orchard. But still the kidnapper struggled, sending a small puff of dust into the dog's face. Paralyzed by the powerful drug, Mitsy relaxed her grip.

With all this happening around her, Christina began to return to the present. She hadn't a clue as to where she was or what was going on. She only knew that her hands were tied and that the Jensen's old dog had its jaws firmly attached to the leg of a howling figure. It only took a moment for her to fathom the danger she was in. She struggled to her feet. Danny came into view in time to see the attacker deliver a swift blow to the old dog's head. Mitsy released her grip and sagged to the ground.

Danny reared back and hurled himself at the attacker, catching him squarely in the chest. Both tumbled to the ground.

"Run, Christina! Run!" he screamed. Christina staggered to her feet and fled into the unknown reaches of the orchard.

Danny's intent was to deliver a round of blows similar to those he'd inflicted on Melvin. But this foe was no Melvin. A violent slap to the head dropped Danny. As he fell, he frantically glommed on to the dark shirt, still hoping to wrestle the maniac to the ground. A loud snapping sound was followed by a groan of pain as the shadowy attacker brought his foot down on Danny's lower leg, shattering the bone. Danny crumpled to the ground, letting go of the shirt.

Voices moved in the darkness toward him. "Over here!" Danny yelled, his voice hoarse. "He's trying to get her! Over here!"

Mitch and Olsen heard the boy's ragged screams. Danny rolled to the side of his motionless dog. She'd never bitten anyone before. "It's okay girl. Hang in there. Help's on the way."

The excitement and fear of the chase had finally taken its toll. The toughest acting boy on the block sank in sheer exhaustion next to his dying dog and began to cry.

Stumbling over roots and falling in ruts, Christina lit out through the trees in her wet nightgown, the grass and patches of mud cold on her feet. She could hear Danny's cries for help. She, too, had played hide-and-seek among the trees. Her willowy body shook violently. The cold, as well as the effect of the hallucinogen, slowed her movements.

Maybe the brief head start wasn't enough. Spurred both by fear and uncertainty, Christina's mind flashed back to the tree house roof. She tried to remember what she'd seen in the face of her attacker that night, when the mask was torn off. The eyes, all she could remember were the eyes, dark, lifeless—like her mother's eyes when she was high on drugs. She knew that if she were caught again, she wouldn't live to tell about the ordeal.

Her hands still taped, she ran crossways up the hill, away from the safety of the house. She could hear grunts coming from her assailant as he chased her through the trees, leaving a bloody path behind him in the grass.

On the relentless killer came, dodging in and out of the trees. A rush of thoughts surged through his brain. Thoughts, traversing time, went back to the jungles of Vietnam. *The enemy is coming through the brush! We helped the allies; the women and children will be raped and tortured, raped and tortured ....I must finish her off before it's too late.*

Christina, even if it meant death, could run no farther. As the sounds behind her grew closer, she searched out a place to hide. There beside her was a low-cut stump—the perfect hiding place. From its base grew a bevy of tall, unpruned suckers. Christina pushed the willowy stems to the side and crawled into the center. The leafy growth gave ample cover.

Mitch reached Danny first; Olsen and three other deputies were only steps behind. The beam of his flashlight rested on the boy lying close to his dying dog. Her tongue hung limp from her bleeding mouth, her ears lay flat, her eyes fixed and cloudy. Danny pointed down a row of trees. "Hurry! She went up there. He's still after her!"

"One of you stay with the boy," Olsen ordered as they rushed off.

Stacey knelt down near Barker, his unconscious friend. The night-vision gear lay two feet from his head, mangled. It was apparent he'd taken a direct hit. The trickle of blood coming from Barker's temple appeared more like a cut from flying glass than from a bullet. A large goose-egg protruded from the brow above his right eye.

Wresting the phone from his pocket, Stacey called for an ambulance. Buseth and his men approached cautiously, still unsure of Bingham's location.

Dear Heavenly Father, Christina prayed, mouthing the words. *I know you can hear me. I'm not going to ask for much—just help me be still and not shake.* She felt her body slowly relax and a ripple of warmth wash over her. Though the shaking ceased, her heart pounded like drums in her ears. Nearby, a muffled "pop" was heard. Her body convulsed at the sound.

Suddenly, Melvin appeared in the nearby clearing, just 20 feet away. His back to her, he was peering down a row of trees. Lights from the city reflected from the clouds, producing a single, feathery glow like that of a moonbeam dancing from Melvin's bald head. Christina's gasp of alarm gave her away. He turned to face her—then both of them turned in the direction of the deep, throaty rumble of a dog moving swiftly through the trees.

Melvin, primed and ready, drew a straw from his jacket. The plant's pollen would *not* completely stop the attack, he knew, but, under the circumstances, it was the best way. Boldly he stood his ground, tensed, anticipating the blow.

The shepherd bounded from the trees, his growl escalated to an all-out roar as he made his final leap. Melvin aimed and puffed the powder from the straw. Sig, duty-bound, plowed through the poisonous cloud. The impact took Melvin to the ground. Sig, blood oozing from the bandage, chomped down on Melvin's arm and held on. Melvin dropped his pistol to the ground and with his free arm proceeded to pry open the clenched jaws of the dazed, disoriented dog. The powerful drug had quickly taken effect.

Like witnessing a high-speed car crash, the scene before her was both repulsive and strangely fascinating. Christina wanted to run, but was frozen to the spot. The violent tremors had returned, and the branches where she hid thrashed through the air above her head. Melvin stood and approached the stump. Parting the vertical limbs with his hands, he pressed his face close to hers and whispered, "It's almost over."

A scream caught in her throat. She struggled to release the sound. None could save her. And this time closing her eyes would not make him go away.

"Buseth, it looks like they've escaped the orchard...." The voice crackled over the radio. "A small jet just landed on the Provo runway."

Buseth's orders rent the night air. "Sweep the area again before you pull out. He could be anywhere. Send all the men you can spare to the airport." His next command was directed toward Stacey. "Now, Officer Stacey, give me the pen!"

"Oh? My friend is lying here bleeding and unconscious...Bingham's escaped...and the only thing you can think of is the damn pen?!"

"You give me the pen or I'll see you rot in a federal prison!" Buseth shouted back.

Mitch knelt and lifted Christina from the stump, where he'd come upon the crying, shivering girl. His strong arms held her tight. "Shhh, it's okay," he reassured her. "No one can hurt you now. I've got you."

Olsen staggered into the clearing and aimed his light beam on the dark figure laying in the grass nearby. Seconds later, two deputies approached, guns drawn, lights darting back and forth through the trees. "What do you have?" one of them asked.

"I found the girl," Mitch said, still holding her in his arms.

"You better take a look!" Olsen shouted. The two deputies stopped beside him, staring down at a body in the grass.

Stacey answered the ringing cell phone. "You shot him, you s.o.b.!"

"You're an amateur, Stacey! A kid playing games against a pro. Do you think I'd fall for your cute little tree ruse? And your buddy, Lieutenant Barker, waiting to ambush me? If it weren't for the feds hiding out there, you'd be bleeding to death right now, your throat slit!" Then it was time to make his point. "Now I'm warning you: if I don't get my property back you'll wish you were already dead!"

"Shove it, Bingham—or whatever your name is! You've killed Deek and now maybe Barker, too."

"Amber...." Bingham shot back, weighing his words, his rhetorical question interspersed by laughter, "isn't that the name of your little sister?...The one that *used* to live in that fancy house with a living, breathing mother and father?"

"I'll kill you if you've touched them! I swear I'm going to hunt you down and kill you!"

"The time's passed for you to do that," Bingham mocked before hanging up the phone.

"You've taken this thing—this vendetta of yours— way too personally, Bingham. I'm pulling my men out. If you decide to stay, you're on your own." Chief Anderson, steering his Cadillac through traffic, had made up his mind. He and his none-too-happy associate pulled onto the exit leading to the Provo airport. A small jet idled on the runway just a mile away, waiting for them.

"You'd better not bail out on me now!" Bingham threatened.

"Too late, it's already done."

"I don't think so." Bingham raised his handgun and fired point-blank. As the Caddy lurched to one side and slowed, he reached across Anderson's slouched body, opened the door, and shoved it out on to the asphalt. The body bounced like a rag doll before skidding to a mangled stop in the middle of the road. Bingham slid over into the driver's seat.

He found the limp body lying face down in a furrow between two cherry trees. Olsen rolled it over. A single bullet hole in the forehead. Long, dark hair fell in strings across her face and down her slender neck. She'd been a beautiful woman, in her mid-forties, he guessed. Her features were fine, but the lines of time and conflict were deeply embedded in her face.

Mitch waited until Olsen came to take Christina from his arms. She was still shaking from her experience. "You won't believe it," is all Olsen could mutter before carrying the girl to the waiting ambulance.

Reluctant to leave her, Danny knelt in the moist dirt at Mitsy's side. Her breathing had stopped. The last few minutes he'd stroked her side and rubbed under her chin, speaking soft and low. Now she was gone.

He lay his head on her still body, his own leg throbbing with pain. "She's dead...she's dead," he whimpered over and over. Officer Grue lifted him up to carry him back to the house.

FORTY

PARAMEDICS LOADED BARKER onto a stretcher. A few feet away, Buseth was trying to settle Stacey down. "I'm telling you, Bingham didn't kill your family. He was just out to scare you. We've been watching him for over a year."

Stacey's eyes bulged and all the blood had rushed to his face. "Listen! You let me go over there myself or send some of your men over right now and find out if they're all right!"

"Give me the pen and I promise we'll protect both you and your family."

"The hell you will! You couldn't even catch Bingham when I brought him to you!" His arm shot up from his side, delivering a glancing blow to Buseth's lower jaw. Buseth crumpled to the ground like a wet towel. Four of his men closed in and wrestled Stacey to the ground—just as Mr. White and half a dozen county rigs cautiously pulled up the lane.

White stepped from his car, followed by his deputies, their guns drawn and pointed at the federal agents. "Officer Stacey's one of my men! Turn him loose and identify yourselves!"

"We're federal agents on special assignment," said one, slowly reaching for his identification.

"What *special assignment* might that be?" Mr. White inquired.

"It's classified." The agent lowered his badge and glanced down at Buseth, still groaning on the gravel road.

"Then we better go down to my office and *unclassify* it before I throw the whole damned bunch of you in county lock up."

The squawk of Buseth's radio broke the mounting tension. "Sir, we couldn't catch them. The plane took off before we could stop it."

Buseth rose to his feet, still dazed, and spouted out his orders into the mouthpiece. "Call Hill Air Force Base. Get a couple of F-16's up to escort that bird back down. If they refuse to comply, have 'em take it out of the air." As one of his men got on the phone, Buseth continued. "Get a couple of men over to the Stacey residence and make sure everything's all right until we make sure Bingham's on that plane."

From the CAT-scan room Barker was wheeled to the operating room, where a team of neurosurgeons prepared to insert an external ventricular drain (EVD) to abate the dangerously high pressure inside his skull. His anxious wife stood as the head surgeon stopped by the waiting area to report his condition.

"Your husband was seriously injured. The blow he received ruptured a tiny blood vessel in the right front lobe of his head. The blood's causing pressure on the brain. We need to drill a hole in his skull and insert a tube to relieve some of that pressure. If that doesn't work, we may need to remove a portion of his skull to allow room for the brain to swell. We need to operate quickly to avoid any additional damage to the brain."

Barker's wife held back the tears. "Will he be brain-damaged?"

"It's too early to tell. We need your signature to proceed." She signed the document and the surgeon rushed off.

Her mind raced back to Deek's funeral, only days before. She couldn't bear the thought of losing Paul. She was desperate to keep him—even if he ended up impaired.

Only a few hours before he had told her he loved her. For several weeks now he'd been acting sentimental, especially when he spoke of the children. Had he had a premonition that this was going to happen?

I should have never complained, she thought. It was a night a week ago when he'd come home late. She'd needled him as he walked through the door—something about whether or not they were still married. It was her indirect way of complaining without it sounding like a complaint. "He's got to be okay," she murmured as she closed her eyes in silent prayer.

In a veterinarian clinic not far away, the operating room had been made ready for Sig's arrival. He was placed on a table and prepped for surgery. IVs were set up and oxygen provided; even a heart monitor was connected. Sig still twitched uncontrollably from the effects of the drug mixture–one that Melvin had blown in his face and the other that the vet had administered to calm him down.

The vet first began to clean and sterilize the old wound on his side that seemed to have torn loose. "These stitches are the cleanest I've ever seen," she remarked, trimming and re-closing the gash.

Her assistant monitored the breathing and heart rate. "He's doing better, doctor. Whatever drug he was exposed to is almost out of his system."

Mitch waited in the front office. Sig was going to be okay.

"I've been hearing stories about you, young man. You're a hero, you know," said the young aide as she wheeled the gurney from x-ray. He didn't feel much like a hero. The pain in his leg coursed all the way up past his hip into his back. His dog was dead, and he hadn't even come close to stopping Christina's assailant. He'd swatted Danny aside like a bug. What made it worse, his leg was broken. "Yeah, some hero all right...."

Kate was just relieved that both he and Christina were safe. "Danny, if you hadn't gone to the girls' room, no one would have known she was missing. And if you hadn't had the presence of mind to let Mitsy go, there's no telling what would have happened. One thing's for sure: Christina wouldn't have gotten away. You saved your cousin. I don't know if I've ever met more of a hero than that." Kate raised a finger to underscore another important point. "Mitsy died a hero's death, too—far better than the alternative you and your father had talked about."

Danny took a minute to review the evening's sequence of events. He'd jumped off the roof; he hadn't thought twice before climbing through the fence to give chase; then he'd knocked the murderer to the ground. Maybe he was a bit of a hero.

Kate left Danny in the good hands of a doctor and made her way to the emergency cubical where Christina lay, curled up under a blanket, sound asleep. "She's a strong girl," remarked Dr. Wendy. "She's not ready to talk about it yet, so I tried to help her understand her feelings—give her some perspective as to what she's gone through the past week. Soon she'll want to talk. I think I should see her Monday afternoon. It might take several visits to get her through this. In the meantime, treat her the same as you always have or she'll feel like everyone's pampering her."

"Thank you, Doctor. I'll bring her in on Monday."

He sat behind his desk, surrounded by Agent Buseth, Officer Stacey and the County Sheriff. "Let's see if we have all the pertinent information on the table, gentlemen," White began. "We think the woman whose body was recovered from the orchard was married to Melvin Briggs. She was shot in the head by who knows who. Chief Anderson's body—also shot in the head—was just scraped off the exit leading into the Provo airport. Bingham was supposedly on a private jet just shot down by two F-16 fighters over the Nevada desert. And Melvin Briggs, the suspect in the murder and molestation of five girls in our community, is at large. Have I missed anything—*other than the fact that Melvin Briggs is actually a federal agent who's been keeping track of our Councilman Anderson and Captain Bingham, who in turn were rogue killers working for the highest bidder!?*"

White slapped his hand down on the desk. "Why the

hell haven't we been told about this before now?"

"Mr. White," Buseth replied guardedly, "this case is highly-classified. I've already told you far more than I'm authorized to." Buseth glowered at Stacey, who hadn't spoken a word about the pen full of chemicals. "Suffice it to say, our operation is nearly complete and we'll be pulling out as soon as we wrap up a few loose ends." His eyes darted again in Stacey's direction. "We don't know where Melvin Briggs is, but we *will* continue to look for him. If the evidence you have against him holds up, we'll be glad to turn him over to you when we find him." Buseth stood to leave. "Here's my number. If you need any more information you can subpoena my superior. I guarantee it won't do you a bit of good, though."

With Buseth out of the way, White made his move. "I need to talk to Officer Stacey privately, if you don't mind, Sheriff." As the sheriff rose to leave, White made one more suggestion: "Let's make sure we keep a few men on the Briggs home until I get a warrant."

Mr. White waited until the door was closed to speak. "I think you know more than you're saying, Officer Stacey. Let me give you a ride home and we can talk about it."

"That dog took one heck of a beating. Who'd he tangle with?" the vet asked Mitch.

"I'm not sure. Will he be all right?"

"He'll be fine in no time. The effects of the drug are gone now."

"I was afraid I was going to have to shoot him. It was a good thing you came when you did. It was amazing how you were able to get close enough to put him out like that."

"I became a vet because I love animals. It would've broken my heart to see such a fine animal destroyed."

"I need to get going. Stace needs to know how he's doing. You take good care of him."

"Don't worry, we will," she said as Mitch hurried out the door.

Debbie Barker didn't feel strong enough to deal with what she might be up against. She pictured Paul lying at home in a hospital bed, being fed mashed foods while wearing a bib. She could imagine his hands curled up, his muscle tone gone, his eyes lolling to one side, unable to dress himself, walk or control his bladder. He might not even know who she was. Surrounded by relatives who had come to the hospital upon hearing of the crisis, she put her face in her hands. "It's not fair," she sobbed. "It's just not fair."

No one paid heed to the slender man with a baseball cap pulled over his balding head, slumped in his chair, his back to them, listening to their conversation.

Olsen and the other officers had scoured the orchard, looking for clues as to the whereabouts of Melvin Briggs. There were none to be had. They were left to keep the neighborhood calm—and the press out of their way.

Mr. White dropped Stacey off at his apartment. "Get some sleep and we'll talk it over later. I'll see you tomorrow at ten."

Stacey walked up the drive, glad to know Sig was on the road to recovery. He pressed his key into the knob on the back door and twisted. It was already open. Crouching at the door, he drew his weapon and pushed the door open a crack. He didn't know what to do next.

"It was already unlocked, Officer Stacey. I let myself in. Please, join me," came a familiar voice.

The head of ER returned to Danny's room. Kate was there. Walking to the light board on the wall, he flipped a switch, the fluorescent light buzzed on, and he slid the x-ray under the clip at the top. Just as the doctor had begun, Alan stepped through the curtain. "Excuse me, this is my son."

The doctor, mildly perturbed by the interruption, forged ahead. "I was just describing the process we'll use to set your son's leg." Alan looked at the dark negative, showing a prominent separation at the mid-point of the shin.

"I think we need to put him under general anesthetic to set this bone," explained the doctor. "It's a clean break—which is good. I've called an orthopedic specialist, who should be here within the next few minutes. So, with your approval, I'd like to get Danny prepped."

Danny began to squirm. "You're not going to put me to sleep, are you?"

A faint smile played over the doctor's lips, "I believe you'd be more comfortable asleep than awake."

"Are there any other choices?"

"We could give you a lower spinal block to take the pain away from your legs. Sometimes women have the procedure done when they have children." Kate nodded as he spoke. "It's called an epidural. You'll be awake when we pull your leg back into place."

"Cool! I could watch the whole thing. I want the block."

The doctor glanced at Kate and Alan to see if that met with their approval. It did.

Stacey holstered his weapon and entered the darkened front room. Agent Buseth sat leaning back on a chair, one foot resting against the side of the table, his arms folded across his chest. His jaw had the beginning of a colorful bruise. His features reminded Stacey of Deek, but his personality did not. "It was a mistake to talk to White," he said stiffly. "You'd better have kept the information about the chemicals to yourself."

"And if I didn't?"

"I could bring military intelligence down on this little town and quarantine the whole place for months."

Stacey knew he was bluffing. "Agent Buseth, your chemicals are safe—for the time being."

"Good, then I have permission to bring you up to speed. Let's talk about turning the chemicals over to me."

"Start talking."

"I'll bring you positive proof that Bingham was on the plane, and you turn over the pen. Until then, I'll sequester your family in one of our safehouses and keep a close watch on you."

"You couldn't catch Bingham before. If he's still alive, how do you think you can catch him now?"

"Listen, we've invested six years in this operation. Melvin Phelps—or Briggs, as you know him—is one of the best surveillance men in the military. We know he's a pain in the butt. He can't get along with any of his superiors and he couldn't make a friend if his life depended on it. He and his wife have been fighting for years, especially after their daughter disappeared, and we're still not sure if he has anything to do with the murders and kidnapping. We've reviewed the research the FBI has turned over to us and know he's had equipment in every location each of the girls was killed. If he's guilty in any way, we'll make sure he fries for it."

"You still didn't answer my question. If Bingham's alive, how can we stop him?"

"If you'd given me any say in the time and location of the first attempt to take Bingham, he wouldn't have gotten away. I warned you not to underestimate him. He's a cold-blooded killer who's been cooped up in a captain's job for the last year. When your Chief Anderson got him his job on the force, it was the biggest break we've ever had. We were afraid Anderson had retired. He did his last job in Woodbridge, West Virginia, five years ago under the alias 'Officer Oswald.' He and his men liked being in positions of authority in small towns, so they could control their own undercover operations. We know Anderson was paying his Mexican maid extra to bring her very mature 14-year-old daughter to work to—how can I put this?—satisfy his needs. Melvin has proof of it. We just don't know if it was Anderson that killed her or if it was her dad, who's going to trial for the murder next month."

Buseth paused. "I'm getting off track." His body shifted positions—as if redirecting his thoughts. "The military forced Bingham to retire almost eight years ago because of his violent temper and insubordinate nature. He'd been trained to kill during the Vietnam War. The military had created these elite killing machines, men who were practically unstoppable, brainwashed to fight and kill without feeling. Now, 30 years later, our government doesn't know how to deal with them, so they get a little therapy and retire to the 'good life.' Problem is, they don't *want* to retire, so they go looking for a cause that will give them their fix of mayhem. Anderson was one of the leaders of a small group; Bingham was his best. We've suspected either Bingham or Anderson had the 'VN three-five-two' chemical for the last few years, and have been waiting to bring them in so it didn't fall into the wrong hands. You screwed everything up by taking the pen."

"Maybe if you'd let us know what was going on we could have helped. Where did the stuff come from?"

"Anderson and Bingham served in the same platoon. The 'VN' stands for Vietnam; the 'three-five-two' is the three hundred and fifty-second strain we've identified. We think they took the chemical from an enemy lab during one of their raids. It's the most potent strain we've isolated thus far. Melvin was infected with one of the earlier strains when he was shot."

"You're going to feel a little poke now." Danny felt a needle enter his lower back, followed by a cool wave of fluid. Instantly feeling nauseous, he was rolled to his side. There sat his father, clearly concerned.

Danny almost laughed. "You don't look so good, Dad."

"Injections make me woozy."

Soon Danny couldn't feel his legs. A man in green scrubs entered. "Danny, this is Doctor Jacobs. He's the Orthopedic Specialist on call. He'll be setting that leg for you."

"Hi there, buddy. How'd you break your leg at three o'clock in the morning?" the second doctor asked. He peered over his half-glasses to scan the x-ray.

"I was trying to stop a killer from hurting my cousin." Danny thought the words sounded pretty good.

The surgeon sought out the other faces in the room to see if the boy was telling the truth. Then he turned back to Danny. "You tell me the whole story while I put your leg back where it belongs." He glanced at the anesthesiologist. "Is everything ready?" The man nodded.

"This shouldn't hurt, but you might be a little uncomfortable."

The ER doctor took up a position where he could get a good hold on Danny's upper body. Dr. Jacobs clamped on to Danny's foot and pulled, adjusting the leg up and down, side to side. Danny could hardly believe what he was seeing. The part of his leg down by his ankle moved totally independently of the part up by his knee.

Alan leaned over in his chair and put his head between his knees.

"You okay, Dad?" asked the ER doc.

"I'll be fine."

Then Danny started in on the story of Christina and the landlord.

Stacey couldn't quite muzzle a laugh as he spoke the words: "I've heard about Melvin's shot butt."

Buseth, all business, shook his head. "Not everything. The chemical affected him in some strange ways. In some areas his IQ goes off the charts. That's why he's such a good snoop–the man is a genius when it comes to computers and electronics, but he's like a ten-year-old when it comes to dealing with people."

"That explains why he was doing all those stupid things to drive his renters out....Do you think he's capable of attacking the girls?"

"More than capable—quite plausible, actually. He claims it was his wife, though. We're almost sure he's the one that killed her in the orchard."

Stacey rubbed his chin. "You've got some serious problems, Agent Buseth. If you suspected one of your men was killing and molesting girls, and you didn't lock him down, the government has some serious charges to answer to."

"We weren't aware of the connection until you arrested him the first time. When my boss flew into town, we slapped your judge with a federal gag order so we could finish things up without Melvin finding out we were watching him. Otherwise he might have bolted."

Buseth took a drink from his mug and gathered his thoughts. "Now here's the kicker–my boss was Melvin's commanding officer in Nam. He has an unwarranted faith in Melvin none of the rest of us share. We planned on turning Melvin over as soon as we took out Anderson and his men."

"It's starting to make sense now," Stacey said. "But if you'd have been watching closer, that girl wouldn't have been scared to death—and nearly killed."

"Like I said, we had to keep our distance—orders from higher up. Before my boss was promoted, he served in Melvin's platoon. Melvin had saved his life a week before the entire platoon was ambushed and everyone was killed—all except Melvin. My boss was still in the hospital recovering when it happened. Melvin was found several weeks later, with half his butt missing. It took him months to recover. The boss claims he owes his life to Melvin and makes allowances for him. He says things aren't always as they seem."

In less than an hour Danny's leg was set in a bright green cast. X-rayed again and the pictures examined, Dr. Jacobs returned to the room and informed Danny that he would be as good as new in eight to ten weeks. "I'll see you in two weeks. Your mother can make an appointment by calling the office on Monday." He glanced over at Kate, who acknowledged his request. "And Danny, no more heroics for a while!"

Buseth informed Stacey that he'd be in touch after the investigation report on the jet's passengers was in. Stacey stood as the agent started for the door. "Hey, Buseth, sorry about the pop on the chin."

"I should have been more sensitive to the situation. I might've done the same if someone told me they'd murdered my parents and sister. We'll take good care of them until this thing is over. By the way, my boss has taken a liking to you. You're the first man that's ever rung Bingham's bell. And the first outside of our team we've given classified information to. Be careful; we suspect that if Bingham did kill Anderson, he probably didn't get on the plane. We'll do our best to keep you covered."

FORTY-ONE

DON WOKE BEFORE DAWN and stared at the ceiling. He'd wrestled all night with his vivid dreams. The one he could remember best had him dressed in suit and tie, sitting in a church pew, Cecily to one side of him and a small, dark-haired boy to the other. The boy's elbow rested on Don's leg, his chin in his hand as he stared off into the distance. Cecily held a younger boy in her lap, who wiggled and squirmed to get down. Christina sat at Cecily's side, her left hand—with a small diamond engagement ring on the second finger—clasped in that of a handsome young man sitting next to her. She was grown up and beautiful. Her smile was an absolute joy. It'd been quite a dream——a wonderful dream!

The phone summoned him back into the present. Cecily stirred in the cot across the room. He hesitated answering it; this wasn't his house, after all. The ringing stopped. A minute passed before he heard a knock at the door. There stood Pauline, wrapped in a robe.

"Kate's on the phone. She sounds distressed," she said.

As he went to the phone in the kitchen, Don's mind rifled through the myriad of frightful possibilities suggested by a call at such an early hour. "Hi, Kate. What's up?"

"I've delayed calling so you could get some sleep. Before you panic, let me tell you Christina's just fine." Don felt both worse and better in the same instant. "Last night she was kidnapped." Don's already hammering heart grew louder.

"What happened?"

He could tell by the tautness in her voice as she told him what happened that it had been a frightening experience.

"Dad was right! ...Can I talk to her?"

"I'll wake her if you want; she's asleep in the back seat."

"No, don't disturb her. Have her call me when she wakes up."

"Everything will be fine. You take care of things up there and try not to worry. We'll call you later. And Don..." she added for emphasis, "don't you worry. She's safe."

Debbie, her mother at her side, was led to the Intensive Care Recovery Unit. Paul, his face swollen almost beyond recognition, was lying there, still unconscious, his head bandaged. A drainage tube was stitched and tied under the skin of his partially-shaved head, and ran to a container filled with blood and fluid. A larger tube was inserted into his throat. A metal bolt stuck from his head with wires connected to a bank of monitors, which bleeped off digital readings. The surgeon informed her that the pressure on his brain was being closely monitored. Now all they could do was wait. She could stay there by his bedside, but only two people were permitted in the area at a time.

Tenderly, the two women stroked his arms and hands. Then, after offering some words of comfort, Debbie's mom returned to the waiting area so others could come in to spend a few moments with them. A doctor's assistant remained at the bedside.

"You must be Mrs. Barker," the assistant said.

Debbie's gaze again fell on the helpless figure on the bed. She removed her hands from her lips long enough to answer.

"Would you like me to explain what everything is?" asked the assistant, gesturing to the array of tubes and wires. Debbie nodded. "This bolt sends a signal to the monitor, which keeps track of the pressure in his cranium. We like to keep it below 12 ." The monitor read nine. "He's been intubated to help him breathe. A head injury can make the brain confused, and sometimes it won't send the signal to the lungs to breathe. The wire on his finger keeps track of his oxygen level. If he can keep it up on his own we'll take out the tube that helps him breathe. Heart monitors and blood pressure monitors track his vitals."

Debbie listened intently as the assistant continued. "'Posturing' is caused by damage and pressure on the brain. This tube," she said, pointing to the one leading from his head, "is draining excess spinal fluid and blood, thereby relieving excess pressure from his skull. The neurosurgeon was pleased with the results of the CAT-scan they took after surgery. He'll be in to see you soon."

Barker's mother washed her hands in a nearby sink and went in to join her daughter-in-law. "Debbie, your Dad's here with the bishop to give him a health blessing," she said. "Is that okay?"

"Of course."

Don, his brothers and sisters, and their wives, husbands and children were all dressed in their Sunday best. Don had on the suit Kate had given him for his court appearance. The shirt, buttoned to the collar, pinched at his neck. He'd fumbled with his necktie for a full ten minutes, but couldn't seem to get it right. An inmate at the jail named Will Vaughan had shown him how to tie it the time he'd worn it in court. Now his fingers and brain just couldn't do it.

Cecily stepped back in the room, dressed in a long, dark blue dress, which flowed down to mid-calf. Her hair was curled under ever so slightly, the ends barely grazing her neck. The natural beauty of her face was highlighted by a touch of makeup, blush, mascara and lipstick. He'd never seen her in a dress before. Momentarily distracted from thoughts of his daughter, he admired her reflection in the mirror as she put her things away.

"What are you doing?" she casually asked, zipping up her bag.

"Watching you." He turned to face her. The words had caught her off guard. She blushed, then laughed out loud when she saw the tangled clump around his neck.

"Would you like some help with that?"

"You know how to tie one of these?"

"'Course I do. I have four younger brothers, remember?"

Cecily stepped close and began to unsnarl the labyrinth of knots. Don looked down at her soft lips, glimmering with shiny gloss. The lips began to move. "You simply cross the ends, wrap the big end under and over the top, then bring it around, then up again and down through the loop."

The lips stopped moving, and he waited for her to look up so he could kiss them. The phone rang. She drew the tie up to his collar, noticing the rapid rise and fall of his chest. Then, with Maria's call from the other room, the spell was broken. "Don, Christina's on the phone."

Cecily looked up into his face. He paused before turning to pick up the phone on the night table. "Yeah, Kate told me all about it. I'm so happy you're safe....I'll be home this evening. We'll leave here as soon as the service is over....Okay, bye, love."

The rest of the household had already left for the mortuary.

Stacey's parents and sister were overjoyed to see him. After the hugs and kisses, Amber finally asked, "Where's the man that was trying to hurt you?"

"Dead, I hope."

"Did you kill him?"

Stacey balked at the question. He measured his answer carefully. "I think his wrong choices were the cause of his death." Stacey had joined the police force to preserve and protect—not to kill. He realized that *if* the captain was dead, it was the hand of justice that had administered the ultimate punishment.

His mother, awash in relief, embraced him.

Stacey turned to his father, a tinge of urgency in his voice. "You need to take Mom and Amber to a federal safehouse for a few days. If the man who's been causing all this trouble isn't dead, you're in a great deal of danger. It'll only be a few days, I promise."

His father reluctantly agreed. The federal agents who'd knocked on his door in the middle of the night were still parked in the street, but they'd supply just so much protection.

While his family packed, Stacey phoned Mr. White. "I'll meet you at the hospital. I need to find my dog....Can we make it eleven?...Good. See you then."

After Alan had retrieved Mitsy's body from the orchard, the family gathered to hold a brief service in her honor. Danny opted to bury her in a corner of the garden. Her rigid body was gently lifted onto an old blanket, and Jake and Alan carried her to the side yard. Kate had brought two shovels from the garage. The tired little family watched as Alan and Jake took turns shoveling soil from the chosen spot.

Don's father hadn't wanted a formal viewing or ceremony, just a small, simple graveside service. Don was surprised at the number of people who'd come to pay their respects. And he was even more surprised—and pleased—that nearly all of them seemed well acquainted with his dad. "You must be Gero's son...I've been hoping to meet you," they'd say. Or "You must be Brother Rodriguez's son...." Don grew more confused by each greeting.

When he and Cecily finally stepped up to peer into the open casket, he asked in a whisper, "Who are all these people?"

"They're members of his local congregation....I'll tell you about it later."

Don gazed down at his father's body—the shell which had once housed his strong spirit. Many of the people lingered, chatting softly, until the funeral director announced that they would be moving to the grave site. "We'd ask the family to remain here to gather in a family prayer...."

As most of the gathering made their way out onto the lawn, the children and grandchildren, Pauline front and center, clustered around the casket one last time. A few of those who remained Don didn't know. Pauline turned to a man she introduced as "bishop".

He began to speak. As he did so, Don's mind wandered, seesawing back and forth between what the man was saying and reflecting on the meaning behind the words. "The family has asked me to conduct this prayer. I've been his bishop the last five years....Gero and I spent many hours talking about his family. He felt he was only just beginning to get to know and understand his children again....He hadn't told you of the peace and joy he found returning to a life centered around Christ. I tell you this because I know he made that choice before he learned he was ill....He credited his change of heart to a good woman whom he met and married. His hope is that some day all of his children can be joined to him—and her—in an eternal relationship....He told me that if you all came to this, his funeral service, it would be the first time in many, many years you would be together....His dying wish was to unite you, his children, together as loved ones....Now, before the casket is closed, I ask you to join me in a final prayer."

The man offered a humble and beautiful prayer. Don could hear his father's sentiments in the man's voice as he spoke, directing his words and thoughts to God.

"Goodbye," Don whispered as the lid was closed and the casket was wheeled out of the room.

The last shovel of dirt had been replaced in the hole harboring Mitsy's body. Two county deputies lingered out front as the family filed back into the house.

Danny had volunteered to pray before the grave was filled in. "Dear Father in Heaven," he'd said, the tears flowing down his cheeks, "we're here to say goodbye to Mitsy. She's been part of our family for a long time. She was getting old and sick. Mitsy never hurt anyone; only barked a lot. She was a gentle dog, and only bit that guy to help Christina. It just wouldn't be heaven without her, so we hope she's there living with you. Thank you for letting us have her so long. Amen."

Stacey was most of the way down the hall when Dianne walked out of the elevator on her way home. "How's he doing?" he asked.

"He's still unconscious. Where've you been? We were worried about you."

"I was detained by federal agents."

"Is everything all right?"

"It will be soon."

Dianne looked down at her watch. "Well, I've got to take off," she said. "You go up and see Debbie."

Up on the fourth floor, Stacey found the intensive care unit half-filled with visitors. A murmur ran through the crowd and most everyone in the room turned to look as he approached.

Stacey wasn't prepared for what he saw. He did a double-take, hardly recognizing his friend. Paul's swollen face and black eyes made him look like he was wearing a Halloween mask. His bed was slightly elevated. He was breathing on his own.

Debbie came over and put her hand on his shoulder. "Rick, good to see you! Are you okay?"

"Are *you* going to be okay?" Stacey countered.

"I'll be fine." She turned to look down at her husband. "Paul's doing much better, too. The doctors say he's regained some reflexes in his left arm and leg that he didn't have when they brought him in. Until the swelling goes down in his head, they won't know what to expect. They think the damage is only temporary."

"If he's made captain," Stacey bantered, trying to lighten things up, "that swelling will be permanent."

Debbie smiled. Moments later, she grew deathly serious. "Where's Bingham? They say he's the one who shot Paul."

"I don't know. The feds think he's dead—shot down in a plane over the Nevada desert." Stacey decided to hold off on the details until later.

"Mitch tells me Sig will be just fine."

"Good, I need to find him."

After giving her a tender hug—and his promise to return soon—Stacey excused himself from the room.

FORTY-TWO

"THAT WAS A BEAUTIFUL SERVICE," Cecily commented when the family met out on the back lawn of the house later in the day.

Don, having pondered what he'd heard and felt, bent down to pick a dandelion. "It wasn't at all what *I* thought it would be like."

"What did you expect?"

"A lot of screaming, I guess...crying."

"Well, it all depends on how you feel about death."

"What do you mean?"

"If you thought death was the end, you'd be upset. But if you believed death was just another step in our progression, in our eternal existence, sure, you'd be sad if someone died, but not so distraught. You'd know it wasn't the end."

Spinning the dandelion stem between his finger and thumb, the yellow bloom just a blur against the green grass, Don lapsed into the world of his imagination. In it he pondered Cecily's words. Why did she always seem to make so much sense? She understood concepts he'd never even bothered to think about. And she was so good—probably the worst thing she'd ever done was get a speeding ticket, while Don had a rap sheet a mile long. They were such different people, culturally, physically, in terms of religion. Yet they shared such a strong friendship and attraction.

Cecily, meanwhile, was entertaining similar thoughts and questions. Why was she so attracted to him—besides his good looks? What was it about him that made her feel warm and safe and loved? She was in love, but how could she think of throwing away all her goals and dreams to marry someone who wasn't of her faith?

For a few long minutes the two of them sat on the grass, reflecting on their hopes—and brooding over their fears. Don's mind was spinning, just like the canary-blonde blossom in his hand. He wondered how Cecily could live by reason and logic, knowledge and understanding, while his life was governed by passion and excitement. She knew exactly where she was going and how she would get there; he took it one day at a time, rolling with the punches and obstacles as they came his way. And she seemed so much more carefree, while he took his responsibilities very seriously. She didn't have the glamor of a Monica, yet he found her to be beautiful. *Maybe we don't communicate all that well,* he wavered. *I don't even know where she wants our relationship to go.*

Don's mind lurched back to reality. "I'd like to get started for home as soon as possible. Christina needs me." Dropping the dandelion bloom to the ground, he pushed himself to his feet and put out his hand to Cecily.

"The poor thing," she said, accepting the hand and easing herself up. "I'd be a wreck, too, after what she's been through."

Don gave a little shake of his head. "The weird thing is, she seems so unaffected by it all," he said. "She's still her precocious, happy self."

The two of them collected their belongings. The family was gathered in Pauline's kitchen, eating the meal the neighbors had brought. Don explained why he needed to hurry back, and mentioned that they should think about holding a family gathering each year. His siblings happily agreed.

Stacey met Mr. White in front of the hospital. "Sorry I'm late," he apologized. "I was visiting my dog."

White got right to the point. "Melvin Briggs—or whatever his name is—has a lot of questions to answer. My men think he killed his wife last night after she was attacked by the dog. Then he got away without a trace. What's going on?"

"If she was bitten by the Jensen's dog, the one that was killed, she's the one who took the girl from the bedroom. I suggest we get a DNA sample from the woman and see where it takes us."

White made a call, then turned back to Stacey. "It's going to take a couple of days to get the results back. In the meantime, we better see if we can find Melvin. We've been to his apartment. The feds won't let us in. Same thing with Anderson's place." He reached into his suit pocket and removed two envelopes. On one was written *Don Rodriguez*; on the other, *Paul and Nancy*. "One of the federal boys at Melvin's place gave us these," he continued, pressing the envelopes into Stacey's hand. "We've checked out Don Rodriguez. He's got a record a mile long. You were one of the arresting officers on his last citation."

So *that's* where he and Don had first met! "Yeah, I know who he is."

"We do too. The note said something about a deposit. We counted five hundred dollars in cash. The second envelope contains nine hundred fifty dollars, plus a note telling this Nancy person that he's sorry for the trouble he caused her. We've located the name of a student at the college with the male's name. Do you have any idea what this is all about?"

"I spent one of my nights on the run in Rodriguez's apartment. He told me that Melvin was peeping in on the previous tenant's wife. That must be their rent and deposit he's returning." Stacey's thoughts raced ahead, tripping over themselves. "We still have a bigger problem than some rent deposits being returned," he muttered. "We've got to find Melvin."

White pointed out his car. "Let's go see Judge Demick and request a search warrant. Maybe that'll get us past the feds."

The displeasure in Judge Demick's face when he opened the door was evident. "This is Sunday afternoon and we just sat down to lunch. Whatever you have to say better be more than just important."

Mr. White fairly beamed as he asked, "Your Honor,

have you ever met Officer Rick Stacey?"

"I'll meet you in my office in ten minutes." The judge then closed the door.

Melvin sat at Judge Demick's desk, tapping at the computer. He had accessed two of the three numbered bank accounts and transferred over eight million dollars to a new account—one so safely hidden, even his superiors would never find it. Hearing the elevator door open and muffled footsteps and garbled voices coming down the hall, he hastened to close the computer. But it was too late; the key was already sliding into the lock.

The door opened and Demick, Stacey and Mr. White filed into the room. Demick had walked most of the way around his desk before he noticed the computer was on. "Someone's been in here!" The chamber door leading to the courtroom shut ever so slowly. "They've been in my computer; it's still on."

Mr. White glanced over at Stacey. "Who knows your password?"

"Just me—and my secretary. But she doesn't have clearance to enter the building on Sundays."

"Who does?"

"The security people...the sheriff's department...and some of the cleaning staff." Suddenly all three realized who it was that had been in the office.

Out in the dark courtroom, Melvin slid open the window overlooking the south lawn and squeezed out onto the ledge. After pulling the window shut, he dropped the nine feet to the ground.

Minutes later, the county deputies had turned up no trace of an intruder—only that Melvin's code had been used to access the building two hours earlier. The code was immediately changed.

White and Stacey left the county building five minutes later, warrant in hand. However, it proved of little value: When the two men entered the upper floor of Melvin's home, they found it empty and spotlessly clean.

Stacey retired to the back window. Through the open garage door he could see the shelf. Nothing on it had been disturbed. The can with the pen was exactly where he'd left it.

"I think we need to stop one more place," Stacey called in to White. "Let's go dig up some answers."

They were soon standing on the Jensen's front porch. Alan answered the door. "I'm Officer Stacey and this is the County Prosecutor, Mr. Jay White. How's your family doing?"

"All alive and home safe, thankfully. What can we do for you?"

"How's Christina?"

Alan shrugged. "Pretty good. She puts up a good front. But I think her emotions are going to explode if she doesn't get them out soon. She has an appointment with Doctor Wendy tomorrow. They spoke for about an hour last night."

Mr. White spoke up. "We'll be glad to help however we can."

"We appreciate the offer. Is that all you stopped by for?"

"Not exactly," replied White. "Two nights ago, Don Rodriguez may have given some disks to your son. They came from the home of Melvin Briggs."

"Yes, Danny was working on them when he discovered Christina was missing."

"Do you know what's on them?"

Alan's face tightened. "He told me they were pictures of sick and dying people."

Stacey and Mr. White exchanged glances. "Do you think he'd let us take a look at them?"

"I'll get him. Please, come in. The computer's there in the study."

Danny fired up the computer. The spate of shockingly grisly images began appearing on the screen. Stacey and White leaned forward, not knowing whether to avert their eyes as Danny scrolled through the disturbing sequence of photos.

"I—I've never seen anything like this," White sputtered weakly.

"Do you still have the other disks?" Stacey asked.

"Yeah, but they've been erased. I stole this one"—he shot a contrite glance in the direction of his father—" and one more the day the shed blew up. I haven't broken it's code yet."

"Do you think you can do it without losing the sound?"

"It might take a while." Once more he looked to his father, who nodded his approval.

"We'll wait," White said. "We appreciate your help."

The two men again stepped out on the front porch. Several questions still lacked answers. "How did you obtain the disks, Officer Stacey?" White asked.

"I was in the home of Melvin Briggs—illegally."

White plunged in, spouting legalese. "These disks will not be allowed as evidence, you know, nor can they be used in legal conversations. They can only serve to help us in our search to answer our questions. Do you understand?"

"I know."

Then he asked, "Where's your squad car and the balance of the missing cocaine?"

"The car's hidden in a cave near Fillmore. One of the bags is buried in the rocks near the car. I understand you saw part of the other scattered in Bingham's office. I think he dumped the other half down my toilet. Sig almost got us caught trying to show me."

"That brings me to another problem. You destroyed a city police car."

"It wasn't my choice, sir."

"We'll have to deal with these issues."

Stacey was careful during conversation not to discuss the sensitive information he'd gotten from Agent Buseth.

Suddenly Danny opened the front door with a grin plastered across his face. "I got in!" he announced as he hobbled awkwardly back into the study.

"Tape three of 15. May 15th, 1994. Port Harcourt Prison, Rivers State, Nigeria...." Melvin Briggs's dissonant voice narrated as color photographs showing the outer walls of a run-down barbed wire compound flashed onto the screen. "I've pressured the guard to let me meet with Kin Ro Sawa, the prisoner accused of being the leader of the Ogoni uprising. Six Ogoni tribesmen are to be hung at these gallows in a little less than an hour...." The photos had been taken from odd angles—perhaps using a hidden camera. The one of a crude wooden structure was followed by a closeup shot of six heavily-guarded men being led from a room, chained both hand and foot. "These men were leaders of a movement to free their people from slavery and oppression of the oil-hungry government." Next came a picture of the six men who were being fitted with black hoods, followed by one showing nooses around their necks. The chronological nature of this particular batch of photos ended with the men suspended below the gallows floor.

Danny and the three men sat spellbound as Melvin told of an autopsy. "I gained access to a video of two Ogoni chiefs in the medical examiner's lab. They were shot at close range, and from an angle which makes it impossible for the leaders of the freedom movement to have slain them. In my opinion, they were killed by assassins. The Nigerian government refused to release the six innocent men, who now have been killed."

Melvin's narration then focused on the Nigerian military junta, which, he claimed, was funded by a consortium of rich oil companies. The images of thousands of people being forced to evacuate their homes to take refuge in neighboring states and the eye-witness accounts of thousands more being killed, raped, tortured and imprisoned were shown in graphic detail. Another batch of photos dealt with oil rigs, polluted waterways and puddles of mud and slurry—many the size of football fields. Starving families, their crops either seized or ruined due to the contaminated ground...refugee camps...disease-ridden villages—the photos kept coming, one after the other, so explicit, so horrid that they would have made the world's worst cynic blanch.

Katie's shrill voice easily pierced the study door. "Hi, Aunt Monica!" she was heard to say.

Danny excused himself from the room; Alan, blurry-eyed, followed. White and Stacey remained in the dark room, while outside the doorway stood a stunningly attractive blonde. Stacey glanced up from the computer. Whoa! A tight pair of dark spandex pants, cut just above the calf, pointed down to a pair of high heels that made the muscles in her calves flex just so. Standing roughly five feet ten inches, she was a life size Barbie Doll, decked out in diamond rings, gold bracelets and necklaces. Her low-cut top accentuated her ample breasts. Stacey listened from the shadows of the room as she spoke.

"I've come to pick up Christina," she announced.

Katie hurried off to get her mother.

Alan sauntered into the entryway. "Monica, you're back," he snipped.

A second or two later Kate rounded the corner and greeted her sister. The two women embraced—though Monica was the more standoffish of the two.

"You're back," Kate said, a touch of foreboding in her tone.

"I want Christina to spend the week with me to meet my fiancé," she gushed. The affected lilt in her voice spoke volumes. Even Stacey, who'd never met the woman—though he might like to, he thought—could see she was orchestrating the performance.

"This really isn't a good time for Christina," Kate began to explain.

"I'm getting married next week," Monica went on, ignoring Kate's comment. "He's going away on business for a few days, and I hoped she could get settled into our condo before he leaves."

Danny stomped from the entry. He had no reason anymore to like his aunt—the witch who'd hurt his cousin so much.

Christina had stood out of sight in the open hallway above, listening. Katie crouched behind her. Finally she stepped out from the wall and peered down at her mother. "I don't want to go," she said matter-of-factly.

"Hi, Christina. Aren't you happy to see me?"

"Not if you plan on taking me with you." Christina, her eyes clear and calm, seemed far removed from the events of the previous week.

"I want you to meet the man I'm going to marry, and

see the beautiful home we'll live in. It's everything we've dreamed of."

Christina bristled at the thought. This was just the latest in a litany of stunts her mom was known to pull. "I'm perfectly happy with what I already have. I'd like to stay here."

Just then Cecily's Jeep pulled to the curb behind a late-model Jaguar. A tall man in his mid-thirties leaned against the passenger door, arms folded, facing the house.

"She's back," Don mumbled. "She's come for 'Tina. She won't even care what's been going on the last few days. That's probably her boyfriend—she's hooked a fat fish this time. I'll never get my daughter back with a bank roll like that behind her." He slumped back in his seat.

"Monica?" Cecily's tone was playful, almost mischievous. She was eager to meet this woman she'd heard so much about. "Let's go see her," she pressed.

"I don't think I'm up to it. I can't afford another scuffle—not tonight."

Inside the house, Kate was defending Christina's choice, stating her case.

"I really don't care what she's been through," Monica scoffed. "This is important to me. Loran's waiting outside to meet her. He owns Rider Ranch Products; he's very wealthy."

Mr. White, perking up when he heard the name, stepped to the window of the study to look out. Sure enough, at the curb under the streetlight was Loran Rider. White knew he hadn't made his money in sales. The company had been a respectable business until his parents were killed in a suspicious small-plane crash a few years earlier. Now the son seemed to have more money than he knew what to do with.

Kate, in an effort to diffuse the situation—and perhaps placate Monica—convinced Christina to at least come outside to meet him. She held her hand out to beckon the girl down the stairs. "Try to be polite," she whispered, meeting Christina halfway. "You don't need to go anywhere if you don't want to."

Monica, miffed at the control Kate seemed to have

over her daughter, tried to cut between them as they reached the porch. "I'll bring her back tomorrow or the next day, after he leaves on his trip," she yammered.

Alan turned on the outside lights and, along with White and Stacey, watched from the top stair. Kate walked to the curb with Christina, Monica flouncing along at the other side. Seeing the Jeep parked at the curb sent a wave of emotion through Christina. She was glad her father was home, but feared the scene was ripe for a full-fledged confrontation.

Cecily watched the woman coming down the front steps and out to the curb. The lights lining the brick fence columns illuminated Monica's every feature. Her curves were to die for; her teeth gleamed, reflecting an orthodontist's dream of a smile. Fidgeting from side to side, she introduced her daughter to the man leaning against the Jag.

"Christina, by next week this will be your new father," she crowed. "His name is Loran Rider."

Christina turned her head to see Don climb out of the Jeep, the words "new father" and "Loran Rider" burning in his ears. Kate, still clutching her niece's hand, pulled Christina a few steps back out of the way. Monica, also sensing the oncoming freight train, likewise cleared the path.

Loran immediately recognized Don from Monica's description, and was hoping to get a shot at the goon who she'd said had beaten up so many of her past boyfriends. Loran stood as tall as Don. Having been raised on a ranch, he could take care of himself.

"If someone's going to replace me, don't you think you ought to introduce me first?" Don growled, extending his hand in an artificial gesture of goodwill. The act caught everyone off guard—including the two men congregated in the study.

Loran slapped his own into Don's and matched his new archrival's squeeze. Then, in a forced bid at psychological warfare, Don pressed his chest slowly up against Loran's and whispered in his ear, "I spent 30 days in jail with Will Vaughan, your right-hand man with a big mouth. Don't screw with my family. You can have the ex, 'cause she ain't worth it—but Christina's *mine*."

"Get out of my face!" Loran brayed, shoving Don away. "*Nobody* threatens me."

Stacey was about to intervene when Mr. White stopped him. "Hang on. I think they're through. Looks like Loran just lost the first round. Who's the other guy?"

"Don Rodriguez."

Christina pulled away from Kate and stepped between the two men. "Nice to meet you, Mr. Rider." Turning to her stunned mother, she then asked, "So, are we ready to go, Mom?" Monica hadn't expected to see Don—and when he did arrive, she couldn't believe he'd kept his temper. And what was even more inconceivable was that Loran had just backed down. Still pleased, she, Loran and Christina climbed into the car. Christina rolled down the back window. "I'll be back soon, Daddy," she called out. "Don't worry, everything will be fine."

Bewildered, everyone watched as the fancy car's taillights disappeared around the corner.

The dimly-lit scene was like an after-hours roomful of museum statues: Don standing, stunned, on the sidewalk; Cecily watching him, paralyzed; Kate, her head down, her thumbs pressed against her temples.

Up on the porch, Mr. White shattered the mirage when he turned on his radio to instruct the deputies parked in an unmarked car across the street to tail the car and to keep a close eye on the girl.

Loran sent the 12-cylinder engine screaming through its gears. "He's a punk!"

"Slow down, Loran. You're scaring me," whined Monica. He took a glimpse through his rearview mirror of the young girl in the backseat. There sat the "punk's" daughter, riding in *his* car.

Monica's hand on his knee worked its magic. He shifted down to a lower gear and grumbled, "Sorry, I don't know what got into me." Almost in the same breath, he picked up his phone and, pushing button number "1" in his address book, spat, "Loran here...meet me at the office in fifteen."

He put down his phone. "I need to take care of a little business, babe. I won't be gone long. You and Christine do a little catching up while you take a dip in the spa."

"My name is Christin*a*," came an emphatic voice from the backseat.

Alan guided Don back into the house. Stacey greeted him, shaking his hand. "Good to see you again." Gesturing toward White, he added, "Oh, this is a friend of the family, Mr. Jay White. We've been looking at the disks Danny opened. He's done a great job...." At the mention of his son's name, Alan excused himself.

White shook Don's hand. "Say, do you know Loran Rider?"

"The bozo my ex-wife's about to sap?"

"That's him."

"I know who he is, but that's about it. I shared a jail cell with his hired thug, Will Vaughan. I'm more concerned about my daughter right now. She needs me by her side—and the help of a professional—not her coke-snorting mother or the slimeball she's with."

"I think we can help you with that," White assured him. "By the way, what did you say to him to get him so upset?"

Don glanced at Stacey and back at Mr. White, trying to figure out what was going on. "I don't think I like this conversation much."

"I think we might just be able to help each other, Don," Stacey suggested. "Your ex-wife has custody of Christina, right?" Don nodded. "You suspect she's doing drugs?" Don nodded even more emphatically. "Maybe we can bring Christina home for good."

The men continued their conversation as Cecily and Kate talked about Monica.

Meanwhile, Danny sat moping in his room when Alan tapped on the door. "Whoever it is, go away," he muttered.

"It's your father." There was a long pause and the door slowly opened. Danny kept his back turned. "It hurts, doesn't it?" said Alan. The boy didn't say a word. "You two've become best friends and you think you might lose her."

"It's not fair. Monica just thinks Christina's her property. She thinks she can do whatever she wants with her."

"I know. How do you suppose you can help Christina?"

"I could get rid of Monica."

"I don't know if that's an option. Do you think maybe your cousin's feeling the same way you are?"

"Probably," Danny stammered.

"Hey, I don't have the answers, but you just might come up with a few. You're one of the smartest guys I know." Danny wiped his eyes and turned toward his dad. He'd waited to hear those words for a long time. His father *did* recognize his abilities. He decided to give it some thought.

"Thanks, Dad." Danny threw his arms around his dad. Alan felt good; his son hadn't given him a good squeeze in a long time. Danny felt even better.

Cecily waited outside the study for Don to finish with the mysterious visitors. A feeling of inadequacy had struck, finally having set eyes on Don's ex-wife. She imagined herself standing in front of a mirror next to Monica. Her own hips were wider, her breasts smaller, five or six inches shorter....Could Don possibly be satisfied with her looks? Would he always be staring at other women behind her back?

At last the men emerged from the study and the visitors left.

"What did they want?" she asked curiously.

"I can't talk about it right now. Can I walk you to the Jeep?"

Why was he trying to get rid of her so quickly? Don took her hand as they trudged down the front steps toward the vehicle. "She's gorgeous," Cecily murmured.

Don stopped in his tracks and, using Cecily's hand as a lever, swung her around to face him. He gently reached up under her blond mop of hair and took her face in his hands. The words came out soft and tender. "I guess it all depends on how you view beauty. If you think it's only on the surface, you're right, she's very attractive." Cecily stared up into Don's face. The shadows cast from the front lights revealed a depth of sincerity in his eyes she'd yet to see from him. Butterflies cascaded down from her ears and into her stomach as he spoke the words, "I'm falling in love with you, Cecily. Your beauty goes far beyond the surface—it comes from the heart. If a loving God does exist, he closed the eyes of other men and saved you for me."

Cecily melted into his gentle embrace. His lips found the side of her neck, then her cheek, and finally her lips. Sweet, soft, warm, tender. She leaned in to him as his hands swept along her neck and down her back. Reaching around his neck, she held him tightly. Her knees buckled under her, and she clung to the remarkable man she had come to love. She felt good, cuddled there next to him, together, as one.

FORTY-THREE

THIRTY-SIX HOURS STRAIGHT without sleep was taking its toll. All Stacey wanted to do was go home and crash. He rode in the passenger seat of Mr. White's car, frazzled, gazing out the window. A few times a minute White would check his rearview mirror, watching the car following them. "We'll get back at it tomorrow Stacey. It looks like those feds'll let you sleep with both eyes shut."

It was the first touch of humor Stacey had seen in the man. "Yup," was all he could manage.

Mr. White let Stacey out in front of his apartment. Stacey trudged up the stairs, unlocked the door and headed for the kitchen.

Suddenly a spiked object drove deep into Stacey's right leg. Shocked with pain, he lurched against the wall. Looking down, he saw a blade sticking out of his thigh, connected to some sort of spring-loaded contraption. Attached was a note with the words *little turd* scribbled across it. Through the open door, Stacey yelled down to the street where his federal friends had parked for the night. He then removed the note, slipped it into his pocket, and yanked the blade from his thigh. The blood poured down his leg as he limped to the bathroom for a towel to tie off the wound.

The agents cautiously entered the dwelling. Seeing the trail of blood and the spring-trap, they quickly placed a call to Buseth.

For more than an hour Don had shared his dreams with her, future visions that seemed to align with her own. After the conversation with Mr. White, he'd finally been able to see the brighter possibilities that lay ahead. He'd even talked about attending a church meeting or two.

Cecily, still cuddled up against him on her couch, could feel the rhythmic thump of his heart. Soon he'd have to go home. She nestled closer.

"We need the HAZMAT unit....No sir, we're in the process of sealing off the area now. I expect it was Peck's work....He's been stabbed. We're not sure if the blade was infected....Nope, we still haven't recovered the source." Buseth hung up his phone.

Stacey was confused. "Who's Peck?"

"Colonel David Ray Peck—'Bingham' to you. He was known in Virginia as Hales, and goes by at least ten other aliases. Now we'll see about your injuries."

Stacey felt light-headed. Blood was soaking his pants. His leg throbbed with pain.

"That doesn't look too good," muttered Buseth. "The bullet that killed your detective Derickson had small traces of 'VN twenty dash three-five-two' on it. The trace is what killed your friend, not the bullet itself."

"You think he might have infected me?"

"Let's hope you have his only source of the chemical."

A semi truck bearing a 60-foot trailer pulled up in front of Stacey's apartment. Automatic hydraulic feet descended and pumped up from the ground, leveling the four sides of the trailer. Four men in protective suits and breathing equipment got out and unfolded a stretcher. Entering the kitchen, they scooped up Stacey and carried him out. An automatic ramp lowered from the back of the trailer and they marched him up the ramp. A pair of heavy doors slammed shut behind them.

A mask was placed over Stacey's face as he was prepped for surgery. He quickly slipped into unconsciousness.

Christina awoke in the most beautiful place she'd ever slept. It was like the movies: king-sized bed, plush carpet, a walk-in closet the size of a normal bedroom. The night before, they'd relaxed in the marble hot-tub with gold faucets and mirrors on the ceiling. Then they'd eaten the best ice cream—imported from Italy—Christina had ever tasted. She'd managed to push the ugliness of the orchard away from her mind and had done her best to keep the peace with her mother.

Loran hadn't returned before Christina went to bed. She and Monica had caught up on everything that had happened in the month they were apart. Monica went first, telling about the European vacations, all the fine food they ate, the clothing and jewelry he'd bought her. Finally Christina drifted off to sleep while listening to her mother tell about her visit to Neuschweinstein Castle in Germany. Christina didn't get a chance to tell her mother about her experience with Melvin, and her mother hadn't asked.

Easing herself up out of bed, Christina padded into the kitchen, where she fixed herself a bowl of fruit. She was anxious to get to school. Timidly knocking on the door to her mother's bedroom, it finally opened a crack, enough to see her mother's scantily dressed body and the dark, sunken, faraway look in her eyes.

"Mom, I'm going to be late for school."

"Shhh—I'll be out in a minute," croaked her mother.

"Who is it?" Loran's deep voice emanated from the bed.

"Go back to sleep, baby. I've got it."

A few moments later Monica emerged wearing a silk robe. "Honey, you don't need to go back to the public school. Loran said you can go to that private school on Foothill Drive."

"Mom, I don't want to go to some fancy school. I want to be where my friends are." The volume of her voice climbed. "You can't just start deciding what my whole life's going to be like."

Monica reached over and clamped her hand over Christina's mouth. "Let's take this conversation to the kitchen," she coaxed.

Christina pulled away. She was losing control. "I have a life, too, one that I'm happy with!...you might think the only way to be happy is to have lots of money and get high!"

Monica had heard enough. She drew back her arm and let loose, slapping her daughter across the face. "Don't you dare talk to me like that, young lady!"

Outraged and near tears, Christina glared into her mother's eyes. They were similar to those she'd seen once before, on the tree house roof—deep, dark, empty. Her hands began to shake as she remembered.

"I can't deal with this right now," Monica announced, storming from the room.

Afraid, hurt, embarrassed...Christina needed to get out of there. Her only thought was to return home. She headed for the outside door. Glancing back, she could see her mother's bent body leaning over a coffee table. Christina knew exactly what she was doing.

Even in the early-morning hours the police station was abuzz. Just coming in, Mr. White learned that Olsen had called in to report a vehicle in the river. White arrived to find a wrecker trying to pull the heavy, water-logged load from the muddy embankment. Just then, the wrecker's cable snapped, sending the load back into the water.

"I can't get hold of Stacey," Olsen yelled over the roar of the river and the noise of the wrecker.

A second, larger rig arrived. The operator climbed across the bottom of the overturned vehicle and hooked his cable to the front frame. Returning to the bank, he pulled down on his hydraulics. The cable tightened and the vehicle's front end again began to lift from the swollen river. It rose straight up, teetered, then slammed to the ground. The force of the water inside the vehicle blew the driver's door off its hinges. As it burst open, the bloated body of a man in his mid-twenties slumped halfway out the door. White made a mental guess as to who the man was. Mitch opened the passenger's door and rifled through the glove box, scrounging through the wet papers.

"Looks like it's registered to William Vaughan of

Spanish Fork." Along with mud and debris from the river, several beer cans littered the floor.

"Let's get the coroner on his way," Olsen ordered. "See if we can figure out where he went into the river."

Don clocked in at seven-thirty. There was a backlog of work to get done, plus he needed to be with Christina when she went to see Doctor Wendy. If Mr. White's plan didn't work, it'd take a passel of money to get his daughter back. He looked forward to seeing Cecily at lunch. All morning long he found it hard to keep his mind on anything but the two young ladies he cared so much about.

The mile-and-a-half walk to Kate's house was well under way before Monica had even realized Christina was gone. The deputies offered the girl a ride, but she refused. Kate pulled to the curb and waved them off before opening the door for Christina to climb in. Kate's phone rang a few minutes after the two walked in the door.

"Kate, it's Monica. Have you heard from Christina?"

"She's standing here next to me with a welt that resembles a hand print on her face. How dare you, Monica?" Christina had never seen her so protective. "Do you have any clue what this child's been through the last few days? Do you?"

"I guess I don't."

"Pure hell, that's what! Don't you dare come back here until you get some help. Alan and I will spend every penny we have taking away your parental rights." Kate slammed down the receiver.

He awoke to the sound of a metal door closing. Rolling onto his side, he peered out the window into a dark, empty room. The stainless steel countertops were bare; the men in white suits had vanished. An unknown voice came from a speaker mounted on the wall. "How do you feel, Mr. Stacey?"

"Like I just slept on a slab of cold concrete."

"You're free to go. It appears you were not infected

with any chemicals. You can step through the door on your left when you're ready to leave. You'll probably need the crutches you'll find under the table."

Stacey sat up and stretched his arms and back. He slid from the table, his right leg now fitted with a brace. He actually felt quite refreshed from the drug-induced sleep.

"If you feel good enough to drive, you'll find an automobile with keys in the ignition and the paperwork in the glove box. Do as you please with the car. You'll also find on the passenger seat a phone and your radio and weapon." The metal door buzzed. Stacey picked up a single crutch and started to exit. The voice once again blurted from the box. "Your friend seems to be recovering quite well and your dog is still resting at the veterinarian's. You may call Mr. White and tell him you're back."

"Did you find Bingham?" Stacey asked as he opened the door.

"Agent Buseth will be in touch with you soon. I'm sorry I can't discuss the matter any further. We're sorry to have inconvenienced your community. Please see a doctor in the next few days to have your leg checked. Goodbye, Mr. Stacey. And good luck."

Stacey opened the outer door and limped down a set of metal steps. Stepping off the last one, they hummed and retracted. The trailer's four hydraulic feet whined and withdrew at the corners, its diesel engine roared to life, and the big rig rolled away down the dusty road. Stacey, leaning on his crutch, glanced behind him to see the captain's Lexus parked alongside the road. Not another person or vehicle was in sight. He hobbled to the car and opened the door. Everything was exactly as he'd been told it would be. Settling into the leather driver's seat and swinging his stiff leg inside, he started the car and picked up the phone. His first call was to Mr. White.

"This is Stacey."

"Feeling better, Officer Stacey?"

"Yes. I'm parked on the edge of the orchard."

"Good. Let's meet and discuss the love note you received from your dear Captain Bingham."

Mr. Bill Penrod sat in his corner office, absentmindedly staring down onto Main Street. For five years he'd been bank president, starting off as a lowly teller 22 years earlier. That was back in his college days. It didn't take long to make loan officer, then he was promoted to assistant vice president at his hometown branch. Here, under his watchful eye, the bank flourished, even through the tough '80s. When the branch president retired, he was made president.

The town had grown—and so had the bank, having outperformed every other branch in the chain. He gazed fondly at the photo of his wife and children on his desk, feeling a little less guilty each passing day. Perhaps, finally, after a long stretch of dark days, he was in the clear. The blond-haired teller no longer disrupted his daily thoughts, and no one from upper management had called to find out why millions of dollars were being shuffled from one account into many smaller ones.

His secretary buzzed him. "Mr. Penrod, a Mr. Phelps with the federal government is here to see you." His heart jumped, then seemed to stop. Suddenly flushed, small beads of sweat began to break out on his wrinkled brow. Was this to be the day that everything fell down around him?

"Send him in, Ms. Lund." He wished he could crawl into a crack.

Dressed in suit and tie, a slender, balding man in his mid-fifties limped into his office. He carried a dark brown briefcase in one hand; the other was tucked in a sling under his suit. He set his case down and took a small black booklet from his suit coat pocket. Opening it up, he lifted the identification and stuck the badge in Penrod's face. "Agent M. Phelps," he chirped. "Mind if I sit down?"

"No, please."

Settling into a chair, Agent Phelps's body momentarily sagged to one side. Catching himself, he straightened up to compensate for the missing portion of his backside. "I'm a surveillance special agent assigned to a task force, Mr. Penrod. We've recently been monitoring the movements of a young lady who worked for you."

Phelps's presence was generating the desired effect. The banker fought to keep his wits about him, but he was betrayed by the sweat now trickling down his face and by the heavier, more irregular breathing. "I'm not feeling so good—haven't all day..." moaned the banker. "Must be a touch of the flu..." He lay his head on the desk, imagining himself behind bars, "property" of a 300-pound tattooed muscle man named "Monster"; he'd lose his wife and family, all because of his infidelity; and, his financial resources wasted on attorney fees and alimony, he'd have to resort to living in a ratty apartment the rest of his life—if, that is, he ever got out.

"Relax, Mr. Penrod. This visit's unofficial. Did you know Detective Kiser Derickson?"

Penrod raised his head from the desk, unfurled a handkerchief from his pocket and dabbed at his forehead. Now he was confused. "He was one of our customers. Yes, I knew him."

"He was killed by a dangerous man named David Ray Peck. Your town knew him as Captain Daryl Bingham." Mr. Penrod began to feel sick again. His mind raced back to the night in the field.

The agent went on. "His girlfriend was your teller. We picked her up at the Salt Lake International Airport on her way to Barbados. Bingham was killed two nights ago—a plane crash. Maybe you heard about it on the news." Mr. Penrod nodded. "I don't want to cause you any grief, but I have some of the footage we shot of her...uh, interacting with you. Would you like to review those with me?" Phelps placed his case on the table and removed a laptop computer.

"I don't think it'll be necessary," the banker stammered. "I've been trying to forget it ever happened."

Phelps smiled and reached again into his suit pocket. "I have something here that may help *me* forget it happened, too." He placed an envelope on the table between them. "If you follow these instructions, you'll never see or hear from me again." He latched his case as he stood and walked out of the room. "Goodbye, Mr. Penrod."

After executing the customary wet kiss and gingerly climbing in the towel-draped backseat, Sig gave a "good riddance" glance through the window. He was back covering his master's back. But this time, it appeared, they were traveling in style.

Stacey pulled into the driveway of his parents' home. Buseth was waiting inside the garage as Stacey opened the door and limped inside.

"Right on time, Officer Stacey. Everything is set up to trace the call. With any luck, we can intercept him before he eludes us again."

"It won't work. He's too good to get caught by a phone call." The phone rang. Buseth gave Stacey the signal to answer it.

"How's the leg, *Officer* Stacey?" Bingham taunted. He used his best tough-guy impression—and did a darn good job of it. "Next time I call, I'll tell you where you can find me to return my property. Don't let the feds come. I know they're listening in." Buseth indeed was giving hand signals to his men as they scrambled to relay the information by computer. "You'll know why when I call you again at two tomorrow morning. You'd better get that phone of mine charged." The line went dead.

"A miraculous improvement," is how the doctors described Barker's health update. Nearly every tube and monitor had been removed. Only the bolt and drain remained.

His doctor stopped by during rounds. "I'm here to tell you, you're one very lucky man." He opened the chart. "When you first came in, I didn't know if you'd ever walk again. I've seen men who had to start from scratch with a blow like the one you took. Do you even know what hit you?"

"Probably a bullet. It got stopped by the night-vision device I was wearing."

"I think if you continue to recover at this rate, we'll have you out of here in a week or so."

Barker smiled up at Debbie, who gave him a wink. Taking his wife by the hand, he gave it a squeeze.

The tailor pinned and marked the expensive silk suit where the alterations needed to be made. All the while Buseth continued to review the plans with him. "If you follow my instructions exactly, we can wrap up this mess and let you get back to a normal life."

Stacey gave himself the once-over in the mirror. If he could lose the sheepish grin, get a haircut and a shave, and some jewelry that White had borrowed from a downtown connection, he'd come out of there looking like a prosperous man. He turned to Buseth. "I have an undercover operation to attend to this evening. I'll do exactly as you wish *if*," he added for emphasis, "if you stay out of my way and keep Bingham at bay until I've finished."

"Agreed."

Mitch sat in the Taurus, spearheading a stakeout in front of the fanciest condo in town. In it, Monica was walking on eggshells around a very angry Loran. She couldn't understand why he was so tense—even after doing her best to satisfy him.

He threw the last of his things in a suitcase and carry-on bag. His tone was threatening. "I'll be gone five days. I don't want her here when I come back."

"You promised she could be part of the family," pouted Monica, rubbing her body up against his.

"I've changed my mind. She'll be too much trouble."

"What'd Don say to you, baby? You scared of him?"

Loran pushed her away and delivered a back-handed warning blow. "I ain't scared a' nobody. Just make sure she isn't here when I get back!"

The sharp whack had sent her onto her backside. She could hardly believe he'd hit her. Even Don, at his angriest, had never laid a hand on her. True, she'd slapped a few men when they got a little too fresh, and she'd lost control with her own daughter a few hours before, but *she'd* never been hit. "I won't be here either when you get back!" she shrieked as he started out the door.

"Good! You'll save me the cost of your habit." The door slammed behind him.

FORTY-FOUR

The view from the third-floor corner office in the new County Building was small-town spectacular. "Technically, Officer Stacey, the money deposited into your account is yours," White explained as he sat at his desk overlooking the well-kept grounds. "If we had any way to prove it had been used as drug money, it would belong to your department. My suggestion would be to use it to replace the car you dunked in the river. And maybe set some aside for new tires and to pay for cleaning up the mess you left in Bingham's office. That would be a nice gesture."

"White, you've got a deal. I think the Lexus will make a nice undercover vehicle, don't you?" Both men agreed.

The room became silent. "The coroner found traces of brine shrimp in Will Vaughan's lungs," White informed Stacey. "Probably from an aquarium. Our men couldn't find him last night. We could have saved his life, you know."

"From what I've seen, it was only barely worth saving."

White grinned. "The funny part is, Don didn't know a thing—he was only bluffing when he went chest-to-chest with Loran."

"That bluff worked like a charm. We need to nail Loran—if we can prove he's our killer."

White gave a thoughtful grunt. "We need a sample of water from the aquarium in Rider's office. I know your womanizing skills are a tad rusty, but see if you can get Monica to help you with that....We'll be releasing the bodies of Jau Fei and Leah for burial in a couple of days. Oh, one more thing: I'm recommending you to the city as the new detective, and your commanding officer Lieutenant Barker to be the new Chief of Police. It's time to bury the old tradition of the council filling that spot."

"Debbie says Barker's recovering. I need to drop by and see him before the day's over."

"Who do you think should fill the council seat?"

Stacey thought about the question. "I have the perfect person in mind. I'll let you know."

Cecily waited for Don to finish the heavy load of orders. He was late again. She found her thoughts constantly returning to him.

Don had already suffered more than his share of trials. But just that day she'd learned of some great news. Hardly able to contain herself, she decided to walk down to the powder shed and see how her blue-collar guy was doing. As she drew near the shed, Don was on his way out. When he turned, a big grin spread across his face. The place where he wore his mask was about the only spot on him that was clean. It didn't matter to her. She jumped into his arms, her feet swinging off the ground, and gave him a smack on the mouth. "Guess what!" she bubbled. "Ralph decided to hire someone new for the powder shed. He wants to put you full-time in sales. He said you've paid your dues—shown *true grit*, pun intended!" She kissed him again.

"Great! Hey, you're getting all dirty."

"I don't care," she kissed him over and over again. "Now let's get Christina to her appointment."

Stacey stepped off the elevator onto the second floor of the medical center's west wing. Barker, feeling much better, had been moved to his own room. He poked his head inside. Debbie turned as she fussed over her husband. "Rick, come in! We've been talking about you."

"What'd I do, now?" Stacey joked, limping over to the bed. He'd learned to get along without the crutch, but hadn't removed the brace from his leg. Though painful to walk, he needed to be at his best for a possible date that night.

Stacey brought Barker up to date, including Mr. White's recommendation that he be the new Chief and the planned undercover sting.

"You remember the discussion we had the other night before all the fireworks began?" Barker asked.

Stacey clicked his tongue. "Nope. What discussion?"

"The one about lining you up with Debbie's sister Tess."

"Oh, yeah. You going to hold me to that? It was spoken under duress you know," he said, trying to weasel his way out.

"If you want, you can meet her first. She just finished college and is back here living with Debbie's folks. She'll finish her student teaching next month. Debbie can invite her over to see me the day after tomorrow. You come over after work—see what happens."

Debbie broke in. "Why don't you come by at, say, six?"

"Okay." He'd tried to step lightly around the topic, but friendship had gotten the best of him. He'd do it; maybe then they'd quit bugging him. He wondered what this unmarried schoolmarm looked like. Debbie was attractive, nice smile. She wasn't exactly his type, but her sister couldn't be all that bad.

Stacey glanced at his watch. "I've gotta run. The tailor said my suit should be finished by now." He left the room and waited at the elevator. The door opened and, deep in thought—and forgetting his etiquette—he barged in, tripping a young woman in the process. "I'm so sorry," Stacey said as he helped her up.

"Oh no, I should have been watching where I was going," she apologized, pulling a rich crop of brown hair back from her beautiful face just as the elevator doors closed.

"...You're in a safe place. Your father is sitting next to you, holding your hand. Christina, you can wake up any time you want." Doctor Wendy's soft, composed voice wafted into the girl's subconscious mind. "I want you to go back to the night you were chased through the woods." Christina's eyes moved rapidly beneath her eyelids, her breathing rapid and shallow. "You're on the roof now, with your rope secured." Don could feel Christina's nails dig into the fleshy part of his hand. "You're leaning back, ready to fall." The young body gave a jolt at the suggestion; it began to shake.

Tears rolled down Cecily's cheeks as she listened to Christina relate the terrible experience. She marveled at the courage the girl had shown. Don's body, too, was tense with the extremes of hate for Christina's attacker and love for his innocent daughter.

"Tell me what happened next, Christina," Doctor Wendy urged. Christina's breathing became even more rapid.

"I see him hanging over the edge of the roof...He grabs me...my shirt's pulled partway up....I let go of the rope with my good hand and scratch at his eyes. They're...looking at me through the mask." Christina clenched her teeth as she spoke, her lips still moving but her jaw drawn tight. "I hate those eyes...they're cold, black...like death. I dig in with my fingernails....Then he screams and pulls away...lets go of my shirt."

Christina opened her hand. A sliver of blood began seeping from one of the marks left by her fingernails as they sunk into her father's skin.

"The mask comes off in my hand...I start to fall. I can see him...the moon is behind his head." She screamed and opened her eyes....

Melvin's attorney arrived for a special appointment with Judge Demick. The two spoke casually about dropping charges against his client. "I'm confident the DNA test results will exonerate Melvin. Furthermore, you'll find a very generous donation made to a trust fund for the families of those girls murdered by his late wife. Here's the information you can release at a press conference. It will help polish your image; make it better than it was before this whole thing began."

Demick opened the document and began to read.

"What about the rumors of chemical agents in our town?"

"I don't know anything about that, Your Honor." The attorney gathered his things to leave. "And by the way, the funds are also there to make sure that the relatives of Melvin Briggs get a proper burial. May we never cross paths again."

The tailor had done a fine job. Stacey could be on the cover of GQ. And, if he walked slowly, he could stride with hardly a limp, although the new leather boots squeaked when he walked.

Next Stacey drove to the jeweler's shop. The Rolex watch and diamond rings felt hideously unnatural, but they sure looked fine. A heavy gold chain around his neck seemed a bit much, but the jeweler assured him it worked well with the suit. In his pocket he'd already placed a thousand dollars, which he now folded into a gold money clip with the initials R.B. embossed in diamonds. He decided to wait at his parents' home for the call. With Loran out of town, he knew Monica would be out on the town.

"What did you see?" Doctor Wendy asked. Christina gazed around as if she'd just come out of hibernation.

"It was a woman!!" she said between gasps for air." I could see her long dark hair. It was flapping around as I was falling. The eyes belonged to a woman!" Christina bowed her head and began to cry. "Melvin went to jail twice—and it wasn't even him!"

Don reached over and took her in his arms. This time he was giving comfort instead of receiving it. "It's okay, Christina. You didn't do anything wrong."

Careful not to let Sig leave dog hair on the new suit, Stacey awaited the call. Sig seemed to understand, pouting for only a moment before returning to his bed. Rifling through his father's closet and picking out a few of his nicer shirts and pants, he then drove to the four-star Excelsior Hotel in downtown Provo and reserved the presidential suite on the 14th floor.

Then Mitch's call came. "Looks like it's time, big guy. Your hunch was right on the money. Her girlfriend just picked her up. My guess is they're headed to Lamar's. It sure would look good if you walked in at the same time."

Sitting on the bed, Christina talked and—for a change—Danny listened. Kate had suggested that the best way to help his cousin was to listen and empathize with her. Together they laughed as Christina recounted all the scary, sad and silly things that had occurred over the past weeks. It was a mix of elation and sorrow. She cried as she told him how much she wished she could get her mother back— not married to her dad, but free of the bad habits that made her so selfish and angry all the time. Danny listened on into the night. Alan resisted the urge to shoo them into bed. They both needed to start the healing process.

Monday night was ladies' night at the club. Although he never went there off duty, Stacey knew the place well.

Lamar's was only two blocks from the hotel. He pulled up in front. Mitch told him the girls had just swung into the lot at the rear. He watched as they rounded the curve by the front door. Then he stepped out and handed the bouncer a twenty to park the car, flashing his wad of bills.

The guy just looked at Stacey, clearly confused. "We don't park cars." Stacey pulled another twenty from the stack as the girls looked on. The bouncer shrugged, "Guess I could make an exception tonight."

Stacey stepped aside. "After you two fine lookin' ladies," he said in a Texas drawl, tipping his cowboy hat. The two women looked him up and down like a slab of meat. Monica's friend poked her in the ribs as they entered. From behind, Stacey reciprocated, twice giving the tantalizing ladies the once-over. *This is going to be quite an assignment*, he thought, following them to the bar.

Mitch strolled into the club a few minutes behind Stacey, who was already engaged in conversation with Monica and her friend. Probably six or eight feds, trying to pass themselves off as cowboys, circled the room. Monica seemed oblivious to the ruse. "So where are you from, cowboy?" she asked.

"The big state of Texas." This was going to be too easy. He glanced around the place again, noticing he was the envy of every guy in the room. The two most attractive women in the bar were already jockeying for his attention.

"The initials R.B. must stand for an important name," Monica said, having paid close attention to the money clip.

"Rick Bennett." He offered her his hand. "I think I may have overdressed for the occasion," he said. She ogled the rock in his ring, then slowly shook his strong hand. She was dressed in a tight pair of jeans–like most everyone else in the joint—a blouse—which seemed more buttoned down than up—and a shiny pair of boots.

She looked him over again. "I think you look just fine. My name's Monica and this is my friend Pamela. Buy you a drink, Rick?" That was the signal for Pamela to get lost. After all, she was the one who'd insisted Monica get out to see what else might be available—if, that is, she really intended to be gone when Loran returned.

"Honey, I'll let you buy me a soda. I've got an important meeting set up for tomorrow. My broker tells me these Mormons don't take too good to drinking. I've got to be at my best if I'm gonna buy the biggest chain of gas stations in the state now, don't I? Why don't I buy *you* a drink or two. Might help loosen things up a bit?"

The music started. Pamela leaned over to them, nearly falling out of her blouse. "I think three's a crowd. Besides, I came to dance." She wasn't ten steps away when another cowboy approached her. She moved to the floor with him to strut her stuff. Stacey and Monica found an empty table.

"How long you plan on being in town?" Monica asked.

"If I make the deal, I'll be leavin' tomorrow, after I find me a condo to buy. Then I'll be visitin' every now and then to keep an eye on my investment."

To Monica it sounded perfect. This guy seemed custom-made for *her*—someone to take care of her financial needs yet out of the way more often than not. She could keep that condo warm and friendly for each time he returned.

"Want to dance with me, Rick?" Monica's voice was soft and breathy.

Stacey looked over at Pamela. "Honey, if you dance like she does, I don't know who wouldn't. I got only one little problem. I own a ranch, see. Last weekend, when I was out ropin' with the boys, one a' my longhorn bulls got a bit too close to my leg. Took several layers of stitches to put it back together. I came here for two things, one of 'em I already found."

A provocative smile crossed her lips. "And what *else* were you looking for?"

"I never carry any with me on my jet; airports aren't a safe place these days. I'll tell you what it is—after I search your *body* for a wire." Monica's smile widened. Stacey could see the wrinkles of hard living through the skillfully applied makeup.

"I think you've found both things you're looking for, cowboy." Monica reached over and put her hand on his thigh. Rick started. He hadn't expected her to be so forward so fast.

"That's the leg with the stitches, honey."

"I'll be gentle."

Mitch called Olsen from his cell phone. He was just putting the finishing touches on the room Stacey had rented. "Looks like they're on their way."

"That boy didn't waste any time."

"From where I was sitting, it looked mutual."

"We're on our way out," Olsen assured him.

This time the bouncer was more than willing to bring the car around, and again was well rewarded for his effort. Stacey drove two streets over. "I had no idea the place was so close to my hotel or I would've walked."

"Nice car."

"Just a rental," he drawled.

Stacey tipped heavily to have his car parked. It hurt to see the cash go so easily. Monica tried to guess how much he was carrying. Loran couldn't hold a candle to this guy. Rick had a more distinctive touch of class; he was also more of a gentleman. If she were lucky, she'd get away with a few pieces of nice jewelry from Loran. He didn't let her close to his cash or credit cards. She was into her supplier so deep she didn't know if he'd even talk to her. He used to do trades with her, but those days were long past.

She hadn't taken a hit since noon, when she'd used the last of her supply. She knew a few of the boys at the bar were good for a few hits in trade for a one-night stand, but that would have been her last resort. She needed to figure out how to get this guy to shake loose a little cash— maybe wait until he was asleep, then just slip out with his cash and cards. But that'd ruin any chance for a long-term relationship. Maybe she could play "hard-to-get" and see what he might give her. But she didn't want the main chance to blow up in her face. She was almost 30 and was losing her youthful beauty. He was young and ruggedly handsome. She hoped he wanted more than a one-night stand and a good high.

Stacey was trying to figure out how to proceed. This was the first time he'd been involved in such a bust. He knew he could get her on possession, and hoped to get a shot at her dealer. But here he was, about to give the performance of his life while a gallery of his friends looked on from the other room.

Monica didn't waste any time helping him off with his jacket. He glanced around to see where he could give the best show. Huddled around a small black and white screen in the next room, Olsen and two other deputies were soon joined by Mitch and Mr. White. "Lucky guy to pull such an assignment," one of the deputies whispered. "Good thing he's not married. A man could lose his wife if she ever saw *these* tapes."

Stacey needed to slow things down a bit. "You know, it may be better for the long haul if we take that hit now." Monica eagerly agreed, and pretended to look for it in her purse.

"I must have left my stash home," she lied. Her counterfeit pout was followed by a poorly-acted show of elation. She let out a zesty "Ahhhh!" and said, "I know a dealer who works close. I could call him and have him deliver. There's an extra charge, but you don't take any chances that way."

Rick handed her his phone. "Let's do it, honey."

Monica dialed. "Jimmy, Monica." Stacey turned away, a sick feeling sprouting in the pit of his stomach. "I know...I'll take care of the entire thing tonight. Send me triple anchovies with the white sauce. I'm in room 1482 of the Excelsior. I'll put an extra hundred in it for a rush order." She looked at Rick for approval. He nodded.

Olsen and the other men could hardly believe what they'd just heard. Everyone bought their pizza from Jimmy. He had the best sauce, prices and service in town.

FORTY-FIVE

THE COUNTY INTERROGATION rooms were designed to be either too hot or too cold, depending on the suspect being questioned. Monica sat at a table, mascara running down her face and blotting onto the ruffle of her blouse. In contrast to her earlier bluster and bombast, she'd now adopted a poor-little-girl tone. Her once-dainty nose was red and swollen from sniffling and wiping. Discarded tissues filled the small wastebasket next to her.

The examiners judged Monica to be "hot-blooded," so they'd chosen to barbeque her with a cold grill. Turning the thermostat down, they'd kicked back to wait. After a half hour or so, Monica had settled into a steady shiver. More than from the cold, she was shaking from anger. She'd lost control when the big Texan stuck his badge in her face. Now she couldn't even remember his name. She *could* remember asking him for a loan, which she promised to pay back in sexual favors.

Stacey, White, an assigned public defender and a female guard watched from behind the glass. Stacey yawned—convincingly—and lied, "I could use an hour or two of rest before the sun comes up." He was expecting an important call in less than an hour.

"Me too," said White. "Let's see if she'll talk yet." All three men entered the room.

Stacey couldn't help but offer a sympathetic grin. "Monica, do you remember who I am?"

Her voice was scratchy, her expression pathetic. "The cop...from Texas."

"I'm Officer Rick Stacey. This is Mr. White. He's the

county prosecutor. This being your first arrest, we're willing to offer you a deal. We need two things: your testimony against Jimmy and your cooperation in our investigation of Loran Rider."

"We broke up," she croaked before her teeth began to rattle.

"No one in his office knows that yet. All you need to do is go in to feed his fish. We need a sample of the water from the tank."

"That's it? Just water and my testimony?"

"Not exactly. We're going to recommend to family court that you lose custody of your daughter. You need to be willing to relinquish that right, then complete a drug rehabilitation program. If you successfully complete the program and find a job, you'll get regular visitation rights."

Monica renewed her sobbing and nodded her head in agreement. Mr. White slid the paperwork across the desk for her to sign.

Walking out the east door of county lock-up, White was all smiles. "You did a good job, Officer Stacey." Looking forward to a little shut-eye, he got in his car and pulled from the parking lot.

Buseth motioned Stacey to an unmarked van. Handing him a cell phone, he said, "You're cutting it a little close Stacey." Stacey peered inside the vehicle. Two other men sat crouched at their computer stations. The phone rang at two o'clock precisely.

"How do you like my car, Bup?" spat Bingham. Then he ended the call by yelling into the phone, "See you at sunrise, turd-brain!"

The technician shook his head. Stacey bristled at the words. It wasn't so much the threat. It was Bingham's familiarity, his breach of an unwritten human code of conduct. Only one other person in his life had ever called him "Bup."

"What did he mean by that, Stacey?" queried Buseth.

"I have no idea." He *had* to lie. He knew if the feds even got close to his grandma's house, Bingham would kill her. The floodgates to his mind reopened. He pictured the humble farmhouse; the momentos his grandma held dear; the photo she kept in the front room, the one of him with his grandpa and the note that said "from Bup." The image of Bingham being there with his grandma made him shudder. There was no other farmhouse for a quarter of a mile. He needed to protect her. This confrontation would be hand-to-hand—and to the death. But Stacey had one advantage in the showdown: he had something Bingham wanted more than anything else.

Buseth pressed harder. "Stacey, what did he mean?"

"I'm not sure. The only person I know by that name was an old high-school buddy we called 'Bup.' I don't know what he'd have to do with anything. Well, thanks. I need to get home, feed my dog, catch a few hours of sleep before sunrise. Maybe I'll grab one of my old yearbooks and see what Bup's real name was." That seemed to appease the agent.

The feds followed Stacey to his parents' home and came in while he scrounged through his closet. Extracting a yearbook, he slowly flipped through the pages until he found someone he hadn't seen or heard from in years. Pointing, he said, "That's him, I think...yeah, it's him."

Buseth glanced up to see two other men come into the room. "Agent Tovar, I think you and Officer Stacey have already met," Buseth chuckled. Tovar gave Stacey a casual nod. "He'll be spending the night here. Two of my men will be outside, so you can get some good rest." Satisfied that all was in order, Buseth, yearbook in hand, left the house.

Tovar followed Stacey to the kitchen, where Sig was hoping to get a meal. The requisite two cans of dog food came down from the cupboard. Stacey slid them toward Tovar, who was standing near the can opener. "Could you open those for me while I get his dish?"

Tovar started to do as he was asked, when suddenly he found himself face down on the tile floor, staring at the baseboards. A shooting pain ran up and down his arm and shoulder. "I'm sorry to do this to you again, Tovar," Stacey hissed as he yanked an extension cord from the wall beneath the table and hogtied the agent, then removed his gun and phone. "I can't take any chances Buseth will screw things up. I'll do my best to keep the chemical out of Bingham's hands."

Stacey called Sig and, after the shepherd had gulped down the food, the two of them slipped from a back room into the night. Twenty minutes later they left Melvin's garage with the paint can, the pen safely stored inside. Careful to use the cover of trees, they headed for the river. Thirty minutes later, Stacey pulled the keys to the Mercury from the tail pipe of the old car and revved it up. If he hurried, he'd make it to his grandma's house by sunrise.

An hour later, Buseth returned, primed to question Stacey about his bad information, only to find Tovar struggling to free himself from the electrical cord. Both men were furious. Barking orders and demanding that his men learn who this "Bup" fellow really was, Buseth lost his temper and kicked a hole in the wall. It didn't do much to cool his rage.

Stacey raced down I-15 toward Fillmore. Two hours later he crossed the lava fields to where he'd left his squad car. Burying the paint can under the rocks near his shotgun, he then backtracked the long miles to his grandma's house, praying he could coax Bingham away without her getting hurt.

The valley was bathed in early-morning light. An orange glow peaked out from the mountain tops as Stacey turned the corner just outside of town. Reaching her lane, he slowed. His heart raced. Sig, sensing his master's anxiety, paced back and forth across the backseat.

When Stacey pulled up onto the gravel drive, he found Bingham there, arrogantly seated on the back porch swing, his arms folded across an automatic rifle. The man went right into his bullying routine. "Looks like the wolf got to grannie's house first....Get out of the car. Leave the dog inside, if you want to keep him alive," Bingham warned, rising to his feet. "I'd just as soon see him dead, but his time will come. And maybe he'll suffer at seeing his master go down first."

Prepared in case he had to make a fast getaway, Stacey turned the ignition switch to *accessory* mode, ordered Sig to wait, and stepped from the car. "Doesn't look like it took much to shake the feds," Bingham said with disdain. "Smart move."

"You let me see my grandmother," Stacey called out, "and you can have the pen."

Bingham's stance was threatening. "The pen first."

"You think I'm stupid enough to bring it with me?"

"Guess not."

Sig began to bark and paw at the door. Stacey moved closer as Bingham glowered over at the car. "I think I'll kill the dog first." He lowered the barrel of the automatic weapon and sighted on the car. At that instant, Stacey lunged for the gun and the two men wrestled for control of the weapon as round after round fired off. One bullet hit the vehicle, some whizzed into the air, most thudded harmlessly into the ground. Finally one connected with flesh. The gunfire stopped, the ammunition spent. Stacey's leg burned, but only from the pain of the knife wound. Bingham's foot bled from a bullet. The scuffle was a stalemate. Bingham held the butt end of the rifle, Stacey the barrel end.

Sig nervously continued to paw at the door until his foot hit the electric window button. The window inched down. Again he pawed, and again the window inched down. He bit at the glass and returned to pawing.

Now, Bingham, with a burst of energy, yanked the rifle free, at the same time kneeing Stacey in the wounded leg. The shooting pain in his leg and the searing barrel against his neck brought Stacey to his knees, gasping for air.

Inside the car, Sig forced his shoulders through the ten-inch crack and hung by his hips until he wiggled free, dropping to the ground. Bingham caught a glimpse of the dog's savage fangs. Frantic, he swung the rifle from

Stacey in the direction of the airborne dog, catching him squarely across the skull. Sig gave one yelp, and crumpled to the ground in a heap.

The captain reached down and pulled a knife from his boot. In a move he'd practiced thousands of times, he seized Stacey by the front of the neck. Slowly, he turned his adversary around and threaded the razor-sharp blade through the skin at the base of his neck.

Buseth stood in the safehouse, explaining to Stacey's mom and dad what danger their son was in, and how imperative it was that they find this Bup guy. Hearing the name, the parents knew exactly where their son was. Their eyes met. What should they to do? Buseth easily picked up on the signal. "You know where he is, don't you? ...I'm telling you, he won't come home alive unless I get a team to help him. It may be too late already."

Mr. Stacey, concerned for the life of both his son and his aged mother, caved in. "He's at my mother's home in Fillmore. My dad used to call him Bup."

"Get the chopper up! Move, move!" Buseth hollered into his radio.

"You're finished, Officer Stacey. I'd take you in to see your dead grannie before we go, but I didn't have it in me to kill that smelly old dog that wouldn't leave her side. He's already suffering—and I didn't want to put him out of his misery. You should have seen the old lady squirm when I slit her throat." Stacey fought for control. If Bingham had killed her, he couldn't change it now; and if it was just a ploy to get him upset, Stacey wasn't about to play along. He wouldn't give him the satisfaction.

Bingham eased into the back seat of the Mercury, all the while keeping the tip of his knife shoved up against the top of Stacey's spine. He was a professional. Bingham, too, had been a recipient of a purple heart for combat wounds. Three times he'd been awarded that distinguished honor. After recovering from each wound, he'd returned to the battlefield. His present lifestyle and personal code, however, no longer reflected those days. Now money and greed ruled. And he played on a different team.

Stacey would have to deal with Bingham on his own terms. One false move and Bingham would send the blade through his neck. He hoped to get Bingham's hand off his throat long enough so that he could tuck and roll. Then again, the move could prove futile—and deadly. Regardless, he believed the blade would find its mark the moment Bingham regained his property. A chance might come when he handed over the pen.

"Where's the kilo of coke I put in your car?" Bingham snorted. "I could use some money. It seems someone raided my accounts."

"It's with the pen."

"Splendid. Maybe then I can stop playing the good little captain and put it on the street so I'll have enough dough to get out of the country. Now drive!"

Stacey steered the old car along the dusty roads toward the lava flows. No one would be there to help. It'd be him and Bingham, alone.

FORTY-SIX

The Jet Ranger hurtled over the mountains and valley floors, Buseth and his four best men jammed into the chopper's small cabin. The flight would take about 35 minutes. The sun was already well above the mountaintops when they sighted the town. Buseth ordered the pilot straight in, producing a massive dust cloud in the field next to the farmhouse. The men stormed inside, ignoring the old German shepherd locked in the bedroom.

"They're not here!" one of them yelled.

Buseth chomped at his radio. "Get this bird back in the air!"

"It's in here." Stacey pointed at the mouth of a small cave. "It's buried under the rocks."

Bingham smirked—for the first time in a while. "Let's go. And remember, the slightest move and I play butcher with your throat."

Stacey needed to know something. In the cave he knew he might not come out of alive, and with nothing to lose, he asked his question. "How did you become so calloused that life has no value?"

"Power and money are the only things that matter," Bingham countered. "With my pen, I have both. Now, dig it out—slowly."

Stacey sidled up to the pile of rocks, leaving room to roll if his rival's grip loosened. Bingham, anticipating the reward of his efforts, could no longer hold back from gloating. "After I infect you, you'll beg me to kill you. First you'll feel your joints start to get stiff; then the muscles'll freeze like ice; and in the end, when it reaches your brain, you'll still be able to think without being able to move. Those Vietnamese boys did me a big favor when they built this biological beauty. The contents of the pen could kill thousands. A few years ago in Africa, a few drops in a community water well nearly annihilated an entire village."

Stacey slowly dug the paint can from its hiding place and removed its lid to reveal the pen. He thought of his friend Deek, a loving father, husband; he thought of the thousands who'd already suffered painful deaths—and the thousands more that would suffer. Who was he to make a difference?

Slowly raising his hand back up over his shoulder, he waggled the pen like a fat worm luring a fish. As he'd wagered, Bingham's left hand disengaged from Stacey's throat to grab it. In the instant Bingham's fingers clamped down on the prize, Stacey yanked the pen from its cap, tucked his body and rolled away from the blade. Reversing his momentum, he then lunged back, drove the pen tip deep into Bingham's leg, and once more rolled out of reach.

Startled by the turn of events, Bingham's eyes bugged out. Then as the chemical coursing through his veins took hold, he staggered toward his nemesis, his eyes now reflecting anger and pain, and his own pent-up fear of death.

"I'm a dead man," he whispered, his voice raspy. "Do you realize what you've done? I'm a dead man."

Wrenching the pen out and raising its poison tip, he limped forward, his feet dragging through the rocks and sand. Stacey backed away into the cave, the huge man's lumbering silhouette drawing ever nearer.

Bingham came on, his mind flashing through the thousands of horrifying images painted in the recesses of his memory—the same images Melvin had transferred to disk. He stumbled toward his enemy, now backed to only a few feet from the narrowing walls of the cave. Bingham dropped to his knees and began wildly brandishing the pen in the hope of connecting with Stacey's flesh.

The images he could still see now spun at drunken angles. Bingham continued to close the gap, his body torpid, his face writhing in agony and hate. "You'll be joining me in hell, Stacey," were his last words, as a deafening gunshot blast reported and echoed from wall to wall.

"I don't think so." A squeaky voice rang through the cavern. A flashlight beam played across Bingham's body, still crouched in a statue-like pose, pen raised, ready to strike. "Melvin Phelps—or Briggs, if you prefer." The man thrust his hand forward. "I don't think we've met."

Stacey took Melvin's smaller hand and shook it vigorously. "Rick Stacey."

"I know, Officer Stacey. You didn't leave me much time to find this place. I almost didn't get hidden before the two of you came in. Nice roll you did. I was afraid I was going to have to take a chance at shooting him with the knife at your neck."

Noticing the blood oozing down from the wound, Melvin pulled a handkerchief from his pocket. "Here," he offered. "Hold it against the cut and you'll be just fine." Melvin motioned for Stacey to step around Bingham's body. "Don't touch him, we wouldn't want you contaminated."

Out in the sunlight, a chopper swooped in over the ancient volcano and set down next to the Mercury. Buseth jumped from the noisy bird and started on a run toward the two men. "What are you doing here?" he demanded.

Melvin's prickly, abrasive tone deflected the question. "Just taking care of a problem you can't seem to solve. Now, while you get your team here to finish up, I'll take the chopper and deliver Officer Stacey to his grandma."

Buseth raised his hand in the stop position. "You're not going anywhere," he fumed. Melvin pushed the button on his phone and handed it to Agent Buseth, who raised it to his ear. "...Yes sir. We should have it cleaned up by nightfall....Yes sir." He hung up the phone.

"Have a couple of your men bring the Mercury and Officer Stacey's squad car back to the farmhouse," Melvin ordered. Then he and Stacey climbed in the chopper.

"My grandma's okay?"

"She's fine."

As the helicopter lifted off the ground amid a blinding tornado of dust, Stacey turned and thanked his rescuer, and asked, "How did you find me?"

Melvin's voice could be heard over the whine of the helicopter. "Simple. I followed you to the parking lot where you left your grandma's car. After some research, I decided I'd keep an eye on your grandma. She was the weak link in Buseth's plan. She's quite the woman, you know. It took a bit to convince her I was one of the good guys. She's been staying with a neighbor the last few days. When you snuck out of your folks' house last night, I had a hard time keeping up with you. I must say I was surprised you hid the pen in my garage. It was a good thing the big car was easy to spot at four a.m., or I wouldn't have found you again. We watched you pull the car onto the lava fields from the air. I knew you wouldn't take the pen with you to your grandma's. After you left, it took me a half hour to find your hiding spot. That's when I hid myself in the rocks and waited."

"It's a good thing." Stacey pondered his foe's end. "What did the chemical do to Bingham?"

"You injected so much of it in his system it made his blood set like steel. I probably didn't even need to shoot; he was nearly frozen when my pellets hit him."

The chopper blew another cloud of dust as it landed in the lane leading up to the farmhouse. Grandma Stacey opened the screen door and stepped out on the back porch. Sig stood on one side of her, his head cocked, a painful lump above his ear, and grandma's old shepherd stood—teetered, actually—on the other.

"Goodbye, Officer Stacey," Melvin said. "I hope we meet again." The bird lifted up and pulled away as Stacey ran to his grandmother's waiting arms.

After a good, home-cooked meal and lots of catching up, Stacey hopped into the squad car and started for home.

FORTY-SEVEN

Judge Demick canceled his appointments for the afternoon. He'd personally taken charge of the arrangements for the burial. A local clergyman would officiate at the graveside service.

DNA tests had proven that Jau Fei was the killer. Demick couldn't comprehend what would make a woman want to kill her daughter and then turn her demented or tormented mind on other young girls. As he commenced the news conference, there still seemed to be more questions than answers.

Driving north up I-15, Stacey turned on the radio. A news broadcast announced the dismissal of all charges against Melvin Briggs and ended by mentioning that a brief graveside service would be held that afternoon for his wife and daughter.

A follow-up report cited an anonymous donor who had contributed a large sum of money to the families of the deceased girls. This report followed the news conference, where Judge Demick explained how he'd been under a federal gag order, which had kept him from telling the prosecuting attorney about the government's undercover operation. He also alluded to the unfortunate plane accident that had claimed the life of Mapleton's own Captain Bingham, who also had been "involved" in the investigation. There was no mention of chemicals or high-tech espionage, nor any hint to the whereabouts of the enigmatic Melvin Briggs.

Christina insisted that her dad take her to the service

that afternoon. She felt a kinship to the body she'd found buried under the shed. Don agreed. Maybe seeing the killer buried would help ease her anxious feelings and bring closure to the strange chain of events.

A handful of people, including Don, Cecily, Kate, Christina and Officer Stacey stood around the open graves. The service was brief. No one cried. Only a haunting emptiness washed over the mourners as they considered the terrible waste represented by the two caskets, laying side by side.

Walking hand-in-hand with Cecily and Don back to the car at the close of the service, Christina turned to her Aunt Kate. "I'd like to stop by and see my mom, if you'll take me."

"If it's okay with your dad, we'll go right after your appointment with Doctor Wendy." Don, sandwiched between the two ladies he most loved, readily agreed.

Stacey, meanwhile, walked away from his car, making his way up through the trees. There he waited. Within a couple of minutes Melvin appeared. He looked different in a suit and tie. After striding out into the clearing to pay his respects, he walked back to where Stacey stood.

"Officer Stacey, I expect you're looking for a few more answers."

"You knew I'd be here."

"As you knew I would," Melvin said, smiling. "Let's find a place where we can sit. This may take a while." The two men seated themselves on a shady bench and, without prompting, Melvin began his narrative.

"I met her as I was finishing up my tour of Nam. Her village was raided by the enemy just prior to our arrival. She, along with three other girls, had been raped over and over. We had come too late to stop the other mothers from executing their daughters. They weren't willing to raise any 'bastard children' born of the violated girls. Most of the mothers were already burdened with the care of their own children, having lost their men to battle.

"I happened to be the one who saved Jau Fei from her own mother. She was beautiful. I felt sorry for her, knowing that as soon as my platoon left the village she'd

451

be killed.

"Three days later my unit was ambushed. We'd been behind enemy lines setting up monitoring equipment to track the Viet Cong's movements. Jau Fei pulled me from the massacre and found a native doctor, who removed the bullet from my butt. She nursed me through my injuries and throughout my recovery. The Viet Cong were just figuring out how to use chemical warfare. I was hit by a bullet contaminated with what the U.S. Army later named the 'VN three-fifteen' strain."

An involuntary smile creased Stacey's mouth, a grin he quickly squelched. "But why would she kill Leah?"

"I'll get to that later. Jau Fei attended to my every need until another unit arrived. By then I'd fallen in love with her, but the unit that rescued me refused to bring her out. She was brokenhearted when they put me on the chopper. I felt the loss, too, especially as I lay for two months in a military hospital. They quarantined me for a while before sending me home.

"I didn't know the determination of this girl, Jau Fei. And I had no idea she'd come for me rather than waiting for me to return for her. Somehow she survived 70 miles of jungle, passing enemy soldiers, friendlies, land mines and poisonous snakes to find me. We were married before they flew us home to complete my recovery.

"I learned later that Jau Fei had the same doctor who treated me give her an abortion. We tried to have children for over six years before we were blessed with Leah. By the time she was two she had long, curly, black hair. She got the curls from me, believe it or not. I continued working for the military, mostly with computers and surveillance. I became the best they had. I officially retired when Leah was ten.

"I was invited to work part-time for a special task force dedicated to tracking a few rogue military men who were killing for hire. By 1994, I was assigned to track your Chief Anderson—he went by the name Oswald then. He'd landed a job as a cop so he could know when someone was on to him. At the same time he was blackmailing a banker to help launder money from the oil companies, then he'd send the funds to his hired hands to do the dirty work overseas. He chose a small-town banker because they're more easily intimidated and less likely to draw attention. He moved to Mapleton in the latter part of '94 to start over again. My family and I followed him here.

"We discovered that the 'VN twenty-three fifty-two' strain was being used in Nigeria to kill off a tribe in the delta region. We suspected its use was linked to Anderson."

Stacey interrupted the account. "I have five of your older disks."

"They won't do you any good," said Melvin. "You can't get into them without the code I wrote."

"We've already been in two of them. We saw what the chemical did to those people."

Melvin was shocked. "Who broke my codes?

"Danny."

"Christina's cousin?"

"Fourteen years old—as smart as they come."

"He packs a good wallop, too." Melvin rotated his jaw back and forth. "I'll need the disks back."

"Fair enough. Did one of Anderson's men murder those chiefs in Nigeria?"

"We're not sure. Our evidence leads us to believe they were assassinated—we just don't know by whom. It could have been Bingham. We think he's the one that got away with the 'VN twenty-three fifty-two' after his platoon busted an underground lab."

"It looked like some very bad stuff."

"It was. Now, let's see, where was I? Oh, yeah...I was monitoring Anderson, who had a Mexican maid at the time. He paid the woman extra to bring her 14-year-old daughter to the home while she cleaned. Jau Fei must have gotten a glimpse of one of my recordings of Anderson raping the girl. I didn't realize it until a few weeks ago when I figured out she was after Christina. Jau Fei was going crazy as early as seven or eight years ago. Some type of coping mechanism, I suppose. In her mind, the girl had been violated and needed to be destroyed. Just as her mother wanted to do to her.

"Leah and I had a special relationship. Because I was at home most of the time, she spent a lot of her time with me. Her mother kept a nursery of all sorts of exotic herbs and plants. She'd extract the drugs, get high, then wander from the house; she'd be gone for days. I tried to get her help, but she always refused. She would get violent and—being every bit as strong as me—slam me around. During the last few years she'd beat me once or twice a month. That's what happened the first night I was arrested for the attack on Christina. I'd asked Jau Fei how she hurt her eye. It was then she slammed me into the corner of the door, before disappearing again. If I'd told you about her, you would never have caught her. I needed her to come back so I could turn her in."

Melvin swallowed hard, as if seeing again what he was about to reveal. "Just before Leah disappeared, Fei threatened to kidnap her and take her back to Nam. She actually accused me of molesting my own daughter. I admit my work does take me in and out of questionable places, but I've never peeked at young girls. She purchased plane tickets and they both disappeared for more than a week. Then Jau Fei returned, alone. I always assumed she'd taken Leah with her to have her mother care for her, but she didn't. I tried to locate her for more than three years before we gave up.

"I probably should have divorced Jau Fei after Leah disappeared, but I kept hoping she'd tell me where I could find my daughter. And she was buried here the whole time. I'd kept my eyes on the whole world, but didn't know what was going on in my own backyard." Melvin shook his head, struggling to hold back the tears. "I think I knew deep down she was dead. I just couldn't face the fact."

Stacey had been affected by Melvin's sad tale. "I'm sorry for your loss. I wish there was more I could do."

"You've done a lot already, but I think that spirited little Christina has done the most. She's helped me start to heal a wound that's been festering for five long years."

Another series of questions came into Stacey's head.

"So you never peeped at the girls? What about the tenants before Don and Christina?"

"No, I'd been reviewing my records to see how the other murders might be tied to Jau Fei. I have monitoring equipment close to each of the locations where they took place. Somehow, she followed me as I set up my equipment. As a child, she learned how to sneak around without being seen or heard. She'd usually be out of the house whenever I was home, except to return late at night to sleep on her bamboo mat in the middle of her room. When I wasn't home, she'd pace the floors endlessly. The carpets were practically worn through. The noise drove more than one of my renters away."

"So who's the anonymous donor that gave money to the victims' families?"

"Truth be told, Bingham and Anderson both left behind sizeable numbered accounts. My superiors agreed to let me disburse it as I saw fit—inasmuch as the men don't officially exist."

"Where did the guy I shot in the woods go?"

"We were keeping close tabs on you, knowing you were in Bingham's doghouse for ringing his bell like you did. For years we'd been trying to pin down the person who had control of the chemical. We finally assumed it was either Bingham—"Peck" is his real name, as you may know—or Anderson. We put our bet on Bingham, since he was wrapping up a money deal here at the bank. And by all our calculations, he was getting ready to run again. We picked up his blonde girlfriend on her way to Barbados and planned on busting him—until you came along and screwed up our plans.

"The best we can tell, Bingham took the hand gun away from his woman the night Detective Derickson got shot. According to her, she's the one who laced the bullet with the chemical. Bingham didn't know anything about it. We think he was only trying to wound your detective so he could get away without being detected. Together, the two of them were responsible for Derickson's death, so she'll be locked up for a very long time."

"What about the rat in the restroom?"

"Christina saw my rat in the restroom the day we suspected Bingham's woman was getting ready to leave the country. My sources informed me she was in the County Building where I was working as a janitor. She picked up a marriage application and was arguing with Bingham on the phone in the ladies' room. I followed her to her car before I returned to get my rat. Christina happened to see it pull out when I attempted to retrieve it....Let's see, you asked where the guy from the woods went." Stacey nodded.

"Well, we were keeping an eye on Bingham, and all the while he was trying to locate you. He was getting reckless, careless. Anyway, he and Anderson guessed your dog was responsible for the cattle drive. They decided to take a closer look. We sent our men in to make sure you didn't get hurt, using a well-trained dog to help find you before Bingham's team did. He wanted you dead, by torture at his own hand, if he could. When the two dogs began to fight, one of Bingham's men came to investigate. Our men took him out without a sound. When it became obvious that your dog was taking a serious beating, our dog's trainer tried to call him off, but the mutt failed to respond. He put him down before your dog was killed. It broke his heart. That's when you shot the other guy. We watched you help him until you passed out. Then we slipped away with both of them."

"Is he dead?"

"Does it matter?"

"Of course," insisted Stacey. "If I killed a man I ought to know."

"He's just fine." Melvin was a good liar. He brought a small flask from his jacket and took a drink. "I'm retiring for good this time." He put the flask back in the jacket pocket and took out an envelope. "Will you give this to your friend Don Rodriguez? Tell him good luck with Cecily. They seem like a perfect match."

"What makes you think he's my friend?"

"You spent the night with him in my basement." Stacey looked surprised. "Like I said, we were right on top of you—literally. We didn't want you hurt."

"What's in the envelope?"

"I have no living relatives. My wife caused Christina and the other girls' families so much grief. This is the deed to my house. Tell him he can sell it or live in it, I don't care. I never want to go back in there again. My heart died in that house. Fei sucked the life out of it the day she killed Leah." Melvin pulled a card from his pocket. "My boss wants you to call him. The pay's not that great, but you'll get one wild education."

"So what are you going to do?"

"I'll go back to Nigeria. Since you've seen my tapes, you know what those people are going through. If anyone can use my help, they can. If I can prove that their government is a partner in genocide, I might be able to put a stop to it. I became acquainted with a man named Kin Ro Sawa before he was hung for a crime he didn't commit. Don't ask me how I got into the prison to interview him—that's another story. Kin Ro's son is trying to carry forward the people's freedom movement. My boss let me keep a little cash for my covert operation....Say, maybe you could join me."

Stacey, having been caught up in Melvin's story for nearly an hour, stood to shake his hand. "One last question. Then why were you peeking into the downstairs bathroom when all that fancy equipment could have done it for you?"

"Everyone always assumes the worst. I fixed the leaking water heater and started the washing machine while I *watched* for more drips," Melvin lied. "I know I don't have much of a personality, but I'm not such a bad guy. The chemical took more than my backside. The specialists tell me I'm a genius in some areas and dumber than a box of rocks in others. I suffer from an obsessive-compulsive disorder—I'm a prisoner to my passions. A goofy idea burrows into my head, it gets stuck there, and I'm compelled to follow through with it. I snoop into anything I get my hands on. I guess that's why I'm so damn good at surveillance. I knew when I started the washing machine that she'd know I was in the apartment. I just couldn't help myself. The note said it needed to be started—so I started it. It was the same with my job at the County Building. Demick's computer was protected by a password and I couldn't rest until I found out what it was."

Stacey, preparing to leave, placed his hand in his pocket, then turned to Melvin. "I almost forgot. Barker asked me to give you this. Said you'd know what to do with it." He dropped a crumpled knot of gold chain attached to a medallion into Melvin's bony hand and walked away.

Stacey jogged stiffly from the parking lot up to the hospital doors. He couldn't wait to get to Barker's room to tell him about his talk with Melvin. And the advantage of being there before Barker's sister-in-law arrived was worth the pain. That way, if he didn't like her, he could duck out without being rude.

The elevator door was closing as he rounded the corner. As he raced to catch it, slipping in just as the door was shutting, he caught his foot on the rubber door slides and fell in face first, staying upright by bracing himself against the elevator's back wall. The door rebounded open behind him. Then he looked up. Inches in front of him were the startled eyes of a beautiful woman, her back pinned up against the wall. She squirmed a bit, and moved to the side—either to get away from the stumble-bum or to let Stacey regain his composure, he wasn't sure.

"It's you," he said. It was the same woman he'd bowled over a few days before. "Sorry, it's this bad leg of mine."

"What happened to it?" she asked out of more than curiosity.

"It's ...a long story. Maybe when you have a day or so to talk about it."

"I have time."

"Weren't you coming to visit someone?"

"I'll be free in five minutes or so. My sister just wanted me to meet her friend...."

EPILOGUE

TWENTY DAYS LATER

"WELCOME BACK **CAPTAIN** BARKER!" The banner in the squad room was scrawled in bold black and blue paint—to commemorate the colorful lump that still graced the side of Barker's skull.

"So, will you be Mapleton City's newest detective, Officer Stacey?" Barker asked, trying to sound official.

"I'll only promise to stay on a temporary basis. That federal job seems like the offer of a lifetime."

"She's under your skin, isn't she?" Barker chuckled. "I still can't believe you and she up and left so fast. You were there less than a minute! Debbie and I were worried sick all evening."

"Yeah...well...."

"Who kisses better—her or Sig?"

"I'm breaking him of the habit."

MAYOR JENKINS, read the sign on the door. Several people had congregated inside the office.

"We sure did admire your husband, Mrs. Derickson," the mayor began. "The council voted unanimously on an appointment for you to fill the council seat. Would you accept the part-time position?"

"I'll need a day or two to think about it. I'm not sure how I'm going to support my family."

"You could always run for mayor when I retire next year. You'd have my full support....Of course, it doesn't pay much, either!" The kindly old gentleman gave her a wink.

"I'm honored. I'll call you back after I talk to the kids."

On her way home, Dianne pondered the weight of her responsibility. Deek's life insurance would be enough for a short while, but with six children....

She missed him terribly, but couldn't keep from smiling at the thought of his own crooked smile, his dumb jokes, the way his curly hair stuck up in all directions when he got out of bed in the morning. Pulling into the driveway, she leaned back in the seat, thinking good thoughts, savoring the memories of the man she loved.

A tap came at the window. "Mrs. Derickson....I have a certified letter for you. I need your signature." The postal carrier passed his clipboard through the window, waited for her chicken-scratch signature, and went on his way.

It was a letter from her bank:

Dear Mrs. Derickson,

You will find a deposit in a new trust account in your name. At the current interest rate, you will earn approximately three thousand dollars ($3,000.00) per month. My instructions are to transfer those funds each month to your regular checking account. Separate accounts in the names of your children were set up to assure them a college education.

These funds were transferred from a numbered account in Switzerland. The benefactor would like to remain anonymous, but hopes you accept this gift with his best wishes.

Sincerely,

Bill Penrod
Branch President

Author's Notes
The Inspiration Behind the Story

Several years ago a young man came to me looking for a job. I hired him, putting him to work at the dirtiest, most loathsome task imaginable. "Don" proved himself hard-working, dependable and, despite his lack of transportation, always punctual.

Several weeks passed, and a position came open in our sales office. Our newest employee was invited to apply for it. Having already shown such outstanding work, the choice was not at all hard: Don was moved to the sales floor.

With this job promotion Don was able to afford an apartment, and we allowed him the use of a company vehicle to travel to and from work until circumstances permitted him to purchase his own car.

Shortly after he moved into his basement apartment, Don, during breaks and at lunch hour, repeatedly was heard accusing his new upstairs landlord of spying on him, essentially snooping into his personal life. At first I attributed this persistent talk to him adjusting to his new home, but after the second week of his voicing such suspicions, I began to wonder if perhaps my new salesman himself wasn't some sort of psychopath.

In desperation—and having had some experience in surveillance—I offered to inspect his apartment to see if there was any validity to his wild claims. My reasoning was simple: If the landlord proved to be spying, Don needed to move out immediately, both for his own good and so we could restore peace to the workplace. If not, I needed to decide how to terminate a deranged employee before he drove my entire office staff crazy.

My offer accepted, one day during lunch we drove over to the apartment. The landlord appeared to not be at home. After an extensive search of the walls, ceilings, flowerbeds and heater vents, I had found nothing. Don simply shrugged and asked if I thought he was nuts.

Early the following day as I pondered his termination, Don came into my office to tell me that just that morning his landlord had stood waiting at Don's truck to ask who he had brought home for lunch the previous day. At hearing this a smile spread across my face. Could this be the simple case of an overly inquisitive, highly meddlesome–and perhaps lonely–fellow? I assured Don that the landlord's own curiosity would in short order be his downfall. Glancing around my office to assess my creative assets, I handed Don an empty box and an old army coat, with the instruction to cover the box and carry it home, perhaps acting a bit suspicious.

When the nosy landlord called his edgy tenant that night and waited with baited breath for him to reveal the contents of the box he'd toted into the house, Don's feelings of impotence and paranoia magically transformed to ones of strength and vindication. Don countered with a casual "Nothing" to the landlord's question. And from that curt, modest reply was cultivated empowerment. Don then was able, over the following weeks, to use his own imagination and the available meager resources within his grasp to drive a snoopy landlord to his knees.

From my imagination came the ensuing storyline, a plot revolving around a complicated character full of obsessions and deceit—a mind so entangled in secrecy and sorrow that he became consumed by his own passions. I further sought to enrich the intricate narrative by weaving in a varied cast of main and supporting characters, all living in seeming ignorance—nevertheless in the shadow—of an extant tribe of people living in the far-away, fertile regions of Nigeria, a poverty-stricken people brutalized by a corrupt military regime in conspiracy with a powerful, greedy oil cartel.

Before long the story began to scream at my thoughts, loudly demanding to be put into words. Thus was born *The Landlord*.

Kay Dee Books
ORDER FORM

Company: _____

Name: _____

Address: _____

City: _____

State, Zip: _____

Phone: ( ) _____

Email: _____

Contact: _____

Single Book:
$7.99 plus $2.50 for shipping and handling

Total _____

**Use this handy page for ordering: fax to (801) 225-1690
or mail to Kay Dee Books P.O. Box 970608
Orem, Utah 84097-0608 USA
or online at www.kaydeebooks.com**

*Prices and availability subject to change without notice.
Please allow four to six weeks for delivery.*